Praise for *The Skeleton Key*

'An intricately plotted thriller, full of detail and invention, with
impeccably realised settings and characters as monstrous as they
are believable. Above all it is a completely addictive story of
two families destroyed by success. Erin Kelly is a genius'
Jane Casey

'Kelly's deftly etched depiction of human relations shows how our
nearest and dearest often spark in us the most intense of emotions'
The Times, Thriller of the Month

'Moody, propulsive, and one of the most intriguing set ups I've read in years.
Erin Kelly doesn't put a foot wrong in this atmospheric, original thriller'
Gillian McAllister

'Gloriously gothic – a richly layered, utterly compulsive
read. I completely lost myself to this book for a few days.
This is Erin Kelly at the height of her powers'
Lucy Foley

'A feat of real ambition and imagination – original, suspenseful,
and with complex characters that spring irresistibly to
life on the page, this is Erin Kelly at her finest'
Louise Candlish

'Erin Kelly excels at twisted family dynamics and
toxic, compelling characters, and this glorious slice of
bohemian gothic showcases all her strengths'
Ruth Ware

'Spearheading a new wave of *Succession*-esque fractured family tales . . .
Erin Kelly's *The Skeleton Key* is the ultimate entertaining thriller'
Evening Standard

'Scary, eerie, moving and compelling: a beautifully-
plotted, gorgeously-written triumph of a thriller'
Nicci French

'A twisted treasure hunt with a fatal family secret at its heart.
Powerful, playful and deeply disturbing. I loved it'
Sarah Hilary

'Kelly's realisation of periods stretching back to the 1960s is
flawless, and her saga of sex, art, fame, money, egos and damaged
children is intriguing, but it's the psychological thriller strand
centred on Frank's daughter '
Sunday

Also by Erin Kelly

The Poison Tree

The Sick Rose

The Burning Air

The Ties that Bind

He Said/She Said

We Know You Know
(Hardback edition titled *Stone Mothers*)

Watch Her Fall

With Chris Chibnall

Broadchurch

Erin Kelly

The Skeleton Key

HODDER

First published in Great Britain in 2022 by Hodder & Stoughton
An Hachette UK company

This paperback edition published in 2023

2

A CIP catalogue record for this title is available from the British Library

Paperback ISBN 978 1 473 68092 0

Typeset in Sabon MT by Hewer Text UK Ltd, Edinburgh
Printed and bound in Great Britain by Clays Ltd, Elcograf S.p.A.

'Hodder & Stoughton policy is to use papers that are natural, renewable
and recyclable products and made from wood grown in sustainable
forests. The logging and manufacturing processes are expected to
conform to the environmental regulations of the country of origin.

Hodder & Stoughton Ltd
Carmelite House
50 Victoria Embankment
London EC4Y 0DZ

www.hodder.co.uk

For my parents
With love and with thanks
for not being like Nell's

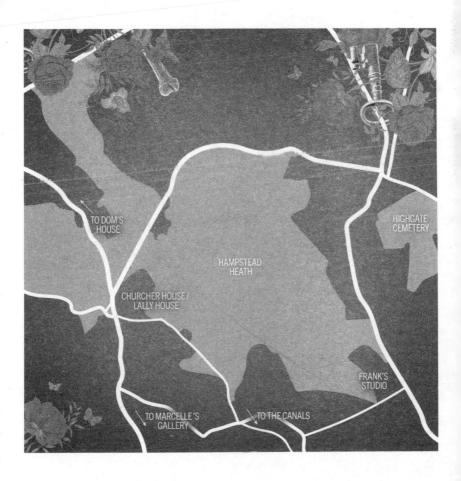

AUTHOR'S NOTE

When I was a child my favourite picture book was the 1979 treasure hunt phenomenon *Masquerade*, by artist Kit Williams. On every page, riddles were posed, and intricate, dreamlike paintings depicted Jack Hare in his quest to deliver a jewel from the moon to the sun. Each picture was bordered by letters that held a clue to the location of a tiny hare, wrought in gold, studded with precious stones, and buried somewhere in England.

By the time I was old enough to read *Masquerade* the prize had been claimed, but that didn't stop me loving the book. The paintings seemed to offer up some new detail every time I looked at them. The page I loved best was a double-page spread of a little girl sitting in a field of dog roses while Jack Hare galloped past. I envied her so much: she was in the story, as I longed to be. I thought that if I looked at the picture for long enough I might fall into it, and, in a way, I did. The book became part of me, as only the stories we read in childhood can.

Masquerade spawned many imitations but nothing caught the public imagination in quite the same way. As I grew up, I wondered how the book would have been received today, when code and algorithm and GPS coexist with ink and paper and boots on the ground.

In 2010 I got my answer. Forrest Fenn was an American antique dealer whose memoir *The Thrill of the Chase* contained nine clues to the whereabouts of a million-dollar treasure chest. It was another study in the human impulse to uncover secrets. The internet meant that hunters could trade theories in real time. They also laid false trails, for just as strong as the need to lay secrets bare is the compulsion to keep them. 'Forrest fever' gripped America.

Fenn was mobbed at conventions and his home became a fortress as hunters tried to scale the walls. By the time the haul was found, in rural Montana, five hunters had died in their quest; the 'lucky' winner was subject to death threats and forced into hiding.

Kit Williams's paintings are still a source of wonder and fascination to me. I want to stress that it is his work that inspired me, and that all of the characters in this novel, and their deeds, are purely of my imagining, as are the 'Bonehunters' you will meet in these pages.

FAMILY TREE

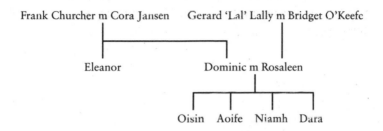

Frank Churcher m Cora Jansen   Gerard 'Lal' Lally m Bridget O'Keefe

Eleanor   Dominic m Rosaleen

Oisin   Aoife   Niamh   Dara

PROLOGUE

Vale of Health, London NW3
May 1992

We all have a before-and-after. A watershed moment that changes the direction of our lives, and forms who we are. For the lucky ones the experience is positive: a child, a relationship, a job. For others, it's divorce, bereavement, the narrow escape from accident or illness.

Mine starts in GCSE French.

It's early spring and the trees are dancing outside the classroom window. Suzy waits till the teacher's back is turned and says, 'Bunch of us going for coffee at the Dôme after school. I know it's not easy for you to get away but could you ask your driver to maybe wait outside?'

Obviously I should say no, but lately Suzy's started to drift away from me. It's not just the fact that I can only socialise in my room that's losing me friends. According to my mother, I've been getting very spiky and sarcastic since Ingrid 'took an interest' in me. My mother has a gift for euphemism.

'Ooh, I wonder why?' I responded.

'I rest my case,' she said.

I'm about to reply to Suzy with a *Yeah right* or *I wish* but she's pretty much the only one who's stuck with me over all this, and I decide on the spot that I'm not going to lose her as well.

'Actually, he's not coming today,' I say. 'They've decided to cut me a bit of slack.'

'About time,' she says. The teacher turns to glare at us and we both dip our heads to the page.

No one seems suspicious when I insist on leaving by the side gate. Most girls whose parents collect them have to idle on the kerb outside, but Ahmed is allowed to drive on to the forecourt, just to be on the safe side. As five of us walk along Hampstead High Street, swinging our bags, it's him I feel bad for.

When the others roll up the waistbands of their skirts to make them shorter, I copy them. I don't even like my legs very much, but the breeze playing with the tiny hairs on my thighs feels like freedom.

The Dôme is a fake Parisian café, ochre walls and nineteenth-century French signs everywhere. The others greet the waiter by name as he shows us to what is clearly their usual table in the window. What I really want is a Coke but I don't want to look gauche so I order a cappuccino. When it arrives it's too thick and sweet and I can't finish it.

I tell myself my jangled nerves are guilt and caffeine, and not anxiety about Ingrid. There's no way she'll be waiting for me. This is the first time in over a year that I've broken my after-school routine. For a long time I would see her every day through the tinted car window. Sometimes she'd lean on the road sign, other times she'd be sitting on a car bonnet or lurking behind a tree, but it's been months since any of us last saw her. There's a payphone on the wall and coins in my pocket. I should call home: tell my parents I gave Ahmed the slip, for his sake more than mine. But that would draw attention, expose my lie.

Suzy and I part ways at Whitestone Pond and I walk the last quarter of a mile on my own, each unaccompanied step a victory for liberty. I turn left on to the Vale of Health, a hook-shaped street of Victorian villas and apartment blocks at the edge of the Heath. There are no shops or pubs or churches; it is a hamlet, not a village. The pond at the bottom isn't the kind you can swim in but it's quiet and overhung with green. It's the kind of place where the houses have blue plaques commemorating the artists and writers who lived and met here in the nineteenth and twentieth centuries. My house is a one-minute walk down the hill. There are grassy banks instead of pavements; the lamp-posts look like old-fashioned gas lights. Our house and its twin are the first two on the left. I'm close enough to see the pink suds of cherry blossom in the front garden.

At the gate stands Dom, shielding his eyes as he looks up the road.

'They've formed a search party,' he shouts, and then, with relish, 'You are in *such* deep shit.'

'Worth it,' I shout back, and flip my middle finger at him.

It's the smell that gives Ingrid away: unwashed hair and the charity-shop funk of musty clothes.

'At *last*,' she says, her breath warm on the back of my neck. 'I've had my birdy eye on you.'

Before I can think, '*Birdy?*' the knife goes into the top of my thigh. It feels more like a punch than a cut and my legs grow hot. As the blood cools it makes itself known only as liquid: I am mortified to have wet myself.

There are three more slow punches.

When I fall, Rose swoops from nowhere to catch me and Dom seizes Ingrid. 'Get off my sister!'

I look up to see his arms hooked through Ingrid's. Her dirty hair is parted in the middle. She's wearing a man's dress shirt that's much too big for her tiny frame, and stained pink velour tracksuit bottoms with diamanté studs. A vein on Dom's neck throbs with the effort of restraining her. Ingrid can't weigh more than seven stone, and Dom's tall for twelve, and sporty, yet this is a struggle between equals. They both have the strength of someone trying to save a life. They both think that's what they are doing.

'I need the missing bone,' she pants. 'I need to put her back together again!'

'Shut up, you mad bitch!' says Dom.

He pulls her arms tighter behind her back and she drops her weapon. A bread knife, old and scratched. The steel glints before turning red in the spreading puddle around me.

'What shall I do?' Rose asks Dom. 'Shall I get my mum or stay and help you?'

The pair of them look to the house and back again.

'I think you're supposed to apply pressure to a stab wound,' says Dom. 'It stops the bleeding.'

'What, with my hands?'

'I dunno,' he says desperately. 'Take off your jumper, maybe?'

She bundles up her school sweater and pushes it against what increasingly feels like a bruise.

'I was only trying to save her!' wails Ingrid.

This time Dom ignores her. 'I think there's less blood coming out.'

A cycler courier huffing his way up the hill leaps off his bike while it's still moving. 'Shit. Do you kids need a hand?'

Talking to a stranger, Dominic has the authority of a man twice his age. 'Go to the first house on the left,' he says. 'Knock on the door and tell the woman who answers – her name's Bridget – to call an ambulance and the police. Tell them Nell's been stabbed by Ingrid Morrison and we need her up here.'

'Police, ambulance, Bridget,' says the cyclist. He circles tightly around and is gone.

A moment later Bridget comes into view, what looks like a superhero's cape flowing behind her. I grow suddenly cold, as though a cloud has covered the sun.

'Oh, Nell,' she says, kneeling beside me. 'It's OK, poppet. It's OK.'

'Shall I . . . ?' The cyclist gestures to Ingrid. Dominic nods; the cyclist takes over the restraint. Dom sinks into a cross-legged position, his knees level with my eyes. My blood looks black on his grey school trousers. Now that the grown-ups are in charge, he is a child again.

Ingrid has gone limp in the cyclist's arms. She is making ugly, meaningless noises.

'I'm thirsty,' I tell Bridget.

Her training kicks in. 'That's a sign of shock. Here.' Her cape reveals itself to be the throw from my mother's sofa. She wraps it around me as she examines the wound. 'Mother of God, she's got the femoral artery. Rose, keep that pressure up.'

4

'Did we do the right thing?' asks Dom. He takes my hand. 'Bridget, she's *freezing*.'

'You both did brilliantly,' says Bridget. She puts one hand to my forehead and the other to my wrist.

I hear a siren sing in the distance.

'Have we saved her life, Mum?' asks Rose.

Bridget, who has always said it's better to remain silent than tell a lie, doesn't reply.

'You've killed my sister!' cries Dominic to Ingrid. 'You should've been locked up years ago!'

The siren closes in.

'No.' Ingrid shakes her head. 'I was trying to *save* a life. All I've ever wanted was to bring Elinore back.'

The siren dies. Strobing blue light turns everyone into aliens. The ambulance door slams and I see the black boots and green overalls of the paramedic at a sideways angle. My last thought as I close my eyes and slide backwards out of the world is how vain is the cause I am about to die for.

For the woman Ingrid is trying to save has never existed outside the pages of a book.

PART ONE

I

Kilburn, London NW6
December 1969

It ends in blood and shattered bone but it does not start that way. It starts with ice and fire.

December is biting hard but the pubs are warm and Guinness thaws the veins. It is the shortest day of the year, the sun set at half past three, and Frank and Lal, and Lal's girlfriend Marcelle, have been drinking in Mulligan's since before it got dark. The guys are six months out of art school and supplementing their dole money by recreating Old Masters in chalk for tourists. They did eight hours today, knees throbbing after all that time on the cold cobbles of Covent Garden. *Mona Lisa*, crowd-pleaser. They're a good team, so well-matched in talent that even they can never tell who drew what.

Frank is waiting for the idea that will launch him on the art world. His father, the Admiral, says it's not too late for Frank to go back to his engineering degree and follow him into the Navy, but he'll have to find him first.

Frank turns out his trouser pockets. 'Ten bob left,' he says.

'Will we get a carry-out?' asks Lal.

A minute later, bottles clink in Marcelle's string bag. Outside, the dustbins lining the road sparkle with frost. Lal and Marcelle walk ahead. She's a bit scrawny for Frank's liking. Give him a dolly bird, dimples and curves, any day of the week. It's no bad thing they have different taste in girls. A friendship like the one he shares with Lal is too rare to risk for a woman. They were both running away from their own institutions – a career in the Navy

9

for Frank, the priesthood for Lal – and, when they collided, recognition was instant. They both understood what it took to leave, and also that you never quite could.

'Would you look here,' says Lal, coming to a stop. 'Firewood.'

Someone has thrown out a set of four dining chairs, stuffing spilling from cracked leather. Frank and Lal take two each. The front door opens to reveal Cora, the artist who lives on the top floor, and whose curves and dimples Frank has been admiring for months.

'Hey, man. I was just about to claim them for myself.' Cora smiles. There's a gap between her two front teeth and she's had it filled with gold. Like most girls, Cora addresses Lal as though Frank's not even there. Lal's all lean muscle and dark curls, and women can't get enough of it. For the most part, female attention goes over Lal's head. He's winning a game he's not even playing.

Frank sees an opportunity. 'Shame to light two fires when we could all sit around one,' he says. 'We've got drink,' he adds when Cora hesitates.

'Cool,' she replies.

There's no door to Cora's rooms, just a beaded curtain made of beer can ring-pulls that tinkles as they part it and step into a different world. They pass Cora's bedroom, directly above Frank's. Moonlight slants across the brass bed whose springs and headboard creak and bang in the night, suggesting that, unlike most girls, Cora practises free love as well as preaches it. In her sitting room, the fire in the grate is almost out. An old bottle serves as a candlestick for a flickering taper. A record, something folky and plaintive, is playing on an unseen turntable. Her stuff is a mess of contradictions: she has the I Ching, half a dozen astrology textbooks, the Bible and the Qur'an on her shelves and a deck of tarot cards is laid on a silk scarf as though a reading has just been interrupted. It should be chaos but it hangs together beautifully; this place is more museum or curiosity shop than bedsit. Cora calls herself an artist but to Frank's mind she is more of a maker. She sews, she is a potter, she paints. She *flits*. She's older than them

– late twenties, at a guess – and she's still living hand-to-mouth. Lal's got the same feckless streak, only in his case it's the drink that will be his undoing. Since leaving art college Frank has been gripped by a panic that his talent stops at the wrist. When his idea finally comes to him, he'll apply himself with a discipline that would make a naval officer look like idle.

Frank has rigged all the electricity meters, but when he flips the light switch, nothing happens.

'I'm out of bulbs.' Cora lights more candles, one from the other. Frank rescues a loose lock of her hair from a flame. It's so soft, it feels as if it might turn to mist in his hands. He holds it for a second longer than he needs to and when Cora turns her eighteen-carat smile on him he thinks, *maybe*.

Lal throws a seat cushion on to the grate and the fire throws back a cloud of soot.

The record Cora's playing suits an open fire. The instruments are acoustic, traditional: guitars, Irish-sounding drums, twisted tales about murdered virgins, haunted castles, talking ravens and vengeful knights. Lal up-ends the half-bottle of Tullamore Dew that was full just a few minutes ago.

'Who *writes* this hey-nonny-no crap?' asks Marcelle.

'Like, they're folk songs,' says Cora, not taking offence. 'The whole point is that no one *knows* who wrote them. It's history, it's in our blood. These songs, they were captured just before they died, like . . . like – butterflies caught in a net and pinned.'

Marcelle takes Cora's enthusiasm and returns it with a slow blink.

'It was a whole *scene*,' says Cora. 'Edwardian scholars went to the countryside and got the workers to sing all the old songs from the fields, just before the industrial revolution ended the *old ways*.'

'Ah, the good old days of rickets and child mortality,' says Marcelle. Frank tries to catch her eye. Any more piss-taking and Cora might throw them all out.

'Well, anyway,' says Cora. 'Loads of cool musicians are redis-covering them. It's all part of a movement, going back to a time when things were more *real*.' She gestures to a mural she's painted on the far wall. 'I'm making a map of English folklore. You've got the Pendle witches and vampires up north, King Arthur down south . . .'

Witches and vampires don't sound particularly real to Frank but he'd happily declare a belief in pixies and elves if it got Cora into bed. There's a blank pad beside his armchair. He takes a stick of charcoal from his pocket and begins to sketch her. He starts with the perfect hood of her eyelid. Her hair flows from his hand like water.

On the beanbag, Lal loses his battle with his eyelids.

'I'm off,' says Marcelle. 'Big meeting in the morning.'

'Anything exciting?' asks Cora.

Frank shades the swell of her lower lip then smudges the charcoal.

'I've got to find the new *Alice in Wonderland*, so if you've got an ingenious idea for a ground-breaking children's book you could have on my desk by ten o'clock tomorrow morning, that'd be great.'

Behind the door to Cora's rooms hangs a beaded curtain made of beer can ring-pulls. It tinkles as they part it and step into a different world.

Cora gets up to change the record. 'Now this song – "To Gather the Bones" – is *really* special,' she says.

It sounds to Frank like more of the same. Jingle-jangle guitars and is that a *recorder*? Privately he thinks those Edwardians would've done well to let the songs die out, or the singer here would've done well not to go digging in the archive. It's about a young woman, murdered by her husband, whose lover has to bring her back to life. The chorus is insistent; it lodges in his brain.

Flesh will spoil and blood will spill but true love never dies
Gather the lady's bones with love to see the lady rise

As the verses play out – something to do with skeletons, something about true love, something about witches – an idea begins to take shape. It is almost ready to shoot down Frank's arm and on to the page but then Cora sighs, 'So romantic,' and he seizes the moment. Shyly, he shows her his sketch.

'You've done me as Elinore from the song!' she says. 'The music spoke to you.'

'Not just the music.' He leans forward.

On the beanbag, Lal snores, his breath surely flammable. Firelight renders Cora's skin in jungle stripes of dirty gold. A lump of coal jumps from the fire and crackles on the hearth.

Flesh will spoil and blood will spill but true love never dies
Gather the lady's bones with love to see the lady rise

'Cora. You must know how lovely you are?'

This time when Frank catches her hair, he winds it around his finger, bringing their faces closer together.

The idea, if it's any good, will still be there in the morning.

2

Vale of Health, London NW3
31 July 2021

I stand at the top of the shallow hill as though it were a diving board and take a deep breath. It's always this way, coming home. It always passes. The Vale is pretty in all seasons but it saves its best dress, green lace over grey stone, for summer days like this one. I can tell Billie's impressed, because she's looked up from her phone.

'I cannot *believe* you grew up here, Nell,' she says as we walk along the grassy banks that serve as pavements. 'I reckon some of these cars cost more than *Seren*.'

In the residents' parking bays are a Lexus, a shiny Range Rover and a Tesla. *Seren* is the narrowboat where we live and she cost me ten thousand pounds.

'D'you know what, I reckon *most* of them did,' I reply. 'There are probably sound systems in some of these that cost more than *Seren*.'

The hedge fund managers are encroaching because this is London, but for the most part these houses stay in families for generations, and tucked behind a dirt track there's a caravan park that travelling showpeople have occupied for a hundred years; it's not unusual to see a fairground ride, folded in half on the back of a lorry, reversing through the rickety gates. It's all rather enchanted. Shame I have to walk past the place where I was attacked by a maniac to get there.

It is a beautiful morning, the kind that makes it hard to believe that the past year and a half really happened. Groups of teenagers play music on their phones; families carry hampers and pairs of women in activewear power-walk behind coffee cups as though being dragged along by the caffeine inside.

The few people wearing masks have them slung around their chins. Not me, though. I keep mine over my nose and mouth and my headscarf covering most of my hair. My grey-blonde roots are on show but the brighter ends – I haven't been to a salon for two years, part of the general giving up of middle-age, the great letting-go of lockdown – are under wraps.

Behind fogged sunglasses I scan for the presence of Bonehunters. When I was little, before the hunt for Elinore migrated online, they were easy to spot. They often carried a ragged Ordnance Survey map or a notepad or an actual copy of the book. They also often wore socks with sandals. Even if they were conventionally shod and empty-handed, the Bonehunters shared a particular way of looking at the landscape, eyes everywhere at once, bodies often turning three hundred and sixty degrees to take in as much information as possible.

And when they saw me, they would get a certain look on their faces: a greed for what I might know, despite the fact that my parents made a point of going public with the fact that only they were in on the secret. It is a mask that makes all its wearers look the same.

Almost every new acquaintance who finds out I'm a Churcher puts on the mask at some point.

You can tell me. I can keep a secret.

We've all had that shouted at us at parties, although I think I'm the only one to have it whispered across a pillow.

Parking on the Vale is a bunfight on a good day, but I've never seen it this rammed. There are half a dozen vans emblazoned with the Crabwise Films insignia, a red crab looking askance at black lettering. Lal's ancient blue T-Bird – *how* is it still roadworthy? – is parked across a flowerbed in the front garden to make room for them all.

A car draws up alongside us. It's only when a police officer climbs out of the driver's seat that I register that it's a patrol car.

'*Shit!*'

It comes out louder than I thought and his smile vanishes. 'Can I help you?'

'Sorry,' I say. I have a complex relationship with the Met police. I need them, mistrust them, resent them and respect them all at once. 'I wasn't swearing at you. Well, I was. But not at *you*. Just the sight of you. Of a police officer. You know. Has someone – is there – are you responding to an emergency?'

His neck protrudes from his heavy black vest like a turtle's. He looks me up and down, evidently making a spot judgement about whether I'm a nuisance or a fool. He goes for the latter. 'Nothing like that, love. We like to pop in when there's a film shoot going on. Nine times out of ten someone blocks a driveway or something.' He looks at the Crabwise fleet. 'Let's hope they've got tolerant neighbours.'

'They've put up with worse,' I tell him.

'Right. Well, you take care.'

Billie and I keep walking. 'Did I look *completely* deranged?' I ask her.

She grimaces. 'Do you really want me to answer that?'

'No.'

We close in on the spot where Ingrid attacked me. At sixteen I was a year older than Billie is now but a tenth as streetwise. She cranes at the opposite bank as though expecting to see a puddle of fresh blood.

'Does your scar hurt when you go past it?'

I have always been honest with Billie about what happened to me, largely because most of it is in the public domain and I wanted her to get my take on things rather than find out from some loser online. She knows about my criminal record too – but not about Richard. Only the people who were there know about him.

'Who am I, Harry Potter?' I ask, and she laughs. Outwardly I keep it together for Billie's sake, but when I look down I see that I am holding a key between each finger, the way I do when I walk along the towpath alone in the dark.

3

As we approach the house, Billie starts to drag her feet. 'Are they *all* going to be there?' she asks.

'The whole dysfunctional clan,' I confirm.

Billie goes to bite her nails, remembers she's got acrylics on, and gnaws at a knuckle instead. Her nails, like all armour, only emphasise her vulnerability. She used her wages from her summer job – she works part-time at a cattery, reckons it'll be good for the CV – to pay for a manicure this morning. She'd never say, but she did it to impress Cora and Rose and Bridget. I don't have the heart to tell her it'll have the opposite effect.

We sidle through the gap between Lal's T-Bird and the houses, three storeys of red brick and tile. It's been a year since Billie's only previous visit, a barbecue snatched between lockdowns last summer.

'I'd forgotten how posh it all was,' she says, looking up. 'How *massive.*'

'If you focus on the fact that it's two different houses it's not quite so intimidating,' I say.

Technically the houses are semi-detached, but that suburban term doesn't do this place justice. Two imposing Victorian villas are joined at the hip, as are its residents. My parents, Frank and Cora, or Sir Francis and Lady Churcher to give them their official titles, live on the left-hand side. Their best friends, Lal and Bridget Lally, live on the right. My brother Dominic is married to their daughter Rose. The girl next door. It's a family joke that if the Lallys had had a son I'd have married him and how pleasingly symmetrical this would be. I'm about to tell Billie that I can't think of anything worse when I see something worse.

To my left, there's a clacking of branches and seconds later Stuart Cummins is standing opposite me, his eyes wide in his shiny face. Despite the heat he wears a threadbare but spotless navy three-piece suit, complete with pocket square and tie.

We stare at each other for a few stunned seconds. I don't know why either of us are surprised. He was bound to be here today and so was I.

'Should I . . . ?' asks Billie.

'Go,' I tell her. We've drilled this. If ever they come after me, she is to make herself safe before anything else. She sidles into the gap between two vans, but not before showing me the reluctance on her face. She wants to stay and fight.

'You shouldn't be here,' I tell Stuart.

His sandy hair is a little thinner but apart from that he is unchanged. His oily skin – his face always looked polished to a shine – has acted as a preservative.

'I'm not breaking the law,' he says. 'This is public land. I'm not under any restrictions, I have every right to be here.'

He's as nervous as I am, I realise.

I look him up and down. His hands are empty, but I frisk him with my eyes. He could still be carrying something. He opens his single-breasted jacket to show me the flat lining inside. 'You haven't needed to be afraid for years,' he says. 'You *know* that.'

But his tone suggests he wants me to argue rather than agree. I refuse to be drawn in. I put my head down so far that I'm basically walking at a forty-five-degree angle. He steps in front of me.

'Just answer me this. Is it true?'

I step to the right. Stuart steps to his left.

'Is Elinore the prize, Eleanor?' Up close he smells of old-fashioned soap.

I put my palm right up in his face, just as I learned in self-defence, and shout, 'NO!'

18

The police officer from earlier is by my side so quickly it's as though he's popped up from a manhole.

'This man is harassing me,' I say.

'That's hardly fair,' protests Stuart. 'I asked you one question.'

'He's got form,' I say. 'Look up Stuart Cummins in your criminal records database thingy.'

I wait for Stuart to retaliate – he could just as easily tell the policeman to look me up and that would hardly endear me to him – but to my relief he seems more concerned with his own exoneration. 'It was a long time ago,' he says.

The policeman straightens up inside his vest. 'Can I take your name and date of birth, sir?'

When Stuart supplies it, the policeman presses a button on his radio.

'Dave Chisholm here,' he says. 'Can you do me a PNC check on a Stuart John Cummins, DOB 18 August 1955.'

A colleague narrates Stuart's history. PC Chisholm's eyes widen as he takes it all in.

'I served my time and have publicly renounced my claim on Eleanor's bones,' says Stuart. 'I am categorically no longer a threat.'

'That's correct.' Chisholm sighs. 'But you're clearly an intelligent man. Let's have a bit of sensitivity and common sense, shall we? Give the lady a bit of space. Hampstead Heath's pretty big; it's not hard. This is a friendly warning, but if you approach her again I'll have to put you on a first notice.'

'This is police harassment,' huffs Stuart. Chisholm's face darkens, but, before he can muster a retort, his radio goes again.

'Any unit for an i-graded call,' says the fuzzy voice. 'Domestic assault in progress on Squires Mount, NW3. Caller reports sounds of a serious disturbance.'

Squires Mount is so close I can almost see it. 'I've got to respond to this,' PC Chisholm says, then turns to Stuart. 'I mean it. Keep your distance. I won't be so friendly next time.'

Stuart walks backwards until he's swallowed up by the scrub of the Heath. 'I only wanted to know,' he says. 'I deserve to know. This is an *utter travesty*.'

I find Billie pressed in the gap between two vans.

'Well done,' I say.

'Did they nick him?'

I shake my head. 'But I think they've scared him off.' I put my hands in my pockets so she won't see how badly they're shaking. Just another day in the life of *The Golden Bones*. 'Come on, let's go.'

I crook my elbow. Billie threads her arm through the gap and together we head for the safety and seclusion of my parents' house.

4

Apparently, though, it's not going to be that simple.

'I'm sorry – you are?' Standing at my parents' garden gate, framed by an arch of roses and jasmine, is an officious young man with wireless headphones around his neck, a walkie-talkie clipped to his breast pocket and a clipboard in his hand. I read the lanyard that swings on a scarlet ribbon – BARNEY BADGER, PRODUCTION ASSISTANT, CRABWISE FILMS – and the question of why this stranger is trying to keep me out of my parents' home is briefly overtaken by the question of why the hell anyone would call their kid Barney Badger.

'I'm Nell.' I don't explain Billie.

Barney Badger runs his pen up and down the clipboard. 'I can't see you on the call sheet. Do you have ID?'

He's looking at my hands. They're permanently cross-hatched with cuts, and when I have a tan, as I do now after a summer on deck, the old scars glow white.

'Are you serious?' I hand him my driver's licence and pull down my mask so he can compare my face with the picture.

'Eleanor *Churcher*!' he says, blanching.

Frank is fond of saying that fame is meaningless: all it means is that more people have heard of you than you have heard of them. Which is fine for him: he chose fame, in the latter half of his career, at least; he chased it. But having any kind of profile, even if it's against your will, means that strangers know more about you than you do about them. Fame gives *other people* all the power.

'I am *so* sorry,' Barney splutters. 'I didn't recognise you? *Eleanor*,' he says, as though he's worried he might forget again.

'I go by Nell.'

He finally registers Billie. 'Is this your daughter? She's not on the list?'

If I don't answer, I haven't lied. I correct him with a withering glance that stops his questions. I should probably come up with a word for what Billie is to me, but that's the whole point: there is no legal definition. Is she my stepdaughter? Am I her guardian? Not officially. But Barney knows I'm a Churcher now, and, while I distance myself from my name when it suits me, I use it when I need to.

'I don't need your permission to enter my own home.'

'We're asking everyone to wear lanyards? For security?'

He drapes red ribbons around our necks with the solemnity of an Olympic official.

'Well,' I say, straightening the lanyard, 'glad to see they're taking it all seriously.'

Barney ushers us down the side return into the back garden. The entrance is blocked by a great big fridge of a man in a black bomber jacket with the word SECURITY stretching from shoulder to shoulder.

'Shane, this is Eleanor Churcher . . . um, plus one,' says Barney, and the fridge steps aside, and I step into the sanctuary of my childhood garden.

Or rather, I don't.

The back garden usually offers soft green seclusion: our houses are surrounded on all four sides by the Heath, which is open public land, but on our property high fences are obscured by even higher trees. Today it has been invaded. A platoon of twenty-somethings in denim and grey marl weave their way around filming equipment. Cameras, monitors and microphones sprout from the ground like strange dark plants. The terrace that runs the width of both houses and looks down on the shared lawn is covered by thick black noodles of cable, duct-taped to the flagstones in little black Xs. The wooden fence that marked the boundary between the two family homes blew down in the big storm of 1987. Because we children were in and out of one another's gardens so frequently, and because it looked better that way, it was never replaced, although when Frank and Lal had one of their legendary arguments Frank sank a couple of six-foot fence-posts, grey concrete spires, so he could rebuild the barricade higher than ever. The row burned itself out before he finished the job, and these days Lal grows sweet-peas around the posts.

On the terrace there's a pile of twenty or so copies of *The Golden Bones* in its shiny new gold-leaf cover. The edges are sprayed gold too. Stacked high, they glow like ingots in a vault.

A label on the topmost book reads STRICTLY EMBARGOED UNTIL 2 AUGUST. I peel it off, pick the book up and stare at the picture, as familiar to me as my own face. A painting of Elinore, or strictly speaking a painting of Cora, in her long blue dress, looking over her shoulder as she runs from danger. The title has been updated with new line of text: 50TH ANNIVERSARY COLLECTOR'S EDITION. There are other changes too, such as a QR code on the back cover to take readers from the page to the screen. I flip it open: each book has an individually stamped number that will grant access to the treasure hunt app when it goes live on Monday morning.

The longer I hold it, the heavier and more dangerous it seems, as though the paper is turning to precious but poisonous metal in my hands.

5

When *The Golden Bones* was published in 1971 it was the most ambitious, expensive picture book ever made. It is artwork and legend and riddle and game, and it was inspired by a record Cora played Frank the night they got together.

The song was called 'To Gather the Bones'. My parents' generation listened to a lot of rock music that had its roots in folk, full of legend and magic. 'To Gather the Bones' was based on ancient lyrics, the knowledge of whose origins had evaporated like mist over the English countryside. Its unhappily married heroine, Elinore, takes a lover, Tam; upon discovering the affair, Elinore's husband murders her and scatters her bones throughout the countryside. A passing witch casts a spell allowing Tam to resurrect Elinore if he can piece her skeleton back together to prove his love. Tam spends the next seven years gathering his dead lover's bones and arranging them on his bed. As you do.

Even by the grisly standards of fairytales, adultery, murder and dismembered human remains don't sound like the ingredients for a bestseller, and there was every chance *The Golden Bones* would have been a very costly failure that ended Marcelle's career in books before it had really begun. But it was more than just a book. It was a treasure hunt, with clues to real-life English locations buried in the pictures. Each page had a verse from 'To Gather the Bones' etched around the edges. There was prose, too, that expanded the song into a storybook, but the pictures were the map. Readers guessed by looking at the pictures, which were photorealistic but otherworldly, so rich in detail that you could lose yourself for hours even if you didn't want to complete the treasure hunt. The central key was some esoteric formula to do with the shape of the clouds in each picture in relation to the number of birds in the sky – it always soared over my head – which pointed to words in the song, which turned out to be anagrams of further riddles to be solved. Those riddles were a hotchpotch of logic puzzles and maths, art and music, folklore and mythology, astrology, astronomy, religion. Riddles were hidden in anagrams, coded in ciphers and spelled out in acrostics.

On the last-but-two page of *The Golden Bones* is a picture of Elinore, her restoration not quite complete. She wears a ragged dress, her blonde hair is matted and greying, and decaying flesh falls away from the bones beneath. It was recently voted the most terrifying illustration in a children's book, beating off competi tion from the Jabberwocky, Struwwelpeter, and the Grand High Witch.

Cora, jill-of-all-trades that she was back then, made Elinore's bones from cheap nine-carat gold and flawed precious stones. Seven sets of bones – head, two arms, two legs, ribcage and pelvis – each no more than two inches long, were fitted with hooks and hinges so that when reunited they would make a tiny articulated skeleton. The seven pieces were assembled and photographed just once, then immediately dismantled. Then my parents threw Frank's ancient canvas tent in the back of their orange Morris Marina. They took a little tour of England and returned ten days later with filthy clothes and seven rolls of film, each documenting the burial of a different bone. The photographs were developed in a darkroom Frank built especially for the purpose, then sealed in a deposit box, along with the latitude and longitude co-ordinates of all the burial sites. Not even Marcelle saw them.

Lal wasn't trusted with the locations either, back in the day. His drinking made him a liability. In fact Frank only shared the deposition site of the golden pelvis – when they took on this anniversary project together. My brother knows too, now, bringing the total to four: Frank, Cora, Lal and Dom.

The Golden Bones was reprinted nine times in its first month. In America, it sold a hundred thousand copies in the first week. The fact that it was all but untranslatable didn't stop it from being a huge hit in Germany, Brazil, Italy and Japan. Its success enabled my parents to buy this house on the Vale of Health, one they'd often walked past when they were young and poor. In fact, the day the book went to press, Frank had proposed to Cora underneath the big oak tree that grows on the other side of the boundary and whose sky-high branches overhang the shared garden.

It was a good job they bought somewhere big, because three rooms were needed just to deal with the correspondence. Frank read every letter and sent a better-luck-next-time response in mirror writing, a gimmick whose painstaking requirements he quickly came to regret. Lal, who was a non-paying lodger at the Vale for the first few years of my parents' marriage, began helping out with the replies – it took him just one draft to replicate Frank's distinctive hand – and before long he was writing them all. Every morning the postman would deposit bulging grey sacks of letters on the doorstep and Cora would return the previous day's mail-bags to him, empty and folded flat.

For most readers the book was a diversion, something to while away an evening or even just an *objet* to be laid on a coffee table. For a hard core, it became all-consuming. Treasure-hunters worked alone, in pairs and in teams. Some bought multiple copies, sure that the answer was locked in a pattern that would reveal itself when a dozen books were laid out in a certain way, open at certain pages. Obsession with the book was cited in divorce proceedings. Family homes were lost as people spent thousands of pounds on travel, or quit their jobs, the quicker to save Elinore. They worked with an urgency that suggested they were trying to find a real-life vanished girl. Pretty, young, blonde, Elinore was the archetype of the Missing White Woman Syndrome years before the phrase was coined.

The hunters saw themselves as comrades as well as rivals. By letter they formed a dense circuitry of connections and eventually, led by Renée and Eric Glemham, a married couple in Little Rock, Arkansas, they formed an association, Elinore's Army, with its own quarterly magazine (which has since migrated online, and is now curated by their children). They called themselves the Bonehunters. They held conventions in chain hotels off interstate highways. They shared news, helped each other crack ciphers and got into heated debates about how to interpret clues. One mystery they discussed time and again was why Frank had, in scattering the jewels, built conflict into the process. Over the years they would come to understand that, for a man like him, that was part of the fun.

6

The seeds of conflict Frank scattered still flourish today, although these days Bonehunters argue on the internet, where conversations are faster and more furious than they were in the airmail days. ElinoresArmy.net is a gathering place not only for *Golden Bones* fans but for armchair treasure-hunters from all over the world. They call it a forum but it's more like a Facebook page: a constantly evolving series of posts, videos and comments. I've always been astonished by how many treasure hunts are ongoing at any given time. None of them ever breaks into the public consciousness the way *The Golden Bones* did.

Stuart Cummins is bound to be a member of ElinoresArmy.net but most of them hide behind false identities. Their names tend to be inspired by the book, and their avatars are often pictures of Elinore. Generally you can glean whether they're a threat from the content they post. Today, the mood is one of cautious jubilation. Emojis punctuate the text: excited faces, gold trophies, books, keys and the sassy red dress lady. As the film crew perform their maypole dance around us, I check in to see if Stuart has posted details of our little altercation.

@BON35: Two days to go, crew! Do we think the rumours about the prize are true?

@goldengal: It must be the missing bone. What else could it be? You know Churcher. He never likes to confirm or deny

@Elinore&Tam<3: She's coming back to life! I can feel it in my heart! See the lady rise!

Elinore&Tam<3 is not hiding behind a picture from the book. It's Jane Jones, another infamous Bonehunter. About the same age as my parents, she has been there from the start. The years have not been as kind to her as they have to Stuart but on the forums they hang on her every word. Just as vampires are believed to acquire strength and status with age, the longer Bonehunters have been actively seeking Elinore, the more highly regarded. Unlike a vampire, Jane Jones was able to cross a threshold without permission.

@BelleDame: You're letting Frank Churcher take you for fools all over again. The man's a born liar

Billie is reading over my shoulder. 'Are they right about the prize? Is that what Stuart was on about just then?'

I don't encourage her interest in *The Golden Bones* but I don't lie if she asks me about it outright.

'Yes. They're finally going to give the last bone away. They're filming the announcement and it's going to be on telly tomorrow night.'

'*Sick.*'

'Obviously if you tell anyone I'll have to kill you.'

'Cross my heart,' she says.

A new user has joined the forum. Welcome @LetterstoIngrid

'That is not funny,' I mutter to my screen. I watch the three dots ripple as LetterstoIngrid types. There are no words: just an emoji, a picture of a skull and crossbones.

@BelleDame: Haven't seen you here before. What's the story behind your username?

@LetterstoIngrid: New to the forum but a long-term Bhr! Just wanted to let you know I'm in contact with IM and she's devastated to miss out on today

This happens periodically: someone claiming to know or even *be* Ingrid. For some Bonehunters she has become a cult figure in her own right. Usually I can shrug it off – no one can get to Ingrid where she is now – but today, so soon after seeing Stuart, it trails a cold finger down my spine.

> @Ur098: As if you have. Security around IM is watertight since you-know-what (knife emoji, picture emoji, blood emoji)
>
> @LetterstoIngrid: It's an utter travesty the way she's been kept behind bars

An utter travesty. It's only minutes since I heard that phrase from Stuart's lips. It's bloody him, I know it.

> @BON35: Please can you stop posting about IM. True Bonehunters know her theories have been utterly discredited. Get off the forum and make space for those of us who actually follow the clues
>
> @Ur098: Well said @BON35

I creep around the side return to look at the street. Sure enough, there he is on the opposite pavement, sun bouncing off his head as he tap-tap-taps on his phone.

7

In 1972, the first correct guesses came through. A physics teacher from Bradford dug a tiny golden skull from a field on a Whitby clifftop (something to do with Dracula). A month later, two readers unearthed two bones in as many days – the left leg in Chanctonbury Ring in Somerset (something to do with Satanism) and the ribcage in Lavenham in Suffolk (something to do with burning witches). The finders gave interviews to the press, laying out their solves in mind-bending detail and vowing that they would never part with their treasure.

When there was a long lull between solves, Frank would give an interview to reignite interest (and sales). In 1973, my parents were photographed in the travel section of a bookshop, Frank's finger pointing to a guide to Cornwall, where Elinore's left arm was buried (something to do with a mermaid? I forget). The newspapers invited their readers to study the picture for clues, there was another spike in sales, and the bone was found the following week, although Frank would later regret setting the precedent of a hint left *outside* the book.

He would also come to regret hiding what I suppose you'd now call 'Easter eggs' in the text. For example, if you took the first letter of every word on the page describing Elinore's wedding night, you'd get CORA GIVES SPECTACULAR HEAD. I mean, where do you even start with that? When Dom and I were growing up, kids our age got wind of this and of course delighted in telling us that our mum was a slag. They never said anything disparaging about Frank, which was . . . ironic.

Tentative plans were made for the finders to lend their bones to the Victoria & Albert Museum when all were accounted for, so that devotees might file past Elinore, pieced together under glass. But that exhibition was not to be.

An eccentric art collector from the Philippines took a shine to Elinore. Fritz Velasco was the heir to a canned food fortune, an adored only child. His father had sent him to school, and then university, in England. While a student at the London School of Economics, the young Fritz had developed, not the business acumen his father had hoped for, but a very particular anglophilia; he was drawn to Arthurian legends and the naffer Pre-Raphaelites. *The Golden Bones*'s collision of pretty pictures, mythology and logic puzzles called to something inside him. He claimed many times that he had solved all seven clues on their own but wanted to give hunters who had not had his advantages in life the chance to own something extraordinary. No one believed him for a second, not least because he refused to share his attempted solves. His claims had all the credibility of a fifteen-year-old boy who absolutely *has* got a girlfriend but you wouldn't know her because she goes to a different school.

Fritz Velasco was a man used from boyhood to getting his way. What he lacked in hunting skills he made up for in tenacity and the depth of his pockets. Velasco hired Jonathan Reid, an old school friend who was setting up as a private investigator, to infiltrate the Bonehunting community. One by one, Reid approached the winning readers and made them offers they couldn't refuse. There are some crossword aficionados and amateur astronomers in England who live in *very* nice houses because of him.

But no one could solve the final mystery. By 1974, the only bone to remain unclaimed was the pelvic girdle, its coccyx studded with garnets. These days Jonathan's son has taken over the PI firm, and Fritz Velasco lives the life of a recluse in a Manila mansion, surrounded by a priceless collection of art with a bone-shaped hole at the heart of it.

8

The Golden Bones was still selling steadily when I was born in the spring of 1976. Frank and Cora named me after the girl in the book, as a thank-you for the life she had enabled them to live. When I first challenged my parents on their choice of name, Cora said, 'But yours is spelled completely differently.' As if that would make any difference to someone like Ingrid! Reality didn't get in her way, so why should spelling?

Frank was beginning to tire of the game. He had money, but the reader correspondence left him little time to spend it. His peers from the Slade were beginning to exhibit in the major galleries. He wanted to be taken seriously as an artist and he was being written off as a puzzle-setter, a trickster even. No one ever talked about the art, only the treasure.

And then, in 1977, a Bonehunter died.

Pete Winship was a London taxi driver who exemplified the phenomenon that cabbies, who back then had to memorise the entire *A–Z*, had enlarged pre-frontal cortexes, the part of the brain that deals with information and memory. A trivia buff who had taught himself German in the taxi queue outside Paddington station, Winship was a regular at the conventions. He had used the clouds-and-birds formula to arrive at these words.

Divine rules kiss over barbed eight
High in a grove of wise souls
A knight's move west of where Arthur's men halt

There is a certain kind of mind to which a riddle like this is catnip. Connections are made, classroom knowledge raises its hand saying *me, sir, me*, the eye is drawn to a reference book knowing that *this* is the volume that will prove the theory. That Winship was able to find meaning in these words is astonishing to me, especially considering that this was a pre-Google era, that his education had stopped at CSE level and that his research never took him farther than his local library. This is what he made of the poem.

Divine rules he understood to refer to ley lines – mystical paths that string ancient monuments together. *Kiss* referred to a point where they met; *barbed eight* he took to mean Thorney Island, the original site of the city of Westminster, *eyot* or *ait* being an old English word for an island in the Thames. On a map, two ley lines meet north of – or *over* – Westminster. They come together in Swains Lane in Highgate.

High in a grove of wise souls, Winship read as Highgate Cemetery. Actually, even I can grasp that one. *Grove* is too similar to *grave* to be a coincidence and Frank even gave the hunters the word *High*, as in Highgate. Highgate is one of London's so-called 'magnificent seven' nineteenth-century cemeteries: that the treasure being hunted consisted of seven bones was seen as relevant.

The last line, though. I could never have cracked that one. *A knight's move west of where Arthur's men halt*. From this Winship wrung the idea that *Arthur's men* were the twelve knights of the round table. Rather than heading to the West Country, traditionally considered the Arthurian seat of power, Winship fixated on the number thirteen: the king plus his knights, their *move* of course being the L-shaped one-two-three on the chessboard.

Winship wrote to Frank, declaring his solve and his intention to dig. He posted the letter at ten p.m. under a full moon, then drove from the postbox to Highgate Cemetery, which he entered by scaling the fence. Once inside, he located the thirteenth tomb from the entrance and counted two headstones across and one down. It was an old Victorian grave, housing no one of note, the words barely legible. That grave, Winship believed, was the final resting place of Elinore's last bone. He made fast progress with an ordinary garden trowel. The earth loosened its hold on the headstone and it toppled on to Winship, crushing the breath from his lungs.

Frank released a statement expressing his regret. He confirmed that Winship had got the wording of the riddle right; his mistake had been in its interpretation. The statement was carefully phrased: our steadfast family lawyer Leslie Napoleon saw to that. Frank went on to say that as a mark of respect, and for Bonehunters' future safety, he would call off the search. Under cover of darkness, he retrieved the golden pelvis and deposited it in a bank vault along with the original paintings and all his notes. He was, of course, distraught that a man had lost his life, but relieved, too. Now he would have time to spend his money. Now he would have time to paint again.

The fever broke and the fans moved on. A few Bonehunters still wrote to Frank and to each other. Some said Pete Winship's solve had been correct, and Frank had murdered him to get the bone back and sold it to Fritz Velasco in Manila – as if he needed the money at that stage. Others said Pete Winship had never existed in the first place.

The die-hards believed that the calling off of the search was part of the game, a ruse to dissuade the half-hearted hunter. That Frank was sick of clueless hobbyists getting in everyone's way. These hunters saw clues everywhere, regarded Frank's every utterance or gesture as information. They pored over old press photographs and divined meaning from the shape of the knot in his tie, or the direction he pointed his knee when his legs were crossed. While Frank maintained his silence, the Bonehunters traded theories and their solves and passed them around until the ideas mutated. By the time Ingrid discovered the book in the 1990s, Elinore and her whereabouts had become whatever the reader imagined or wanted her to be.

9

'Hi, Auntie Nell!' My eldest nephew, Oisin, emerges from behind a monitor and reaches down for a hug. Marcelle swung an internship for him as part of the TV deal. The poor kid started university – media studies, to Dom's abject despair – in the middle of lockdown. Even skivvying for a TV show must be a breath of fresh air after a year on Microsoft Teams.

'What's *this*?' I ask, squeezing a ridiculous bicep. Our little boy has turned into a monolith. He got the Lally curls and the Churcher height and athleticism, but, where Frank and Dom are lean in a *Chariots of Fire* sort of way, Osh has the huge arms and shoulders boys these days seem to think is required.

'Just been training,' he shrugs, clearly delighted that I've noticed.

Dom and Rose's children were carefully planned at five-year intervals, so each could have full parental attention during those vital early years of development – no screens until they could read one of Bridget's books in full. Rose is a child psychologist slash artist slash writer. She writes comic-strip non-fiction about mindfulness for teenage girls. Rose was raised as though the Vale was a little exclave of Ireland: I used to be fascinated by her wardrobe, the miniature wedding gown she wore for her first Holy Communion, the green velvet dress she wore to get her Riverdance on. Her kids have Irish passports and traditional names to match, spelled to fox the English. Oisin, Aoife and Niamh, pronounced Osheen, Eefer, Neev. Little Dara's name is pronounced phonetically but by the time they get to him, people have lost confidence in the alphabet and he's been called all sorts, from Darren to Dory to Tara.

Oisin adjusts his headphones, releasing springs of dark hair. 'You parked in London at the moment?' he asks.

'You don't park a boat, you moor it. And yes, I got this lovely little spot, between Ladbroke Grove and Kensal Rise. You should come and visit before I have to move on.'

'Is it safe?'

I get why he's asking. My family are never happier than when reminding me how vulnerable I am on the water. They have a point, but also they don't. *Seren* is essentially a floating shack, and a determined nutter could crowbar the hatch open in under a minute, but isn't that true of all but the most expensively secured houses? And then there's the trust you experience on the waterways. It's the only community where I've ever felt safe, mainly because none of them knows who I am. Or rather, they know the real me; who I am on a day-to-day basis. It's my background I conceal.

'We look after each other on the canals,' I say. 'You get to know people even when you're on the move. And if I don't feel safe . . . I just go.' He's clearly not convinced. 'Come round this evening, have a beer on deck.'

'I wish. We'll be working through the night in the edit suite. This goes out tomorrow evening at nine; it's all a bit of a race against time.'

'Well, you're always welcome.'

'Thanks.' His eyes travel over my head to Billie, who's facedown in Snapchat.

'She's *fifteen*, Osh,' I tell him.

He pulls back from me, offended. 'Jesus, Nell. I know that. I was checking she had a lanyard on.'

I've done him a disservice, judging him by the standards of my own youth. I'm sure Oisin's hard drive is as mucky as any boy his age, but he was raised by two feminist parents rather than an adulterer and a narcissist, and moral values were modelled for him in the home rather than being something he had to cobble together from outside influences.

'Right. Sorry.' Rose is big on apologising to children and young people. She says it builds mutual respect and teaches them that mistakes are learning opportunities.

'No biggie,' he says. 'Here, come and watch the guys.'

Everyone calls Frank and Lal 'the guys', even their grandchildren. Oisin guides me around a laurel bush so I can see the filming up close. 'The guys' are in earnest but inaudible conversation with a woman a bit younger than me, late thirties maybe. Red hair in a top knot, double denim and Converse.

My father is dressed as An Artist, just in case the knighthood, the retrospective at Tate Britain, the string of honorary doctorates and now being the subject of a documentary about his work wasn't making the point strongly enough. He's elegantly dishevelled in rolled-up shirtsleeves, a skinny red cravat and an old waistcoat. His silver hair is swept back and his beard is trimmed to a point. I can smell him from here: Guerlain Vétiver, the resiny, peppery scent he's worn my whole life. The one time he came to visit me on *Seren*, the place reeked for days afterwards.

Lal – who was offered a knighthood too but refused on the grounds of regarding himself as a soldier of the Irish Republic, a move that put Frank's nose out of joint for *months* – has puffed out with age, and his once glossy curls have the texture and colour of wire wool. He's in a polo shirt with a Tu by Sainsbury's label poking from a curling collar and what looks like an egg stain on the left breast. If he were trying to illustrate that he is secure enough in himself as An Artist to not dress the part, he couldn't have chosen better. But it probably just didn't occur to him.

'Who's that they're chatting to?'

'Polly Dean,' whispers Oisin, watching with naked adoration as she runs a highlighter over a printed page. 'We call her PD because she's a Producer-Director *and* her name's Polly Dean!'

'Is Aoife alright with all this?' I ask him. Aoife is Dom and Rose's thirteen-year-old. She gets overwhelmed by things other children don't even notice. She has special needs – a rare developmental disorder named after the double-barrelled doctor who identified it – but Rose thinks labels are unhelpful past the point of diagnosis. Instead we talk about her individual challenges, the learning difficulties and the emotional dysregulation. We all love her fiercely.

'The grandmas took the girls into the village for an ice-cream,' Oisin says. Our joint matriarchs were never 'the girls', even when they were young. They were Cora'n'Bridget or Bridget'n'Cora until Oisin was born, and then they became 'the grandmas'.

'Here.' Oisin hands me a pair of headphones so I can listen in. I hold them up to my ears, headpiece under my chin.

'Is there a word for your relationship?' PD wonders aloud as people peer into monitors and flash lights. 'I mean in the sense that two of your children are married – is there a word to describe joint fathers-in-law? Father-in-laws?'

'Outlaws,' they say in unison. Even their laughter is syncopated.

'Your friendship has endured longer than most marriages,' says PD.

'Well,' says Lal, 'we've too much dirt on each other to end it.'

He's not entirely joking. Cora tells me that Frank used to take Lal's empties to the bottle bank so Bridget wouldn't see how much he was drinking. And if Holy Lal didn't approve of Frank's affairs, he certainly turned a blind eye to them.

'We're basically brothers,' says Frank. 'I don't know if we could survive without each other now.'

Lal scratches his nose. 'Hey, Frank. What if, after all this time, it turns out that we're each other's muses?'

'Truly, he is my very own girl with a pearl earring,' says Frank affectionately.

They can argue as passionately as lovers about *anything*. In the past they came to blows over, off the top of my head: the first Gulf war, Van Gogh vs Gauguin, the Maastricht Treaty, religion (multiple times, in multiple ways, although Lal's Catholicism and Frank's equally staunch atheism have both softened over the years), *Let It Bleed* vs *Exile on Main Street*, Brown vs Blair, abortion (no prizes for guessing their respective stances on that one), poached eggs vs boiled, assisted dying, and manual vs automatic cars; and each man's conviction that *he alone* knows how to correctly lay a bonfire is legendary, although I'd like to see either of them try to keep a stove burning overnight on a narrow-boat in January. As recently as Christmas 2017 the guys had such a heated, stand-up row about who was the best James Bond that Lal put his back out and Frank lost his voice mid-rant. They were best friends again while the rest of us were still surveying the smoking rubble. I honestly don't know if it must be more exhausting to know them or to be them. They've been on an even keel lately, but before that it was as though they sat astride a seesaw for over fifty years, their fortunes never seeming to rise at the same time.

IO

Vale of Health, London NW3
1972

FRANK UP

'Darling!'

Frank opens his eyes to see a flushed Cora shaking him awake.

'Frank! Someone's found the skull! You've got a journalist call-ing to interview you in a moment and the book's going to be reprinted *again*. That'll make it the twenty-sixth reprint!' She gives him a kiss that's longer than it needs to be and he can sense what's on offer but she knows what he wants to do first. 'Go on,' she says. 'Go and tell him.'

Frank runs downstairs to break the news to Lal.

Not many brides would put up with their husband's best man being a lodger in the new marital home, but nothing fazes Cora. Frank likes having Lal around, not just for the company, but as a witness to his success. Perhaps it will even kick Lal into touch: show him that it takes more than just talent, it takes hard work and application of that talent.

LAL DOWN

Five postbags today. Lal's got a callus on his forefinger from wield-ing the letter-opener. He has a list of wrong answers, but not a list of right ones; if he's never heard them, they go straight to Frank. He can't be trusted not to blow the secret, apparently.

He starts the response, always done in mirror writing as a little

41

compensation prize. Lal's left handed and has a flair for looking-glass letters and now he can forge Frank's hand as easily as he can form his own.

His life is this house, that book, the pub, Mass on Sunday, the odd girl. Although lately he seems to be drawn to types who criticise his drinking. English girls can be so uptight.

It stings that he doesn't know the secret. Frank is wrong not to trust him. He can drink till dawn and still make it to Mass on Sunday morning. No matter how big the previous evening's session, he hasn't missed a Sunday or a Holy Day of Obligation since he left home. What's that if not an example of a man who can hold his drink?

Sure at the end of the day, Lal's happy for Frank. He really is. If *The Golden Bones* had been his idea he knows he'd have looked after Frank the way Frank's looked after him.

II

There's a lull in the interview. I return the headphones to Oisin and wander over to Shane the security guard. Billie trails after me.

'Alright?' he asks from on high. The guy literally blocks the sun. I come up to his armpit.

'I'm not being funny,' I ask him, 'but why've they got some kid on the door while you're out here guarding the camera crew? There's a guy out the front who really shouldn't be here, and if he tries anything funny, Barney Badger isn't exactly a brick shithouse, is he?'

Shane looks blank. 'Stuart Cummins?' I ask. 'Surely you've got some kind of blacklist?'

'I'm not personal protection,' he says. 'I'm here for the insurance company. There's valuable artefacts to be taken into account.' He nods backwards at the house. My heart sinks: I feel stupid – no, ashamed – for even thinking they might have hired him to keep me safe.

'There's a video on the Bonehunter forum,' Billie says, in that too-loud way people do when they've got headphones in.

A crew member losing a wrestling match with a tripod shushes her.

'Sorry,' she says, louder than ever.

I look over Billie's shoulder. On her phone are two sets of perfect teeth, two baseball caps and two shapeless royal blue T-shirts printed with a gold skeleton with the pelvic bone missing.

43

'I know these people,' I whisper.

Lisa-Marie and Porter Glemham are the exhaustingly peppy siblings from Arkansas whose late parents founded the magazine *Elinore's Army*. They aren't the only second-generation fanatics: love for the book seems to be passed down, like a family heirloom, or maybe a hereditary disease. Lisa-Marie and Porter are admins for the Bonehunters' Facebook page as well as for ElinoresArmy. net. Marcelle once worked out that if the Glemhams had charged for all the PR they've essentially given Frank for free, it would run to hundreds of thousands of pounds. Naturally, Frank can't stand them.

Billie gives me an earbud so I can hear what they're saying.

'. . . So two years ago, we booked our flights to England for the fiftieth anniversary of the greatest armchair treasure hunt of all time. We were going to do a tour of all six known burial sites. But then . . .'

'Needle scratch!' interjects Porter, and they both mime a DJ mixing a record.

'*Then*, right,' says Lisa-Marie, 'we got wind that a film crew were making a documentary about *The Golden Bones* and with a little sleuthing we learned they're actually filming at Sir Frank Churcher's house on the Vale of Health, London NW3, today, right now, so we are *en route* and hoping for an interview with the great man himself! If you're interested in coming along, we'll be meeting at Hampstead Tube station at eleven.'

Fantastic, I think. Any remaining Bonehunters who *didn't* know where Frank lived do now.

12

Our first close encounter with a Bonehunter came when I was nine and Dominic was six. A woman calling herself Mary put a professional-looking card through our letterbox offering her services as a babysitter. It was only when Cora checked with the neighbours – not just Lal and Bridget, but other families in the Vale – and found that ours was the only house to have received such a card that she became suspicious. Something about the covering letter had also rung a bell: a turn of phrase, perhaps? Being Cora, she could not be more specific than that.

Bridget solved the riddle. She combed the archived correspondence, comparing details, and spotted that the telephone number 'Mary' had given also appeared on letters by a persistent Bonehunter called Jane Jones. Cora telephoned the number and let 'Mary' know that she was lucky she wasn't calling the police.

Perhaps she should have.

Jane was playing a long game. Over the following months, she adopted another *alter ego*, Anne, and got cleaning work in a handful of houses on the Vale, including the Lallys', so that by the time she approached Cora for a job she came with glowing references from people Cora trusted. Cora had never met 'Mary' and had no reason to be suspicious of 'Anne'.

Jane was sprung when Cora caught her trying to pick the lock on Frank's study, a camera swinging from a strap on her wrist. Jane broke down immediately, confessed that she had only been trying to find out the truth and said that she would *die* if she didn't find Elinore's last bone.

Cora sacked Jane and changed the locks. This time the police *were* called. Jane got a rap on the knuckles. She didn't die, but she did leave us alone.

And then, a few years later, along came Ingrid.

Ingrid Morrison had an IQ of 145. She won a scholarship to St Paul's School for Girls, obtained three As at A-level when those were still the grades of an outlier, and a place to read philosophy and literature at the University of Warwick. During her first term, what had been a perfectionist work ethic mutated into something else. She stayed up all night pursuing complicated logic problems that went far beyond undergraduate-level study, and then punched through another threshold, from reality into madness. She became convinced that one of her tutors was sending her coded messages through the text of Hegel's famously impenetrable *The Phenomenology of Spirit*.

That tutor flagged Ingrid to student welfare and a stay on a psychiatric ward followed. In hospital she begged for reading material, but, in hands like hers, ideas were considered loaded guns. A well-meaning doctor steered Ingrid away from heavy-weight text that might feed her imagination and gave her a picture book instead, one that he had enjoyed during a convalescence from a childhood illness. It was an unusual picture book: it had something to offer adults as well as children.

It doesn't take a genius to see where this is going.

In the time it took her to read *The Golden Bones*, Ingrid transferred her obsession from her tutor to Elinore. The doctors were so pleased that she no longer carried a torch for her tutor that they overlooked the wildfire taking hold inside her. She solved four of the seven clues *on her own,* correctly identifying the resting places of the skull, the ribcage, the left arm and the right leg, with only her lightning mind and a poorly stocked hospital library to guide her.

The doctors thought it was nice that she had a hobby.

The inpatient became an outpatient, and *The Golden Bones* became Ingrid's life. She abandoned her degree, and drifted from unskilled job to unskilled job. Who has the energy for a career when they have a missing girl to find? She devoured all the back issues of *Elinore's Army* magazine and through their contacts pages amassed penpals across the world, connecting with those who didn't believe the search had truly been called off and sharing increasingly outlandish speculation about the missing pelvis. Most of them were to do with Frank: it was a scam, he was a fraud, he'd quietly slipped it to Velasco for a king's ransom – but over time those theories began to centre on me.

Ingrid combed the song collections and libraries that had so fascinated scholars nearly a century earlier, and Cora in the sixties. She ran her white-gloved fingers over pages my mother had touched in Cambridge colleges, private libraries, Halsway Manor in Somerset, the British Library, and the Bodleian in Oxford. She found links to the 'skeleton myth' going back to Danish and Celtic folk songs, and at one point got very excited by the ancient Egyptians. What was Ingrid looking for? Well, the hunt rewarded research, and she thought that she could crack it where no one could. That the clue was not in the book but beyond it. No one had ever thought like that.

'Because it's bollocks,' said Frank, when he was trying to explain what she had done to the police.

Nevertheless, she persisted, as the slogan on the T-shirt goes.

Ingrid's mission took her all over England but it was three miles down the road from us, in Cecil Sharp House in Regent's Park, that she struck gold. In their vast archive of traditional English songs, she found a slim pamphlet containing an earlier – and therefore arguably more authentic – transcription of 'To Gather The Bones'. This version included four extra verses and made the better-known one read like an episode of *My Little Pony*. The Cecil Sharp Verses, as they came to be known, continued the narrative beyond Elinore's resurrection. She bore Tam a daughter, but died in childbirth. The good old witch said that to bring Elinore back to life for a second time, she would need to take a bone from the baby. Tam offered his own life, but it was sacrifice or nothing. He closed his eyes so as not to see his baby torn apart; when he opened them, Elinore was nursing her little girl. The moral is probably something to do with men trusting women. You can see why this ending was omitted from the recorded version. Not exactly one for Top of the Pops.

Despite (or perhaps because of) their grisliness, the Cecil Sharp Verses appealed to Ingrid. An idea lodged itself in Ingrid's mind: the notion of a daughter sent to save her mother. And, as I was the daughter of the woman whose likeness filled the book, might I be a person of significance in the hunt?

On her next rereading of *The Golden Bones*, the last line of the book spoke to her.

With every kiss Tam gave her, Elinore grew stronger, and he kissed her every day. A year after her final bone was found, she gave birth to a daughter. The child carried gold within her, as all children born of a great love do.

If not quite a throwaway line, the word 'gold' was a hasty metaphor for goodness, bashed out on a typewriter hours from deadline. The story itself had always been secondary to Frank. The pictures were all. Ingrid, however, took it to mean that the golden bone was implanted under my skin.

These two pieces of 'evidence' were the basis of Ingrid's conviction that my actual, very much not-made-of-gold pelvis belonged to Elinore, and that the only way to bring her back to life was to gouge it from my body.

13

Ingrid – once the shining star of the Bonehunter community – gradually lost her lustre as people realised quite how far from Frank's intended search she had drifted, even by Bonehunter standards. The shunning drove her underground. This was in the early nineties, when most correspondence was still of the ink and paper kind. There were no public posts to warn us what was happening, and by definition the people still in touch with Ingrid were not the kind to sound the alarm.

The first I knew of her was the day she approached me on East Heath Street, the road that links Hampstead village with the Vale. I was fourteen and on my way home from school, REM playing on my Walkman, foam headphones over my ears.

'Elinore!' she called, and naturally my head turned her way. I recognised her as a Bonehunter and gave my customary response: head down, cross the road, quicken my pace.

'I knew it,' she said, and clapped her hands together like a child.

She began to loiter at the school gates. I told my teachers and my parents, who told me to ignore her and she would go away. They always did in the end. But Ingrid was different. She was suddenly everywhere I went, asking me nonsensical questions about bones and burials and gold, her eyes roaming my body more invasively than any man's. One day she ambushed me at a zebra crossing and thrust a leaflet for a private orthopaedic hospital into my hand.

'What's this for?' I asked her.

She laughed as she hopscotched across the stripes. 'Someone your age would hardly get a double hip replacement on the NHS, would they?'

Leslie Napoleon tried to get her arrested for harassment but the police dismissed her as a batty eccentric, then gave us a number to call if it ever got serious. Stalking wasn't a crime then. The laws that would have protected me would not come into force until 1997. So my parents took out a civil injunction against her. She was banned from going within fifty metres of me. To be on the safe side, I was driven to and from school in a minicab and chaperoned everywhere I went.

'The worst thing is the lack of spontaneity,' I overheard Cora saying to Frank, a few weeks into the regime. 'It's such a drag, all these curfews and chaperoning.'

'Leslie says we should scale down our parties this summer,' said Frank. 'Reckons it's too much of an open house.'

'You've *got* to be kidding me.'

'Wish I were,' he replied. 'Fucking Bonehunters. There's nothing they can't spoil.'

And for the next couple of years that was how it was, until the day I gave my driver the slip and nearly paid with my life.

Afterwards, when the police searched Ingrid's flat, they found an extra-large Jiffy bag with a pre-paid shipping label addressed to Velasco's company in the Philippines and a hand-written note saying that she didn't want any money, as for Elinore to rise again was a prize above gold. She really did think she was putting Elinore back together. She had clearly thought about the dimensions of my pelvis rationally enough to procure the correct postage and packaging materials, yet she still believed it could slot into a little gold skeleton that sat in the palm of a hand.

How did you reason with someone like that?

The next – and last – time I saw Ingrid was at her trial, nearly a year later. She looked like a textbook 'care in the community case', as we called them back then, with her mismatched clothes and her wild hair. She was clearly desperately ill but her intelligence shone through; she was as articulate as any of the barristers as she led us through the 'evidence' that had provoked the attack. There was a clear through-line of logic; she was almost convincing. She professed her regret throughout. 'I had to do it! I had no *choice*.' When the prosecuting barrister asked her how she thought a real human pelvis could possibly complete a tiny gold skeleton, she threw up her hands and said, 'Magic!' and then, 'Love!'

It was chilling to see someone so bright spout such abject nonsense.

She was discovered not guilty by reason of insanity. A psychiatrist diagnosed her with a personality disorder and schizophrenia and sent her to a psychiatric hospital. By then I had come to feel sorry for her.

A shiny-faced man in a three-piece suit had sat quietly in the public gallery throughout the trial. When the verdict was announced, he stood up and shouted, 'I'll put her back together again, Ingrid! I'll get that bone if it's the last thing I do!'

'See the lady rise!' responded Ingrid as security dragged him from the gallery and her from the dock.

'For fuck's *sake*,' said Cora.

In hospital, on medication, Ingrid's resolve to save Elinore was undimmed but broadcast only to her doctors and fellow patients, where the words bounced off the walls of the ward. The Bonehunters rose as one to condemn her actions, and to reinforce their commitment to a 'bloodless solve' in the *Elinore's Army* magazine.

My parents celebrated by throwing a party.

A month or so later, I was at home on my own when a young female police constable came to tell me that the man who'd called out to Ingrid at the end of the trial, one Stuart Cummins, had been hiding coded messages about me in long, rambling letters to Ingrid. 'Nothing for you to worry about, Miss Churcher,' she said. 'We've made sure that Ingrid won't have any more contact with the outside world. All letters and visitors are banned with immediate effect.'

A high-pitched ringing started up in my head. 'Let me get this straight,' I said. 'You're telling me that there're *two* people who think *this*' – I poked my own hipbone so hard it hurt – 'needs to be cut out and sent to the fucking Philippines? And one of them's just walking around out there?'

'Cummins is in Ingrid's thrall but we don't believe he's a threat,' she said carefully. 'Their conversations have been theoretical. There's no premeditation of any crime in their correspondence and he's got no previous.'

I gripped the doorframe with tingling fingertips. 'Ingrid didn't have any *previous* before she started on me, did she? No thanks to you lot. What if he tries to finish what she started?'

She shook her head. 'He's a bit of a saddo, really. The male equivalent of one of those lonely women who get engaged to serial killers.' She followed this up with a nervous laugh.

She was trying to reassure me; I saw her as flippant. Nothing was harmless when it came to *The Golden Bones*. Nothing was funny. That laugh released the tight spring of anger that had been coiling inside me for years. I caught her by her shoulders, the metal on her number cold under my hands as I bounced her head off the doorframe. Her hair painted a single red brushstroke as she slid down the white gloss.

A second later, I was dialling 999 on the hallway telephone, asking for an ambulance, and then I phoned Leslie Napoleon.

Assault on a police officer is something that the courts take really, really seriously. In mitigation: I had been through hell, and there was paperwork – reams of the stuff – to prove it. I had confessed on the spot, and sought help. In aggravation: the police-woman sustained a concussion that took her out of active duty for six months.

Leslie worked his magic. I did three weeks in the young offenders' section of Holloway prison and the rest of my sentence was suspended for two years. The day I was released was the day my compensation from the Criminal Injuries Board came through. That felt like money I had earned: I spent it on an Interrail ticket (forging my parents' signatures on the permission forms) and got as far from Ingrid – and my family – as I could.

I did not know that the threat remained. Years later, after he came back for me, we found out that the ban had been but a speedbump in the Stuart-Ingrid correspondence. A hospital orderly with a coke habit to fund had been only too happy to act as a go-between. While I had been travelling, Stuart had crossed the line from harmless saddo into something far more dangerous.

Ingrid's brief to Stuart Cummins was that he continue to delve into the folk song archives she had not been able to visit before she was put away. A sign – *any* sign – that there was another interpretation of 'To Gather the Bones', another lost ending, and the need to remove my bone would disappear. Any further confirmation, however, and efforts would need to be redoubled.

Despite an exhaustive search that took him the best part of three years and the expense of which led to him giving up his one-bedroom flat for a room in a shared house, Stuart drew a blank.

It broke his heart to have failed Ingrid.

Their conversations then turned to philosophy: the ethics of murder, of sacrificing my life for Elinore's. Ingrid sent him back to the British Library, this time to read Nietzsche and his theory of Master Morality that values consequences over ethics. So, one teenage girl (me) might sacrifice her life. But if the consequence was that Elinore was restored, violence was justified. After all, few people had heard of Eleanor Churcher and fewer still loved her. Elinore, on the other hand, had devotees all over the globe, deeply invested in her fate.

Stuart, to his credit, countered with a Kantian argument that killing was always prohibited even when the action would bring about more happiness than the alternative; but Ingrid was a persuasive writer, schooled in debate, and over the course of their correspondence she wore him down.

Soon their letters turned to the practical matter of finding me, and there they both faltered. I was living hand-to-mouth in

Europe, sporadic postcards to my family the only sign I was alive at all. It was the last time I ever felt truly free.

He found me the first time I appeared in public. Unlike Ingrid, he didn't get close enough to break my skin. Just my spirit.

After that, he too spent some time away. No psychiatric hospital for Stuart but a few months' detention at Her Majesty's Prison Gartree. Upon his release he was banned from approaching me but there was nothing to stop him continuing Ingrid's work. And thank goodness for that. Because he unearthed something that undermined Ingrid's rationale. A private collector of old sheet music discovered a dossier that became known as the Northumbria Papers, a set of drafted verses and letters written in 1903. They showed that the hallowed Cecil Sharp Verses were a pastiche, written by some twirly-moustached Edwardian who thought the fad for unearthing folk songs was sentimental.

I don't know if Stuart ever got word to Ingrid about the Northumbria Papers, but I do know that he renounced Ingrid's cause. He didn't darken my door again.

Until today.

14

The filming pauses while someone checks Frank's microphone.

Barney Badger sets a couple of glasses of red wine on the table in front of them.

'If he's here, who's out the front?' I ask Oisin.

'It's fine, we're doing shifts,' he says. 'Melanie's out there now.'

'What's this?' asks PD.

'Just a bit of set-dressing?' says Barney.

Frank slides the glasses out of Lal's reach and says, 'He's in AA.'

Lal rolls his sleeve up: he's got the date of his first day sober inked on his forearm, 21 June 1997, surrounded by a Celtic knot similar in style to his own illustrations – that seemed to make up ninety per cent of the tattoos everyone had back then. 'Twenty-four years dry,' he says proudly.

PD glares at Barney. 'Get. Rid.' Barney and the wine dematerialise. PD looks at her notes, then back at Lal's tattoo, and asks, 'Wasn't that the day after—'

'Hoooo, yes,' says Frank.

'Sure it was the session to end all sessions,' says Lal. 'Might as well go out with a bang as a whimper.'

'More of a detonation than a bang,' says Frank.

Lal chuckles. 'I'd say.'

There is more faffing around with light readings and sound checks. PD says, 'We're filming "as live" as time's so tight, but any mistakes we can edit out in post, alright?'

Someone shouts 'Roll!', a clapperboard snaps – I didn't think they still did that – and the atmosphere shifts as filming starts in earnest.

'You famously called off the treasure hunt in the seventies,' PD is saying, 'So why have you resurrected it now?'

'The obvious answer is that it's the golden anniversary.' Frank spreads his hands. 'Fifty years! Where did that go?'

'The days are long but the years are short,' says Lal.

Frank steeples his fingers. 'I had my reasons to turn my back on the work when I was a younger man, but now I've got the distance to acknowledge and to appreciate what it meant to so many people. But that alone didn't make it worth revisiting the project. I wasn't interested in a nostalgia trip; I started to think about how I would do it if I were starting out now and that's how we had the idea for a game, a computer game that would let readers interact with the story and join in the hunt in a different way.'

That 'we' is a stretch. The app was a hundred per cent Dom's idea.

'Unlike many people my age, I embrace tech.'

Does he bollocks. Even when Dom was managing a hundred staff, Frank still asked him to come round and set up his iPad. And Dom *did* it.

'I don't believe that screens are killing creativity,' he continues. 'I think they're revealing incredibly exciting new ways to create and connect. And, with technology being my son's area of expertise, we thought it might be rather a fun family project. If the past year has taught us anything, it's that time spent with loved ones is precious, and that exploring is precious too. One of the great things about the original treasure hunt was that it was a multi-generational thing. Entire families spent evenings together, trading solves. This new iteration marries that with a good old-fashioned walk in the English countryside – and if a screen incentivises our children to get out and about again, what's the harm?'

'We all piled in this time,' says Lal. 'It was good craic, even when we were doing it all over Zoom. We got the wives and kids involved, you know.'

'Obviously we had different teams in different countries but the germ of it's the same everywhere, and that was all of us. We've an impressive set of skills between us. Setting the puzzles, getting the look right – even got the grandchildren testing it out.'

'Did they ask you to be part of it?' Billie whispers, her breath hot on my ear.

'I politely declined,' I say, out of the corner of my mouth.

'And I tell you what else,' says Frank. 'It was a good thing, after all these years living in each other's pockets, to have something new to chat about over dinner.'

'So talk me through how the competition will work,' says PD.

Frank holds a copy of the anniversary edition of *The Golden Bones* to camera. 'Each copy has a QR code to take the reader to the app.' He points to the code on the cover then opens the book with the flair of a presenter on a shopping channel. 'And inside there's a unique serial number that will allow access to the hunt. This time, the prize is not physically buried. Rather, the player has to solve a series of clues and riddles to move on to the next location. They have to take their devices to the exact spot, rather like Pokémon Go, if you're familiar with the game – and there they will be able to claim a digital cache, a little golden key, that will reveal the next riddle. There are seven riddles for each territory. The first correct solves in each territory will win a replica of the original Elinore: a gold articulated skeleton.'

He smiles, knowing that his next words will form the clip that goes viral.

'And the first correct solve *worldwide* will receive a replica *and* the original missing pelvic bone, the one that has evaded capture for half a century.'

When this is broadcast tomorrow night, the Bonehunters are going to break their little corner of the internet.

'Why take the hunt worldwide?' asks PD. 'Obviously there have been dozens of armchair treasure hunts, but none on this scale.'

So he can flog fifty-quid books – and therefore apps – all over the world, I think.

'The treasure-hunting community is global,' says Lal. 'We want to open up the opportunity to as many people as possible. We like the idea that a player in, say, Germany or New Zealand or India is as likely to find Elinore as someone down the road.'

Frank takes over. 'And where possible we've made sure that the caches are reachable by public transport, and they will always be on land that's free to access. We don't want to price anyone out of the game.'

Apart from the people who can't drop fifty quid on a book, of course. Or don't have a smartphone. But who cares about them?

PD spins her pen between her fingers like a baton. 'Are you worried about people sharing solves online?'

'If you want to give away all your hard work then more fool you,' says Lal. 'But we're looking forward to a bit of healthy debate.'

'And what do you expect to happen to the original golden pelvis? I believe that the collector Fritz Velasco, who holds the other six golden bones, is currently offering a reward of . . .' she glances down at her notes '. . . four hundred thousand pounds?'

'The finder is of course free to sell it to Mr Velasco.' Frank is grinning: he knows the bunfight nature of the hunt is great publicity. He's missed this. 'They may decide they would rather own a piece of history. But if the past fifty years have taught me anything, it's that people mostly want to see those bones reunited.'

Dom told me that Fritz Velasco has bulk-ordered multiple copies from each territory and has enlisted a bunch of students to join the hunt on his behalf, a move that reminds me of Veruca Salt's daddy buying all the Wonka bars and getting his factory workers to look for the golden ticket.

PD turns a page on her clipboard. 'I'm interested to see that you, Frank, own the copyright to *The Golden Bones*. If it was such a joint effort, why not credit the others?'

'Legally it's very complicated, in terms of intellectual property.' He looks deeply regretful, before brightening. 'But the main reason is: everything the four of us – myself and Cora, Lal and his wife Bridget – own is for our grandchildren. The money we'd spend on lawyers and so on to evenly distribute the copyright could put one them through university, or get them on to the property ladder.'

'What's mine is his, and what's his is his,' says Lal, then pulls a face that suggests there was an edge in his voice he wasn't expecting.

Frank laughs to show what a good sport he is. 'I like the idea of Elinore being able to look after the next generation as well as she's looked after us,' he says. 'I mean, it's impossible for kids these days to get into a nice little flat in London the way we did, isn't it?'

Beside me, Billie makes a growling noise. For a girl like her, owning *a nice little flat in London* is about as feasible as owning a nice little flat on the moon. Then her face changes, as though someone's just whispered a shocking truth in her ear. She turns to face me.

'Did your *parents* pay for *Seren?*'

'They offered, but I wanted to stand on my own two feet.'

I thought my answer would increase her respect for me, but instead I see it draining from her. 'You're *mental*,' she says.

I shrug. Obviously I get where she's coming from. Since the day I left home, I haven't taken a penny from my parents. Money from *The Golden Bones* is blood money. I acknowledge of course that the book gave me a privileged childhood. It paid for my education and Dom's, not to mention lawyers and drivers and burglar alarms. But the day I left home I turned the tap off behind me.

Dom and Rose live in a five-bed listed property in Hampstead Garden Suburb. Dom does well but they had help with the deposit. I don't judge them for taking the money. They have a different relationship with the book, and of course, they have children. I've got to admit that my resolve has wavered a couple of times since getting Billie, but after Richard I swore I'd do the right thing, no matter how uncomfortable.

'Nearly done,' says PD. 'Are you worried about the hunt spilling into violence?'

'Another reason for making the caches digital is that you can't come to blows through a smartphone,' says Frank. 'And if the locations are compromised in any way, we have back-up clues, and we can change the locations at the tap of a keyboard.'

PD sets down her pen. 'And are you worried about your own security? In the past, family members have been subjected to—'

'Are you taking the piss?' Marcelle appears from nowhere, like the witch who emerges from the mist in 'To Gather the Bones'. 'You were told at the outset that is *totally* off limits.'

'We can edit that out,' says PD, but I notice she doesn't tell the cameras to stop rolling.

15

PD finally yells *cut*. The crew perform their maypole dance of cables and poles. A camera moves and a snaking black cable becomes a tripwire. I jump over it and into Frank's view.

'Thanks for coming, darling,' he calls across the garden. A warmth fans through me. I guess that no matter what they have put you through, no matter how many moorings you slip your rope around, as long as they are alive, your parents are home. 'That's my Eleanor,' he says to PD.

'Ah!' The way she swings her smile my way reminds me of a lighthouse. Her teeth are white but her pupils flare black and I can see the muckraker behind the arthouse film-maker. 'I'd *love* to catch up with you later, Eleanor.'

I bet she would. 'I prefer Nell,' I say, then turn to Oisin. 'Where's Dom?'

He nods backwards to the kitchen. 'He's doing some last-minute stuff on the app. There's coffee and breakfast stuff too.'

'Let's go,' I say to Billie. If anyone can reassure me about this LetterstoIngrid business, it's Dom.

On the way to the house we pass a raised bed of tomato plants, the fruits in various traffic-light stages of ripeness. If you look closely you can see some spikier plants in the middle. I pinch a leaf between my forefingers. This, along with Guerlain Vétiver, is the other scent of my childhood.

'Those plants look like . . .' says Billie, and I raise an eyebrow.

'Yup,' I say. 'That's my mum's finest organic marijuana.'

'They grow weed in their garden?' she says, delighted.

'Don't get ideas. Come on, let's go inside.'

My parents' kitchen spans the width of the house, just as the Lallys' does theirs, only, where Lal and Bridget kept the original doors, my parents had bifolds put in to facilitate the flow of bodies at parties. Every five years they rip out an expensive kitchen and install a new one (and throw a party to christen it, naturally). This navy blue DeVOL has been here since long before the pandemic so its days must be numbered.

'Jeez,' says Billie, as we enter. 'How many people are they expecting?' Every inch of the marble surfaces, including the induction hob, is hidden beneath a spread. There are Danish pastries, *pastéis de nata*, milk in steel jugs and huge fruit platters under stiff net cloches. There is even champagne in a huge ice bucket, green and gold bottles studded with condensation. Clearly Cora is making up for lost time. When we were little the 'season' kicked off with the Lallys' St Patrick's do in March. Frank and Cora hosted an August bank holiday barbecue when the funfair came to the heath and Bonfire Night marked its close with two rival pyres, Frank and Lal competing to see who could get a metal dust-bin full of smashed frames and lighter fuel to burn brightest for longest.

'Dominiiiic!' I sing bad opera into the belly of the house.

My brother is nowhere to be seen but his tech is here as his representative. The kitchen table is piled high with devices, the iPad charging and the laptop blinking with pages of bewildering code. Around the machines are books, printouts and files. Papers spill from an archive box on a chair. There are even a couple of old grey postbags, doubtless full of decades-old letters.

A note rings out from Billie's phone, a rich tone that sounds as though someone standing beside me has just struck a golden glockenspiel.

'Look, it's Dom's app.' She taps an icon on her screen, and an avatar of Elinore, a digitally revived young Cora, fills the screen, only to turn immediately into a skeleton whose bones scatter to reform the words Two Days To Go.

'Do you think they might give me a book?' she asks shyly.

'Best not take one of those. But I'll get you one,' I say, even though the thought of having it on the boat makes me nauseous. 'I'm just gonna go to the loo. Don't go outside. Or talk to any of this lot.'

'Stranger danger,' she says, not looking up. 'Got it.'

I look over my shoulder before leaving the kitchen. PD is talking to Barney Badger and gesturing at me, a look on her face that I would recognise anywhere. A mask that makes all its wearers look the same.

I need someone level-headed (so that rules out either of my parents) to talk me down from my paranoia. I text Dom.

Where are you bro? I need you

He fires a reply straight back. *Meet you in mums kitchen in 5*

The downstairs loo is for the crew, so I use the family bathroom on the first floor. I see that Cora's changed everything on the huge landing around again. Cora doesn't have furniture, she has *pieces*, and she doesn't rearrange furniture, she *curates* a *space*. All her pieces are *narrative*, patterns and prints inspired by mythology from around the world. There's a new Egyptian-looking console table outside my parents' room and a love-seat in Liberty fabric at the foot of the stairs to the attic.

The landing window that overlooks the front of the house is the original stained glass; you can't see into the house from the outside, but if you press your eye up close you can use it as a spyhole on to the street. I look through a little pane of untextured red glass, squinting with one eye as if it's a monocle. Standing opposite the house, under a streetlamp, holding his phone but looking dead ahead, is Stuart. He can't possibly see me, but it feels as though he's staring into my soul.

16

I slide the bolt on the family bathroom as if he were running after me. It's a surprisingly calming place. The towels are new but everything else is the same. My old rubber ducks are in a string bag ready for Dara's next bathtime. I use the loo, phone in hand, knickers around my ankles, then flush, wash my hands and take myself to the back bedroom. I'm carrying myself defensively, low to the ground, like a cat.

My childhood bedroom is the nicest one, which is just as well since it was a prison for so long. It's at the back of the house, with views over the heath. It's the kids' room now, for when they stay over: twin beds with flamingo-print bedclothes for Aoife and Niamh and a racing car bed for Dara. On the shelves, volumes of *Diary of a Wimpy Kid* and *Dork Diaries* sit beside my old Judy Blumes, and of course Bridget and Lal's Selkies series: the original 1970s editions and the slick TV tie-ins.

Gathering grey fluff on the top shelf is a row of identical books. *The Ghost Bell* was Cora's solo foray into picture books. Real stained-glass panels were reproduced on acetate, each page more elaborate than the last, overlapping to reveal clues. After the success of *The Golden Bones*, Marcelle's publishing house were desperate for a sequel. Frank wasn't interested but Cora was; an old Lake District tale about bells that rang for a drowned bride had fired her imagination. I think Cora, who has never been comfortable living in the real world, thought that she was tapping into some kind of English race memory: that we'd all be swapping our rotary washing lines for maypoles and Morris dancing. She hoped that she could build on the phenomenon of *The Golden Bones* and invite everyone into the misty glens with her.

It was not to be. *The Ghost Bell* tanked. It was such a spectacular failure that for years publishing houses used it as an example
of how not to do things. It's one of the reasons Marcelle left
books for art. It was beautiful, but lacked the complexity, not to
mention the reward, of *The Golden Bones*. Another project – a
full and exquisite set of glass tarot cards – was stocked in Harrods
but even their customers wouldn't pay the asking price of £1,000
for something so niche.

I pull a first edition – well, they're all first editions, there was no
reprint – of *The Ghost Bell* from the shelf. The spine cracks in a
way that tells me I'm the only person ever to open it. There's
something tragic about a book no one ever reads. Maybe Cora's
bad luck is one reason – apart from keeping my profile low – that
I keep my work modest. I've got the skills for large-scale pieces –
the work I've done on custom windows is probably my best – but
I'd rather scratch a living with integrity and keep my ego separate. And besides, if I went bigger I'd need a workshop, and a
permanent mooring, and all the things I've spent my adult life
trying to avoid. I have occasionally thought that Billie gives me
the perfect excuse to put down some roots, but that would be
tempting fate. The minute I drop anchor is the minute they'll take
her away. I keep cruising because then they can't catch us. The
more I sink in, the more I invest, the more I have to lose. My
awareness that this is bullshit magical thinking at its worst doesn't
stop me thinking it.

I used to watch Cora at work in my teenage years when this
room was my prison and I saw each season roll around twice, fists
on the window ledge, watching the trees sway on the Heath. I
resume my old position now, my hands finding a remembered
flaw in the woodwork. At the end of the garden is her old studio;
a one-storey cottage really. She used to call her work 'pottering'
and I'd play a game with myself, trying to predict which skill
she'd be honing on any given day. I loved to watch her work; to
marvel at the illusion of a woman with four arms as her hands
flew over her loom or her potter's wheel. The studio is where she

taught me to work with glass. I thumb the raised scar on the edge of my hand from the one and only time I tried to cut without scoring first.

When Cora couldn't work any more and Frank's prostate put the kibosh on his affairs, he moved all his stuff from the contentious place in Gospel Oak to that studio. Through its French windows I can see canvases, stacked white-on-white against the walls, and the orange tongue of his yoga mat, rolled out for his next sun salutation.

A squeaky floorboard behind me pulls me back into the house.

'Alright?' says a voice that has become all too familiar.

'Hello, Barney,' I say, without turning around.

'The downstairs one's busy?'

I nod to the family bathroom, marvel briefly at his stream, and am pleased to hear the taps go when he's done. He joins me at the window.

'You know Cora made picture books as well?' I proffer *The Ghost Bell*. 'She gets overshadowed by Frank.'

He declines the book; I replace it in its outline of dust.

'So are you inner circle,' he asks, 'with the treasure and that?'

I shake my head. 'My parents were of the opinion that if I never knew, I could never tell.'

'And you never had a go at solving it?'

This gets a laugh from me. 'I could never get my head around the puzzles.'

'That's the side of it I *like?*' says Barney. 'No offence, but the pictures are a bit fairies-at-the-bottom of the garden for me? I like his other stuff, though, a lot.'

He gestures up at the painting to our right on the landing. It's Cora, one of the first paintings Frank did in his 'new' style. One day, frustrated that every painting of his wife looked like Elinore, he swapped his fine sable brushes for thicker ones made of hogshair. Using heavy, viscous paint, he vandalised his own work, painting over the photo-realistic – if flattering – flesh with slap-dash gestures in khakis and mauves, more suited to a rhinoceros hide than human flesh. The result was an intimate, candid portrait of a woman in early middle age. When she sat for it, Cora had probably been only a couple of years older than I am now, and I recognise in my own loosening jaw and breasts the way time is beginning to pull her curves into hammocks of skin. A reworking of this picture was the centrepiece for *Intimacies*, Frank's comeback exhibition, a collection of female nudes in this new style.

The opening night was a perfect showcase of Churcher-Lally dysfunctionality.

It was on Midsummer's Eve, 20 June 1997, and when Lal had told PD it was the session to end all sessions, he wasn't lying. He ended up in hospital.

Rumours flew that Frank had slept with all his sitters.

Cora was high as a kite, Bridget brittle with the stress of trying to keep everyone together.

And *The Golden Bones* had overshadowed it all.

Jane Jones and Stuart Cummins, convinced that the exhibition was secretly a series of clues to the last golden bone, had crashed the party. It was the first time they met.

Neither of them had an invitation, of course.

She had a disposable camera.

He had a knife.

'Don't suppose *you* fancy being interviewed?' Barney asks, with such studied casualness that this must be what he's been building up to. 'We've got Dominic's take on it, obviously. But it'd be good to get your views on the phenomenon, on your dad's work? Now and then? And – how it affected you, growing up?'

The thought of the Bonehunters dissecting the footage, trying to find clues in my facial expression or the stone in my earring or reading my body language like runes, spikes the hairs on my arms.

'Thanks, but no.'

'Well, if you change your mind . . .' he says.

'I really won't.'

His walkie talkie goes *chchchchch*. 'Barney, how long's it take to have a piss?' barks PD. 'You're supposed to be chatting up the daughter.'

'I'm actually with her now?' He drops his voice even though I'm right next to him.

'It's OK,' I say to the radio. 'He was just going.'

17

Dom's not in the kitchen, just Billie, taking a selfie – fingers splayed in a peace sign, mouth drawn in a pout – in front of a ziggurat of chocolate brownies.

'How much can I have?' she asks. For a second I think she means the champagne in the bucket next to her. As far as I know, she doesn't drink. I worry, though, that she's inherited her parents' addictive personalities – it's not even noon – and, if I'm the first one to put a glass in her hand, what I could be setting in motion.

'I don't know if now's . . .' and then I follow her gaze and realise that she's simply eyeing the feast. '*Oh*. As much as you like, honey.'

Billie pumps her fist. 'Get *in*.'

She drinks two glasses of orange juice standing up, then piles her plate high. She says she was never greedy when she was little but at the foster home you ate fast or you went hungry, and then during her short stint on the streets she got to know real hunger and it flipped a switch inside her. She doesn't talk about it much but once let slip that there was a day she only made two quid begging at Paddington station and had to choose between food, tampons or a shower. (She stole the tampons, ate chips from a bin and paid for the shower.) This was a few months before I met her. She had only just turned thirteen. Thinking about it makes my eyes fizz and burn.

'What's all that?' Her gaze lands on a cardboard archive box to my right. I stick my hand in as though it's a lucky dip. The first thing I find is a scrapbook of yellowing cuttings. These headlines are familiar, our fucked-up family fable. It's weird to think of the old sketches and plans, the things Frank said he would never unearth, being released from the vault, let alone filmed for television.

TREASURE HUNT TRAGEDY is from the *Daily Mail*. There's a picture of the golden skeleton and another of Winship holding a toddler, all dimples, bowl cut and dungarees.

That's pretty hard to stomach but the next cuttings, both from tabloids, are worse.

ARTIST'S GIRL STALKED BY NUTTY FAN cries the *Mirror*. They've illustrated it with a shot of the book and Ingrid's mugshot, more frightening to me than any illustration.

GOLDEN BONES GIRL BANGED UP says the *Sun*. The headline is sensational but they used an old school photograph of me, taken a couple of years earlier, in which I look as if butter wouldn't melt.

Time, which has felt less linear than normal all morning, loops a little tighter.

'This is nothing interesting.' I slide it to the bottom. 'Let's see what else is there.'

I sift through old pictures, including a rare sketch of my mother with all her clothes on. There's a copy of *A Dictionary of Faith and Folklore* with Frank's mad-professor scrawls in the margin, then an ancient hardback AA roadmap of Britain covered with ballpoint scribbles, some locations circled and ticked, some with ticks, some with question marks beside them, others crossed out. I squint to decipher them. *Ley lines,* I can make out, *solstice, vernal equinox, ancient burial ground.*

'Billie, look!' Every now and then I forget to hate *The Golden Bones* and excitement catches me out. 'These are Frank's original plans for the book. It's like finding the original lyrics to *Sergeant Pepper* or something. No wonder they hired a security guard. Bonehunters would kill for this; they must be worth a fortune.'

I set it carefully back in the box.

Under that, there's my naked mother again, Cora on the cover of the *Intimacies* catalogue. Billie takes it from my hands and reads from the opening page.

'*Is realism a lie? In his new collection of paintings, Frank Churcher engineers a head-on collision between fidelity to appearance and the ugly, pulsating essence of humanity. Urgent gestures in viscous oil share the canvas with forensic portraiture, inviting the viewer to . . .*' She shakes her head and sets it to one side. 'I'm sorry, but what a load of *wank.*' She moves swiftly on to another dog-eared book. 'This is *De Humani Corporis Fabrica Libri Septem* by my man Vesalius.'

I chastise myself for thinking the words sound funny in Billie's broad London accent. Why should they? The posh schoolchildren who still learn Latin are no more Roman than she is.

She leafs through the reproduction engravings. 'It's a banger. We did it in history.'

'Did you now? When I was at school we just seemed to do the Tudors and World Wars on a loop.'

'I'm doing history of medicine for GCSE.' Her eyes rest on a pen-and-ink brain. 'It's well gory, I love it. Is this where Frank copied his drawings from? Because these pictures are like four hundred years old and the anatomy's all wrong.'

'No. He actually had a skeleton.'

She sets the book down. 'Shut *up.*'

'Not a real one. Should've made that clear. One of his art school friends was a prop-maker and they made fibreglass skeletons for horror films. Frank used one of them, so he could draw it from all angles. There's a really good picture of him doing it, let me see if it's here.' I leaf through the archive box. 'It was really convincing, even up close. It *felt* real, not like a prop. They called it Gertrude, after one of the nuns at Lal's school.'

'And what became of Gertrude?'

I sift through studio portraits and snapshots. 'Oh, she was one of the family for years. Frank actually had her mounted in a frame on the wall for a while, up on the landing, right up until, ooh, ten years ago. We used to take the bones off the pins and play with them when we were little.' I flash back to happy afternoons with Dom and Rose, arranging Gertrude in various poses; we had one we called Disco Dancer, the *Saturday Night Fever* stance of one hand pointing, the opposite leg out, and another called The Buddha, which unsurprisingly involved crossing her legs. We'd shout things like 'I need the right ulna' the way other kids might say, 'I need a oner,' when playing Lego.

'Normal.'

'It was for us. Although, by the time Dom had kids he'd changed his mind, he wouldn't let them near it. I think he has a policy of, whatever we did in our childhood, he tries to do the opposite. Ah, here it is.' I pull out an old black and white photograph of Frank at his easel, a paint-spattered smock over his flares. On a table at his side is a ribcage. On the canvas is a half-finished picture of those same bones submerged in a river, weeds binding them to the bed, fish swimming through their arches. I hand it to Billie. 'I swear, skeletons could be my specialist subject on *Mastermind*. Adults used to think it was hilarious. They'd quiz us, like, how many bones in a foot, or tell us weird facts. The collective noun for bones is a "humility". In the nineteenth century, poor people sold their bones to medical science to pay for their funerals. The crossbones in a skull and crossbones are made from a femur, which is a—'

'Thighbone,' she interrupts, setting the picture aside. 'And there're twenty-six bones in a foot.'

I love this side of Billie; the deep wells of knowledge inside her. 'Gold star. But do you know why the skull and crossbones used those particular bones?'

She shakes her head.

'They thought that the femur and the skull were the last parts of a skeleton to decompose.'

Even Billie, with her biologist's strong stomach, grimaces at this. 'Did you genuinely never find it creepy?'

'I knew she was fake,' I reply. 'The only time I even noticed she was there was when friends came round and got weirded out. But then when Aoife was about three she got one of her phobias about it.' Another flashback now, the same landing twenty years later,

Dom and Rose out for the evening and me trying to calm a terri-fied Aoife who cried so hard she threw up all over me. The poor girl has a rotating stock of debilitating phobias – buttons, balloons, sirens, daffodils, sand – or perhaps it's one metaphobia with a thousand different faces. There's a system Dom and Rose use now to talk her down from the brink, numbering her distress on a scale of ten to one, but she was too little then, only recently diagnosed. 'Frank was an absolute dickhead about it, told Aoife to snap out of it. Even without her special needs, who forces a toddler to look at a skeleton? So I took matters into my own hands and took her down.'

'What happened to Gertrude?' Billie's moved on to a plate of sandwiches, opening them all to see what's inside, rejecting cream cheese and celery.

'I wrapped her in recycling bags and threw her in the bin. Bye-bye, Gertrude.' I brush imaginary dust off my palms.

'Must have been quite the shock for the bin men. What's this?' She parts two triangles of bread to reveal a black paste.

'Uh . . . black olive tapenade. I made sure she was all taped up in bin bags. The bones would've just got chewed up in the lorry. I think fibreglass shattered pretty easily.'

'Oh, my God, that's *delicious*,' she says, mouth full. 'You could've sold her.'

I shrug. 'You know I don't accept any money that comes from anything to do with the book.'

'And you're gonna keep that up forever?' she asks. She would never come right out and ask me to take a handout so she could have a better life, but she must think it.

'It would take a lot.' It's a big deal, me saying this. People have asked me this question my whole adult life and this is the first time my answer has deviated from a hard no. Still, Billie shakes her head in frustration. It is so far from her experience – God, it's so far from most people's experience – that I don't expect any adult to understand, let alone a fifteen-year-old who grew up in poverty – who still doesn't live far off it, to be honest. But I'm proud to have built a life – a strange life, an insecure life, but one with integrity – without taking a penny from Elinore's bony hand.

18

Dom clatters in, phone in hand, white sticks in his ears. Always lean, he's solid gristle from eighteen months going nowhere over a Peloton.

'Why are you dressed as a Land Girl from World War Two?' he says.

'Get bent.'

He gives me a one-armed hug which I reinforce with both arms around his waist. You couldn't say my brother is my best friend – we only see each other a couple of times a year – but there's a unique bond, a shared history, that I could never replicate with anyone else.

Also, winding him up is one of the great pleasures of my life. I pounce on an orange tidemark around his collar. 'Are you wearing *make-up*?'

He rubs his neck. 'They made me when I did my piece to camera earlier. I looked like a corpse under the lights.'

'Did they psychoanalyse your relationship with Frank?'

He grimaces. 'God, can you imagine? No, I was more talking about the development process, investors, how the pandemic affected the experience economy and so on.'

'Did you *thrust*?'

'Piss off.'

Until recently, Dom was a management consultant in the City. Going into management consultancy was quite a punk move when you come from a family like ours. I am genuinely proud of him. But when he got his first job – a training scheme where he worked with lots of other young men called Dom (or Josh, or Toby), some boring business magazine singled him out as 'one to watch'. The reporter described him as a 'thrusting young graduate'. It has never stopped being funny.

He opens a cupboard next to a fridge and takes down a large plastic box full of smaller cardboard boxes. 'The old dear must have some paracetamol in among all this,' he says.

I peer over his shoulder. It looks like the stock room of a small pharmacy. Statins, antacids, Xanax, co-codamol; and that's just the top layer. 'Are these all Cora's?' I ask, horrified. 'What's actually wrong with her?'

'I know,' he says. 'The irony is, if she'd ease off on the self-medication, she could probably ditch half of these. I do worry, but she won't listen. Ah, here's the good stuff.' He pops two paracetamol caplets from a blister pack and swallows them dry.

'What's the matter with you, anyway?' I ask.

'I'm hungover. Apparently I was being uptight yesterday so Dad and Lal took me to the Duke last night and got me shitfaced. Do you know they had a *literal* pissing contest last night? At the urinals? It was quite something.'

I hold up my hand to his face. 'Please stop talking.'

'And before that, I hadn't slept for a week. If it's not the coding it's the marketing. It just never bloody *ends*.'

I scan his face. The unequal division of labour has scored new grooves under his eyes and across his forehead. Frank is the face of this app but Dom has been the driving force. He gave up a stellar career – with stress, yes, but also security – and developed an app from scratch. I hope he's not going to be one of those people whose dramatic pandemic life change doesn't work out.

And now I'm about to add to his worries. My hand closes around my phone in my pocket but, before I can do anything, Billie grips my wrist and stage-whispers, 'Can you ask him for me?'

'Hello, William,' says Dom, making her smile. 'Ask me what?'

'Billie was wondering if she could have one of the new books,' I say.

'Please,' she adds. 'I can't *wait*.' She opens the app on her phone and shows him the golden skeleton. That distinctive chime sounds again.

'You pre-ordered!' he seems genuinely touched. 'Of course you can have a book. Um, it's a bit tricky 'cos it's embargoed till Monday morning but I'll sneak one out to you later, OK?'

'Nice one. I'll get a ton for that on eBay.'

He knows she's joking, although she probably *could* name her price.

'But you do know you can't win?' he says. 'Family are ineligible. Sorry.'

Far from being disappointed, she lights up like a bulb. He's included her in the family. *Thank you*, I mouth.

'Hey,' I remember, reaching for my bag. 'I've got something for you.'

He knows what it is by the care with which he undoes first the tissue paper, then the bubble wrap. I'm gratified by the gasp he lets out before holding it up to the light. It's a suncatcher in the shape of a skeleton working on a laptop. The body is two shades of glass, the deep amber of honey and the crisp pale gold, shot through with bubbles like champagne, and the laptop is a gorgeous iridescent gunmetal.

'That's you, that is,' I tell him. 'It's a one-off; I didn't do it from a pattern.' I want to remind him how long my makes take me, that the love I can't show with money I give with my time.

For a moment, he doesn't speak; when he does, he's choked.

'I love it. I *love* it. Where will it be safe?' He looks around the kitchen, every surface given over to *The Golden Bones* in one way or another.

'Literally nowhere,' I say, and then, because he looks like a man whose circuits are about to malfunction, hold my hands out. 'Give it back to me. I'll bring it round next week.' I re-wrap it and slide it into my bag.

'Why do you need me, anyway?'

'So,' I begin. 'Please don't call me paranoid, but I was online and I saw—'

'WHAT DO YOU MEAN, A CRISIS?' he suddenly bellows, apparently at me.

It's only when I see his earbuds flashing that I realise that he's just answered a call. 'But how did they – when – OK, Leelo, no, I *am* calm. Walk me through it.'

Leelo is his lead coder, a keyboard whiz – based in Estonia, in charge of the detail that turns Dom's idea into reality. Dom looks dazed, as though he's taken a punch: with two days to go until the app launches, this can't be good news. Dom frowns at his laptop and says, 'Yup, yup,' a lot, and, 'Right. Find out and call me back in five.'

'What's happened?' I ask.

'Problem with the server. Leelo's lost the past two days' work.'

'Bonehunters,' I say. They've tried to sabotage everything Frank has done since *The Golden Bones*, and there's a strong overlap between the kind of mind that is drawn to complex puzzles and mythology and the kind of mind that can make things happen from behind a keyboard.

'Looks like an outage rather than a hack,' says Dom. 'Sorry, you were saying?'

'Stuart's outside.'

'Oof. You OK?'

'The police say they can't do anything.'

'You called the *police*?' Dom's expression changes. 'Did he threaten you?'

'Not in person. But I think this is him.' I call up LetterstoIngrid's posts, and the video on the forum that Billie showed me. 'Can you get those bloody Americans to take it down? It's freaking me out.'

'The Glemhams aren't that bad,' says Dom. 'I've been in touch with them a lot about the app, actually. They're annoying but basically benign. They play by the rules. They're still trying to solve the location of Elinore's pelvic bone but they're doing it in good faith; they accept that it's in the vault. I'm more worried about them interrupting filming than anything else. I've seen the shooting schedule; there's no margin for error.'

'If they're such good guys, why do they allow all this speculation? *Any* mention of Ingrid is not in keeping with the spirit of treasure-hunting.'

'Money,' says Dom ruefully. 'Their advertisers pay for eyeballs. They can't afford to lose any traffic.'

'Amazing.' It hasn't taken me long in my brother's company to slide back into sarcastic teenage mode. 'I'm so glad the most traumatic event of my life is making someone money from Grammarly ads.'

He squints at the code rolling past on his screen. 'The Glemhams don't make a *profit*,' he says, without looking away. 'They lose money on it. Honestly, you don't need to worry. If anything, it's a good thing. If the Glemhams weren't hosting those dodgy chats they'd end up on Reddit and Quora with the nutters and incels.'

'What, keep your enemies close?'

'I mean, yeah. A bit.' Dom stretches his arms over his head, revealing burgers of sweat under each armpit.

'But what if Stuart's really in touch with Ingrid? If those old stories have come up again?'

Dom holds me by the shoulders. 'Nell. It's been decades since there was a threat to you. You know Leslie had Ingrid checked out before all this began? She isn't allowed any contact with the outside world. Hasn't been for years. It's not going to be her.'

19

There's a screeching noise in the garden.

'What the hell's that?' I leap to my feet. It's not Stuart forcing an entry but someone dragging a large black box on wheels across the terrace. My already elevated heart rate spikes further and my eyes travel to the cupboard housing Cora's personal pharmacy. If I weren't responsible for Billie, I would seriously consider taking a leaf out of my mother's book and floating through the day on a cloud of Xanax.

'I can't hear myself think,' moans Dom. I pour him a coffee. 'Get it away!' he says, when I bring it to the kitchen table. 'You know what you're like, with your gift for spillages. You'll manage to get it on every document and in my hard drive in one swift movement.'

I see that he's regressed too, to when I was a kid and I couldn't cross a room without stubbing my toe. Living on a boat teaches you to be steady on your feet. But that's what coming home means, doesn't it? You're always going to be who you were then.

'Was the kitchen table really the best place to commandeer?' I ask him. 'It's a big house, there's lots of rooms. Why not work in Frank's study?' I nod to the room off the hall, the administrative hub during the postbag years.

'It's full of memorabilia. And the wifi's shit everywhere else.' He nods to the router flashing blue on the sideboard.

'Next door?' I suggest.

'Well, that was the idea, but Dara poured a Fruit Shoot over *their* router last month and they didn't get round to replacing it. They've been piggybacking off Mum and Dad's wifi ever since. As have half the fucking crew, today. Have they not heard of unlimited data? Some of us have a fucking app to launch!'

As if to prove Dom's point, Barney Badger enters the kitchen with his iPhone in one hand and a bright yellow charger in the other. 'I'm down to four per cent?' he says, and bends down to the plugboard. 'OK if I just—'

'For fuck's sake!' shrieks Dom. 'That's the fucking *router*! Do you want to disconnect me? Do you have any idea what'll happen if my connection drops? Literally *any* other plug in the house except that one. Go on, fuck off.'

'Yeah, no, cool,' says Barney, and disappears into the hall.

Dom rolls his eyes. 'You know the really sad thing is, *that's* what Oisin aspires to be.'

'Do you say that to Oisin?' I ask. 'Because you of all people should know what it feels like to have your father sneer at what you do.'

Dom looks chastened. 'You're right,' he says. 'It seems to be a Churcher man thing, doesn't it? The Admiral disappointed in Dad. Dad disappointed in me. *God.*' He runs his hand through his hair and then looks at his hands, as though he's expecting a whole chunk to have fallen out. '*Media* studies, though,' he says, making me laugh.

'Look, if anyone can break the chain, you can. You're a brilliant dad, Dom. Involving Oisin in the app, not to mention the way you are with Aoife.'

'Well, I've certainly been more *present* lately,' he concedes. 'Possibly at the expense of the whole "provider" thing, though.'

He chews his lip the way he used to when he was little and waiting for something to be over with: a penalty in football, a piano exam. *The Golden Bones* has been such a money-spinner that I had never associated this new project with risk.

'Dom, you haven't sunk your own money into this, have you?'

'Only in the sense that I'm living off a fraction of my old earnings and even with our best projections the company won't turn a profit for another three years,' he says, and then, when I draw a horrified breath, 'No, don't worry. Most of it's been funded by venture capital. I won't lose the house if this goes tits-up. Just my reputation, my sanity, the last two years of my life and my independence.'

Interesting that he thinks of his project as establishing independence, as I'd have thought that a project linked to *The Golden Bones* isn't exactly going it alone, but I know better than to voice my judgement. It wasn't easy for Dom growing up in a household of artists. He's got a brain like a computer but whatever it is that connects ideas to the hand, the ability to effortlessly replicate images on a page that fed into me from both our parents, passed him by. He's always been insecure about it; felt like an outsider. Frank's obvious disappointment in him didn't help. Dom would never say it, but I think there's a part of him that envies what happened to me. It pressed me deep into *The Golden Bones*'s sages. *I'd* never say it, but I wonder if part of his motivation in creating this app is to stand inside the circle at last.

I try again. I pull up the screenshot from ElinoresArmy and wave it under Dom's nose. 'Just in case. This LetterstoIngrid person. Can't you get their email or something? We can prove it's Stuart and then we can get another restraining order or whatever.'

'On the grounds of what? There's no explicit threat to you. And even if there was, no, I *can't* "get their email or something". You'd need to ask the Glemhams for the IP; I can't see the back end of their forum, can I? And a troll like this is probably hiding behind a VPN.'

'A what now?' I know my way around the internet as well as most women in their mid-forties, which is to say, I'm on it all day but mystified by what happens 'backstage'.

His phone flashes again, and within seconds he's saying, 'Leelo, sorry about that.' I can hear the panic in her voice through Dom's earbuds. He pinches the bridge of his nose as he listens. I'll take this up with him again when he's done.

'Hey, listen,' I ask Billie, 'what was Dom on about just then, with all those letters? VIP and all that.'

'VPN and IP,' she says. 'The IP address is basically the address of an individual computer – it's like a trace you leave behind on every website you visit.'

'So if the Glemhams can find out the IP address, we can just turn up and see who this is?' I feel like a Victorian mystified by the workings of a light switch.

'Well, it's not always accurate. Sometimes you can get it down to the door number; other times it gives you like a hundred-mile radius. Also there's the other thing Dom said, a VPN – that means you can hide your IP address so no one can trace it.'

'And that's legal, is it?'

'Yeah. Loads of people have them.'

'Normal people, or terrorists?'

She laughs. 'You can watch telly from other regions is the main reason I can think of. Also it's more secure.'

'God. It almost makes me nostalgic for physical stalking.'

My phone vibrates with a reminder that pulls me back into the world outside this house. 'Are you working on Thursday?' I ask Billie.

She checks her iCal. 'Nope.'

From the corner of my eye I see Dom pressing his hand down in a 'quieten down' motion. I lower my voice. 'Make sure you keep it that way,' I tell her. 'We've got Eyebrows at half-past one.'

Eyebrows is our name for Jill, Billie's social worker. She draws skinny dark brown arches above her own sparse brows, presumably to save her the effort of keeping them permanently raised in judgement.

'Can't you put her off?' Billie groans. 'She's such a downer.'

Dom's a bundle of nervous energy, listening to Leelo, working his mouse with one hand while the other drums maddeningly on the table, or clicks a pen lid until it blurs, or thumbs through Frank's old art catalogue like it's a flipbook. His kinetic energy is physically catching, like those mediaeval villagers who started dancing and couldn't stop. I turn my back on him. I have enough jitters of my own without absorbing his.

'She's not my idea of fun either, but we missed the last two because we were travelling,' I say to Billie. 'We can't get away with missing a third. I wish your dad would get his arse in gear.'

'Does Eyebrows still think Dad's working as a hospital porter?' asks Billie.

Dom glares at her. 'Can you not?' He presses his earbuds dangerously far into the ear canal.

'Pretty sure she does,' I whisper.

It was a good cover during lockdown. No one was going to question a key worker, exhausted from frontline work, the girlfriend stepping in to help with the kid. But Dylan's been AWOL for a year and a half now, and it's getting harder to explain away his absence with every visit.

'When did you last see him?'

'Got a text on my birthday from someone else's phone,' she says. 'At three a.m., when mine was on flight mode. When I rang back it turned out to be some random whose phone he'd borrowed.' She brightens for a second. 'But it does show that he memorised my number.'

'Ssshh!' says Dom.

My heart twists at how low her expectations are, how far she can make the crumbs go.

'He hasn't posted on Facebook for over a year,' says Billie.

'Oh, he never does,' I say. 'I mean – what's his status update gonna be?'

'Another tooth fell out, hashtag goals?' suggests Billie.

'Found a new shooting gallery, hashtag blessed?'

Billie laughs, spraying orange juice and pastry crumbs everywhere.

Dom erupts. 'Will the two of you just pack it in! My head is about to explode here!'

He looks twice as hungover as he did five minutes ago. And he looked like crap then.

'Bad news?' I ask, our earlier row forgotten.

He waves me away with his hand. His chin is puckered, as if he's trying not to cry.

'Sorry. We'll go next door. Call me if you need me. Come on, Bill.'

I grab my coffee; Billie takes her plate. I leave him staring at the wall. Shit. If this goes wrong, there's so much more at stake for Dom than 'just' his professional pride.

All those years he was jealous of my association with *The Golden Bones*. You don't know until you're in. It's not a privilege, it's a curse.

20

Going from Cora's kitchen to Bridget's is a matter of crossing a few flagstones. 'Hello?' I say, turning the door handle. 'It's me, Nell.'

No one appears to be in.

'It's nice here,' says Billie, and I realise it's her first time at the Lallys' place. 'Friendly.'

'That's actually a really good word for it.'

This is as much my home as the house I grew up in. When we were kids, our parents were pretty much interchangeable. It wasn't unusual for Lal and Bridget to go off on a book tour and for Rose to stay in my room, or for my parents to take themselves off on holiday and for us to camp out at the Lallys'. Their kitchen is cool and dark, and as chaotic as my parents', but not because of the filming. It's always like this, clutter on every surface. The walls writhe with William Morris and Laura Ashley prints that were all the rage when they decorated in the late seventies, an ersatz Victoriana that just happens to suit the place, so they left it that way. The kitchen has the same appliances and dark pine cabinetry piled with wholefood cookbooks as when I was little. One wall is panelled in oranged pine tongue-and-groove.

'That bit looks like a sauna,' observes Billie. 'And it feels like a totally different time of day to next door,' she observes.

'I know what you mean.'

The whole house seems to absorb light and matter. Lal and Bridget aren't poor but they never throw anything away. Once I punctured a tyre on my bike on the way to Sunday lunch and, when I mentioned it, Bridget nipped up to the huge attic and fetched not just one inner tube but a selection of them, as though she had a small branch of Halfords up there. You'd never think she used to be a nurse. Growing up, that attic was a deadly place, containing an overspill of artists' materials, lye and lead paint and all manner of toxins. The story is that it's still full of such stuff, which is why the little ones aren't allowed anywhere near it, but the truth is that, as well as being a holding place for a half-century of crap, it's also where they dry out – or *cure*, as they like to say – the marijuana they grow in the long borders.

We sit on the church pews that flank Bridget's table and like any good mother and daughter ignore each other in favour of our phones. Billie's watching videos of puppies falling over on TikTok. I log on to ElinoresArmy and immediately wish I hadn't.

@LetterstoIngrid: The bloodline continues! Apparently Eleanor Churcher has a daughter now. They live on a boat, never settling in one place. Why do you think that might be?

There are no responses but it was only posted thirty seconds ago. A bad energy starts to gather at the base of my spine.

Stuart only saw Billie for a few seconds, but Bonehunters have made life-changing assumptions in less time than that.

And how does he know about the boat? I've only mentioned it to Oisin. Did one of the crew overhear me, then feed this information back to Stuart?

No one in the boating community knows about my family.

No one outside the family knows about Billie.

No one else except Dylan.

I met Dylan at a Christmas party in 2019. I'd woken up that morning thinking how nice it would be to get laid – probably a combination of the lights and mistletoe on the boats and some kind of perimenopausal last hurrah impelling me to fertilise my last viable eggs – and that night I met him, a funny, charming, tousle-haired man who'd never heard of *The Golden Bones* (trust me, I can tell).

It wasn't until I woke up in his council flat and saw the bandy-legged thirteen-year-old child standing in the bedroom doorway that I understood he was a father. Over stewed tea and white toast with Billie, I learned that he barely knew it himself. She had been living with Dylan for only five weeks; before that, she'd met him as many times. Her mum, Christie, had been just fifteen when she'd had Billie and only seventeen when she'd OD'd in a stair-well. With Dylan long off the scene, Billie was brought up by her beloved nan, and, when she died, there was a spell in foster homes – and the streets – while Social Services traced Dylan.

From that first conversation, there was a sense that this kid and I *recognised* each other. She was bright but furious, well-meaning but impulsive.

Billie didn't give me the whole truth about Dylan that morning. Already she was thinking in terms of getting me to stay. A couple of months later, *Seren*'s hull needed blacking and I moved in temporarily. Two months later – complications at the shipyard – I was still there.

And then, lockdown, Dylan's long hours spent in the bath-room, the disappearing money, the little squares of foil and the blackened teaspoons.

I gave him two weeks to sort himself out and took Billie to stay on the boat.

When we returned, Dylan was gone and the flat had been sublet to a family of Bulgarians. We weren't a brilliant couple, what with Assaulting a Police Officer (me) and Affray, Fraud and Possession with Intent to Supply (him), but the fact that we *were* a couple went a long way for Eyebrows. The stability of a nuclear family effectively wipes out our criminal records. So as far as she's concerned we're still together.

I'd love to adopt or even just foster Billie but continuous cruis-ing is deemed unsuitable for a child who needs stability. They should have seen us in lockdown. They should have seen how learning to pilot a boat and work the locks built Billie's confi-dence. They should have seen how hard she worked, how she sat on a freezing canalside to catch free wifi so she didn't miss any lessons. They should have seen us bingeing on *Real Housewives* and playing Uno and sharing memes that made us laugh until we couldn't breathe.

I look at her now, swollen with love and worry as she bites into a *nata* and closes her eyes with pleasure as the custard oozes out. Billie opens her eyes to find me staring at her. 'Why're you looking at me funny?'

I flick on a smile. 'No reason.'

21

'Can you copy those videos and send them to me?' I ask her.

'Get your own TikTok.'

'I'm too old.'

She knows something's up. 'Why d'you want TikToks of dogs, anyway?'

The real reason is that the longer I keep her distracted, the greater the chance that this post about me having a daughter will be pushed to the bottom of the ElinoresArmy page where she won't see it.

'I think Aoife would like them,' I say, which is true; it's just not the reason.

'Oh,' she says. 'Yeah, sure.'

On the forum, the responses to LetterstoIngrid's post about me, Billie and *Seren* are getting heated.

@BON35: Pack it in the lot of you. You should be ashamed of yourselves

@Yorick: Admins, can you step in? This is not in the spirit of the treasure hunt

@LisaMarie: Agreed. Can we keep on topic here, guys? I'm taking this down. Kids are not fair game

The screen flickers and the posts about my 'daughter' disappear.

Thank you, BON35, thank you, Yorick. It's good to know there are at least two voices of reason out there. I check out both their profiles. BON35 has posted a few Russian novels' worth of content over the years. You wonder where people find the time. Yorick is less prolific, but what he lacks in productivity he makes up for in passion. There are accusations of murder and wrongdoing stretching back a good fifteen years. He clearly belongs to the subset who think the *very* worst of Frank. Hundreds of them have accused Frank of murder over the years: he murdered Elinore, he murdered Pete Winship, he murdered every Bonehunter who died without knowing Elinore's fate. Yorick's earliest post is from 1999, a cached page that takes ages to load and when it does it's from the earliest days of the net, a crude headline and eye-melting pages of Times New Roman font on a black background.

@Yorick: When Elinore's last bone is found, the truth will come out about Frank Churcher

@Yorick: What he did to Elinore is the least of our worries

@Yorick: He is a literal killer

'He seems nice,' I say.
'What?' Billie looks up from her puppies.
'Nothing!' I say brightly.
They continue in that vein for another fifteen years or so, culminating in an explosive post from 2016.

@Yorick: I know things about the treasure hunt that would make your eyes bleed. One day, when the time is right, I'll blow the lid off everything

That last post seems to have tired Yorick out, because as far as I can see nothing has stirred him until LetterstoIngrid joined the forum today. He might bear a grudge against Frank but he's our ally against Ingrid and I will happily take that.
Underneath, the discussion is still raging.

@BelleDame: I don't understand why she would be in touch with you and not me

@LetterstoIngrid: Because you let her down last time. You got found out

@BelleDame: I put my neck on the line for her when no one else would. Where were you then?

I realise with a rush of bile that BelleDame must be Stuart. Which means Ingrid has somehow garnered herself another disciple. If Stuart is BelleDame, then who the *hell* is LetterstoIngrid?

@LetterstoIngrid: We both want the same thing. Are your DMs open? I can send you proof – and some pretty explosive new information

@BelleDame I simply don't believe you

@LetterstoIngrid She's got her birdy eye on things

All the blood in my body drains abruptly to my feet. That's almost exactly what Ingrid said the second before she plunged the knife into me. It was such an odd turn of phrase that over the years I've come to believe I misheard, or misremembered. It's a detail I've never mentioned to anyone. If she convinces Stuart, then what?

@BelleDame: Opening DMs now

Shit shit *shit*.

@BON35: Too right. Keep your crackpot theories off the forum

But BON35 is wrong. If history is repeating itself, as it seems to want to, then it's when Bonehunters go dark, when the mainstream Bonehunters can't police them, that the trouble really begins.

22

I've tried not to picture their procession from the Tube to the Vale but the little blue dot on the map in my mind is moving steadily closer.

'I reckon they'll be at the top of East Heath Road by now,' I tell Billie.

Rose enters the kitchen, wraps a bony arm around my neck and rests her chin for a second on top of my head. Like Dom, she was there through all of it. She gets it. We say we're basically sisters but we're not. we're nicer to each other than that.

She knows something is wrong as soon as she sees me.

'Has there been a scare?'

'Stuart's out the front,' I say.

'That creepy fuck. Well, this is the worst bit as far as you're concerned. After the TV show airs and everyone knows the actual golden bone is the prize, you'll be off the hook. Are there any others?'

'Yes,' I say. 'They're *marauding*.'

'Oh, God,' she says. 'I *hate* it when they maraud. Marauding is the *worst*.'

I can't help but smile. I glance at the tiny pair of underpants she's holding. 'I know you're skinny but even you'll struggle to fit into those.'

Rose's dress hugs her ribs and skims a belly flatter than a mother of four's has any right to be. Like Bridget, she's what you'd call handsome rather than pretty; a proper Pre-Raphaelite stunner with the long red-brown hair, heavy brows, strong jaw, wide shoulders. Frank once said that Cora and I were the kind of girls you like to paint naked but Bridget and Rose were the kind of women you wanted to photograph in clothes.

And still he wonders why I prefer not to call him Daddy.

Rose sighs. 'They're Dara's. He hasn't worn clothes in three weeks and I can't have him running around with his willy out in front of the cameras. Have you seen him?'

I shake my head. 'Are *you* alright?' I ask, noticing the two spots of high colour stain her pale cheeks, her lifelong tell.

'Bit frazzled, you know.'

I wonder if it's a good thing or a bad thing to tell Rose that Dom's having trouble with the app and decide to leave it. For all I know, it's sorted already.

Her gaze sweeps the back garden and comes back to land on Billie. 'Hello, there,' she says formally. 'How are you?'

'I'm good,' says Billie.

'Still working at the cat shelter?'

'It's more like a cat hotel?'

'And they don't mind the nails?' She eyes Billie's green talons with distaste. 'They *can't* be hygienic.'

Beside me, Billie shrinks. I make a *fuck's sake* face at Rose. This is not like her. She's supposed to be about empowering teenage girls, not knocking them down. But she's already moved on. 'I'd better locate Dara. Especially if your man's out there.'

There's a weariness in her voice I've never heard before. She's probably been absorbing Dom's stress and managing Aoife as well as the other kids pretty much single-handedly for the last however many weeks, so I decide to give her a break. I'll tell Billie later that Rose is not herself at the moment – none of them is – and she mustn't take any crap they give her today personally.

Not that she seems bothered. She's taken her plate on a little tour of the kitchen, examining everything as though she's in a museum. A splintered plank in the tongue and groove has been framed and a little white card has been stuck next to it with what must be the world's longest-serving piece of Blu-Tak.

Title: TOXIC MASCULINITY, 1997
Artist: Gerard Lally
Medium: Fist on pine
*The artist rejects the conventions of figurative art to make a bold
statement about repressed anger.*

'Is that your writing?' she asks.

'It's an old joke,' I tell her, and it is, although it was a good few
years after he threw the punch that I figured enough time had
passed that we could laugh about it.

23

Vale of Health, London NW3
1985

FRANK UP

At four o'clock in the morning, Frank and Cora wake to find Bridget shivering at their bedside, a weeping Rose in her arms. All Frank's senses are suddenly on high alert and he can smell spilt whiskey on Bridget's clothes and urine on Rose and from next door come the sounds of glasses smashing. 'He doesn't know what he's doing, God forgive him.'

'Are you hurt?' says Cora.

Bridget shakes her head. 'He missed.'

But he tried. That's a first.

Cora folds back the bedclothes and Bridget and Rose curl in beside her. The women look to Frank, who nods in answer to their unspoken question. They've had the drying-out clinic on speed-dial for the six months since Lal decided it was safe for him to start drinking again – in moderation this time, of course. Except, there is no moderation for Lal. Everyone but him understands he's in the grip of a disease.

Frank watched with – not satisfaction, he's not *that* much of a sadist, but it was reassuring to have his old friend on the same page as him, neither of them making art. And if Frank is honest, yes, more than once he's been the one to suggest the pub. But this is the first time Lal's gone for his wife, and next time it might be the child, whom Frank loves as though she were his own.

In the kitchen, Lal is surrounded by broken crockery and glass.

'Where's my slag of a wife?' he slurs.

'Let's go for a drive,' says Frank. 'Clear your head.'

LAL DOWN

London streaks past the car window. Lal vomits into the carrier bag on his lap. Load of fuss about fucking nothing.

When Frank slows before a gate and Lal reads the name of the clinic he tries to take the wheel from Frank. 'You bastard,' he says, but they're already at the door. 'Yeah, yeah, yeah,' he says, raising his hands in surrender. If they're going to take him for a fool he might as well play along. What he'll do is, he'll go to the clinic, sleep it off, do a lap of the grounds and come out again. Anything to keep them all off his back.

24

There's a giggle from under the table and Dara rolls out, naked, then does a kind of victory breakdance, spinning around on his back on the dusty floor. I hold out my arms, waiting for him to say, 'Auntie Nell!' but instead he charges past me to Billie, who is at best indifferent to toddlers, and flings his arms around her legs.

He nods. 'I've got my *willy* out,' he says solemnly.

'Eww,' she says, pulling away. Dara is nonplussed rather than upset. As far as he's concerned, Billie is an adult, and he's never met an adult who didn't fawn over his blond curls and street moves.

'Dara,' I say, 'is it true you don't know how to put your own underpants on?'

Now he is profoundly affronted. 'No! I'm really good at it.'

I aim for a sage nod. 'Go upstairs and show Billie, then.'

She gives me an incredulous look. 'Do I have to?'

'Yes.' I smile.

She climbs the unfamiliar staircase without taking her eyes off her phone.

'I've got my *willy*—' Dara tries again, but Billie cuts him off.

'Not interested, kid.'

I find Rose in the garden. 'He's upstairs, getting dressed.'

'Oh, thank goodness.' The release of tension makes her lose a couple of inches in height.

Under an apple tree, Frank is watching playback of his interview on a monitor. I touch his arm in greeting and he puts both his hands over mine.

'How's it hanging, Franco?'

'We're still persisting with the first-name terms, are we?'

'I beg your pardon. *Sir* Francis.' I give a little bow.

'That's more like it,' he says. 'It's going well, I think. All a bit military precision but I still got my steps in.' He taps his smartwatch to show me he's done 15k this morning. 'It's the same team who did Lal's doc, although they're hopeful that mine will reach a wider audience.'

'You can't help it, can you?' I ask. 'You'll go to your grave trying to outdo him.'

'A little competition is a healthy thing,' Frank chuckles, then looks me up and down, takes my dungarees and headscarf. 'I didn't realise the Women's Land Army had re-formed.'

'Hilarious.'

'Is that a fashion hole or a poverty hole?'

I follow his gaze to my knee. 'It's a laziness hole. I ripped them going through Enfield lock and I can't be arsed to replace them.'

'Darling, if you need money, you will say, won't you?' He searches my face. 'It's just that you've never taken anything from us and your brother stands to make a few bob out of this if it goes well. Obviously I'll leave you enough of my work to make you comfortable when I go, but if you need cash in the meantime, just say the word.'

'You don't need to leave me anything.'

'It just doesn't seem fair for Dom to profit when you haven't. Especially when you're the artist, after all. Even if you don't have a degree.'

Here we go. 'I don't need a degree.'

'They'd have *loved* you at Goldsmith's.'

Frank still cares desperately that I didn't go to art college, even though he is the reason I didn't. I'd seen his obsession with having the right letters after his name and being owned by the right buyers and attaching the right meaning to his name my whole childhood. I thought it was ugly. I wanted to do the work but not be part of any world except the one I created for myself. Can art-for-art's-sake get any purer than that?

'Do you know,' he says, 'their schedule is so tight I have to factor in breaks for a piss?'

'How *is* the old prostate?' I ask him. There's something benign but inconvenient going on down there.

'Size of a coconut,' he says. He makes a great show of stretching upwards then touching his toes, as if to prove that his prostate might be showing his age but the rest of him is well preserved. 'I was up all night, forcing out a useless dribble of . . .'

'That's actually enough information, thank you.'

'I'm having a full screening next week,' he says meaningfully. If anyone else said this my mind would immediately leap to worst-case scenarios, but with Frank I'm not worried. One of his greatest pleasures in life is having expensive doctors tell him he's the healthiest seventy-three-year old man they've ever seen.

'Seen all the stuff in there?' He nods at the house. 'We basically emptied the whole vault on to the kitchen table.' He pauses for a second. 'Well, not the *whole* vault.' His words conjure the last golden bone, sitting cold in a cellar in a bank somewhere. Picturing it, I have the ridiculous notion that it – *she* – will be cold, now she's not insulated by all that paper. I'm thinking like one of *them*. 'Lal came over for breakfast, helped me look through it. There were things no one had seen for fifty years. Stuff from when you were little, stuff from the nineties. And obviously Lal's had so many "lost weekends" that some of them he was seeing as though for the first time.'

'I saw them,' I say. 'It was quite the trip down Memory Lane.' I take a deep breath. 'Stuart's outside and the police can't legally move him on.'

'Stuart must be pushing seventy,' he says dismissively, as though he is a whippersnapper of fifty himself.

I show him the conversation between BelleDame and LetterstoIngrid. He has the same reaction as Dom. 'He's not actually saying he wants to hurt you.'

'Still, though. Just the fact of him bringing up Ingrid's name. It could give people ideas.'

'Bastards.' Frank pauses to consider. 'I could pay for security for your boat. Would that make you feel better?'

If he were at all interested in the way I live he'd know how ridiculous his suggestion is. How would you guard a boat that's always on the move? Does he intend to pay a live-in bodyguard, when there's barely room for me and Billie and my work stuff? It's such a Frank Churcher solution, to throw money at the problem, that I start to laugh. Within seconds it's turned into tears. I go to cover my eyes but Frank catches my hands.

'Oh, Eleanor. I'm sorry,' he says quietly. 'I never have apologised for what the book did to you, growing up. Obviously it was unintended consequences, but still.'

I have waited so many years for this. I never expected acknowledgment to come, let alone apology. When I did dare to hope, I thought it would be preceded by a declaration, a ceremony even. And here he is, dropping the words lightly in a garden full of strangers. Relief freights my tears, makes them hot and heavy. He has finally owned the damage he did me. No more defensiveness, no more denial. It must be this project with Dom; working so closely with his son must have somehow humbled Frank and mellowed him. And the anniversary will have made him reflect on the things that he got wrong. I open my mouth to tell him what his apology means to me.

'So come on. A five-minute piece to camera. Just for *once*, don't throw it all back in our faces?'

Ah, *there* he is. Manipulation and pass-agg blame. The Frank Churcher we all know and love. I take my hand off his arm and leave before I say something I regret.

25

Vale of Health, London NW3
1977 (Lal up, Frank down)

FRANK DOWN

Frank's easel sits in what used to be Lal's room. He can afford the best materials that money can buy. He spends all his time up here, staring at the wall. As far as everyone knows, he's so devastated by the death of Pete Winship that he's too depressed to paint, but the truth is more shameful than a man's death. Frank has no ideas. Nothing will come. No matter what he reads, where he travels, what he watches, who he meets. In the house next door, Lal is churning out pages and pages every day. Frank is coming face to face with the prospect that he peaked in his early twenties.

Eleanor toddles in officiously with the post. They are down to a handful of letters a day. Frank leafs through them. It's the usual stuff. One calling him a murderer, another desperate to know the whereabouts of Elinore's pelvis, a couple of begging letters from charities. There's one from the editors of the *Elinore's Army* magazine asking him to come to their inaugural convention. He feels so wretched that for a moment he almost considers saying yes.

LAL UP

Lal has never known happiness like it. He'd almost given up on being an artist. And now here he is, his wife writing at one end of the kitchen table while he paints at the other. The clack of typewriter keys and the ping of the carriage return echo in the almost empty house. Frank gave them the deposit for this house as a wedding present but they can barely afford any furniture.

'What?' She catches him staring at her and smiles.

'I just can't believe we get to do this. That we get to live here.'

That makes Bridget tighten her lips. 'Do you never think Frank's lording it over you a bit? That he likes to feel superior?'

Lal shakes his head. 'Sure it's called generosity, Bridie my love.'

'Or control?'

Lal just laughs. He shows his wife the cover he's designed for their new book and in her gasp the disagreement is forgotten. The pair of them are too excited by what they are creating to stay cross about anything for long.

26

Vale of Health, London NW3
31 July 2021

Salt water blurs the figure waving at me across the garden. I blot my eyes with my sleeve and the figure sharpens its line into Marcelle, Frank's 'work wife', sitting in the swing chair with a MacBook Air on her lap. She looks me up and down.

'Digging for Victory, are we?'

I am going to *burn* these dungarees.

Marcelle tilts her chin to me.

'Nice try,' I tell her. 'But if there's one thing I hope we can take away from the pandemic it's the death of the air-kiss.'

'I've never heard anything so ridiculous in all my life.' She pulls me down to her level and says an exaggerated 'mwah' an inch from my cheek. 'I'll make a luvvie of you yet.'

I've always got on with Marcelle. I sit in the seat and it swings a little.

'How are you?' I ask. 'How's Harriet?'

'I'm very well. Harriet's at the place in Southwold.' Marcelle and Harriet keep their marriage fresh by living in different houses. 'I invited her, but she said she'd rather eat her own feet.'

I've always liked Harriet as well.

'How was your summer?' she asks.

I don't like the finality of her question. It's not even August yet – there's another month before Billie starts school – but she makes it sound as though the sunshine is already being packed away.

'It's been good,' I say. 'We took a couple of weeks off, cruised up to Oxford. Really nice community up there. Saw a lot of old faces. The weather was shit, but everyone was just so happy to have a bit of freedom back.'

Marcelle's not really listening. 'Did you think about that tender?'

A few months ago, Marcelle put me forward for a job designing windows for a multi-faith chapel in a big new academy school.

'Can you tell Frank I've got no interest in raising my profile or carrying on his name?'

'It wasn't Frank. I did it without telling him.'

'Why? You're not my agent. I don't want an agent.'

'Well, you *should*. You've got all that talent and you're squandering it on—'

'I like the way I work.'

'My generation of women saw ambition and visibility as their *duty*. Christ knows your mother never made the most of her talents. Content to sit in a dream world while the men had all the glory. Doesn't that bother you?'

'I try not define myself against either of my parents, to be honest.'

Marcelle sees she's wasting her breath and changes tack. 'Isn't it *divine* to see London opening up again? Do you know, I went to an opening last week? First one since the apocalypse. Speaking of openings, have a look at this. I'm literally wearing the *same jacket*.'

She gestures to her screen, where grainy home-movie footage is playing. She's in her art gallery. She's right, she does look the same as always; big round glasses, curly brown hair. It was as though she waited all through her twenties for the sharp suits of the eighties to come and, once she was there, she stuck to it.

'You haven't aged a day,' I said. 'Have you got a portrait in the attic?'

'I wouldn't be a very good art dealer if I didn't, would I?'

I sit down next to her, out of the sun's glare. The quality of the video is poor but the gallery was well lit, and the mirrored pillars that held up the ceiling make the space look bigger than it really is. 'Hang on,' I say, catching sight of one of Frank's nudes on the wall. 'Is this *Intimacies*? That show is *haunting* me today.'

'It's haunted the lot of us over the years,' says Marcelle. 'I had someone tape it on a camcorder and totally forgot. It's been languishing on a shelf for decades, I'd never even watched it but I gave it to Oisin and he digitised it. Isn't he clever? I had it written into the contract that the producers include a few seconds of this, so that we underline Frank's legacy as an artist, nudge his selling prices a little higher.'

'Always be closing. Is Stuart's little outburst coming up?' I say it flippantly but my heart is racing. 'He's outside, you know.'

'Of course he is, the little worm. And no, he's not on here. Oisin edited it out. That's the *last* thing we want to dwell on.'

On her screen, everyone is smoking indoors. There's Cora looking surprisingly gaunt; there's Bridget looking like something from a magazine. Between two huge canvases, both depicting the same female body in different poses rendered in khaki slashes, a much younger woman leans against the wall.

It takes me a good few seconds to recognise myself.

I am twenty-one, tanned from three years living on the run. My sunbleached, white-girl-travelling dreadlocks – what was I *thinking?* – are piled high on my head and I'm wearing a tie-dye shift that I got for a few hundred pesetas from a market in Sitges. There are multiple silver hoops in my ears, one in my nose, and silver ropes at my neck and wrists.

Someone passes in front of the camera and I have gone, replaced by a very beautiful woman crying into a tissue.

'She came round!' I say with a jolt of recognition. I'm about to tell Marcelle what I mean by that – that she was one of the women who turned up on our doorstep – they were, in their own way, worse than the Bonehunters – but Marcelle doesn't need it explaining.

'Ah, lovely Adeola,' says Marcelle. 'She fell hard. He got some bloody good paintings out of her, though.'

The camera does another sweep of the room, capturing for half a second the misery on Cora's face. We all had our demons to battle that night. The picture shakes as whoever was filming climbs on to a chair to film Frank's speech over a sea of heads. I can remember that speech as if it were yesterday.

'You can just about hear the bit where Lal calls him a prick,' says Marcelle.

After the speech Frank takes a glass of champagne from the waitress with hair the colour of marigolds in July. He flirts with her – I'd forgotten how shameless he was. The screen freezes and a little wheel spins on the waitress mid-laugh. There's a gap between her teeth, the kind Cora had filled with gold. It's called a diastema and some cultures think it's lucky. I inherited it but insisted on getting braces to close mine up – anything to differentiate me from Elinore. I put my tongue against my two front teeth where the gap is beginning to reappear. I won't have it fixed again. The waitress also has a missing premolar and a row of black fillings that a teenage Rose once called 'poor people teeth', causing all three of us to be subjected to a long lecture on privilege and compassion from Bridget.

'Fucking computers,' says Marcelle, hitting the space bar. The film stops buffering and the camera moves again through the crowd. The party thins out, as launches always do after speeches. I watch myself slip away through the fire exit to the safety of Suzy's car. The dance goes on: and then, without warning, I see Richard and the shock sets fire to my skin.

In a baggy green suit and white T-shirt, he looks different from the Richard I knew, or rather the one he presented to me. I never saw him the way he looks on the tape, highlighted hair and designer stubble like a bad George Michael impersonator, but I'd know him anywhere. I find myself blushing to the roots of my hair. I hate that this is my reaction to any mention of Richard. Why must my face broadcast my feelings? Whose side is my skin on?

'Nothing else really happens,' says Marcelle. She fast-forwards through the final moments. I see Lal swigging champagne straight from the bottle in triple time, which would look funny if I didn't know how close he came that night to drinking himself to death. The camera lingers on the open door to the gallery kitchen, then cuts off.

Marcelle closes the laptop, then looks up to see me rolling someone's abandoned glass against my cheeks to bring down the burn.

'Are you having a hot flush? Because if you're in peri I can put you in touch with a marvellous gynae on Wimpole Street. You're only supposed to stay on HRT for five years but I've been on it for thirty now and it's *fine*.'

'Um, thanks?' I take the card she gives me.

'Two words: *vaginal oestrogen*,' she says.

'Thanks,' I say, pocketing it. 'I'll bear it in mind.' I spot a few cubes of ice in the bottom of her glass. I scoop them out and press them against my cheeks, which are blazing so bright the ice melts and falls like tears. Marcelle looks on knowingly.

'You promise me you'll call them next week?' she asks.

I close my eyes and nod. There's no prescription in the world for shame. Richard always did know how to call my blood to the surface.

27

It's a cold, bright Valentine's Day. The glass hearts on my market stall blow crimson kisses on the old stable walls. The air smells of chocolate peanuts and falafels and my money belt rests heavy against my thighs. It's been a good day: a coachload of Italian exchange students cleared me out of Big Bens and red buses. A glass suncatcher strikes me as a pretty dumb purchase for a teenager on the move but I take their money anyway. It's not my problem if they give their mama a paper bag of smashed glass as a souvenir of their time in London.

A big bear of a man with a couple of silver threads in his dark hair stops to examine the kids' suncatchers: Pokémon and the Simpsons. 'All made by hand here in Camden,' I say, then leave him to it. Some people like to be sold to; others hate it. I wonder who he's shopping for: son or daughter?

It is eight months since Frank's *Intimacies* opening. Nothing and no one has been quite the same since. The changes are positive – Lal's sobriety, Rose and Dom's relationship, Frank being in demand – but the dynamic has altered in a million subtle ways and we have yet to wear in new grooves.

I look different these days. The dreadlocks are gone. I wear my hair dark red and my eyeliner heavy. I don't know where Stuart Cummins is now, only that he can't be within two hundred metres of where I am at any given time. So far he has complied with that directive, and the other component of his restraining order, which is that he may not write to, or contact in any way, any member of

109

my family. I'm based in Camden now, sharing a market stall in the old stables with Martina, a girl I trained with in Prague. She makes beautiful glass sculptures of flowers and speaks only in the present tense. Martina's my landlady as well as my boss. I have the sofabed on her narrowboat *Jitka*, moored on a bend in the Regent's Canal.

Daddy Bear clears his throat. 'I'm looking for something for my niece,' he says. 'She's nine. Mad about Hello Kitty. You don't have any of those?'

I take a moment to study him. His navy suit is off-the-peg – it doesn't quite sit right on his generous frame – but the cashmere scarf tucked into his collar is the real thing. I fold my arms. 'Are you a lawyer working on behalf of the Hello Kitty people?'

He grins. 'I am very much not a lawyer.'

'In that case, I might be able to help you. I've got a template in my workshop. But you'd need to order it; I don't have any in stock.'

He rocks on his heels. 'Can you get it done by Wednesday?'

I make a mental inventory of the glass I have in stock and the shifts I'm working over the next few days.

'If you give me a deposit, I can.'

He slides a pristine ten-pound note from a fat wallet. When I go to take it, he holds on to it for a second longer than he needs to. He holds my eye and gives me a smile that sends a jolt of long-ing to my groin. Really? I think. This guy? This middle-aged man in a Next suit?

I open my order book. 'What's your name?' I ask.

'Richard,' he says. The phone number he gives me has a weird code. 'It's a carphone,' he says.

'Ooh, *fancy*,' I say, then go red. I sound like a sarcastic teenager. 'Well. Thanks for the order. I'm Nell, by the way.'

'I'll see you on Wednesday, Nell.' He winds his way across the cobbles, through a sea of Invicta rucksacks, leather jackets and stripy tights.

*   *   *

Every other morning I go for a swim at the council pool, as much for the washing facilities as the cardio. I use the dryer at the pool to blow my hair long and soft. When I get back, Martina is cutting glass at the workstation, opalescent lilac glass that she's making into crocuses. She watches me hang my damp kit over the stove to dry.

'What is the occasion?' she asks, stroking her own hair to draw attention to mine.

'Just felt like a change,' I say, but my cheeks are glowing.

Daddy Bear (or rather Uncle Bear) arrives in a herringbone coat with an upturned collar that makes him look distinguished and for the first time that term feels like a reason to be attracted to someone, as opposed to mistrustful of them.

'She'll love it,' he says, when I dangle the cartoon kitten on a chain.

'I'm so pleased.' I take extra care with this one, cutting the bubble-wrap to size and making sure the ribbon on the tissue paper sits symmetrically.

'What's her name?' I ask as I hand it over.

He looks blank. 'Whose name?'

'Your niece. The Hello Kitty fan.'

'God. Sorry. It's Lauren. I thought you were asking if . . .' He trails off, distracted, agitated. 'Well. Thank you. So much.' He walks away, stops, takes another step, then turns on his heel. 'Would you like to go for a drink with me tonight?'

I check his wedding ring finger as a reflex.

'Footloose and fancy free,' he says.

'Do you mind me asking how old you are?'

He flicks his eyebrows. 'Thirty-six,' he says. 'I'm guessing there's a bit of an age gap.'

'I'm twenty-two,' I tell him.

'If it makes a difference, I'm *really* immature.'

My eyes travel from his upturned collar to his shiny shoes. 'You *look* like a grown-up.'

'Don't let the suave corporate exterior fool you,' he says. 'I'm basically a nine-year-old. I literally still read *The Beano*.'

I can't help but laugh. 'I knock off at seven.'

'I'll see you in the Hawley Arms at half past.' He holds up the paper bag with the suncatcher in as if to seal the deal.

'I've never been on a date with a nine-year-old before. What're you drinking, if I get there first? Orange juice? Ribena?'

'Ribena.' He wrinkles his nose. 'I don't drink anything with *bits*.'

When I get to the pub, he isn't reading *The Beano* but the *Evening Standard*. Foam tracks the walls of his almost empty glass. I buy a Kronenburg for myself and a pint of blackcurrant squash for him, which he drinks with a straight face.

Five hours later we're in a bachelor pad in the north London hinterland of Whetstone. The flat has all the charm of a motorway service station hotel.

'I've just moved in,' he says apologetically. 'I never know what to do with pictures and such, so I just don't do anything.'

The part of me that isn't mentally undressing him is draping an Indian throw over that sofa, propping a big Venetian mirror against the wall. Then he slides a finger under my bra strap and the room falls away. On the blank canvas of his bed, Richard kisses me until I'm deranged with longing. He is tall and broad. His hands are soft and dry, like expensive leather.

A week later, I'm back there; *still* there. I've only left his place to work.

Every morning, he cups those soft hands around my face, his thumbs at the corners of my mouth, the pads of his fingers finding the pulse at my temples. 'Where did you come from, Nell?' he says. 'Who sent you to me? What did I do to deserve a girl like you?'

Two months into our relationship, there is colour on the walls of Richard's flat and plants on the windowsill.

When I tell him about *The Golden Bones* and everything it has done to me, I don't look Richard in the eye but focus on the potted basil above the kitchen sink. He holds me as I cry and cry.

'You deserve better.' There is a catch in his voice, as if he might be about to cry himself, and, wretched as dragging it all out again has made me feel, there's comfort to be had, because no one outside my family – maybe no one *inside* it, not really – has ever loved me so much that my pain became theirs.

28

Vale of Health, London NW3
31 July 2021

'Eleanor!'

My mother's voice, issuing from the terrace, turns every head in the garden. I suppose the name *Elinore* has lodged in everyone's mind today; it pricks at every ear.

'Come!' She holds out her arms to me. Her Paisley kaftan billows like butterfly wings. The cords that fasten the neck and the cuffs have tiny silver bells on, so she jingles as she moves.

I follow her into Bridget's kitchen and watch her lower herself into a rattan chair. I think the same thing I always do when I see her after a while. How are you still alive? She's touching eighty and looks it. Her eyes and face are the same dark pink, her eyeballs covered by a lacework of veins, while white flakes float on the rough red sea of her skin. Her features seem somehow unmoored, as though they might begin to drift around on her face. The clothes that used to look artistic now droop as though they, too, just want to collapse on the floor, and when she raises her arms for a hug it looks as if it pains her. I bend down and lean in. She smells of yeast and weed, overlaid with the patchouli oil she's always worn, as much a part of her as Frank's Vétiver is of him.

When we have disengaged, she looks at my clothes. I brace myself for another comment about my helping the war effort, but she says, 'Girls like us need a nipped-in waist. You can't carry off that straight up-and-down look when you've got curves.'

'Thanks for that,' I say. 'Which way back did you come? You didn't see Stuart Cummins, did you? No one was taking photos of the girls or anything?'

'Eleanor. The girls are *children*.'

I hold out my phone so she can see what they're saying online. She grunts. 'You know what they say about the internet. Tomorrow's fish-and-chip paper.'

'No one says that.'

I could scream at her naïvety. I've heard people from normal families describe the feeling they get over Christmas, an irritation that creeps in after three or four days cooped up together. With Cora, I can reach that state in ten seconds.

'If you must know, we *did* come the back way.' Cora splays her fingers as best she can. 'Why should spending an hour on my *feet* hurt my *hands*?' Instinctively I massage her gnarled fingers until I feel them go out of spasm. It is this ping-ponging between irritation and sympathy and what I suppose is probably, despite everything, love, that makes spending time with my family so exhausting.

Bridget enters, brisk as ever, nodding her hello. She still wears tight bangles on her upper arms, as if to emphasise that she still has the frame of a teenager, even if the skin on her arms is pinched into tiny pleats. Like Rose, she has a lean, spare body. She dresses in fitted, stretchy clothes that allow her to spring into action at a moment's notice. Everything about Bridget's appearance says efficiency, business, urgency, whereas everything about Cora's – her impractical long hair, the swathes of fabric that wrap her round and slow her down – says: leisure, pleasure, we'll deal with it tomorrow.

Bridget could pass for my age until she turns around and you see the lines of a woman who smoked and sunbathed. Note the past tense. Like Frank, Bridget knows when to stop.

Cora says, in a nauseating baby voice, 'Will you be mother, Bridget?'

Instead of getting busy with a tea set, Bridget opens a little Indian-style tin on the counter that says SUGAR and contains a pouch of tobacco, a packet of Rizla and a twenty-quid deal of weed. I try not to look judgy but I must fail, because:

'It's *medicinal*,' says Cora defensively.

I can hear Aoife and Niamh giggling in the hall outside.

'Even so. You're not going to smoke that in front of the girls?'

'Oh, Eleanor.' Cora rolls her eyes. 'As far as they're concerned it's just a cigarette.'

Aoife might not be observant but Niamh is, and I knew what the adults were smoking when I was younger than her. I bite my lip as Bridget gets to work, unfolding the Rizla and crumbling tobacco into its crease.

'Nell!' The girls enter in a scent cloud of coconut sunscreen and sugar, mouths sticky with ice cream.

'I like your costume,' says Aoife.

I am never wearing these bloody dungarees again. 'I like your clothes too,' I tell her, and I do, although their matching outfits are more appropriate for Niamh's eight years than Aoife's thirteen: flamingo-patterned T-shirts under denim playsuits, white knee socks and Velcro trainers. The outfit looks almost obscene on Aoife, who has shot up since I last saw her, and filled out too. She sits on my lap as she has done since she was a baby. Her legs are longer than mine and reach the floor: I'm holding a woman, not a girl. Rose leans over to clean her mouth with a baby-wipe, and she smiles a gappy smile that steals my breath. She is *so* like a young Cora – far more than I ever was – that it makes me fearful. If the more suggestible Bonehunters catch a glimpse of her, they are bound to pour their obsession into her, and then what might happen?

Cora misreads my expression. 'I know,' she says. 'It's not easy, standing next to a reincarnation of your younger self.'

'Not about you, for once.' I appeal to Bridget. 'Do not under any circumstances let this one appear on camera,' I say, smoothing Aoife's flaxen hair. 'She looks just like Elinore.'

'Way ahead of you there,' says Bridget. 'They can't broadcast her image without a release form and Rose won't sign one.'

I watch her sprinkle cannabis buds into the joint with a life-time's expertise. On my lap, Aoife performs one of her repetitive movements with her hands, winding an imaginary bobbin up again and again. It looks as though she's distressed but it's actu-ally how she soothes herself.

Niamh opens Bridget's fridge and turns her nose up at the contents: fruit and veg and a brick wall of Pepsi Max cans. 'Have you got nicer food at your house, Grandma Cora?' she asks.

'We've got everything you could possibly want.'

'Come on, Aoife.' When she offers her hand, Aoife takes it and lets herself be led across the terrace to a world of sugar.

'How's Aoife getting on?' I ask Bridget when the girls have gone.

'Up and down. Coming out of lockdown's been a shock to the system. All her old friends are growing up and it's heartbreaking to see her getting left behind.'

I wonder, then, if maybe I've been too hard on Rose. Maybe she's cold to Billie because of envy rather than snobbery. Maybe, even with her psychologist's training, it's hard for her to see this girl with no advantages outshine her own daughter. It's compli-cated and it's not attractive, but I think maybe I get it a little more than I did.

Bridget sparks the joint for Cora, who closes her eyes and takes a long drag.

'You know that's not good for your brain, Cora,' I tell her.

She waves my words away with the smoke. 'That's all that genetically modified skunk the kids do now. This is pure, organic, old-school grass.'

'Or your lungs, then. Especially at your age. You're incredibly lucky not to have lung cancer already. Could you not at least vape it or something?'

Cora closes her eyes and blows a perfect smoke ring. 'Why don't you have some,' she says. 'Go with the flow.'

I get to my feet, start furiously washing cups in the sink rather than snap at her. Bridget joins me with a tea towel. 'Your mum does care, you know,' she says in a low voice. 'In fact the more she cares the *more* she retreats. Rose says she has an avoidant personality: we can't force her to confront what she can't cope with.'

'That's a bit convenient for her, isn't it?'

'It is what it is,' says Bridget. 'Listen, I'm aware how much like Cora Aoife looks. I'm aware of why you'd be so worried. We're all looking out for her. And for you.' She boops me on the nose with her tea towel.

'Oh, Bridget,' I say. 'Where would we all be without you?'

She laughs. 'I shudder to think.'

29

LAL UP

Frank pours red wine from the bottle into a cut crystal decanter. Cora stirs gravy with the baby on her breast. The smell of Sunday lunch fills the Churchers' all mod-cons kitchen. The glass before Lal is opaque with paint. He's doing a watercolour of the landlord's Cavalier King Charles to pay off his tab. The doorbell goes and Frank returns with two women: Marcelle and another Lal knows is Irish before she opens her mouth.

Oh, there's my wife, he thinks. There's no drama, just a sense of certainty and calm, as though Cupid's arrow is infused with some kind of muscle relaxant. Their eyes meet; she smiles as if to say: *that's decided, then. Grand, so.*

'Everyone, this is Bridget O'Keefe,' says Marcelle. Lal almost corrects her: *no, I'll be calling her Bridie and she'll soon be a Lally.* 'She's working as a nurse at Great Ormond Street, where she's famous for telling the children the most incredible stories. I hope she'll soon be a bestselling children's author. With you, Frank, as her illustrator.' She hands Frank a slim typewritten manuscript.

'It's Sunday lunch, Marcelle,' says Frank, setting the pages aside. 'I didn't invite you here to talk business.'

Lal can read what's really being said. He's preparing this Bridget one for rejection. Marcelle should know better.

While Cora interviews Bridget and Marcelle wheedles Frank,

119

Lal sneaks a look at Bridget's pages. It's a modern kids' adventure story that incorporates Irish myths. It calls to Lal's boyhood and inspires him to draw a picture that mixes Celtic art with something looser and more kinetic than his usual lifelike work. He slides it across the table to Marcelle.

Her double-take ends in a smile. 'I think this could be the beginning of a beautiful friendship.'

FRANK DOWN

Lal's illustrations reignite the old envy in Frank, as fresh today – despite everything – as it was in art school. After lunch, he corners Marcelle.

'I've been thinking. You're clearly ambitious for Bridget's books. Maybe getting a name like me on board would give her a leg-up?'

Marcelle almost laughs. 'I've found my man.'

'In that case, I'm happy for him,' Frank says through gritted teeth.

30

Vale of Health, London NW3
31 July 2021

Billie enters with a shy, 'Alright?'

Bridget and Cora look her up and down in perfect unison, then exchange a glance I hope Billie doesn't catch. For all their performative free thinking, for all their artistic 'lack of judgement' and bohemian ideals, when these old women are actually challenged by a girl with a baby-fringe kiss-curl glued to her forehead, a glottal stop and acrylic nails, they can be as snobbish as any golf-club executive. They like their working class people horny-handed sons of the soil, dead and in folk songs.

Billie tries valiantly to stifle a cough.

'See?' I tell Cora. 'It reeks in here.'

Cora clicks her tongue. 'Bridget, in our sitting room there are some of those organic soy candles,' she says. 'You couldn't bring one here? We could burn it, cover the smell.' Bridget leaves by the double doors and Dara enters, a book clasped to his chest which he holds out to me.

'We found a picture book with Aoife on the front, in with Daddy's stuff.' He picks his nose and goes to wipe the results on to the front cover of the *Intimacies* catalogue. That night, gatecrashed as it was by *The Golden Bones*, was always going to prey on our minds today, but I didn't expect it to keep manifesting itself like this. It's starting to feel uncanny.

'Oh, no, you don't,' says Cora, guiding his little fat hand away. 'That's worth a fortune.' She puts the thing down. 'They all went missing on the night, there are hardly any left.'

My mind whips the dustsheets off an old memory. 'Didn't Jane Jones try to get one? She got it into her head there were clues in the pictures?'

'That's right.' Cora is wearing her I'm-going-to-change-the-subject face, as she always does when that night rears its head.

'How valuable?' asks Billie, but no one replies.

'I tell you what, if Jane knew this was here she'd break down the door to get it.'

'Why do I have to wear clothes and Aoife doesn't?' presses Dara.

'*That*,' says Cora, clearly grateful that he has moved the conversation along for her, 'is not Aoife. Here, play on this.' She pulls her iPad from her bag. Dara puts his thumb to the home button and swipes expertly through the tiles.

'Does Rose know he can unlock that?' I ask.

'They're a godsend, those things, aren't they?' says Cora, as Dara slides to the floor, slack-jawed. 'Wish we'd had them when you were little.' She peers at the catalogue. 'God, look at that. I think I was in my forties when he painted that, and I thought I was old and past it. I'd give a year of my life to have that body back. Not to mention my Elinore body.'

'You were *thicc*,' says Billie.

'Excuse me?' Cora frowns.

'Thicc with two "c"s, not thick "c-k". It's a compliment,' I say. 'It means skinny waist, big bum, strong thighs. It's how they all want to look now.'

'Well' – Cora thaws a little – 'I'm glad *something* about me has come back into fashion. My figure was all the rage when I was life modelling.' Her eyes glaze over. 'God, that could be a tough gig. One side of your body being burned to a crisp with one of those electric fires and the other side getting frostbite.'

'Weren't you nervous getting naked in front of strangers?' asks Billie.

Cora scoffs. 'We weren't uptight about that sort of thing. We were the *free love* generation.' Cora talks about free love as if it was a two-way thing, so I presume she gave Frank a run for his money and was just more discreet about it. Certainly we never had any lovestruck *men* weeping on the doorstep. 'Anyway, aren't you Millennials all Snapchatting sexties to each other?'

'I'm fifteen! I'm not a Millennial, I'm Gen-Zee.' Billie clutches her bosom in mock outrage. 'The Millennials are actually our common enemy.'

Cora's laugh is throaty and real. Perhaps there's hope for her and Billie yet.

I check ElinoresArmy for the latest and what I see chills my blood.

@BelleDame: Explosive few moments here. Not only have I verified that @LetterstoIngrid is genuine, I've also seen evidence that the Northumbria Papers are fakes!!!! Meaning that Ingrid's theory about Eleanor Churcher being the 'host' for the missing bone is valid! I should never have doubted her; she truly is the greatest Bonehunter who ever lived

I think I'm going to puke.

@BON35: I've never heard such codswallop in all my life

@Elinore&Tam<3: Who would do such a thing?

@LetterstoIngrid: Someone in the Churcher camp who wanted to hide the truth?

@BON35: What is wrong with the pair of you? We are literally two days away from a totally new incarnation of the world's greatest ever treasure hunt. We're as sure as we can be that the last golden bone will up for grabs. Pack it in, both of you

@goldengal: Post evidence here if you're so sure

@LetterstoIngrid: All in good time. I have to protect my sources

@BelleDame: Ingrid was right all along. I'm just going to come right out and say it. I've been going through the archives. Now

that we can discount the Northumbria Papers I'm seeing the
Cecil Sharp pages clearly for the first time in years. There's nothing to suggest that the carrying of the bone can't continue down
the bloodline

@BON35: Er, 'bloodless solve' mean anything to you?

@BelleDame: It's time to put Elinore back together again.

I begin to shake all over. Where's Dom when I need him?

Bridget sweeps back in with a three-wick candle in a dusky
pink glass. Knowing Cora, it will have cost more than a week's
state pension. Her gaze falls on Dara on the tablet. She glares at
Billie. 'If Rose sees—' she starts, but Cora says,

'Calm down, it's *my* iPad. Anything for a moment's peace.'

'Fair play.'

Billie turns her attention to the catalogue and starts leafing
through that. 'What might something like this be worth?'

Bridget puts a lit match to the wick. 'There, now.' Her eyes land
on the catalogue and her focus narrows, an eagle zooming in on
prey. 'I'll take that,' she says, and snatches it from Billie's hands.

'Bloody hell, Bridget!' I say. 'She was only looking.'

'It's *rare*,' she says.

I realise with dismay that she thinks Billie's on the take, fishing
for a slice of the Churcher riches, when really she's just curious
about how the wealthy behave, and why shouldn't she be? Bridget
picks the attic key up from the hook that's out of the children's
reach and climbs the stairs. I hear the attic door turn, like she
doesn't trust Billie, like she thinks she's going to sell it off on eBay.
The message could not be clearer if Cora and Bridget had spoken
it aloud. *That girl is not one of us, and she never will be.*

Fortunately for Billie, she hasn't picked up on this. Her attention is back on her phone.

'Those Bonehunter guys,' she says. 'They're at the top of the
road.'

31

I picture dozens of them in a pincer movement, surrounding the house. I look out of the window in the hope of seeing them but the Crabwise van is parked right up against the glass.

'We'll have a better view from my place,' says Cora. 'Dara, I'll swap you one item of contraband for another.' She takes the iPad away from him and gives him a Twix. We parade back across the terrace to the tinny sound of Porter Glemham's commentary. The crew must be watching too – they appear to have downed tools, all heads bent over screens.

Dom's not in Cora's kitchen but Niamh and Aoife are, making light work of the brownies. Niamh's been at Lal's Pepsi Max. There are two empty cans next to her. If an eight-year-old can be a hedonist, she is.

'Where's your daddy?' I ask her.

Niamh points to the ceiling. Above us, the light fitting shakes as Dom paces the floor of my old bedroom.

He'll want to know about the commotion outside, but I don't want to endanger whatever he's doing to save the app. 'What kind of mood's he in?' I ask.

'A shouty one,' says Niamh.

'What's a cunt?' asks Aoife.

'He must have been saying "can't",' I improvise. 'Maybe they can't fix the server just yet.'

Aoife buys it, even if Niamh doesn't.

Outside, PD springs into action, dishing out orders. The crew funnel around to the side of the house. 'You,' she says to Shane the security guard. 'Get out the front and scare them off.'

'With respect, you're not my client, and . . .' I don't catch the rest of his sentence.

PD gesticulates so hard she's almost dancing. 'I don't care what your brief is! If they film even a second of the reveal on their phones, then our exclusive is fucked.' I can't hear what she says next, but there's no mistaking the shift in Shane's body language, and, although no one in the garden would be able to see it, there's no missing the passing of cash from her hand to his.

'One minute,' says Shane, disappearing around the side of the house.

Upstairs, Dom lets out a roar of anger.

'Can we go out the front?' asks Niamh.

'No,' I say. 'You know you've got to be careful of people with cameras. Go and clear up the mess you made of those brownies.'

The girls decline rebuilding the stack of brownies in favour of eating the outliers. Rose comes downstairs. She looks awful: like her own ghost.

'What's up?' I ask, my voice pitched at a frequency I hope the girls can't hear. 'Have you had a row?'

I'm astonished, and a bit appalled, by how unsettling the idea of Dom and Rose fighting is. It takes me back to those nights listening to arguments through floors and walls, unsure whether it was my parents or the Lallys, feeling equally unsafe at the thought of it being either of them.

'No, he's yelling at Leelo. It's bad. I don't know what he'll do if all this . . .' She gestures at the kitchen table. 'What's happening outside, anyway?'

I bring her up to speed with the Glemhams and their entourage. From out the front we hear Bridget's voice. 'Dara, put them back *on*.'

'Jesus take the wheel,' says Rose, heading for the front door.

'I'll come with you,' says Niamh.

'*Stay. In.*' Rose's forefinger pokes the words into her daughter.

'That is not fair.' Niamh sidles mutinously towards the exit.

'Girls,' I say, desperate to keep them – especially Aoife – out of view, 'I have a really important job for you. Go upstairs, and *only* if Daddy comes off the phone, tell him the Bonehunters are here.'

Niamh folds her arms and raises her eyebrows.

'Seriously?' I ask, but I fish in my pockets and find a two-pound coin for each of them.

'*Thank* you,' she says, and turns to go, but Aoife hesitates.

'Bonehunters are scary,' she says, her chin starting to shake.

I glance up at the ceiling where Dom still paces above us. The last thing any of us – most of all Aoife herself – need right now is for her to melt down. And the repercussions if that were to be caught on camera? Just the thought makes the hairs on my arms rise.

'It's nothing to worry about!' I say, cheerful as a children's TV presenter. 'It's all part of the fun! I just don't want Daddy to miss out, OK?'

I watch them go up the stairs in their matching clothes, Niamh repeating my reassurances to Aoife and leading her by the hand, the big little sister.

If Dom can't be here, then at least I can get a bird's eye view for him. I put my hand in my pocket for my phone but then I realise it's next door on the kitchen table, next to the rapidly warming bottle of champagne. 'Can I borrow your phone?' I ask Billie. She hands it to me. I hold it up to a clear pane and hit record, then hand it back to her.

'Be right back,' I say, and head back next door. After retrieving my phone from the pine table, I glance up and see that the attic key is still missing. Bridget's kept it with her, presumably in case Billie has designs on the catalogue. I'm not going to let this go.

On my way back across the terrace, I almost collide with a youth in a grey hoodie, a quiff of fair hair poking out of the front, surgical mask up to his eyes. He's wearing a lanyard, so he's crew; but he's got his phone trained on *Billie* through the open back door.

'What the fuck are you doing?' I ask him. He dances on his toes like a boxer about to land a punch, then disappears around the

Lallys' side return. I bolt into my parents' kitchen and slam the door shut behind me. The noise makes Billie turn around.

'You're missing all the action,' she says.

'Did you see that kid? On his phone? Did he talk to you?'

'What kid?' I realise that to her of course he's an adult, as is anyone with a job.

'Guy in a hoodie, with a lanyard,' I correct myself. 'Sort of maybe Oisin's age.'

She shrugs. 'I was watching the window.' She picks up on my fear. 'Why? What's wrong?'

I'm put on the spot. If I tell her and it turns out to be nothing, an already vulnerable kid will be further traumatised for no reason. If I don't tell her, I'm doing what I always said I wouldn't: I'm treating her like a baby, downplaying the risks, overprotecting her. I'm sure real parents would instinctively know what to do in these situations but I have no idea what I'm doing.

'Nothing,' I say, and instantly feel it was the wrong call. I join her at the window, searching not for Stuart, for once, but for the crew member who just tried to film her.

'Here we go,' says Billie. In the corner of the window and the corner of her phone, there's a flash of royal blue as the Glemhams approach the house, followed by a crowd of maybe two dozen. Some of them are holding copies of *The Golden Bones*; a handful carry placards.

The Glemhams lead their disciples in song.

Flesh can spoil and blood can spill but true love never dies
Gather the lady's bones with love and see the lady rise

When I was little I went to a Church of England primary school and on Palm Sundays we'd do a procession from the school to the church, waving little crosses and singing hosanna. That's what the encroaching crowd reminds me of.

Flesh can spoil and blood can spill but true love never dies
Gather the lady's bones with love and see the lady rise

Directly outside the window, a female crew member, surgical mask around her neck, pulls off her hood to reveal spiky blonde hair. A girl, not a guy: but, irrespective of gender, no one should be taking photos of Billie. A chill runs through me: what if one of the crew is a Bonehunter undercover? What if the call is coming from inside the house? The blonde girl climbs into one of the Crabwise vans but I won't forget what she looks like and the first chance I get I'll ask her what the hell she thinks she's playing at.

As the Bonehunters get closer, the words on the placards come into focus. Their mood is hopeful: SHE WILL RISE and AT LAST and THE TIME HAS COME. They no longer remind me of primary school children; rather, they look like superannuated versions of the Woodstock hippies, which I suppose some of them are. There's Jane Jones, in a Per Una maxi dress and a necklace of seashells. She closes her eyes and waves her hands in the air; a white-haired man in socks and sandals holds a tattered copy of *The Golden Bones* aloft.

'They don't seem that scary,' remarks Billie, as the singing grows louder. 'Bit weird, but not *threatening*.'

I watch as Jane Jones and Stuart Cummins greet each other like the old friends they are and a cold finger runs down my spine. Wherever there are Bonehunters, there is threat. Their obsessive love can become even stronger hatred in the time it takes to turn a page.

32

'Can I stop filming?' Billie asks me.

'Sure,' I say. 'WhatsApp it to me?'

In the garden, Oisin is rubbing the back of his neck, a stress release that's pure Dom. 'If they get round the back, we're fucked,' he says, gesturing to the mob out front.

PD addresses her assembled crew. 'We're going straight to the final scene. You two, stay here.' She gestures at Barney Badger, filming the crowd with a handheld. 'Come on, move it! We're on a fucking clock here!'

Everyone else funnels down the side return, the girl in grey included. I rush to the garden to intercept her but she's out the back gate before I get a chance. I collar Oisin and point to her retreating back. 'Who's that?'

'Melanie,' he says. 'She's on sound.'

'She was creeping around earlier. Taking pictures of Billie. Is she freelance or on the payroll?'

'What? Why?'

Because a Bonehunter could pose as a freelancer, or Richard could more easily plant a freelancer than a staff member is why, but I pull family rank and reply, 'Just tell me.'

'She's staff.'

Less likely, but not impossible. Film crews work famously punishing overtime: even a staffer could probably do with an extra few quid.

'Some time this century, Oisin,' barks PD.

'Sorry,' he says, and follows the rest of them. I trot at his heels.

'What is this final scene that's so urgent?' I ask him.

'I dunno, they've been really cagey about it.' He looks at his schedule. 'Dad's supposed to be part of it, though.'

'He's still trying to save the app.' I point to the window where Dom's silhouette paces back and forth. 'I'll get him.' I dash off a text.

Don't crash the app because of this but we're all being summoned to the final scene out the back, and apparently you are a vital cog in the machine?

Two grey ticks tell me it's been delivered. I wait for them to turn blue.

I find Melanie just inside the garden, winding a cable on to a reel.

'Melanie, is it?' I ask. Oisin flinches.

'Hi!' she says brightly. 'Don't worry, we'll be out of your hair soon.'

'Why were you taking pictures of Bi—' I stop myself giving away Billie's name just in time and I'm not going to use the word *daughter*. 'Pictures of the girl who was in the house just now?'

She looks to Oisin in confusion.

'Sorry, this is my aunt, Nell. She thinks she saw you round the back just now.'

'Not me,' she says, but she's faltering.

'You were taking pictures of the book, then. The serial numbers. Or the catalogue. Were you after that?'

'What catalogue?'

'Don't act like you don't know. Can I see your camera roll?'

'I'm really not sure what you think I've done,' Melanie says, but she's getting out her phone, ready to share. A little *too* ready: clearly she's already tidied up. I didn't come down in the last shower.

PD yells across the garden. 'Don't let me keep you, Melanie, it's not as if we're broadcasting tomorrow or anything.'

'I've *got* to go,' says Melanie. 'You can have a look later.' She looks less enthusiastic now.

'I don't trust her,' I tell Oisin. 'Did you see how shifty she looked?'

'We'll sort it out afterwards.' He looks anguished. 'I've *really* got to go.' He vanishes through the gate on to the scrub of the heath.

If the crew think they're safe from the Bonehunters out there, they're wrong. The Vale of Health pond cuts access off in one direction and East Heath Road in the other, but anyone with a decent sense of direction or working phone would be able to snake through the pathways in the bracken and arrive at the back of the house in minutes. And Jane knows both these properties inside and out.

I hang back for a bit to check ElinoresArmy. No one has posted Billie's name or her picture.

Yet. That Melanie could be doing anything out there.

Before joining the others, I check my phone. Dom still hasn't read my message. I look at the video Billie shot to see if we've got a line-up of the Bonehunters. 'Oh, you are *kidding*,' I say. She had the camera trained on the crew and my family, not the Bonehunters like I asked her. Or did I? Now I think about it, I'm not sure I gave her specific instructions, just expected her to read my mind. Looks as if we're all feeling the pressure today.

I stand, not on the public land of the Heath, but in the gateway, on Churcher property, so that even if they come round the back no one can (legally, anyway) film me.

Lal gives me a one-armed hug, holding his Pepsi Max at arm's length. 'Good to see you, girl,' he says. 'How's the wean?'

'Wean!' I say. 'She's fifteen.'

'*You're* still a wean to me,' he says.

Frank wanders over. 'Nice to see the jailbirds bonding, but if you hadn't noticed, we've got a film to make.'

I exchange a glance with Lal: how shall we play this? Telling

Frank to fuck off when he's in what we call one of his heightened states can go two ways: it can defuse the situation or it can escalate it into a full-blown diva tantrum.

'Please,' I say. 'Lal doesn't count. I'm the only hardened criminal around here. Come back to me when you've done three weeks' porridge and then we'll chat.'

33

The Duke of Wellington, Hampstead
1983

LAL UP

'I promise you I'm not being racist, sir,' says the barman, bold behind his row of brass beer pumps. 'It's illegal for me to serve an intoxicated person.'

'When I first came to this country, *son* . . .' Lal leans across the bar for emphasis '. . . there were signs outside the pubs saying no dogs, no blacks, no Irish. The signs may have gone but the prejudice remains.'

Lal returns to the table and slumps opposite Frank, who's been eking out the same pint of Guinness for lord knows how long.

'Shame to let it go to waste,' says Lal, emptying the glass. Usually Guinness hits the spot, as much meal as drink, but tonight it feels as substantial as orange squash.

'Jesus Christ, here we go,' says Frank.

'Will we go on somewhere else?' asks Lal and then shouts over his shoulder, in the direction of the bar, 'Somewhere my money's good enough for them!'

'Let's call it a night,' says Frank, but from the corner of his eye Lal has seen the barman enter the gents, and he's on his feet and through the door before you can say *intoxicated person*. The barman's in mid-flow, chasing a fag butt along the trough of the urinal, when Lal punches him in the back of the skull.

'I'll teach you not to serve me, you English prick.' The barman falls to the floor, limp, dribbling dick hanging out of his jeans. Lal kicks the guy in the ribs until he hears a crack.

FRANK DOWN

Frank is waiting by the phone for Leslie to call. Lal's looking at a charge of Actual Bodily Harm, worst-case scenario five years in prison. Frank's asked Leslie to do what he can to make it go away. Money no object. Marcelle's raging: this is not a good look for a children's illustrator. Bridget's in tears at the thought of losing her livelihood, at little Rosaleen forgetting her dad.

The thought of not having Lal next door brings a visceral terror to Frank. It is almost worse than the thought of losing Cora, or even Eleanor.

The phone rings. 'As luck would have it, the barman's solicitor's an old chum. He can be persuaded to drop the charges.'

The figure Leslie names is modest. Frank would have paid twice that.

34

Vale of Health, London NW3
31 July 2021

Lal and I hold our breaths as we wait to see how my porridge joke has landed. Frank doesn't lose his temper but he doesn't laugh. His silence makes me feel small.

Aoife and Niamh hover at the gate.

'Is your dad still upstairs?' I ask them. Niamh nods. 'Did you talk to him?' Niamh shakes her head.

'Can we watch?' I try to catch Rose's eye but she's got her work cut out holding Dara still.

'Stand here.' I corral my nieces, along with Billie, firmly *behind* the cameras.

'Eleanor!' Frank's voice is brittle. 'I thought you were getting Dominic?'

A glance at my phone tells me Dom still hasn't read my message. A notification flashes from ElinoresArmy.

@Yorick: You mark my words. Before the day is over Churcher will have blood on his hands again

@BON35: Change the record, you've been saying that for years

@Yorick: For good reason

I slide it away. 'He's upstairs, saving the app,' I tell Frank. 'I can go and get him?'

A radio on PD's breast throws out static and Barney says, 'There's more of them? Out the front?'

'So bloody *keep* them there,' shouts PD. 'Are we all ready to go straight into Frank's piece to camera?' I duck as a microphone sails over my head.

'But *Dominic,*' insists Frank.

'Sorry, Frank,' says PD. 'We haven't got time to wait for Dominic. Give it your best; we might only have the one take for this.'

I'm torn between wanting Dom to be part of this and my own curiosity when the clapperboard makes the decision for me. A hush falls over the clearing, exposing the buzz of equipment, the rustling of leaves and the fizzing of Lal's Pepsi Max. A woman balances a camera on her shoulder and points it at Frank; he addresses the lens like a pro.

'Fifty years ago, seven bones were hidden. Only six were found, and after tragedy struck I decided to keep Elinore's last bone safe.' He speaks softly, confidently, as though he were reading a bedtime story, and I can't shake the image of him pacing his studio or bedroom rehearsing these lines: of watching himself in the mirror. 'The rumours are true; the time has come to give readers all over the world another chance to find the missing jewel, and maybe even to put Elinore back together again. But before we launch our new hunt, I'm going to reveal her final resting place, so that readers are free to embark, unencumbered, on a new adventure.'

'Did you know he was going to do this?' I whisper to Lal. He puts his finger to his nose and winks.

'A lifetime ago, a riddle was posed. Its meaning has been the subject of much debate.' He takes a breath, then recites the contentious clue.

> 'Divine rules kiss over barbed eight
> 'High in a grove of wise souls
> 'A knight's move west of where Arthur's men halt.

'Now, the treasure hunter who sadly lost his life was so very close. Yes, I was referring to the intersection of ley lines in north London. Yes, a knight's move west of thirteen was correct. But he was mistaken about the second line. He never should have been in that graveyard in the first place. He became so focused on the notion that the grove of souls was Highgate Cemetery that he became blinkered to other interpretations. In fact, this very heath is the triangulation point of several ley lines far more significant than the ones that converge on Swains Lane. The *grove of wise souls* refers to this very wood. A grove is a wood, is it not? Any good scholar of English folklore knows that the Druids worshipped oak trees as founts of wisdom: that they considered the oaks the spiritual equals, or indeed superiors, of their own human essences. Elinore's resting place is far closer to home than any treasure hunter has ever dared to guess.'

I can't help it. I've got goosebumps. Even I'm getting swept up in *The Golden Bones*, and I can't stand it. When this is broadcast tomorrow night, it should go out with a health warning. The average Bonehunter is about seventy: the excitement could finish off some of them.

He comes to a stop underneath a silver birch. The leaves cast a greenish tinge on his skin. He raises his chin, looking briefly like some kind of Messiah. 'Listed trees, like listed buildings, have preservation orders. They are also numbered. If you could pan up a little?'

The camerawoman tilts her lens before pulling focus on a little silver tag stamped with the number – I can just about read it on the monitor – thirteen. Frank walks to one tree – two to the left – and then forward – one forward. He is standing under the old oak tree, the one where he first proposed to Cora. It used to have a rope swing on it but Lal took it down when Rose fell off it, landed on a rusty nail and had to have stitches.

'And she's here today.'

Cora whips her head towards Bridget. 'Did you know about this?' she asks, at the same time as Marcelle says, 'You fucking *what*?' Bridget shakes her head.

The conversation they have with their eyes is as clear as though it had subtitles. *Why didn't we know about this, what is he doing, this is a bloody stupid idea, shall we tear the men apart with our bare hands when this is all over?*

Frank's composure barely slips. 'I'd like to invite my grandson, Oisin, to do the honours.'

'*Really?*' says Oisin. He flushes with pleasure, then bounds out from behind the camera. He looks to Rose, briefly for permission, who bites her lip – I can read what she's thinking: *it's different for boys* – before nodding. 'Cool. OK.' He cracks his knuckles, then looks around. 'Is there a spade?'

'You don't need a spade.' Frank puts a hand on his shoulder. 'You're not going to dig. You're going to climb.'

From a hollow in the tree, Frank retrieves a blue nylon rope and slings it over the lowest sturdy bough. 'Off you go.'

Oisin hoiks himself up as though he's flying, triceps flexing as he Spider-Mans it up the trunk.

'So Dom was supposed to do this?' I whisper to Lal, who nods. I feel bad that my brother's missed his moment on screen. I decide to make one more check on him.

He's in the kitchen, gulping water from a pint glass.

'Is it sorted?' I ask.

He nods. 'But I think I might be about to die of adrenaline poisoning.' He registers the silence in the garden. 'Where is everyone?'

'I've been texting and texting,' I say. 'They're out the back, doing the final scene.'

Dom starts. 'But that's not supposed to happen for another two hours.'

'They moved it forward so the Bonehunters couldn't spoil it. Check your WhatsApp.'

'And Dad was alright with that? And *Rose* let him?'

I laugh. 'He's the fittest of all of us.'

'But that was supposed to be *my* job.'

I'm taken aback at his pettiness. I didn't realise how much it meant to him that his role was on camera. He sprints down the garden.

'Ah, Dom, he's already started,' I call after him. 'Let the kid have his moment.'

'I'm insured to go up there. He's not.'

Dom covers the garden in about three strides; it takes me twice as long.

By the time we're at the gate, Oisin has disappeared from view and the drone is a shadow through layers of green.

'I should be doing this,' says Dom, to the evident annoyance of the Crabwise crew.

'We can cut that in the edit,' says PD. 'Keep rolling.'

'I'm at the top!' Oisin's voice floats down. 'What now, Grandpa?'

'There's a fork between the two highest branches and a loose flap of bark,' says Frank. 'Prise it carefully away and you'll find a large hollow.'

'Ow!' yelps Oisin.

'Right, that's it, get down,' says Dom.

'No, it was just a splinter,' says Oisin. 'OK, I'm just getting a load of mouldy leaves.'

'Put your hand deep inside until you find it.' says Frank.

'I'm looking,' says Oisin, 'But I can't find— oh, hang on.'

His scream, high and girlish, seems to shake the trees to their roots.

There's a movement above, a dark shape plunging swiftly, then catching on a branch. It's a bird's nest, I think, Oisin's dislodged a bird's nest, and instinctively I find myself sprinting towards it, arms outstretched.

The object that lands in my hands is not a nest. I can name all the bones in the human body. This one, moth-shaped, I would know anywhere. It is a human pelvis.

PART TWO

35

The Latin name for the hip bone is the *os coxae*. The large curved edge is the iliac crest, the point of symmetry is called the sacral promontory and the joint at the front is known as the pubic symphysis. This is what's going through my head as the bone, dirty ivory, rocks like a cradle in my palms.

'Is this someone's idea of a joke?' asks Bridget weakly, then all hell breaks loose.

'What the hell were you *thinking*?' Marcelle yells at Frank.

He answers with a question that he addresses to the heavens, no longer the Messiah but the forsaken son. 'Where's the fucking jewel?'

'Oisin, are you OK?' cries Rose.

'I'm fine, I think?' His voice sounds very far away.

'It's a bone,' says Aoife, and then again, louder, fear shaking her by the shoulders, 'It's a *bone*!' Her screams go beyond language as she burrows into her mother.

'Aoife, sweetheart,' says Rose, 'you've got this. Give your fear a number and we'll breathe through it.' But Aoife's gone, freefalling down to that terrifying place where even her parents can't reach her.

'Oisin!' Frank shouts. 'Keep looking for the jewel. It *must* be up there.'

'Swear to God, there's nothing here,' says Oisin. 'I can put my arm in up to the elbow till I hit solid wood.'

'What's happening?' says Cora. 'I don't understand.' She looks to Dominic, who puts his hand absently on her shoulder but has no words. He's as stunned as the rest of us, and there's no way to think because even if there were no other voices there's Aoife, screaming and screaming and screaming.

'Oh, man. I am *fucked*,' says Shane the bouncer quietly.

'Is *that* what you were supposed to be looking after?' I ask him.

'I didn't know it was a bloody *jewel*,' he says. 'I was just told there was a *clue* in that tree and my brief was not to take my eyes off it. I reckoned it was a piece of paper or summink.'

And PD made him go out the front to deal with the Glemhams. And the CCTV will show him taking a bribe and leaving his post. Despite the chaos, I find a moment to feel sorry for him.

'Oisin, mate,' Shane calls. 'Use the torch on your phone, see if you can catch the light.'

Shane seems to know an awful lot about how to look for something. It's hard to picture a man of his bulk shinning up the tree with the same ease I just saw Oisin climb it, or to believe that the boughs could take his weight.

Hard, but not impossible. That Melanie girl was tall and athletic. Where is she? I scan the faces but I can't see her.

Marcelle is already on the phone. 'Police, please.' She sticks a finger in her ear, the better to hear the operator as Aoife sets Dara off. Naimh bends down to scoop her little brother up and carries him back into the house. Rose follows with Aoife. A camera pivots to follow them.

Bridget puts herself between the lens and her grandchildren. 'Do not get those girls on camera,' she says. 'I mean it. *None* of the kids.'

At PD's nod, the camera turns away.

'Where's the fucking *jewel*?' says Frank again.

I am a still point in the chaos, a bone trembling in my hands that used to be inside a human being.

Not just any bone but the pelvis, the same one that two people tried to cut out of me. One of whom is on the other side of that fence. And where the hell is Melanie?

PD's walkie-talkie crackles. 'I've lost control of the crowd?' says Barney. 'They're, like, all following the noise to where you guys are? What even is it?'

There's a blue plastic bag, the kind you get from a corner shop, on the stone table. Shane tips it upside down. Two oranges roll out. 'Not ideal, but it'll do.' He holds it out. 'To prevent any further contamination of evidence. Drop it in.'

I am glad to let the bone go. Shane hangs the bag from a high branch just inside the perimeter of the garden, at the outer limits of his own impressive reach.

Marcelle returns, phone in her hand. 'I've called in the theft,' she says. 'There's a police officer on patrol round the corner, he'll be here any second. The Churcher house is off limits until they've searched it.'

'Shouldn't you be reporting it as murder?' asks Shane.

'No.' Marcelle is dismissive. 'You can buy human bones perfectly legally. Don't you remember when Damien Hirst covered that skull in diamonds?'

Shane nods. Everyone remembers that skull: one of those rare pieces of contemporary art that goes mainstream.

'Well, that was a real head; he bought it in a shop in Islington. Some poor Victorian who'd probably sold her corpse to pay for her funeral. That's what this'll be.' In an impressive gear switch, she turns boiling fury on to Frank. 'And you! What the fucking hell were you thinking, bringing the actual jewel here? God, if you wanted to make a big flourish we could've had a copy made, but leaving the *real thing* up the fucking tree?'

Dom steps in. 'But no one knew, Marcelle. As far as everyone was concerned, that jewel was still in the vault. Even the crew didn't know. The only people who knew what we were doing today were me, Dad and Lal. We've all been keeping an eye on it all morning.'

'What's that?' says Cora, head turning sharply. We all follow her gaze to a shrub whose leaves appear to be moving of their own accord and watch as a figure shoots out and makes a run for the heart of the Heath. Dark jeans and a grey top, the hood pulled tight around the face, the light blue concertina of a surgical mask covering her mouth and nose. 'That's Melanie,' I tell Marcelle as she disappears into the scrub.

'Who?' she asks.

Oisin jumps out of the tree, sinks on his heels to absorb the impact of landing and breaks into a sprint after Melanie. It's one smooth movement. No questions asked, just a man on a mission.

'Who's Melanie?' Marcelle repeats.

'Um, I am?' Melanie steps forward from behind a monitor. My heartbeat – already fast – hits a new personal high. If Melanie is still here, who the hell is Oisin chasing across the Heath? She holds out her phone nervously. 'Um, I know there's a lot going on right now, but do you still want to see my camera roll? I swear I wasn't up to anything dodgy.'

'You don't know who that was?' I say, but I can tell by her face she's as clueless as the rest of us. More so, perhaps, as she doesn't have the context. I wave her away without waiting for an answer. 'I owe you an apology. Wrong end of the stick.'

She retreats behind her camera, exchanging a look with the rest of the crew that says *nutter*. I turn back to my family.

'Whoever that was in the tree, they were here earlier when you lot were all out the front. They were trying to take pictures.'

'Of what?' asks Dom.

Beside me, Billie is silently absorbing every word. Again, I make the split-second decision to protect her feelings until I know more. 'Er, the archives?' I suggest. I can tell him my real fears later. 'I saw Melanie take her hood down, and the blonde hair . . . I just presumed it was the same person? I was going to have it out with her but then the filming started.'

Shane runs his hands over his face, pulling his skin into great ridges.

'It'll be on CCTV, at least,' says Frank, glancing back at the cameras mounted on both houses.

'Will it cover the tree?' says Marcelle.

Frank stalls for a moment, as though she's asked him to solve a complex equation. Like the rest of us, he's shocked, punch-drunk, doesn't know which way is up. 'Um, it could do,' he says when she prompts him with a kick to the shin. 'At the very least they'll show us anyone coming in and out of the back gate.'

Cora begins chewing on the cords that hang from her dress, like a child sucking her hair. The tiny silver bells clack against her teeth. It is the single most grating sound I have ever heard. 'Can you pack it in?' I ask her.

'Lay off her, Nell,' snaps Dom, but he pulls gently at the cord which Cora has darkened with spittle, and she lets him lead her to the stone table, still laid out with production notes and bottles of water. He slides a garden chair under her like a waiter at a posh restaurant. He's placed her right in front of her ashtray, although I can tell by his distracted gaze that he hasn't noticed it.

Cora has, though. 'If the police are coming I'd better get rid of this.' Her hands steady for as long as it takes to flick the lighter's wheel and rekindle her earlier joint. She drags on it as if it's an oxygen mask. One of the crew slyly raises a phone to capture the spectacle.

'If you share that I will sue you into the next century,' says Marcelle.

The phone goes down.

Dom fans the air as though trying to disperse the smoke from a stuffy living room rather than the open air of the Heath. 'Just put it out when they get here, Mum.'

Billie clicks her long green nails together. It is the second most grating sound I have ever heard, but I don't feel the need to snap at her; I rarely do. Should I send her home? If we all have to give witness statements, are we getting into 'appropriate adult' territory? And, if so, can I do that, or does it have to be Dylan or a social worker? Because once we go down that road . . .

I slide my words from the corner of my mouth. 'Listen, if anyone asks – they won't, but if they do – your dad's away for work, OK?'

Her eyes widen. 'Is this gonna be a problem for us?'

I give her hand a quick squeeze. 'I can't see why it would be.' I speak the words lightly but I chose them carefully. When a child has been let down as many times as Billie has, you learn never to promise what you can't deliver.

36

In the garden, the two tribes – crew and family – huddle at either end of the stone table.

Outside, the crowd close in. A handful of singers are still persisting with their refrain of *see the lady rise* but most of the voices are raised in question and the loudest of all is Stuart's.

'What's happening?' he shouts. 'The Bonehunters have a right to know!'

'Is someone hurt?' That's Lisa-Marie Glemham.

Just when I'm starting to picture them storming the house with trebuchets and boiling oil, the police arrive. We hear the officer before we see him, his words rising above the hubbub.

'Get behind this cordon, the lot of you!' says another voice, this one familiar only to me. 'Yes, that includes you, sir. Phones away. Phones *away*. This is a potential crime scene. You don't want to be up for contempt of court, do you? Then put it *away*.'

'I'll let him in,' says Dom, opening the back gate to reveal a drunk spiderweb of blue and white crime scene tape between the bushes and trees, and PC Chisholm winding it back on to its reel.

'If you could all just – oh, hello again.'

I raise my palm in greeting.

'Wow, there's even more of you than I thought. If you could all just stay where you are while I assess the scene and ascertain what's occurred here. *This* incident was called in by a Marcelle Veasey?' The puzzlement in his voice tells me he thinks this is a coincidence. He'll soon see that when it comes to *The Golden Bones* there's no such thing.

Marcelle stalks across the lawn. 'Where are the rest of your team?' she demands. 'I was very clear on the phone that, monetary value aside, the stolen jewel is of huge cultural significance. This is my client, *Sir* Frank Churcher.' She drops the title as subtly as a suit of armour. 'There's bound to be media interest.'

'Like I said, back-up's on the way,' says Chisholm. 'Where are the suspected remains?'

'It's the whereabouts of the jewel you should be focusing on,' says Marcelle, but Shane shows Chisholm where he's bagged the bone, high in a silver birch.

'Good man, good man,' says Chisholm, then unzips his black rucksack to reveal more police tape and various bags and boxes in compartments. He snaps on a pair of sky-blue vinyl gloves, the kind we all bulk-bought last year. Wearing these, he removes the bone from the shopping bag and examines it closely before sliding it into a clear evidence bag.

A panting Oisin sprints into the garden. There's a strip of police tape across his chest, as though he's just breasted a marathon finish line.

'Oh, no, you don't,' says Chisolm.

'He's family,' says Marcelle. 'He was pursuing the thief.'

'I lost him,' says Oisin. 'I'm so sorry. It's packed out there. I think he went towards the pond but I couldn't swear to it.'

Chisholm takes the details, then talks to his radio. 'We have reports of an IC1 male, grey hoodie and blue jeans, absconding the scene in the direction of Hampstead Heath station. All units on the lookout – whoa, madam, are you OK?'

Cora has gone a very pale green as the effects of smoking an entire joint in one go take hold. I click eyes with Dom. Only our mother could have a whitey in the middle of a jewel heist.

'Does she need first aid?' asks Chisholm.

'I'm a trained nurse,' says Bridget, uncapping a bottle of water. 'Let me look after her.'

Lisa-Marie's voice sails over the fence. 'Please talk to us, Mr Churcher!'

'He never had any intention of doing so,' replies Stuart. 'We were idiots to trust him!'

A lone woman tries to restart the singalong of 'To Gather the Bones' but no one joins in and she doesn't get beyond the first verse.

No one is asking if I'm OK. Not even *Dom*. I find myself fighting tears.

At the table, Oisin hovers between family and crew until a stern look from Rose has him scuttling to our end. On the terrace, Marcelle's talking a mile a minute when Chisholm interrupts her.

'Hang on,' he says. 'The missing item was *supposed* to be found? By a stranger?' He sucks his teeth like a plumber who regrets how much he's going to have to quote you for the job. 'I'm just thinking, if it was put there with the intention of being retrieved . . . Theft means the dishonest appropriation of property with the intention of permanently depriving the owner of it, and the owner has to have possession or control of the object. You've lost control of it by deliberately leaving it to be found. What's to say the clue hasn't just been solved and they've left you a bone as a kind of calling card?'

Frank glowers. 'If you're suggesting that someone solved the puzzle that's eluded tens of thousands of readers on the very night before I decided to reveal it, and that person just happened to have a human bone about their person? No. There's a long history of people who have broken the law – done terrible things – to get this jewel, officer. I don't know who or how but I assure you that a theft has taken place here.' *And my daughter has been put at risk*, he doesn't say. Tears form diamonds in my eyes and a fat pearl in my throat.

'That's a matter for— Can I help you, mate?'

Barney Badger has silently apparated in front of Chisholm. 'I left my phone charging? In the house? It's like a yellow cord? Can I just go and get it?'

'What part of "nobody in the house" don't you get?' asks Chisholm. 'Please. Sit down and let me do my job.'

PD addresses her crew. 'No matter who else comes on the scene, we retain ownership of this story. You hear me?' Her eyes are glittering, and no wonder. Half an hour ago she was making a bog-standard arts documentary. Now she has a true crime film on her hands.

I turn to Marcelle. 'She can't use that footage of me, can she?'

She's already pulled up a document on her iPad. 'That's what I'm trying to find out. You didn't sign a release, but if this turns out to be *news* . . . then they might be able to. We'll move heaven and earth to stop that happening. In the meantime I need to get a press release out about the bone, seeing as this joker' – she nods backwards at Chisholm – 'doesn't seem to understand what he's dealing with.'

And the people who *do* understand don't care, I think, and only then do I understand why no one is thinking about me. The others don't *know* that things have changed. Dom was on the phone to Leelo while everything was escalating online. The only one who knows the new implications for me is me.

37

More uniformed officers arrive and a couple in plain clothes: a stocky white guy with a shiny bald head and a slim Asian woman in a pair of pegged trousers that I wouldn't mind for myself.

'DC Mike Passmore and DS Mehreen Bindra,' she announces as she scans the garden and the Heath beyond. 'If you could just remain where you are while my colleague briefs us.'

Chisholm gesticulates like a traffic controller, to the street, the house, the garden, the tree and at the main players, me and Oisin. Bindra picks up an old copy of *The Golden Bones* and something crosses her face that's nearly a smile. 'I *knew* the name was familiar,' she says. 'We had this growing up. My dad fancied his chances but never got anywhere. Mike, can you take down names and numbers?'

Barney hands Passmore a piece of paper. 'There's a call sheet? With everyone who was here on the shoot today?'

I flinch. Billie isn't on that call sheet, and, while I'll relish my own conversation with the police, I don't want her absence on paper to draw attention.

'Did you get footage of that lot out the front?' he asks PD.

'I'd have to check the time stamp but I'd say we have the crowd on film for the past twenty minutes to half-hour,' she says.

'Good,' replies Passmore. 'We'll need that. It'll help us track down anyone who wandered off.'

Chisholm escorts a woman in a hazmat suit through the garden. It takes her just minutes to confirm that the bone is human. A dark current passes through me and I can tell from the others' faces that they felt it too. She takes it away in a white cardboard box that looks like something you'd store cakes in.

'Where's she taking it?' asks Cora.

'To the lab, for dating,' says Bindra. 'If bones are older than fifty years we class them as archaeological bones, and an investigation, especially of partial remains, is unlikely to yield any real evidential value.'

'Well, there you are, then,' says Marcelle. 'That's what's happened here. It's a stunt by a disgruntled treasure-hunter, and believe you me there are hundreds of them. Ask anyone here. At the risk of sounding like a broken record, darling, devote your energy to finding the jewel.'

'I'm not your darling,' says Bindra.

'Thank God for that,' says Marcelle under her breath.

'And what if the bones are . . .' I struggle for the right word. Fresher? Younger? 'What if they're recent?'

'Anything in the last fifty years is forensic, and then we're looking at a suspicious death.'

Lal makes the sign of the cross.

'What was the missing property worth?' asks Bindra.

'It was insured for a million,' says Marcelle.

'People have staged burglaries for far less,' says Bindra.

'Sir Frank has been a very rich man for years. He doesn't need to commit *fraud*,' says Marcelle, and then, shooting daggers at my father, 'and besides, in placing it in the tree he hasn't so much invalidated the policy as obliterated it.'

'What does this mean for the prize?' Dom chews his lip. 'Does this put us in breach of anything?'

'It's in the Ts and Cs that we reserve the right to change the prize without notice,' says Marcelle. 'So contractually it's not a problem. But readers want Elinore. Without her, where's the appeal? Honestly, Dominic, didn't you *think* of this? You're supposed to be good at risk analysis.'

'Saying *I told you so* isn't helping, Marcelle.'

Passmore hovers near the table. 'Sir Frank, I understand you've got CCTV covering the property exterior.'

'Call me Frank.' My father rises from his chair. 'And it would be my pleasure to show you.'

'That's more like it,' says Marcelle to Bindra. 'Honestly, I can't believe you're falling for it. I mean, there can't be *that* many places selling human bones; it's not like you can pick them up in Waitrose, is it? It'll be a doddle for you to trace it. Focus on the bloody jewel! This is what they *want* – for you to get so caught up in the stunt that you forget about the theft.'

'These are *human remains,*' says Bindra sternly. 'Our next steps are to bring in cadaver dogs to see if there are any further remains at the location. It's not uncommon for body parts to become displaced.'

If she knows how strong the resonance is with the plot of *The Golden Bones* she isn't giving it away, but it's not lost on the rest of us.

More uniformed officers arrive to keep the growing crowds, and then the news crews, at bay. Two dog-handlers lead German shepherds around the Heath and garden. Scene-of-crime officers in hazmat suits crawl over the forest floor with torches that look like light sabres plunged into the ground to illuminate the dark recesses under the trees.

Time stops looping and turns to treacle. After what could have been five minutes or an hour, Passmore and Frank return.

'Bad news, ma'am. The property's CCTV cuts out at 1.25 p.m. The feed just goes dead. So, right at the crucial moment when we think the jewel was switched for the bone, we've got no footage. Looks like someone unplugged it and replaced it with this.'

Swinging from his hand is an evidence bag containing Barney Badger's bright yellow charger, still plugged into his phone.

Dom's jaw falls open.

'You did say any other socket in the house,' I remind him.

'How was I to know the dozy bollock would kill the CCTV feed?'

'Hang on,' says Frank. '*You* told him to unplug it? Dominic, what the hell were you—'

I position myself between my brother and my father. 'Don't have a go at Dom. What if that's what Barney *wanted*? With all those plugs and wires in the garden, there wasn't a spare socket?

But if he came in here and made himself such a pain in the arse that he was told to find another outlet?' I fold my arms in triumph and wait for Passmore to congratulate me.

'The plug for the CCTV, is it labelled?'

Frank frowns. 'No, but it's a short cable, and it's not a stretch to follow it to the hard drive.'

'Mr Badger,' calls Mike. 'A minute of your time. Sarge?'

Bindra marches and Barney slouches over. 'Oh, wow, you've got my phone,' he says. 'Thanks.'

There's a charged silence before Dom explodes. 'Do you realise what you've done, you stupid little fucker?'

'I hope you're going to search him,' I tell Passmore.

Barney spreads his body into a starfish, aiming for insouciance, but his skinny legs are unsteady.

'Maybe he's eaten it?' I tell Bindra as Passmore frisks him. 'You should X-ray him. Or maybe it's up his bum? I know for a fact that men smuggle mobile phones into prison that way and the jewel is a fraction of the size—'

Dom winces. 'Nell, *please*.'

'I'm just saying.'

Rather than taking my ideas on board, Bindra is watching us as though *we* are the ones with something to hide. When Passmore has finished searching Barney's myriad pockets, he shakes his head.

Our fingerprints are taken on a digital reader. Last time, my fingertips were inky for days. They were virgin prints then, unmarked by decades of working with glass. These don't feel as though they belong to the same person.

'We'll need everything you filmed today,' Bindra tells PD. 'And I repeat my colleague's earlier instruction not to broadcast anything. Not so much as a fuzzy picture on Twitter. It could jeopardise the investigation.'

PD's loss is my gain. I feel a knot between my shoulders loosen.

'Well,' I say, 'at least I won't be on TV.'

Oisin clears his throat. 'Auntie Nell,' he says, looking up from his iPad. 'About that.'

38

We gather around Oisin's iPad. There's a video at the top of the ElinoresArmy forum captioned WHAT THE HELL IS GOING ON?

'Good question,' mutters Frank before being interrupted by his own words issuing mineral and sibilant from the built-in speaker.

'Fifty years ago, seven bones were hidden. Only six were found, and after tragedy struck, I decided to keep Elinore's last bone safe . . .'

The camera is trained on the back of his head, thick silver hair curling to the collar. The sightlines mean that this must have been filmed in the shrub where the guy in the grey hoodie was hiding. He tries to follow Frank but I'm guessing he reached the limit of what could be filmed from his hiding place, because Frank soon steps out of view and his speech becomes indistinct. There follows a couple of minutes' footage of branches and bracken. When Oisin's scream – which makes us all jump, even though we are expecting it – comes, the picture shakes and then I run into shot, in my dungarees and headscarf and no face covering, my arms outstretched and mouth wide with horror as I catch the bone.

'Where's the fucking jewel?' shouts Frank on screen.

'Christ alive,' says the real Frank at my side. 'That is *not* how I envisaged telling the world where Elinore was buried.'

Raised voices over the fence tell us that the Bonehunters are watching it too. The odd phrase leaps out.

'She was there all along?'

'You believe that, do you?'

'So Frank reveals the hiding place – and she's not there? That's a bit convenient, isn't it?'

'He doesn't change, does he?'

'The *audacity* of the man!'

'Who would *kidnap* her?'

And under it all the constant repetition of her name. *Elinore, Elinore, Elinore*, as though if they say it often enough they will summon her.

'So they've broken our embargo, revealed the hiding place, stolen the jewel and broadcast its theft in one fell swoop,' says Frank. 'It almost makes you want to doff your cap to them.'

'Can we get the Glemhams to take this down?' Frank asks Marcelle.

'You must be joking,' says Dom. 'They'll be rubbing their hands together at this kind of traffic.'

'It wouldn't actually make a difference,' says Oisin. 'It's already getting numbers on YouTube, Facebook, Twitter. And the comments are on fire.'

He shows us the screen where a new comment box appears every few seconds, too quick to read any to the end before it's replaced by a new one.

A voice rises above the hubbub: English, male, posh-ish. 'Frank Churcher!' he cries. 'What have you got to say for yourself?'

'Well said!' shouts another man.

It is such a strange thing for people to be talking to each other and tapping at their screens at the same time. The frantic nature of it seems to make the world spin a little faster. I would hardly be surprised if the houses and the garden suddenly broke free of the Heath and were whirled away to Oz. I think I would prefer that to this reality.

'Come out and talk to us, you fraud,' says the first man. 'You *coward*.'

We all see Frank bristle but he doesn't rise to the bait.

'What are they saying in the comments?' I ask Oisin.

Dom tries to tilt the screen away from me. 'Don't read them,' he says I snatch it back, a reflex honed by years of grabbing the last biscuit in the tin from under his nose. 'I need to know what they're saying. I need to see everything.'

@BON35: Is that Eleanor Churcher? Whoa! Someone's had a hard paper round

@goldengal: Came back when she smelt the money, didn't she?

Obviously I don't love the comments about my looks, but the idea that I'm on the take lands like a punch to the gut.

@BON35: Nice publicity stunt, Churcher

We all wince in unison because we know how that's going to land.

'Publicity stunt?' shrieks Frank, angling his body towards the crowd. 'I spend fifty years trying to be taken seriously as an artist and some shitbag on the internet has the gall to accuse me of pulling a *publicity* stunt?' There's a grain of truth in this, of course – the reveal itself *was* a publicity stunt – but I know better than to point this out. Abruptly Frank turns his face, and his anger, towards Dom. 'I knew this was a bad idea. I should never have let you talk me into this, I should have left this fucking book in the past where it belonged.'

Dom blinks rapidly.

'Frank, that's not fair.' Cora is suddenly lucid again, like Dom's need for his mum to defend him has pulled her out of her stupor.

Late in the afternoon, the police disperse the Bonehunters (after taking their names). The 'exclusion zone' of the crime scene is widened and the casual rubberneckers are pushed so far from the house that there's nothing worth hanging around for.

The sniffer dogs don't find any more bones.

'That's good, isn't it?' says Marcelle. 'Makes it more likely it was a single bone, bought online.'

I don't share the collective sigh of relief. Comforting as it would be to believe that this is a hundred-year-old bone of someone who died peacefully in their sleep, this is *The Golden Bones* and I have learned to fear the worst.

Erin Kelly

'Can I have a word, Dom?' I say, and pull him to one side. 'What does this mean for me?'

He scratches his jaw, looking over my shoulder at the strangers combing the garden. 'What do you mean?'

'Stuart and his little friends on the internet,' I say. 'Now that the jewel's gone missing, they're going to come looking for me again. I know you said he'd turned his back on Ingrid but he seems to have . . . turned his front to her again now. That person saying they were writing to her reckons they've re-verified the Cecil Sharp verses.'

'What do you mean?' The same words, but his tone is different and I've got his full attention. I show him what's on my phone.

'Why didn't you show me this earlier?' he says.

'I *tried* to,' I remind him.

He puts his hand to the back of his neck and clicks it, as if his head's come loose and he's reattaching it. I know the feeling.

'We'll sort this. OK? I'll find a way to nip this in the bud.'

He's saying the right things in the right way; he's even holding himself the right way, upright with feet planted apart, as though nothing could ever knock him over. But his words ring hollow. He couldn't even protect a piece of gold in a tree, so how does he think he's going to protect me?

Minutes turn to hours.

Lal brings the extension cord he uses for the lawnmower to the stone table so we can all recharge our devices. There's nothing but speculation on the forums, guesses and pronouncements coming from all over the world.

'I'm going to get Leelo on it too,' says Dom, dropping his voice. 'Half her team hack systems for fun in the evenings. If I offer a reward, they'll probably do a quicker job than the Met.'

Bindra's head swivels our way like an owl's. 'I am instructing you not to do that.'

'I just want to feel like I'm doing something,' he says. 'What *can* I do to help?'

'I strongly advise you to make a note of anything you want to include in your statement,' she says. 'No matter how irrelevant you think it seems. You'd be surprised what the memory erases overnight.'

Chisholm reaches the end of his shift and a new constable takes over. The police shield Rose and the three youngest as they get into their car, and give them an escort back to the Suburb. The Crabwise crew go home before the reporters but soon they leave too. Half a dozen police and crime scene officers remain. Frank oversees the collection of evidence. The valuable prints and sketches and the press cuttings the police are content to photograph. They take away old tapes and the postbags, the letters rolling around like tickets in a tombola.

When Bindra is satisfied, she hands out her business card. 'Eleanor, Gerald, Sir Frank.'

'Just Frank, *please*.' He gives her what I know he thinks is a winning, wolfish smile. It bounces back in his face like a squash ball off a wall.

'Dominic, Rosaleen, Marcelle. I want you all to come and give your statements in the next few days.'

Bindra's departure is abrupt but she leaves something of herself in the air; not a scent, more an echo. The feeling you get after standing next to the speakers at a club and your ears ring for hours afterwards.

The sun dips over the houses and the solar-powered bulbs that string the garden flicker on. Moths dance around pearls of light. The new PC unwinds the police tape and returns the Heath to the public. He is not thorough in the undoing, tearing at Chisholm's knots and leaving scraps behind. And then he is gone, leaving trampled undergrowth and trees dressed in blue and white rags.

Frank locks the gate behind him.

'Mother of God,' says Lal, his voice breaking. 'What a day.'

'Drink?' suggests Cora.

39

Cora can move fast enough when she wants to. She's back from the kitchen with a brace of chilled jeroboams in under a minute. '*Champagne?*' says Dom incredulously, as she hands him the bottle to open. 'Could that be any less appropriate?' But he clearly needs a drink as badly as the rest of us, because he twists the cork without further prompting and serves himself first.

'Nell, can I . . .' asks Billie, waving her empty water glass under my nose.

Cora fills her glass without checking in with me.

'*One*,' I say, as the bubbles hit Billie in the nose.

'Yes, don't go getting a taste for that,' warns Cora. I'm impressed that she's backing me up, but she hadn't finished. 'You'll be lucky to get supermarket prosecco on Eleanor's little boat.'

I give her my sweetest, most sarcastic smile.

Oisin's found a six-pack of Beck's from somewhere. He uncaps the bottle on the edge of the table and takes a long glug, draining half the bottle in one go. Bridget watches him, a thick crease between her eyes. Does she worry about Lal's blood in Oisin's veins, just as I worry about Dylan's and Christie's in Billie's?

'What's the latest, Osh?' asks Dom.

He sets his iPad on its stand where we can all see it. Marcelle's face fills the screen, backgrounded by the Strawberry Thief wallpaper of the Lallys' sitting room, and framed by the BBC News channel logo. Oisin slides the volume up and we catch the news anchor asking her if she's concerned about the human remains found near Sir Frank's home.

'I feel that when the bone turns out to be historical, they're going to wish they'd focused their energies on retrieving what is an important part of English artistic and cultural history.'

'When did you do that?' asks Frank, astonished.

'Cheeky little Zoom with a mate at Broadcasting House while the police weren't looking,' she says. 'Someone had to get the word out.'

'That jewel is probably halfway to Manila by now,' says Frank glumly.

'Catastrophising isn't going to get us anywhere.' Bridget is as irritable with Frank as she is coddling with Cora. They've always been the weak link in the foursome. 'Let's put our heads together. It'll take the police a week to get up to speed on the history of the treasure hunt, whereas no one knows it better than us.'

'What we need to do is think like the police,' says Dom. 'Analytically, logically.'

'What we *need* is to think like Bonehunters,' says Lal. 'Mad as a box of fucking frogs.'

'I think the main question is how the hell they knew,' says Dom.

'Well it's not like the filming was a secret,' says Oisin. 'It was in all the trade press, *Broadcast* magazine and so on, and then there were location signs in place from yesterday. A Bonehunter could've put two and two together: *it's the fiftieth anniversary, he's getting on a bit, if they're ever going to make a big announcement about the missing bone it's probably going to be now.*'

'I'll allow that,' says Dom carefully. 'But how did they know the exact location? And that the jewel was hidden there? And the timing of it? That's the bit I can't get my head around.'

'You *must* have written it down,' says Bridget.

'Nope,' says Dom. 'Not so much as a Post-it. And we certainly never emailed or texted about it. We literally only ever discussed it verbally, and only when we were alone.'

'Ah, Dominic, fella,' says Lal. 'That's not strictly true.'

'What do you mean?'

'The pub. Last night. I was a while in the bog.'

'It's all that Pepsi Max,' says Frank. 'I keep telling you, it's wreaking havoc on your gut microbiome.'

'Aye.' Lal pats his round belly. 'Any road, when I came back to the beer garden, youse two were going over it. You've neither of you ever been able to keep to a whisper.'

Dom and Frank look at each other, aghast. 'I've got a horrible feeling he might be right,' says Dom.

Lal shrugs. 'Who am I to give out to someone for messing up after a few drinks?'

'This is what happens when I stray from high-grade vodka,' says Frank loftily. 'I was trying to drink clean. I'm sure the whiskey wasn't *my* idea.'

Dom's shoulders slump. 'No one forced either of us to drink.'

'I cannot believe you would be that careless.' Bridget drums a hard rhythm on the stone stable, as though she's trying to get her anger out through her fingers rather than her mouth. 'So if someone overheard you saying you were going to put the jewel back in the tree, you could well have let slip that you had a security guard looking after it?'

Dom stares into the bottom of his glass like the answer's written there. 'I mean . . . maybe?'

'So they'd have known to cause a fuss, create a diversion,' suggests Bridget.

'Stuart?' I ask. 'Where was he when it was all kicking off? Or Shane himself? Or both of them? Could it be more than one person?'

'That could work,' Dom kneads his neck while he thinks. 'I mean, they all want the same thing but for different reasons, which is Elinore back together.'

'I agree we're looking for some kind of teamwork,' says Bridget. 'Why would the thief hang around to film you catching the bone? If you'd just stolen something valuable and high profile, you'd get as far away as you could, as fast as you could.'

'I reckon Barney Badger was part of it,' I say. 'Unplugging the CCTV. I reckon he was so blatant as a kind of double bluff.'

'Could it be the Glemhams?' asks Cora.

Lal shakes his head. 'I don't think that fits. The Glemhams want the puzzle solved above all else. I know they're a pain in the hole but they're good sports.'

'Have you got any ideas, Cora?' I ask, but my mother's earlier flash of clarity has gone.

'I can't.' She makes a face like she's swallowed a spoonful of bad medicine. 'It's all too horrible to think about.'

'Let's think about the logistics, then.' I turn to Oisin. 'How fit would you have to be to scale that tree?'

Oisin considers. 'It's only the rope and the first couple of branches that're tricky.' There are four empty bottles lined up in front of him and he's slurring a little. 'After that, it's easy. If someone had, say, a two-metre ladder you could do it if you were old, or out of shape.'

'I didn't see a lot of two-metre ladders hanging around the crime scene, son,' says Lal. It's clear that Oisin's only trying to help, but he's also caught up in the drama of it. He's too young to have lived through the worst of the Elinore phenomenon. He knows the stories about what happened to me but he wasn't *there*.

Oisin burps into his fist, then declares, 'Well – it's not *all* bad. The new book's gone to number one on Amazon, just on pre-orders. And on eBay you could get the original for a fiver last week and now it's a hundred quid a copy. And you're number one in the app stores, two days before launch.'

'I suppose that's some comfort,' says Bridget. 'That your hard work is reaching people, Dominic?'

'Hardly,' says Dom. 'I quit my job. I gave a year and a half of my life to this project. All those focus groups, all those brainstorming sessions. And if it's a hit I'll never know, now, whether it's the work I did or some Bonehunter with a grudge.'

I put my hand over his. This is as hard on Dom as it is on Frank. I wonder for a second whether this could be an attack on *him*. I never understood the ins and outs of Dom's previous career, but have a vague idea that management consultancy is basically about fucking people over. An old memory surfaces: when he was streamlining a workforce he used to talk about redundancies in terms of skulls. I heard him on the phone once, talking to one of his Joshes: *How many skulls do we need to lose?* Is there some sacked middle manager who wants to see him fail?

I discount it without bothering to voice it. We all know that this is the work of Bonehunters. We all feel it in our marrow.

The empties pile up: Laurent-Perrier, Beck's, Pepsi Max.

The firefly of Cora's joint dances in the dark.

The night turns on a wheel. Glasses and bottles sail from hand to hand with the urgency of water buckets dousing a fire. We repeat conversations, arriving at the same non-conclusions. One question echoes and echoes.

Where is the jewel?

Where is the jewel?

Where is the jewel?

Is it the right question, though? In my head, another pounds like a baseline. We're all working on the assumption that this is an archaeological bone, a curio, a prop. Someone who died before any of us were born.

But what if it's not?

What if it's not?

What if it's not?

Dom bites his lip, then looks at me. 'Don't bite my head off, Nell, but is there any way Richard Reid could've been at the Duke last night?'

Everyone shifts, ever so slightly, in their seats. Here comes the shame, banging its fists on my cheeks.

'I don't know, Dom,' I snap. 'I don't keep tabs on the man. I haven't spoken to him for over twenty years.'

'I don't think we can afford to discount any possibility, love.' Cora speaks gently; this is the one area of my life where even she treads carefully.

40

Vale of Health, London NW3
April 1999

'The fabled Churcher-Lally Sunday lunch,' says Richard, scanning the street for a parking space.

It's not the first time everyone has met Richard but it's the first time we will have sat around a table for any length of time. I've been the reluctant one: he has been such a good thing for me that I like to keep him separate, where they can't spoil it.

'Oh, here we go.' He reverses smoothly into a tight spot directly opposite the scene of Ingrid's attack. I don't fall apart. I'm dealing OK with that stuff since Stuart Cummins backed off. In addition to the restraining order, he actually renounced his quest. Some new research has come to light that challenges Ingrid's theory, apparently. And having Richard at my side helps.

'I know why *I'm* nervous,' says Richard as we get out of the car. 'But why are *you* all twitchy?'

'Everyone's been *mental* since my dad's show,' I say. 'I mean, even more so than usual. I find myself drinking to take the edge off, then running my mouth off about my parents' failings. Then *they* get defensive. Plus, last time I was there Dom was playing footsie under the table with Rose but he misjudged and I found my brother's foot in my crotch and I choked on the beef Wellington and—'

'Bloody hell, Nell, take a breath,' says Richard. 'It'll be fine.'

'Sorry,' I say, turning the key in the door. 'Hopefully you'll have them all on their best behaviour.'

He crosses the threshold with a bottle of Veuve Cliquot in one hand ('Oh, *you* can come again,' says Cora). In the other is a chunky black mobile phone, which he sets down on the hall table.

'I'd like to address the fact that I *know* this makes me look like a wanker,' he says. 'I've got a vulnerable client – messy divorce. I'm helping the wife prove that he's cheating so we can use it as leverage for a decent settlement. I have to be available for her.'

Cora winds a lock of hair around her fingertip and tilts her head to one side. 'Of course,' she says. She's put back on all the weight she lost last year and looks far better for it.

In fact, it's a good lunch. For all the tensions I told Richard about, one huge source of unpredictability has gone. Lal is still sober, and his new evenness of mood seems to have a calming effect on the rest of them. And, to my personal relief, everyone's feet stay where they're supposed to.

An hour in, Richard's phone starts bleeping. 'Excuse me,' he says. 'I really have to . . .' He turns to Frank. 'It's a bit delicate. Is there anywhere private I can . . . ?'

'Use the study,' says Frank, and nods to the ajar door. Richard pulls the aerial out of the phone as he goes in and closes the door behind him.

'A businessman, eh, Nell?' says Lal. 'I always saw you settling down with some hippy on a houseboat.'

I just smile. In fact, Richard's job has become part of the appeal. In a family where everyone is judged by the art they create, it's nice to spend time with someone whose job is just what they do all day, not an expression of their soul. It's only now they're at the same table that I realise he reminds me of Dom in that way.

'What's it like, dating a spy?' Rose mops up gravy with a roast potato. 'Is he like James Bond?'

'I don't think James Bond takes on a lot of benefit fraud cases,' I reply.

'I hope he doesn't go after the artists,' says Frank. 'In the good old days all the artists and musicians could claim the dole while they were rehearsing or practising their craft. Nowadays they want everyone out being a good little taxpayer from the moment they leave school. It leaves no room for people to grow.'

'Ah, I don't think he goes around persecuting people who draw the *Mona Lisa* on the pavement. It's more industrial than that. You know, someone whose company has them on full sick pay and the guy's out playing football at the weekends.'

Cora's already lost interest. 'What's that bloody cat got?'

Finn McCool, the Lallys' ancient tabby, is pulling at a wire on Richard's recently vacated seat. The wire is attached to a little foam device and a socket that plugs into his ever-present dictaphone.

'It's a thing he uses to record phone calls,' I say. 'Must've fallen out of his pocket.'

'He *is* James Bond!' says Rose.

I hesitate. 'I'd better take it in, in case he needs it.'

When I enter Frank's study, Richard is not on the phone at all, but standing with his back to me. The desk drawers are open: reader letters are spread over the desk. Richard is taking photographs of them with a slim camera. A jolt passes through me, as though I've touched an electric fence.

'What are you doing?'

He doesn't turn around right away. He straightens up first, takes a deep breath and says, 'Nell, I can explain.'

'Are you a Bonehunter?'

When he faces me, his face is like sand that someone's drawn a rake through. 'This isn't how I wanted you to—'

I bring my fist down hard on the desk. '*Are you a fucking Bonehunter?*'

Next door, the chairs scrape across the floor. Richard steps towards me, tries to take my hands. 'I don't want to lose you,' he says.

The others are in. They line up, blocking his exit.

'You'd better explain yourself, sunshine.' Lal steps out of the formation. He's shorter than Richard and fifteen years his senior but he seems to expand while Richard shrinks. I've told him wha

Lal could be like when drunk; for the first time I can imagine him being violent when sober.

'I'm a private investigator.' His voice quavers. 'I work for Fritz Velasco.'

My legs go as if someone's kicked them out from under me; my spine grinds against the wall as I slide to sitting.

'Let me get this straight,' says Frank. '*You're* N20 Investigators, or whatever it's called? The one who's been sending the letters on Velasco's behalf? You can't be. You'd have been a little kid in the seventies.' He clicks his fingers. 'That guy's name was Jonathan.'

'Jonathan Reid was my dad,' says Richard. 'I took the business over when he retired.'

Once again, *The Golden Bones* has insinuated its way through the generations. Frank paces a tight circle. I feel a steadying hand on my shoulder: Bridget, calm as a nurse taking my heart rate.

Dom takes the reins. 'And you've been stringing Nell along so you could get close to the jewel?'

'It started out like that, but—'

'Jesus Christ.' Frank blows out his cheeks. 'The hunt is *over.* The jewel is in a safe and that's where it's going to stay. You can tell Mr Velasco that from me.'

'Do you know what? I'm glad it's in the open.' Richard crouches down to my level. I turn my head away. 'I love you, Nell,' he says. 'If we can ever move on from this, I'll sell the business; I'll cancel the contract with Velasco if you can forgive me. I didn't know how to tell you, I just got deeper and deeper in until—'

'Get the fuck out of my sight.'

My words act as a shove to Richard's chest. He teeters for a moment, raises a leg in a clumsy Cossack kick, before falling on his arse.

'Has he broken the law?' Frank wonders. 'False representation?'

'You can't consent to sex if you don't know who you're sleeping with,' says Dom.

'Jesus *Christ*, Dom,' I say. I look to Rose for solidarity, in the ope she'll tell him off later, but she's staring at her feet.

Richard is now sitting opposite me. 'No, you can't – I wasn't. I *love* you,' he tries again.

'I'm going to call Leslie Napoleon,' says Cora.

'No one's calling anyone,' I say. 'I've had enough of courtrooms and the judicial system to last me a lifetime. I just want him gone.'

'You heard her,' says Lal. 'You've got ten seconds before I punch you myself.'

Richard gets on all fours. If there was room, I think he might fully prostrate himself before me. 'But your stuff . . .' There's a sob in his voice. 'All your things at the house.'

I'm about to say keep them, burn them, when Bridget intervenes. 'You can send them here,' she says. 'By courier.'

'On your feet, sunshine,' says Lal.

Richard wipes his eyes, but he doesn't put up a fight.

When the front door has slammed, everyone gathers around me, blocking the light. I look up at the horseshoe of faces. Frank's sharp features come into keen focus. 'Well. What a nasty piece of work *he* turned out to be,' he says.

The storm that breaks has been brewing my whole life.

'This is all *your* fault.' I don't decide to stand up, I just find myself facing my father, screaming in his face, louder than I knew was possible.

Cora looms into view beside him. 'That's not fair, Nell.'

'*And* yours. You're as responsible for this as he is.'

'Responsible for what?' she says.

'That book! My name! There's *nothing* in my life that isn't tainted by it.'

The defensive squaring of Frank's shoulders is the closest I'll get to an admission. 'We've *been* over this,' he says.

'No!' I shout. '*You've* been over it. You've moved on, with your new paintings. But *The Golden Bones* is going to follow me around for the rest of my life. How can I trust anyone? It all leads back to you.'

I shove my parents aside and run upstairs to my childhood bedroom. I'm acting like a fourteen-year-old but I feel like a baby. I lie on the single bed and howl. Rose lies behind me and spoons me; she passes square after square of toilet paper to mop my tears. Dom sits on the windowsill, clearly floundering for words, but his presence is everything. Neither of my parents come to see me.

By the evening I'm back aboard *Jitka* in Camden. Martina and I sit with our legs over the side, watching crisp packets and plastic pint glasses bob on the water and drinking vodka from a bottle with a picture of a bison on it.

'Thanks for having me back,' I say.

'You are staying here as long as you need.'

'I bet he never even had a fucking niece.' I take a deep swig. The vodka is allegedly made from grass but tastes like ethanol.

'He is *total* prick,' she agrees. 'An insult to Hello Kitty.'

'I hope she wreaks a terrible feline revenge on him.'

'Huh.'

The sun dips over the flats on the opposite bank and the temperature plummets.

'I get blankets,' offers Martina.

An oil spill paints psychedelic swirls on the water's surface. In one of the flats a light goes on, and in a bedroom a woman shakes a duvet into a white cover. A flashback assails me. *Where did you come from, Nell? Who sent you to me?* What a fucked-up choice of words, when he had clearly tracked me down using methods honed on cheating spouses and fraudsters. And what about the sex? Was every second of that a pretence? Did he invoice Mr Velasco for the time he spent between my legs? Was he so deep into his own legend he had started to believe it himself?

When Martina drapes a blanket over my shoulders, I use it to wipe my cheeks.

'I feel like I've got shit all over my skin,' I say. 'Does that make sense?'

She nods her understanding. 'I have a friend in a peace camp in Bristol who discovers her boyfriend is undercover police officer.

She says same thing when it happens. She is violated. We go to see her if you want to talk to someone who knows about it.'

I look longingly at the water. 'The thought of casting off and cruising the Kennet and Avon down to the West Country is pretty fucking tempting right now,' I say.

She sits next to me, her boots poking out from her blanket. 'Then we get someone to look after the stall.'

'I'll drink to that.'

She lights a roll up and carefully taps the ash into a flowerpot.

'He's worse than the Bonehunters,' I say, after a while.

Martina purses her lips. 'I know Richard hurts you,' she says, 'But he doesn't try to *stab* you.'

'Bonehunters, though – they were obviously mad and tried to kill me and all that jazz, but they were acting in *good faith*. They thought they were doing the right thing; I was just a by-product of their obsession. Whereas what he did . . . it was cold, calculating. He knew he was doing a bad thing and he kept doing it. He lied and he lied and he lied.'

A hired barge crawls past us, evidently crewed by a stag party as they're all dressed in old-fashioned sailor suits. One of them pulls down his white trousers and moons at us.

'They all drown,' says Martina enthusiastically. I raise the bison vodka in a toast to their demise.

'It's changed me, you know? I'm not the same person I was this morning.'

'How you change?'

'I'm going to be a good person, Martina.' I pause for a hiccup that recruits every muscle in my body. 'I might not make anything of my life, but I'm going to do the right thing by people. I'm never going to do anything like what he did to me.'

4I

Grand Union Canal, Ladbroke Grove, London W10
2 August 2021

I sit up in bed with such force that the whole boat rocks. Usually, waking up is a lazy swim to the surface of the day. This morning I feel as if someone's yanked me blinking and gasping into a world of bones and books weirder than any dream.

Light through the blinds and the clock on my phone tell me it's not even seven a.m. Billie won't stir for some time. I've got an appointment to see DS Bindra at nine. At the same time, the bookshop doors will open, copies of *The Golden Bones 2021* will start to pass through the tills and the app will go live. Yesterday the *Sunday Times* ran an interview with Dom and Dad, and last night the television programme should have been broadcast to an audience of millions. Instead they repeated their profile of Lal, which I imagine delighted Frank no end.

Oh, and for an hour or two I trended on Twitter, was the most viewed video on the *Daily Mail* website, and have become a meme. Someone even took a photo of me buying milk at the Costcutter on the Harrow Road yesterday morning. I'd forgotten my resolution to abandon the dungarees and gone out dressed pretty much exactly as I am in the video. It won't take a puzzle-solving genius to cross-reference that with the reports of me living on a narrowboat and work out where I'm moored, so I've got to factor a change of address on top of everything else.

swing my bare feet on to the floor and stretch out until my palms t on the ceiling. When I first bought *Seren* she was called *ity*, along with seemingly half the boats on the waterways.

I wanted my boat to have a person's name because I love her as if she's a friend. Seren was the name of my cellmate in Holloway, in for stealing from the pub she worked in. I liked her a lot. I've tried to trace her several times but some people just seem to vanish.

When people learn that I live on a boat they expect it to be full of wind chimes and hippy tat, but, if I say so myself, the interior wouldn't look out of place in a design magazine. Herringbone oak flooring, a vintage rug, some Art Deco tiles I found in a skip that would've cost me hundreds on eBay, and kitchen units painted a shade of sage green that makes me happy every time I look at them. There's no art on the walls but you don't need paintings when you have windows like mine. It's a hot morning and the sun bounces off the canal and turns my stained glass windows into sequins. I designed and installed them. I plumbed in and tiled the bathroom and fixed the solar panels on to the roof. I even built the dovecote shelves that house my colour-coded sheets of glass. The only thing I didn't install was the wood-burner and the fridge. I like to think the Admiral would be proud of me.

I make the bed and tuck it back into sofa mode – Billie has the bedroom – in one practised movement, then flick on my little kettle. I throw open the side hatch. The canal is so green with algae it looks as if you could play snooker on it, but that doesn't stop the moorhens gliding up to the window and diving for the seeds I throw on to the water.

While the kettle boils, I set myself to doing some work, as a distraction. I get out some of my smaller offcuts: it's a shame to waste them when the colours are so gorgeous. I lay out the pieces on the table and a design for a sunflower puts itself together in my head. I might be shit at logic and riddles but I can look at pieces of waste glass and they form themselves into patterns as though invisible hands were assembling them. Within a minute I've sketched a perfect template freehand. It needs a circle of dimpl glass in a rich coffee brown at the centre. I'll go to Lead and L in Camden on the way back from the police station.

*   *   *

I search the socials for #TheGoldenBones. Some of the long-term Bonehunters are thrilled to share their passion, posting fan art and fiction they've done over the years. On ElinoresArmy, not everyone wants to share Elinore with the great unwashed.

@LisaMarie: Whoa you guys! 50k new subscribers in the last 24 hours! Welcome to our community! Can I get a HELL YEAH

@Elinore&Tam<3: Mere Johnny Come Latelys. I'm sorry but this is a slap in the face to those of us who've supported the cause for so long

@BON35: Surely the more people looking for Elinore, the greater our chances of getting her back together again? Does it matter who finds the bone?

@Elinore&Tam<3: Excuse me for caring about her. Excuse me for wanting this to be about love, not money

I shake my head. Jane really needs to get a boyfriend.

I'm still nervous that someone might 'take an interest', to borrow Cora's old euphemism, in one of our girls. A search for 'Aoife Churcher Lally' yields no results bar a very old interview with Frank, and there isn't a single photograph of any of the children, not even a slip-up on an old Facebook profile picture. I'm impressed how well Dom and Rose have protected their kids' privacy. I search the whole web for Eleanor + Churcher + Daughter but all it returns is hit after hit of me and Frank, as though I exist only in relation to him.

I don't want to wake Billie, and nor do I want her to overhear the phone call I'm about to make, so I take my coffee up on to the hull where two tiny picnic chairs are chained to the guardrail. It's early ̣ough that the towpath is clear of tourists but the odd commuter ̣ by on a bike and the joggers are out in force.

̣ ̣orning, Loz,' I say to my neighbour, a gentle giant of a ̣ith long red hair and a Viking beard he sometimes wears in little plaits. He's got a toilet cassette swinging from his hand as casually as though it were a bag of shopping. I know Loz from the Facebook and Instagram boating communities and over the past few months we've fallen into a similar rhythm, the way you sometimes do with other continuous cruisers. He's a person of significance on the battle re-enactment scene. Usually he'll greet me with something like, 'Good morrow, fair maiden,' or 'How goes it this fine day?' Today, though, he looks me up and down as though seeing me for the first time. The expression on his face isn't the hunger for information I've seen on Bonehunters' faces. It's more akin to pity. He's obviously seen the video.

A stone sinks inside me. I've worked so hard to make sure that nobody on the waterways knew about *The Golden Bones*, and now my cover is blown.

I nod an awkward hello and take my phone for a walk along the path in search of an empty stretch of water where I can't be overheard. The Westway roars overhead, a dual carriageway balanced on vast concrete stilts. A mile further in and the spaces would have been gentrified, brought the tourist footfall to the towpath with designer lighting and public art and chain restaurants the way they have in Paddington basin. Probably in ten years they will have, but for now this little stretch of the Grand Union Canal is scrubby and urban and the graffiti is the work of local kids rather than something commissioned by developers. I keep going past the skate park until I find a quiet bank, where I sit on an upturned shopping trolley and call Dom.

'Have you been in yet?' I ask as soon as he picks up. Rose says that we were the only people she knows who do away with the hello and goodbye parts of phone calls, just as they do on films.

'I'm going this afternoon,' he says.

'What's the latest?'

'Velasco's made a statement saying he hasn't been approach about the jewel but that he's having a kind of amnesty, saying t' anyone with information will be rewarded.'

'It does feel like every day no one tries to get it to Velasco it gets a bit less likely, do you know what I mean?'

'It's like when an actual person goes missing,' he agrees. 'They call it the golden hour, although I think it's actually twenty-four hours or maybe even forty-eight. If they haven't been found safe in that crucial time period, the odds just plummet.'

He yawns into the mouthpiece, an over-the-top, big-cat sound that has my own mouth twitching. 'You enjoy yawning too much,' I say, trying to clamp my jaw shut.

'I *what*?'

'It's indulgent. Performative. You're manspreading *with your breath*.'

Truly, there is no greater comfort than winding my brother up. If I can still bait him, I must be keeping it together, right?

'Glad to see you've got your priorities straight,' he says, but he's laughing. 'Listen, whatever happens later – call me when you're done? I want to know exactly what they're up to. *Everything* they ask you. Anything they let slip. Anything that might help us make sense of it.'

'*None* of it makes sense,' I say. A heron swoops to perch on a mooring post. I dig in my pockets for some bird food to throw but find only sweet wrappers.

'I suppose if it did, there wouldn't be an investigation,' he says. 'I can't help thinking someone's setting us a puzzle to solve. It's someone's grand revenge on Frank. He set an impossible puzzle; they're trying to show him how it feels after all these years.'

We end the call without saying goodbye. Just as they do in films.

42

There's not enough diesel in the tank to get me the half-mile to Little Venice, let alone east London. I text the Coal Man, who loops the waterways with all kinds of fuel from diesel to firewood, to ask when he's next on this stretch; he'll be here tomorrow. That will have to do.

Billie emerges from the bedroom in a Rolling Stones T-shirt and, 'Are those my pyjama shorts?' I ask.

'Not any more,' she grins.

'*Bruh*,' I say.

'Oh, my God, Nell, no.' She bends to the fridge and pulls out a carton of Tropicana. 'Please never do that again.'

'Why would you deny me the pleasure of watching you cringe?' I nod at the juice in her glass and she pours one for me without my needing to ask. 'Thanks. Moving day tomorrow,' I warn her.

She sets down her glass and regards me from under hooded eyes.

'I'm sorry, Bill. I hoped we could last here till term starts again.'

'So why *are* we moving?'

I've thought about this; the last thing I want is for her to feel unsafe with me.

'They're clamping down. We've overstayed by weeks.' It's a condition of my continuous cruising licence that we move o every ten days or so. The Canals and Waterways Trust send inspe tors round to check no one's living on a permanent (expens basis on a (relatively affordable) cruising licence. They're toothless, but Billie hasn't worked that out yet.

'Where to?'

'East. It's the only stretch we haven't moored for a while.'

'Bruh.'

'I know, honey.' London moorings are like London parking spots. If you're unlucky you can get all the way to Haggerston, which is halfway to Essex, before there's a gap. Not only is that a long way from the cattery, it's also a *lot* of locks. My biceps and thighs twitch in anticipation of a hard day's push and pull and my heart sinks at the thought of doing Camden Lock, overseen by tourists, any one of whom might recognise me and take a picture of me on board *Seren*. It's bad enough that my image has gone viral, but for my home – my highly distinctive home, which is pretty much always moored on a public towpath – to be in the public domain would break me.

On top of the boat, I check that our bike racks are secure and give the solar panels and the vegetable beds a good tug to make sure nothing's come loose since we've been moored here. I'm hitching a stray cable to the guard rail when one of the other boaters, Ian, walks past, newspaper under his arm. Ian is the kind of man who says 'I speak as I find'. I lie flat behind a window box of lavender so he can't see me, but Loz has no such lucky escape.

'Alright?' says Ian.

'Hail, fellow, well met,' says Loz.

'If you like,' says Ian. 'Here, have a look at this.' I hear the rustle of newspaper. 'Is this your neighbour?' I raise my head as far above the lavender stems as I dare.

I'm on the front page of the fucking *Daily Express*. Loz makes a show of studying the picture, then glances at the boat. I duck again, but not before our eyes have made contact.

'That's not her.'

'Fair enough,' says Ian. 'They all look the same, don't they, ᴐse middle-aged women in their dungarees? I'm off to read all ⸗ut it. Have a good day, mate.'

⸗ well,' says Loz.

⸗n Ian is out of sight, I get on to all fours. 'Thank you,' I say

'Some people have no concept of privacy,' he says, then disappears into his hatch before I can tell him that his kindness has set me up for the rest of the day.

Hampstead police station, the one that dealt with me as a criminal and as a victim, shut down ages ago. Its shell is now in a tug-of-love between the developers and the local community. Kentish Town nick now serves a huge swath of North London that includes the Vale. I mask up underneath my helmet and ride the towpath in blissful anonymity. Tourists dawdle three abreast, making me cycle so slowly I'm in danger of losing my balance. On a bend under the Warwick Avenue bridge, a teenage boy stands in the dead centre of the path, not moving no matter how much I ring my bell. 'Oy!' I shout, one tiptoe to the ground, and he looks up.

'Sorry,' he says. I push off, wondering what was so absorbing. A second later, I hear the unmistakable struck-bone tone of *The Golden Bones* app.

At Camden I take to the roads. There's no escaping Elinore here, either. The bookshop on Kentish Town Road has given her a window display. Someone – a good enough artist to capture the spirit of Frank's original paintings – has painted her likeness inside a gilt frame made of hundreds of golden skeletons, and a stack of books gleams from a table inside a door.

It doesn't stop there. Outside a newsagent, the shopkeeper is replenishing the stack of newspapers in their plastic display cases. It's the silly season: the politicians are on holiday and the reporters seem to relish the novelty of a non-Covid story. The headlines say TREASURE HUNT TWIST, SHE'S BACK (with a picture of Elinore), MYSTERY REPEATING ITSELF (I inwardly salute the sub-editor who came up with that one), FIND THE LADY. And all of them carry stills of me, dumbfounded, with the bone in my hands.

For all that, I don't mind this. Well, not too much. The headlines are tamer and less offensive, than, say, STALKER NUT. The something quaintly reassuring about newspapers, where e are fixed. They are facts, not fears. Pain in the arse thoug can be, reporters are bound by truth to a degree that the keyboard warriors are not.

I dismount near the station. I hear that ping again from a kid on a street corner. And, instead of feeling happy for Dom that it's clearly taken off, I share his dismay. We'll never know if it's morbid curiosity or his skill and hard work behind its success.

I double-lock my bike to the rack. Someone has dropped an empty box of fried chicken on the pavement and a fox has distributed the contents as far as the kerb. Tiny bones, scattered skeletons that people crush underfoot without even noticing.

43

A uniformed officer guides me to an interview room where DS Bindra is waiting for me. I vow to stay focused. My job is to point the police towards the known troublemakers and make them chase the jewel, because that's what we need to get me out of trouble.

The first thing I notice is that cigarette smoke, the overwhelming smell of a police station in the 1990s, has been replaced by something that may be microwaved food or body odour. In the room, the equipment is more sophisticated, than last time I was in such a place including the black bubble of a camera on the ceiling.

I decide to lead the elephant into the room with me. 'I take it you know about my record.'

Bindra's slow blink tells me that she does. 'Do you think it's relevant?'

I squirm in my chair. 'What was done to me, yes. I've never lashed out like that again, so no, that's not relevant. Have you got the jewel yet?'

She smiles thinly. 'Let's get going, shall we, and we can chat after the statement.'

I take her through the events of the day as exactly as I remember them, leaving out a couple of details. I refer to Billie as my boyfriend's daughter in a way that makes it sound as though Dylan and I are still an item. I don't want to tell Bindra that someone else's kid lives with me. I feel like she'd be on the phone Eyebrows. So far the lack of joined-up working between S Services and other agencies has worked in our favour, but F strikes me as the type to dot all her Is and cross all her Ts a check everyone else's grammar as well.

I talk until the air in the room is arid. There's a plastic jug of water on the table. I could quite happily tip it over my head, but I force myself to pour some into a cup and take measured sips.

'So *have* you got the jewel?' I ask.

'That's not our focus right now.'

I almost spit my drink out. 'Why not?'

'The *removal* of the jewel is clearly linked to the depositing of human remains, but we're not pursuing it as a crime in its own right.'

'It's the *main* crime! The bone's a stunt. For goodness . . .' I count to five in my head. 'Did you find out who was behind Yorick and LetterstoIngrid? And BON35? They're never offline, they might know something? Are you looking on all the socials? There's loads of dark stuff on Reddit – are you looking there? Did you find out if Stuart Cummins and Ingrid were in touch? Everyone knows the NHS is at breaking point; I bet it's easier to sneak a phone in to her or whatever than it's *ever* been. This could have major safety implications for me.'

When I finish, I find that I am panting.

'We took your assertions very seriously,' says Bindra. 'Ingrid Morrison's hospital was badly affected by the very first wave of the coronavirus and she's a textbook long Covid case. She's been absolutely floored by it. Still doesn't leave her bed for weeks on end. Between you and me, her psychiatrist used the word "zombie" on the phone.'

'Well, someone knows something,' I persist. 'You need to interview Stuart Cummins. Shane the security guard. Barney Badger. The Glemhams. Go through their emails, see if they were talking to each other beforehand. And have a look at their bank accounts, ⸻e if anyone's got a mysterious payment in Philippine pesos.'

⸻he smiles again. 'They're far more likely to have been paid in ⸻o-currency,' she says. 'I promise you, Miss Churcher, we are ⸻g at all the intelligence. But this is not a theft inquiry. ⸻ remains is proper no-stone-unturned territory. I'm sure ⸻ciate the sensitivity of it.'

She pauses to smooth down an immaculate eyebrow. I refill my cup from the jug.

'We're talking to someone who has excellent connections with the market, whom I believe you also know?'

She means Richard, and she's looking at me for a response. The blush starts at my neck and rises.

'Yup,' is all I'm willing to give her.

'You were in a relationship?'

My whole face is burning. 'For just over a year.'

'And it ended because . . .'

Even my *eyeballs* feel hot. 'You *know* why.' She's going to make me say it. 'It ended because I found out that he was a private investigator working for Fritz Velasco.'

My skin goes *vwump vwump vwump.*

'Good to have it confirmed.' She runs her pen up and down the notebook she's holding at an angle. You bitch, I think. You enjoyed that. I take a long glug of water. A rogue droplet hits my cheek. I swear I hear it sizzle.

'Have you talked to Velasco? He's just as obsessed as Ingrid was, in his own way. He's not mad, but he doesn't mind exploiting the Bonehunters who are.'

'We're following several lines of inquiry,' she says. 'Now. We've covered a lot of your father's professional life, but what about his personal life? Is there anyone else who might have had a grudge against him?'

'If you've done your due diligence on Frank Churcher you'll know about the women. But that was all decades ago. They – and their husbands, come to think of it – they'll all be in their seventies by now; they'll hardly be shinning up trees. Honestly, it's got to be a Bonehunter.'

'He never had relationship with anyone in that community?'

At her suggestion, something inside me screeches to a halt wouldn't have. Would he?

'No. He hated the Bonehunters, no matter how pret were,' I say. 'And, to be honest, usually they weren't. You was mainly sort of sturdy retirees.' I think, then correct myself. 'Maybe it's better to say that I really don't think he would have *knowingly* gone to bed with one of them. But, as we've established, interested parties went to a lot of effort to infiltrate our family.'

'Hmm.' She looks down at her notes. 'Between Ingrid Morrison, Stuart Cummins, Jane Jones and Richard Reid, you've personally been impacted by your father's career and by *The Golden Bones* more negatively than the rest of your family.'

She's looking at me as though there's a right answer and she doesn't expect me to provide it.

'There was some stuff I could have done without, but it is what it is.'

'You have good reason to resent the book. And its author.'

It takes me a beat or two to realise what she's saying.

'You think *I* did it?' I cough up a laugh. 'I am the last person who'd want to call attention to *The Golden Bones*, even if I'd had a clue where the jewel was. I live virtually in hiding. You think I want a video of me on the internet that gets me involved all over again? It's no secret that I think my father can be a dickhead but my brother's actually a good bloke, especially considering who his parents are. I wouldn't sabotage *his* work.'

My voice has been rising in pitch. Bindra pulls a satisfied face that makes me feel as if I've given something away. I start panicking, the way you do when you walk through customs *knowing* you haven't got a kilo of coke in your hand luggage but what if you have? I find myself thinking, what would an innocent person say here? even though I *am* innocent. The best thing you can say about this new blush is that it disappears into the old one, which hadn't had a chance to subside.

'Thanks so much, Ms Churcher,' she says. 'You're free to go.'

She studies me for my reaction. I'm beyond even attempting to control my face.

As she leads me back into the reception area, I ask her about
'Have you had it dated yet?'

She swipes her card and a door clicks open. 'There's a backlog at the lab.' Her eyes slide away from mine. She's holding something back from me. 'We're working round the clock to find out who put her there.'

'Her?' Abruptly the blood drains away, leaving me light-headed.

'It was a young woman's pelvis.'

I picture her skeleton re-forming, building itself up bone by bone. I imagine flesh covering it, just as Elinore's body is restored in the book. And of course it is Cora's face the dead girl wears, or is it Aoife's? Is it Billie's? Is it mine?

I wheel the bike a couple of blocks down to Kelly Street, where my favourite greasy spoon in London faces a row of pastel houses. From the pavement table I order a bacon sandwich with brown sauce and a full-sugar Coke. I'm scrolling ElinoresArmy when a text from Billie fills my screen.

Found something juicy deep in a subred. It's five years old but still

I open the attachment. It's a series of screengrabs of a long, long Reddit thread going back a full decade.

u/439t8gbh: I don't believe the jewel is in a vault. I think Churcher just said that to get rid of all the latecomers that ruined the community. He knew only the die-hard Bonehunters cared enough about Elinore to keep searching

u/Yorick: Typical of the man and his mind games

u/439t8gbh: If I had the solve, you know what I'd do? I'd take the jewel and swap it for a real human bone, then get FC to unveil it. Can you imagine! That'd wipe the smile off his face

u/Yorick: You might just be a genius

My heart flutters to my chest. This is premeditation. Th' evidence that Yorick knew about this. Find Yorick, and you whoever's behind the stunt.

I text Billie back immediately.
YOU might just be a genius more like
She fires back the painting-my-nails emoji.

I email the photograph to DS Bindra, and then send it to Dom, who lets me know that Aoife's having a bad day and he'll get back to me when he can, which could mean tomorrow if she's really distressed. I'm fizzing with the need to discuss this development, to turn things over with another person. Not with Billie: I need to speak freely, talk about every threat, including the ones that might endanger her. She's mature and bright and interested, but she's still a kid. I need someone who wants it found as much as I do, someone already familiar with the hunt, someone I don't have to explain it all to from scratch.

Outside my family, there is only one person who fits that description.

44

I haven't been back to Whetstone High Road in twenty years.
The little boutiques that used to line it have mostly been
replaced by restaurants and nail bars. The chain coffee shop
under Richard's office is new but the second-floor window
hasn't changed, the gold letters N20 ASSOCIATES still shiny on
immaculate glass.

I secure my bike next to one of the huge plane trees that line the
street then put my finger on the buzzer and keep it there.

'OK, OK!' he says, and then, when I let the buzzer go, 'Do you
have an appointment?'

'It's Nell Churcher.'

He leaves me in a fuzzy wall of sound for a few seconds before
answering. 'You'd better come up.'

I take the stairs, feeling the static build on the thin office carpet,
and shoulder the door. At first I wonder if I've got the right floor.
The little ante-room, which used to be floor-to-ceiling paperwork,
is now sleek and minimalist, a black leather sofa and – is he taking
the piss? – a Frank Churcher print the only flourishes. Richard
always did love his tech; he was an early adopter of every gadget
you could think of. Judging by the lip gloss, the desk with its
blinking MacBook is shared with a PA or maybe another investigator. Partner or gatekeeper, she's not there now, so I open the
door into his main office to find him sitting on the edge of h
desk, shirtsleeves, arms folded. He's in his late fifties now;
shoulders and belly are rounder than I remember and his be
more salt than pepper.

'Nell.' His voice takes me back through the years to
when neither of us had lines on our faces. A time of

where we didn't come up for air. 'Can I get you anything? We can go downstairs for a coffee or . . . it'll be lunchtime soon. There's a new mezze bar—'

I snap back to my senses. 'I'll get straight to the point. I've just come from the police station. They don't seem to give a shit about the jewel and until it's located I'm looking over my shoulder. You need to tell me what you know.'

'Nice to see you again too,' he says.

'If Velasco has it, he *has* to go public.'

He scoffs. 'Take it from me, Mr Velasco has not got that jewel. Listen to this.' He presses a button on the phone.

'Richard, it's Fritz Velasco.' The voice is rich, patrician; almost English but for a trace of east Asia in the Rs. 'I can't help but feel desperately disappointed in your progress. I'm wondering if some kind of public statement, an increased reward, is key. We'll talk strategy first thing.' There's a pause. 'I spent the evening with Frederic Leighton and was struck again by the similarities between his work and Churcher's. Sometimes my art provides solace, but sometimes it opens up that part of me that so desperately wants . . .' Another pause, evidently while he gathers himself. 'I have never felt the lack of this jewel so keenly as I do tonight.'

There's a click as the message ends.

'The fuck?' is all I can manage.

'Yup. Man loves a good old-fashioned voicemail,' says Richard.

'*That's* what Fritz Velasco sounds like?'

'What did you expect? Some yapping Bond villain? He was educated here.'

'It's not so much his accent as . . .' I fumble for the right word. 'He sounds so *sincere*.'

Richard looks surprised. 'He's always been *sincere*. He genu- loves your dad's work. Did you think he was cynical? Because tell you, if you were investing in art to make money, *The Bones* is not the way to do it.'

Frederic – Frederic . . .'

'Leighton?' asks Richard. 'A Pre-Raphaelite painter. *Flaming June?*' I shake my head. 'Victorian girl curled up for a nap in a sort of billowing orange dress?'

Instantly I know it: it's fridge-magnet famous. 'He owns *that*?'

'He wishes,' smiles Richard. 'But that's the painter in question. Mr Velasco has the largest collection of his work outside the UK.'

'Huh. I thought he was just a spoilt rich boy stamping his feet because he couldn't get what he wanted. Or that he was obsessed with the hunt, like Ingrid or Stuart.'

'Not at all.' Richard pauses. 'Although he's not above exploiting those people.'

'Meaning *you're* not above exploiting them?'

We hold eye contact for a few searing seconds.

'Anyway, never mind Mr Velasco,' says Richard. 'Shouldn't I be asking what you can do for me? Aren't you the one with the inside track?'

'You owe me!' I erupt. 'This thing ruined my life; it's been nothing but a cash cow for you.'

Richard laughs bitterly. 'I fucking wish!' He points to a filing cabinet, as tall as I am, labelled TGB. 'There's forty years of my life in there. A paper tower of dead ends. I'm nearly sixty and I spent last Sunday lip-reading someone's cheating wife through a Wetherspoon's window when I could've been playing golf. If I found that jewel I could retire. I'd be able to give my kids a head start in life.' He nods to a framed photo on his desk: a palm beach, a leggy brunette wife and two clones at the upper end of the teenage years. Even if this photo is recent, he can't have left it long between our relationship ending and theirs beginning. It ties a little knot in my heart. 'They're *never* going to leave home. One of them wants to open a toy shop and th other one wants to be a *newspaper* journalist, for fuck's sa Talk about dying industries. Why not just be a lute-maker thatched-roofer?'

'Or a stained-glass artist?' I offer. 'Not everyone wants corporate.'

He's about to fire something back but then changes his mind. He rubs his hands slowly across his eyes, as if it's midnight rather than noon. When he's finished he looks even more exhausted. Everyone involved with this hunt is so fucking tired.

'What do you want, Nell?'

'I want you to find out who's behind these avatars. Yorick and LetterstoIngrid.' I write their names on his notepad.

'Yup. They're on my radar too.'

'My brother reckons they're all hiding behind VPNs.' I drop the acronym casually now.

'Well, yeah. Who'd have a public IP address in this day and age? You're just asking to be hacked. But these two do seem particularly impenetrable.'

'And BON35 turns up a lot.'

'Oh, that's Miriam,' says Richard airily. 'She's one of mine. Very active, isn't she?'

I arch an eyebrow.

'I've got a handful of Bonehunters on the payroll, as it were.'

'Of course you have.'

'Miriam's a voice of reason. And the police have already cleared her.'

I'm impressed. Bindra was telling the truth. They are turning every stone they find.

'OK, what about this person? 439t8gbh. It's an old, old Reddit that my – that *I* stumbled across. They suggested planting the pelvis years ago and Yorick said it was a good idea.'

I show him the subred Billie found. It's clearly news to Richard.

'Interesting,' he says. 'I'll do some digging.'

'Do you think Lisa-Marie and Porter Glemham would be able to give your their emails or whatever it is you need?'

Richard swivels from side to side in his office chair. 'I'm not their urite person,' he says. 'They don't think my heart is pure.'

an't think why.'

aps a pen against the edge of his desk. 'How'd you know e different people? Could be one troll with loads of personas. Sometimes there's seven people in the chatroom and six of them are me. I'll set an alert for all three of these handles. Might do a bit of catfishing, see if I can catch any of them out. I'll ask my contacts in the community for help.'

'Right. Well, we should probably swap numbers.'

'No need,' he says, opening his phone and dictating my number to me.

'Richard, what the fuck?'

'I've always kept an eye on you,' he says. 'Not in a creepy way. I just wanted to know where you were in case something like this ever happened and you needed my help.'

'What else do you know about me? Do you know where I live?'

'I know where you're *registered* as living,' he says. 'I also know you don't actually live there, unless you've changed your name to Boyana Dmitrov, which is an interesting way to go dark.'

'So you've tried to *doorstep* me?' I can't picture him on the Nightingale, in his shiny watch and flashy suit.

'I've been worried, alright?'

His concern is the opposite of reassuring. All this time I've wanted someone to take me seriously and now it's happening I miss Cora's head-in-the-clouds denial.

'I might as well confess,' he says, 'I do know about the houseboat, but only because of the post on ElinoresArmy.'

I go cold. If he saw it, who else did?

'Here's my number if you need me. For anything.' He calls my number. As the phone rings, he locks eyes with me, the same way he did that first day. I have to drop my eyes. Richard ends the call, but not before I notice that he's saved my number as Steve.

'*Steve*?'

He looks shamefaced. 'Mrs Reid wouldn't take too kindly to seeing your name in my contacts.'

'Tell her she can sleep easy.' I save his number. His avatar is the same as the photo on his desk: wife and daughters.

I'm half out of his office when he says, 'You know, Nell, would've wanted you anyway. I was never pretending. It broke m heart to lose you. What I did to you is the biggest regret of my life.'

'What, more than not finding that last jewel? If you had to choose between being with me and finding the jewel, you'd choose me?'

He stares intently at his wedding ring.

'Dickhead.' I slam the door on the way out.

45

Billie's at the cattery when I get back to the boat. I text the Coal Man, who tells me he's having supply issues but he hopes he'll be here end of play, soonest.

'*Hopes*,' I mutter to myself. 'Brilliant.'

I can feel myself starting to spiral. I could go for a run or I could do a mindfulness app or I could work. There's really no contest. I dig out the pitch for the window that Marcelle slyly put me forward for, and sketch a few ideas, just as an exercise. It's absorbing – I almost treat it like a proper job – but pen on paper isn't giving me enough friction. I need the resistance of glass, its sharp edges. I need to play with knives and fire. At the same time it needs to be mindless enough that I can let my thoughts wander, which means working to an existing pattern. It might be August, but it's never too early to start on the Christmas stock.

I score, snap and grind the glass for my silver starburst, always a sellout – alternating spikes of clear and nacreous glass, silver finish on the solder. As the pieces pile up, my mind falls still. I move on to Santa hats. Not the most original of designs, but they're steady sellers.

The slowing *tick tick tick* of bicycle wheels heralds Billie's arrival. *Seren* lurches as she heaves her bike on to the roof rack.

'Incoming!' She enters arse first – there's no elegant way of boarding a narrowboat – then turns around to reveal a band of reddened skin around her forehead from her cycling helmet. When she's on board with the hatch fastened, I feel a huge relief, as though someone's pulled a pin out of me.

'How'd it go with the po-po?' She fires finger guns into the 'Have they found it? Do they know who it was?'

I take off my safety goggles as though eye contact makes my lie more convincing. 'I'm not worried.'

She takes a few seconds to decide to believe me – for my benefit or hers, I'm not sure.

'Here.' She opens Dom's app. That unnerving ping reverberates throughout the boat. 'I reckon I've got a solve. I think there's a cache at the obelisk at Trent Park in Cockfosters. It's on the top end of the Piccadilly Line. We could go there and see if I'm right?'

'What was the clue?'

'Oh, it's easy.' She explains it to me: something to do with a triangulation point between three rivers, Earl Grey tea and the length of a shadow cast at a certain GPS location on Christmas Day. She's talking slowly and repeating herself but after a while I just hear the high-pitched *eeeeee* that used to sound ten minutes into every maths lesson.

'You're looking at me like I'm Einstein.'

'You might as well be.' I know some parents are jealous of their children, but one of the unpredicted joys of having Billie is the pure *delight* in watching a kid you're raising soar to heights you could never dream of. '*How* did you work it out?'

She shrugs. 'My nan did the *Times* crossword every day.'

A flicker of surprise – her nan was a school cleaner – crosses my face before I can stop it, and I kick myself. I'm no better than Cora and Bridget.

'Yeah, don't worry, no one else could believe it either. She definitely didn't sound like someone who read *The Times*. She used to do it the day after. One of the teachers saved it for her. What are you looking at me like that for?'

'Nothing. It's just nice to hear you talk about her.'

The shutters come down over her face. I've poked a sore spot. For someone who remembers pretty much everything about her own mid-teens, I often forget the basics.

'Anyway,' she says, fake-breezy, 'it's not about knowledge, really, more about shifting the way you see things. Once you learn, easy.'

'I think I'll just take your word for that,' I say.

She watches me for a few beats, as if to check I'm not going to probe any deeper, then shuffles on to the bench beside me. 'Whatcha making?'

'Thought I'd get in early for Christmas.'

She holds a triangle of red glass up to the light. The false nails have gone, I notice with relief. I never liked to think about the cat food and litter tray gunk accumulating under those acrylics.

'Want to help out?' I ask.

'Really?' She looks doubtful. During lockdown I didn't let her near my work, but the anxiety I had then about letting her loose with a blade has gone. Even though Dylan was AWOL, I was hesitant in case he blamed me for any accidents. It's not that I've observed any great leap in Billie's dexterity or responsibility; it's more that I've grown in confidence as a parent. These calls feel like mine to make.

'Yeah, why not? You're nearly as old as I was when Cora taught me. This is German glass, best you can get.'

I give her the good goggles and wear the scratched-up, second-best pair. She's a fast learner. I imagine that steady hand performing surgery on sick animals, a decade from now. I think I get why Rose used to bake with her kids when they were little, even though the kitchen was trashed and the cakes were lopsided. It's not about them being good to start with, it's not even about them being good at the end; it's about watching them absorbed, developing a skill, being human. If there's one thing that breaks my heart about looking after Billie – apart from her background of course, and the obvious uncertainty about how long I get to keep her – it's that there's no one to share these moments with. It's not the tough stuff I mind doing alone; it's the moments of happiness that cut to the quick of my loneliness.

'You're good at this,' I say. 'I'll cut you in. A pound for every piece we finish, and then when we do the markets you can have another quid for each piece you hand-sell.'

She smiles and I know it's not just because I've included her, because I've affirmed I still want her here at Christmas. No m

how many times I tell her I'm not going anywhere, she's heard
that before and she can't quite trust it. What does it do to a child
when everyone she loves leaves her? For all Frank and Cora's
faults, they were present. There was always someone at home,
and, if there wasn't, we could always go next door.

A rumble of diesel at the side of the boat and a shout of 'Oy
oy!' tells me the Coal Man is here. Bald-headed and tattooed and
about six stone soaking wet, he's one of the few people who *make*
a living on the water rather than just living on it. He prides himself
on not reading the news or having a smartphone, so at least he
won't recognise me.

'Alright, princess, looking lovely as ever, sorry about the wait,'
he says as I pass him the key to the fuel tank. 'I was on a date with
Kim Kardashian and she can't get enough of my body. Up all
night, I was.'

'Where'd you take her? Anywhere nice?'

He shows me his bed: a lumpen feather mattresses on the floor.
'Classy,' I say.

'What?' He grins. 'I let her have the dry side.'

I can't help laughing. The Coal Man considers his work as much
pastoral as practical. He once told me he considers any interaction
where the customer doesn't crack a smile a personal failure.

He finishes filling the boat. 'Where you heading next, then,
princess?'

I point east.

'It's quiet up White Post Lane,' he suggests. I grimace. White
Post Lane, in the wilds of Hackney, can get a bit anarchic. If there
are free moorings it's probably for a reason.

By the time he's done, the sky to the west is starting to bruise.
I don't fancy trying to outrun the sunset or doing the locks or
mooring in the dark.

Billie pokes her head through the hatch. 'Are we going or what?'

'First thing tomorrow,' I tell her.

She salutes. 'Aye, aye, captain.'

46

When you moor in a city, the nights are noisy. Sirens chime the hour; lovers and drunks sing and shout on the towpath. Geese are bastards who think nothing of a three a.m. group honking session. Sometimes whole flocks of them seem to honk their way through the small hours. You get used to these sounds; you tune them out in your sleep. You have to, or you'd go mad.

Then there are other sounds, sounds you wouldn't even register during the day, which at night wake you up as though someone's crashed a pair of cymbals over your head.

My body is alert, sitting up and dressing before my eyes pull focus. I don't know what I heard, only that it meant danger. When the numbers on the digital alarm clock finally sharpen, I learn that it's 2.32 a.m. I yank on some socks, heart jackhammering away, ears pricked. I can hear only white noise: the rumble of the Westway in the distance, the lapping of water on the hull. Then I hear it again. It's a scraping, and a click-click-click that means someone's trying to force the padlock. There is a voice, possibly two, grunting with effort. I can't tell if they are male or female, young or old, British or foreign. I only know that they're trying to get in.

I dim the screen on my phone so its light doesn't shine through the windows, grab the poker from the fireside then creep to the back of the boat where Billie sleeps.

'Bill.' I touch her bare shoulder. Her eyes glitter in the dark for a second before closing.

'No,' she says, and burrows further into her duvet.

'Billie,' I say. 'Wake up, love. I think someone's trying to bre in.'

She's on full, trembling alert. 'What do we do?'

'I'm going to raise the alarm and then we should prepare to get out the back way if need be.'

She glances at the back window. It opens straight on to the water, which glugs like thick black oil. To jump on to the towpath you'd have to do it in a sort of L-shape. A knight's move, if you will.

'Hopefully it won't come to that.'

I call 999 and squeak my emergency – someone is breaking into my home – and my location using GPS co-ordinates. I take Billie's hand and the two of us stare down the length of the boat, waiting to see if the hatch is breached. When a man directly outside her window booms, 'Oi! What the hell d'you think you're doing?' we both jump and scream like girls in a horror film.

'It's Loz,' I realise.

'Go on, piss off!' he says. There's a scuffle on the roof and a metallic clang, then the sound of footsteps heading towards the flyover. I fling open the back window, using the torch on my phone. It's not so much a spotlight as a floodlight that shines on Loz. He's wearing a tartan dressing gown and fluffy slippers, the kind with no heels that are designed for shuffling around indoors.

'Have you called the police?' he asks, and, when I nod, he gestures to his attire and says, 'I'd have gone after them but I'm not exactly dressed to give chase.'

I recognise someone who's nipped out for a late-night wee when I see one. We've all disappeared into the scrub at the side of the towpath when the warning light on the toilet's flashing red and it's a long time till morning.

'Did you see who it was?' I ask. 'Male, female? Old, young?'

'There were two of them, but apart from that . . . I didn't bother with my glasses. I wasn't anticipating any nocturnal crime-fighting.'

'So you don't know if either of them had on a grey hoodie?'

'I couldn't say. Sorry.'

It was a dumb question anyway. As if there's a uniform this person puts on when they're after me.

'I did see them drop something, though,' says Loz. 'Can you . . .' He indicates that I should shine my torch on the towpath. It picks out the long scalene blade of a knife.

Billie goes back to bed but Loz sits up with me until the police arrive. Neither of us touch the knife – my fingerprints have been on enough evidence to last me a lifetime – but we guard it as though it's something that might sprout legs and run off before the police can bag it up. We make small talk about life on the waterways. I can feel him almost vibrating with the effort of not quizzing me about *The Golden Bones* and I am so grateful for it, although I know I will have to break my silence when the officers arrive.

There are two of them and they both look about Billie's age.

'We've had a lot of solar panels being nicked off boats lately,' says the more foetal of the two. 'There's been a spate. It'll be that.'

'No.' Their youth emboldens me. 'I want you to notify DS Mehreen Bindra at Kentish Town police station,' I tell them. 'Let her know this is related to the human remains found on Hampstead Heath last week.'

'We'll do that first thing,' they promise.

I look to the east, expecting 'first thing' to be creeping over the horizon any minute now, but the sky is dark grey as far as the eye can see.

'Why don't you go down and get some rest,' says Loz. 'I'll stand guard.'

I'm about to protest but as he holds the poker aloft like a spear I can see that he's in his element. As I settle back on to my sofabed, Billie calls my name from the bedroom.

'I don't wanna be on my own,' she says.

I slip under the covers and drape an arm lightly over her shoulder. Before I met her, I never knew that you could take comfort from the act of giving it.

I wake up again at around eight to find that Loz is still on duty. In the morning sun he looks endearingly ridiculous, his huge burly frame perched on my little patio chair.

'You must be exhausted,' I say. 'Let me get you a coffee.'

When he stands up, his bones click. 'Methinks I should retire to my own quarters,' he says, then snaps out of his Viking overlord persona. 'Actually – I have a suggestion for you. I hope you don't think I'm interfering, and obviously you're not obliged to take me up on it, but me and a mate are going up the Worcester Canal for a few weeks. He's got a permanent mooring in Horsfall Basin. I told him your situation. He says it's yours for the next month. If you want somewhere a bit more secure to get your head down for a bit. I hope you don't mind me asking on your behalf?'

I wonder if I'm hallucinating. Horsfall Basin, a watery cul-de-sac near King's Cross, is the holy grail of London moorings. They're permanent – no one to move you along – and there's mains electricity, a shower block. A *gate*.

'Are you for real?'

'Yeah. No one deserves this shit.'

I consult my inner judge of character. Distrust is my default setting. But Loz didn't have to do that. He's known for two days who I am and he hasn't mentioned it to anyone, even me. If he had an ulterior motive he's had a dozen chances to take advantage. And if he's a Bonehunter playing a long game, disappearing up the Worcester Canal is a funny way of doing it.

'Thank you,' I say. 'That would be an absolute godsend.'

Ten minutes later, we're on the move.

'Fare thee well,' says Loz as we move off in a rattle of the engine and a cloud of diesel. I take the tiller: Billie is a figurehead on the stern. We enter Little Venice, with its puppet barge and tourist boats; the creamy terraces of Maida Vale slide past. A little kid on a bridge waves at us, laughing with delight when we wave back. We keep waving right up until we get to the Maida Hill tunnel. As its tight dark tube swallows us up I let my hand drop. A shrinking circle of light frames the stretch of canal we are leaving behind. It's too far to see clearly and I hope it's just my imagination that shows me a flash of two figures in royal blue T-shirts bending to examine every boat they pass.

47

Horsfall Basin, London N1
5 August 2021

Horsfall Basin is bordered on one side by private gardens, the surprisingly lush appendages to houses whose brick frontages come right up to the street. A wooden pontoon juts into the water and the boats are moored perpendicular to it. We're side by side with our neighbours rather than the nose-to-tail formation we're used to. Our windows are level on both sides but we gain privacy as well as lose it. *Seren* all but disappears, only her stern visible. We're overlooked by flats and offices that used to be wharves and warehouses. An amenities block has hot showers, laundry facilities and flushing toilets that I don't have to empty out. Within two days Billie and I have become irretrievably spoiled.

It is five days since the jewel was stolen. We have all given our statements to the police but heard nothing back. Elinore is back in the news, just as she was when the book was published, just as she was when Pete Winship died, just as she was when Ingrid tried to kill me. The columnists have claimed it now: what the ongoing fascination with Elinore says about our objectification of women, why Frank encapsulates straight white male privilege, why the perfect woman is one who doesn't speak or age . . . we are moving from column inches to column miles. The dirt on my father has been dug up like – well, like an old bone. The parents have been under press siege, with paparazzi outside their house. They have a security guard (not Shane) and the CCTV is back in action to keep an eye on the Bonehunters, many of whom have discovered *The Golden Bones* for the first time. They're all over the Heath with metal detectors, fighting over patches of ground and refusing, all over again, to believe that Elinore is not there for the finding. Even Dom's place was staked out, with such devastating effects on Aoife that after just a few hours they did a midnight flit down to Marcelle and Harriet's place in Southwold.

Naturally Oisin was let go from the production, but friends on the crew let him know that Crabwise Films have, as feared, decided to turn their arts documentary into something more sensational, with a working title *The Curse of the Golden Bones*. Apparently PD has said the word 'BAFTA' more than once.

Billie stands over me with the kitchen scissors.

'Just chop it off,' I say.

'What if I mess it up?'

'Then I'll pay someone to fix it. But I want it gone, *now*.'

There's a scrunching sound and the next thing I know my head feels weightless and there's a rope of plaited hair in various shades of brown, blonde and grey at my feet. The blonde and the grey are mine: the brown is from a box dye, shade 6.0 natural 'light' golden brown that came out a lot darker than we expected. I check my reflection over the sink. My eyebrows and lashes seem to have faded dramatically but the length gives the illusion of a jawline and I'll happily take that.

'You look like Lord Farquaad from *Shrek*,' she says.

'I don't care if I look like Shrek himself, as long as no one recognises me from that bloody video.'

I leave the boat and put the plait in the communal rubbish bin. When I come back, she's looking at her phone with even more intensity than usual.

'You playing Dom's game?' I ask.

'I'm on a Golden Bones Reddit.' She looks guilty, but not scared. If that daughter stuff has resurfaced, it doesn't look as i Billie's seen it. 'Here's a good one. Apparently Pete Winship nev actually died; he won the bone but then faked his own death to avoid publicity.'

'Pretty sure that rumour did the rounds at the time.'

'They reckon there was a funeral and a burial but there were just bricks in the coffin. Anyway, they want his family to have the jewel, or at least a cash equivalent but . . . apparently they don't want anything to do with it. Seems to have put a few noses out of joint. Like, they can't understand why you wouldn't want to be part of the community.'

'I don't know why anyone in their right mind *would*.'

Billie goes quiet. 'You know there are people on here who reckon your dad murdered Pete Winship? Not, like, with his hands. They reckon he misdirected him to Highgate, knowing he'd have an accident, and then he wouldn't have to keep promoting the book.'

'That doesn't even make sense. There was no *way* of predicting the guy would go gravedigging. What, they reckoned Frank went up in advance and made the tombstone all wobbly by himself?'

'Actually, yes.'

I find a nub of red lipstick under the sink and put it on. Instantly my new dark hair makes sense. A light comes on in the boat next door, *Prevail*, followed by the sizzle and smell of onions and garlic frying in butter. Someone starts to play the violin, a yearning classical piece that I recognise but can't name.

'Nice here, isn't it?' says Billie. 'There's a bus that goes straight to my school.' She says it casually, not longingly, but I feel a pang of sadness that I can't afford a permanent mooring like this, followed by guilt because of course all I need to do is approach the bank of Mum and Dad. Sticking doggedly to my principles when it comes to taking my parents' money has become a big part of who I am, but, in moments like this, doubts creep in. Am I being a good parent in living my values, or a bad one in not providing every comfort? The problem with growing up in a house where conventional morals were dismissed as bourgeois and suburban is that you have to make your own. I think I might err on the side of too rigid and self-righteous, but I'm only doing what feels right for me. Dom seems to get it right, but then he's got Rose to bounce off.

As if I've summoned him, my phone lights up with his name.

'They've arrested Barney Badger,' he says without preamble. Even before he tells me why, I just *know*.

48

The pontoon shakes gratifyingly as I stomp in time with the ring-ing tone.

'N20 Associates?' It's not him but his female colleague.

'Can you tell him Nell Churcher wants a word.'

She transfers the call swiftly: she knows who I am.

'Just wondering why it didn't occur to you to tell me you had a spy in the film crew?' Every other word is accompanied by a stomp. 'Bloody *hell*, Richard. He was in my parents' house. He was in my old bedroom!'

On a yellow boat called *Amerigo*, a net curtain twitches at a porthole. I leave the pontoon and pace on the path, where it's less satisfying but also less likely to alienate my neighbours. 'How do you know he wasn't a double agent? For all we know he's an actual Bonehunter! One of Ingrid's nutters!'

'I doubt that very much,' says Richard. 'He was pretty crap as a *single* agent. We paid him in crypto and the idiot put it straight in his bank account. No one his age gets 10k he can't account for. Talk about falling at the first hurdle.'

'I'm serious. How do you know he wasn't already connected with the hunt?'

'He already had the job when I scouted him. My PA looked through the production company's website. Mr Velasco authorised me to pay him a 10k retainer, and then more to come depending on what he could find out. Which, as it turned out, was fuck-all squared. Anyway, you can congratulate yourself on his arrest, Miss Marple. Apparently it was your insistence that made them take a closer look.'

I allow myself a brief glow of satisfaction before pressing on. 'Did you put him up to that trick with the CCTV?'

'What trick with the CCTV?'

I explain: Richard denies.

'God, could you at least have the balls to own up to it?'

'Why would I lie about that? The only reason I could possibly have for wanting to get rid of CCTV is if I *had* put someone up to nicking the jewel.'

'You're not above that.'

'D'you know what, if I'd known it was going to be hidden in that tree, I might have considered it. I'll consider anything at this stage. But if I *had*, it'd be on its way to Manila by now, and I'd be on the golf course.'

I cannot, in fact, fault this logic. My pacing has taken me to the edge of the wharf. In one of the ground-floor flats, a toddler watches *In the Night Garden* on a huge television. I envy the kid his simple life.

'Hang on, did you talk to him about me?'

'Well, I had to put you in context,' he admits. 'Tell him your history. But I didn't tell him about us, if that's what you were worried about. I wouldn't.'

'That's something, but what I meant was -- you wouldn't have told him I live on a boat?'

'No. Why are you asking me this?'

I tell him about the attempted break-in. The knife on the towpath and how it made me feel.

'Someone knew where to find me,' I say.

'I promise you, Nell, that wouldn't have come from me.'

I've slowed my pace without noticing; I'm all but dawdling now, letting my fingers trail along someone's garden fence. An email alert chimes over the line. 'Speak of the devil, he's just emailed me.' There's the scrape of stubble on the receiver as Richard wedges it under his chin, and the sound of fingers on a keyboard 'They've released him without charge. Don't get yourself worke up over this. The only person this kid is a danger to is himsel hear the shuffling of paper on his desk, and then he says, 'I tr the poster on that old Reddit about hiding the bone.'

Instantly I brighten. 'You found Yorick?'

'Alas, no.'

'Ha ha.'

'The other poster, though – went by 439t8gbh? That account was set up fifteen years ago, an old University of Seattle email address. I traced the poster: no further activity in the last decade. When I made contact he'd forgotten all about *The Golden Bones*. Very keen to discuss the Illuminati with me, though. He's never left the States. I think we can rule him out.'

Disappointment breaks my stride. 'So a dead end, then.'

'But a *known* dead end,' he says. 'Which is more than you had before.'

'I s'pose. Thanks.'

'I'll be in touch.'

'Not so fast,' I say, before he can hang up. 'There's something else you can do for me. Not to do with the *Bones*.'

'Oh, yeah?' There's a face he makes when his interest is piqued: he rounds his mouth and his eyebrows rise into two points. I can see him as clearly as if we were on opposite sides of a desk, or – this thought comes unbidden but inevitable – a bed.

'His name's Dylan Garnet.' I stoop to rescue a ladybird stuck on her back, legs flailing.

'An ex?'

'I always did have shit taste in men.'

'Touché.'

'He should be living on the Nightingale Estate – I'll text you the flat number and stuff.'

'No need,' says Richard. 'It's still *your* official address.'

'Oh – yeah,' I say, but I can't muster yesterday's indignation. 'Well – he's sublet this place and gone off God knows where. I don't want you to approach him or anything. Just find him. Let me know what he's up to, if he's clean, where he's living. Get a phone number for him if you can.'

'What's in it for me?'

'warm, fuzzy glow,' I say, then cut the call.

My phone buzzes before I can put it away.

'Shut up!' I yell at it. 'Leave me alone!'

The curtain in the neighbour's boat starts twitching again. I muzzle my rage with a smile, and retreat into *Seren*'s belly, pulling the hatch to and bolting the door from the inside, keeping my movements slow and controlled so I don't put Billie on high alert.

On the sofa, I automatically check the ElinoresArmy forum, but that's not where the notification came from. There's a private message on my Instagram account, @GlassyNell, one that I use to showcase my work. There isn't a single identifying detail on this page: it's just pictures of stained glass. No surname, no location. My heart leaps. No one ever gets in touch with me this way unless they want to commission a piece from me. A new design to lose myself in is exactly what I need right now.

Are you Nell Churcher? This is Lisa-Marie and Porter Clemham.

My heart sinks. Not a commission. Just more *Golden Bones* shit. Everyone says the Glemhams are the good guys; I'm not so sure. My finger hovers over the 'block' button.

We need to talk to you urgently. It's for your own good.

I look at their account. Their name is a string of numbers, their avatar a plain grey circle. I remember what Richard said about half the people online being imposters. It could be anyone, luring me to a meeting. It could be Stuart, or whoever he's talking to. I block the account, and wish someone would invent a block button for my darkest thoughts.

49

Next morning, I'm in the Horsfall laundry room, watching all our bedding whirl in the machine. I've been systematically washing everything we own, taking double advantage of the washer-dryer and an empty boat. Billie is staying with her schoolfriend Kenza for the evening and I'm relieved – not because I'm tiring of her company but because she needs to go and be fifteen for a couple of days. I worry that in my efforts not to exclude or patronise her I've taken her too far into my confidence. Life has made her an old soul: all the more reason for her to contour her face and do TikTok dances or smoke in a bus stop or whatever it is she does when she's not with me.

It is six days since gold was switched for bone. The book is still a bestseller and the streets are still pinging with digital Bonehunters. A couple of celebrity deaths have knocked Elinore off the front pages, but online momentum continues to build.

The big news in the forum is that a new cache has been found. It was in Trent Park in Cockfosters, by the obelisk. I hope that Billie can at least take pleasure in being right, and comfort in the knowledge that, as family, she could never have claimed the cache.

ack at the boat, I flip the mattresses to air them. In Billie's room ava lamp, fake ivy and a row of textbooks – I find a piece of r torn from a spiral-bound notebook. I don't mean to look at I absorb the lot in one take. I lean the mattress against the vall and take a closer look. Billie has sketched a map of

London, recognisable by a not-to-scale Thames and straight lines of canals jutting from the main curve of the river. Xs are marked at intervals. She must have narrowed down a handful of locations by solving clues. I love that she's doing it for the sake of it, knowing she can't be the one to crack it. Then my eye travels down to the bottom of the page, where her handwriting is neat but cramped.

Boat first OBVS but then – if they get to N for whatever reason
Fins pk nature reserv
Kenzas but only 4 a couple of nights
Heath nr Nell's mum LOL
Archs nr Lee Vally gd shltr
Ally Pally park – nr caff
Outside LDN? Where tho

I'm no Bonehunter but these do not sound like the kinds of places Dom would choose to hide a clue, virtual or real. The Lee Valley railway arches and Kenza's house aren't renowned well-springs of ancient folklore – but that's the point of *The Golden Bones*, isn't it? To connect us with the stories we unwittingly trample every day.

I wasn't snooping before, but I am now. I look between the slats and see if there are any more notes. Tucked in a gap in the bedframe is another sheet torn from the same pad.

Look for dad in case
Do NOT tell eyebrows
If Bhs get Nell just run

And further down:

Paddington Station £2

Paddington Station £2. Where have I heard those words before?

Manna N1 – free
Churches check online changes a lot but free
Salvation army free

The significance of *Paddington Station* £2 punches me in the face. Billie begged all day for two pounds and had to choose between food and a shower.

This is nothing to do with the hunt for Elinore. This is a list of emergency plans if something bad happens to me. Places she can sleep. Places she can shower. People she can call for help. Corners of the city where she would rather bed down on concrete than go back into a foster home.

I slip the paper back where I found it and hope she doesn't realise I've seen it.

I make the beds with lavender-scented sheets, then take a coffee on to the deck. I say hello to the married couple who live on *Prevail*, the bottle-green boat in the next mooring. Moira and Joyce are two white-haired, permatanned women in their sixties. Moira is the violinist, Joyce the cook. The smell of saffron and fresh fish fills the air.

'Love the hair,' says Joyce. 'You look like a silent movie star.'

'Thank you,' I say, still self-conscious, my hand going to the nape of my neck. 'I don't think I've ever moored next to such fragrant neighbours.'

'Hop aboard,' says Moira. 'You haven't lived until you've tried Joyce's kedgeree.'

I make the leap from my deck to theirs without falling in or spilling my coffee. 'Impressive,' says Joyce. 'Get your daughter up ere, there's plenty for everyone.'

For a second I think about confiding in them: say that I don't what I'm doing, my worry that I've overloaded Billie, that mpounding all the damage that every adult she's ever loved e to her. But the water in Horsfall Basin is glittering and ented steam is piping from golden rice and the sun is shining and their assumption that we're a real family is so comforting that I just go with it.

'She's staying with a schoolfriend,' I say. 'Maybe I can save some for her for later?'

Joyce has it in a Tupperware almost before I've finished speaking. 'What is she, sixteen?'

'Fifteen. Just going into GCSE year.'

'Tricky age. Who'd be the mother of a teenage girl? I don't think there's any other love that feels more like hatred, is there?'

My face must show the blankness I feel here.

'The way they save it up all day at school – every catty remark from another girl, every put-down from a teacher, don't even get me started on the boys – and they dump it all on you. While you're drinking wine in secret and crying about where your little girl's gone.'

'But that's our job, as mothers, isn't it?' says Moira. 'She needs somewhere safe to put all her pain, and you just have to suck it up. You don't stop loving her, but you do mourn that little girl.'

Tears spring as I realise that I do mourn Billie as a little girl. I would have loved to know her at the age Dara is now, or Niamh.

Joyce senses that she's hit a nerve, and puts her hand to the tiller of the conversation. 'And she doesn't mind living on a boat?'

'God, no. It's been the making of her,' I say, relieved: conversationally at least, water is solid ground. 'And she's a godsend when it comes to locks.'

Joyce spoons more food on to my plate. 'And how do you manage school?'

'Term-time can be tricky,' I admit. 'So far we've been lucky with moorings but I dread the day we end up in the middle of nowhere and she has a horrible commute.'

'Where does she go?' asks Moira.

I name it, an Ofsted-Excellent girls' comp on the Essex/London border that's given her a continuity as vital as her ⟨⟩tion. Moira and Joyce exchange a glance. Not like the ⟨⟩ this one's eager rather than guarded.

'Is it *not* a good school?' Not having come up 'through the system', not having any mum friends apart from Rose, who wouldn't dream of state-educating her children, it's hard to trust my judgement.

'No, the school's great, it's not that,' says Moira. 'It's just, we have a friend selling a mooring in that area.'

When they tell me what the fees would be, I nearly fall into the water – but with a long-term mooring I could hire a workshop and double what I earn. That window constructs itself in my mind's eye, pieces flying together, and in my vision the sun is streaming through the glass. I wouldn't be greedy or go around craving recognition. It would all be for Billie.

'I would love that. Thank you. Yes, please.'

I look across to the opposite side of the canal where a boater is tying a pink satin skirt to a mast. It dances in the wind. When I bring my attention back to Moira and Joyce, they are no longer looking at me but over their shoulders, towards the gate.

'Friends of yours?' asks Joyce.

50

On the street side of the gate stand Lisa-Marie and Porter Glemham, waving manically.

I feel in my gut that Loz would not have directed them here.

Richard? No. He doesn't stand to gain anything. And he doesn't do anything unless there's something in it for him.

'Excuse me,' I say to my hosts, and jump on to the pontoon so hard it sends a ripple of shockwaves along the planks. 'What the hell do you want?'

They seem open and guileless, no trace of the glassy, greedy look I know so well.

'Love the hair,' says Lisa-Marie through the grille. If she's expecting me to accept the compliment, she can whistle. Commenting on my appearance is an intimacy she hasn't earned.

'We took down the post about you living on a boat because we were worried about you,' she says. If she's expecting thanks, she's not getting it.

'How'd you find me *here*?' I gesture around the basin.

'Like, I get that this feels weird, as someone who's got a history of being stalked,' says Lisa-Marie.

'We basically walked the canals from Kensal Rise to Enfield. We covered a *lot* of ground for a couple of armchair hunters,' says Porter. 'Forty thousand steps a day till we saw *Seren*.'

Well. No one told them. They found me by themselves. I ~~was~~ right to trust Loz. That's a huge comfort; there are still people in the world and I can still recognise them.

'We tried to contact you on Instagram to let you kn⸱ think you blocked us? So we thought we'd *find* you ar⸱ Eleanor, we have to talk to you.'

'Nell,' I say reflexively, defensively, but Lisa-Marie mistakes it as an invitation to familiarity.

'Nell, we're asking you to trust us,' she says. 'We've done everything right by you. On our forum we're trying to *stop* the crazy theories and get folks back on to the actual clues.'

Everyone keeps telling me these are the good guys. I was right to trust Loz. Why not take a second leap of faith? I'm starting to feel as if I have nothing to lose.

'OK,' I say, and buzz them through.

The pair of them look longingly at *Seren* but there's no way they're crossing her threshold. There's a wooden picnic table on the bank. I slide on to the bench, my back to the fence, and motion for them to sit opposite me. Although I've never really thought the Glemhams meant me physical harm – they 'only' facilitate a website that lets people discuss my dismemberment in public – it makes me feel better that they are in the more vulnerable position, backs facing the water. They seem to sense it too, the excitement of a moment ago now laced with unease.

'So,' I say. 'Tell me what I need to know. Don't go too fast, I'm not a Bonehunter and I'm not a tech person. Just give me—' I was going to say *just give me the bones of it* but I bite the words back.

'We found a conversation between a couple of members that concerned us. We took it down, but we felt you ought to know.' Porter hands me his phone.

@Elinore&Tam<3: I'm thinking if the Cecil Sharp verses are real we should examine old theories. I'm still convinced that Intimacies and everything FC has done since is part of one overarching master work. Everything is about The Golden Bones. This is all part of the same treasure hunt

lleDame: I like your way of thinking

ore&Tam<3: Suspicious isn't it the way those old exhib- alogues all vanished? I'm convinced they're the key

@BelleDame: Maybe Churcher wants us to move heaven and earth to find them

@Elinore&Tam<3: It could shed light on your own work

@BelleDame: I'm eager to see anything that could support my theories. Thanks for taking this to me and not you-know-who

I look up from the screen and into the Glemhams' expectant faces.

'What do you think?' asks Porter. 'About the idea that your father's work is all part of some lifelong treasure hunt?'

I blow out my cheeks. 'Honestly? I would be astonished if my father had done something like that. The whole point of *Intimacies* was to distance himself from *The Golden Bones*. He obviously did that thing about Cora giving spectacular head' – Lisa-Marie blushes scarlet – 'and the Cornwall book guide, but he got such grief for both those things, he was trying to move away from gimmicks.'

'Don't you think it's suspicious that they all disappeared, though?'

I remember Bridget snatching the catalogue away from Billie. *It's rare.*

'I can't explain that,' I say. 'But it doesn't mean it's packed with clues. Isn't it more likely that they're taking the scarcity as a starting point and working back from that, attaching meaning where there is none? With respect, they'd hardly be the first Bonehunter to go off on a flight of fancy.'

'Well, that's why we took it down. A flight of fancy might not end well for you. I suppose it depends on the odds of them actually being able to view those paintings.'

'They're never going to be shown,' I say.

'But if one of these people got hold of the catalogues . . .'

They let the threat hang in the air.

'What if I could get one?' I ask. 'Not that I believe for a that *Intimacies* was anything to do with *The Golden Bo* you two think like Bonehunters. If there's anything that can be misread, you'd be able to warn me? Predict their next move? Obviously I'm reaching here, but . . .'

They look at each other, dumbfounded for a second, before Lisa-Marie finally manages, 'We are *so flattered* that you would trust us with that. We're here till Sunday, then we're flying back home.'

'Well, I don't even know where I'd find one,' I say, back-pedalling. 'It's just a thought. But thanks for saying yes.'

'Listen, we're meeting a few people in the community for coffee so we have to head,' says Porter. 'You're welcome to join us?'

'Nah, you're alright.'

They get up to leave. 'Oh! Porter!' says Lisa-Marie. 'We almost forgot. The anagram!'

'Oh, yeah. Nell, it's probably nothing, but a forum member found something intriguing in some old, cached newsletter of your dad's. If you take the first letter of every sentence, then mix them up, you get what really feels like one of his clues. HONESTY HIDES TRUTH'S BONES IN KING'S CHASE. Does that mean anything to you?'

I shake my head.

'Well, like we say. It could be nothing. King's Chase is actually a mall in a suburb of Bristol. We're gonna take a day trip tomorrow.'

'Let me know if you find anything,' I say.

They exchange a glance. 'Er, how? You blocked us.'

Fuck it. I give them my number. I'm going to change it when this is all over anyway.

When they have gone I call Billie. 'Are you home for lunch?'

'Actually? I was wondering if I could stay at Kenza's for another ght.'

'Of course you can.'

t Billie's kedgeree – waste not, want not – and rinse my mug Tupperware in the sink. The beds are made and the boat could do more work on my Christmas stock but I'm out of solder. And that post about the catalogue has set my mind racing. If only I could slide together this kind of puzzle and make it fit, the way I can make a pattern from any old mismatched glass. It might be quicker, and safer, to break the habit of a lifetime and ask Frank a direct question. Did you hide a clue in *Intimacies*? If I get a straight answer at least I can put the Glemhams out of their misery. And it's a beautiful day for a bike ride.

I text Cora.

You in? Thought I'd come round for coffee.

Her reply takes an age.

El

Ele

I imagine clawed fingers tapping at her huge iPhone. I wish she'd let one of the kids teach her how to send voice notes but she's having none of it. I suspect her hearing is going along with everything else and she's too proud to admit it.

Eleanor! What a shame to miss you. We all decided to take ourselves down to Dorset for a couple of nights, get away from all the fuss and bother at home. Apparently the tasting menu at the Pig is out of this world! Soonest, Mummy.

She's attached a car selfie, Lallys in the front, Churchers on the wide back seat of Lal's T-Bird. All the better: I can look at the catalogue and try to decipher any clues for myself beforehand. I have a full set of Bridget's house keys from cat-sitting years ago. Before I have a chance to change my mind, I snap on my helmet, sling a backpack over my shoulders and set out for the Vale of Health.

51

Gospel Oak, London NW3
1993

LAL UP

When the estate agent has gone, Lal takes a moment to appreciate the way light floods through the Crittall windows and throws a rainbow on to the white-painted floorboards. The only furniture is a sofa that folds out into a bed. The rest of the space is seven hundred square feet of potential. Lal chose it for the location as much as anything else. This converted warehouse in Gospel Oak is within walking distance of the Vale but far enough away to feel like a new beginning.

Frank wouldn't accept any repayment for the deposit on the Lallys' house. It was a gift, he says. It's your place now. But Frank is in a bad way – it is a decade since he painted – and Lal wants to repay his friend's early generosity, his foresight in marching him to rehab, and bring him home to paint again. He can't wait to see Frank's face when he hands over the keys.

FRANK DOWN

Frank's up early but the newspaper's already on the mat. He turns straight to the arts section. The pull quote jumps out at him.

Trust me, The Golden Bones *doesn't even hint at the greatness* *nk Churcher's capable of, but he hasn't painted in a while. I've* *ally rented him a wee studio, see if the muse visits him there.'*

Frank lets out a roar. It was bad enough being the recipient of Lal's charity but it was at least tolerable when only *they* knew about it. But now here he is in the *Sunday* fucking *Times* telling everybody that Frank is blocked and making it sound like he can't even afford a fucking bedsit in Gospel Oak. He hammers on Lal's back door with the paper open at the offending page.

'Lal! Get down here and explain yourself.'

Lal comes downstairs in a loosely belted dressing gown and unlocks the door from the inside.

'Fuck you,' says Frank. 'Why would you belittle me like this?'

Lal is barely awake.

'I can see how it reads, but . . . I gave the interview when I still thought I was doing the right thing. I forgot I'd even said that, to be fair. Will you have a coffee?'

'Fuck off with your shitty instant coffee,' says Frank. 'How am I ever going to be taken seriously as an artist now?'

'You've got the wrong end of the—' begins Lal, but Frank slams the door in his face and the rest of his sentence is muffled.

Right now he wouldn't give a damn if he never saw the guy again.

52

It's a hot, sweaty ride up Hampstead High Street, but the thought of my parents' well-stocked fridge propels me up to East Heath Road. I check the family WhatsApp for the new code and neutralise the burglar alarm. In the kitchen I stand in front of the fridge as though it's an air-con unit, observing that, even though there are only two of them, my parents have four different kinds of milk. Frank has pre-portioned smoothie mixes in pouches. I blend the one with the most obscure and therefore most expensive ingredients – blue algae and alfalfa lacing the usual blueberries and kale – with ice, then drink it so quickly it gives me brain freeze.

I can't remember the last time I was in this house on my own. It's much nicer without Frank and Cora in it.

The Lallys' back door is opened with a huge brass key, probably the original Victorian. It makes a satisfying clunk and tumble. The house smells strongly of rosemary and faintly of marijuana. I look for the attic key but it's still not back on its hook, which sends a tingle through me. The catalogue can't have been *that* valuable. Unless Jane is right? And Bridget knows?

The smell of cannabis on the top landing is eye-watering, even ith the door shut. Sickly-sweet and dusty. It takes me a few goes nsert the key in its hole as the line of communication between rain and my hands seems to be down. I reach my hand into rkness to find the light pull – a bit of string – and yank hard, I remember doing. Two bare bulbs blink on, not giving out much light but scattering moths. I let go a sneeze that shakes my whole body.

Cannabis buds in bunches are strung across the ceiling, much as you'd find lavender in a Provençal kitchen. I'd forgotten how huge the space was: it takes up the whole footprint of the house. And almost every inch of it is piled waist-high – almost head-high in places – with *crap*. Children's tricycles with wheels missing. Bridget's notebooks from nursing college. A thousand plastic flowerpots. There are bags upon bags of clothes, some labelled – BABY GIRL 6–12 MONTHS. It is eight years since we had a child fitting that description in the family. Are Dom and Rose planning on having *more*? They certainly can't be saving them for me. And there are books and books and books in different shapes, sizes and languages, so many that I don't know how this floor could possibly be holding them up. I count one of the piles. Do they really need twelve copies of the first Selkies book in German? Living on a boat has made me clutter-intolerant. I sneeze as I open a shoebox. It contains the place settings for Rosaleen and Dominic's wedding. A crumpled Hatchards carrier bag holds ten copies of *The Ghost Bell*, each bookmarked with a faded receipt. The thought of Bridget bulk-buying her friend's doomed book just to get the numbers up brings a lump to my throat.

How can I look systematically for the catalogue in here? There are a couple of pathways, tributaries carved through the trash. The floor has not been filled in – how could it, when it seems that they started laying down junk the day they moved in and never stopped? Instead it is wide beams striped with grey fluffy insulation. There's a valley leading to a back wall, either where a path has caved in or recently been forged, it's hard to tell.

I use the light on my phone to get a better look and the first thing I see is the catalogue, right in front of me, resting on top o a headless rocking horse. I sneeze again, then slip it into my ruc sack. I'll go back to my parents', fire up the coffee machine, study it over a flat white.

Turning to leave, I hit my head on a light bulb and it swings, a sickening pendulum of light. For a second, it illuminates something on the far side of the attic, at the end of that dip in the junk pile.

Some force that doesn't want the best for me compels me to grope my way through the books and the bags and the mess to a little pile of – the part of my brain that wants to protect me says, how sweet, they've saved all Rose's baby teeth, but the closer I get the more obvious it is that these aren't teeth. They are the right colour, very pale ivory, but the wrong shape. The word *metacarpal* whispers itself in my ear. I pull the black plastic bag that the tiny bones have spilled from and more come tumbling out. Knobbled white truffles of vertebrae, the flat mushroom of a patella.

I'm sure that you can buy individual human bones in curiosity shops in Islington, but a whole skeleton?

I smooth out an old picnic blanket as best I can and go into a kind of autopilot, except that 'autopilot' suggests a level of detachment I don't feel. My whole body is flooded with adrenaline and it's with trembling hands that I piece together the awful jigsaw, the strange skills of my childhood sharp despite their long sleep. The smallest bones I don't attempt but the larger ones I do. Humerus, ulna and radius make a right arm. I lay the scapulae out and balance the sternum on top to lay the foundations of a thoracic cage.

There is no pelvis.

This is the rest of the girl in the tree.

I peel off the plastic bag covering the skull. The tape has gone brittle with age and gives easily. In art, people hold skulls as though they are one single entity – picture Hamlet, holding Yorick's entire head on one palm – but here the jaw has come way from the cranium and it takes two hands to reunite them, nds which are shaking so much that the teeth chatter like a prop n a ghost train. Eventually I still myself and the top teeth align the bottom and my tongue tells me who this is. Not in words.

Rather, it finds the tiny gap between my two front teeth and then travels to my left premolar, present in my mouth but missing from the smile in front of me. Black fillings line the molars. This is a smile I have seen only recently, frozen on a computer screen behind a looping pinwheel. My mind's eye stretches freckled skin over the bone, pokes blue glass beads into the voids of her eye sockets and pours strawberry blonde hair over her head like honey. This is the waitress from Frank's *Intimacies* opening.

53

Animal self-preservation kicks in. I go back to the kitchen, fetch a bag of vinyl gloves and a pack of antiseptic wipes from under the sink and wipe my fingerprints from every inch of the skeleton. Then I scoop it up, bones falling through my arms like beads from a broken necklace, and stuff it all back in those bin bags, which I also wipe down. If only knowledge could so easily be erased.

I tip a pile of books on top of it – *her* – then throw the picnic blanket over them. In my haste to get away I almost put a foot through the gap between two joists but I get out and lock the door behind me. I wipe the door handle. I turn out the light on my phone, and curse when I see that I've run the battery down to five per cent.

My next moves are dreamlike: it seems that I float downstairs, lock the back door, weightlessly enter my parents' house, and it's only when I'm back in the kitchen, staring at the dregs of a smoothie I drank in another lifetime, that my feet touch the floor again.

What. The. Fuck?

The bone in the tree came from a girl who was at a party where a man with a knife said that Ingrid would never forgive him if he didn't leave with a bone. When he couldn't take me, did he take her instead?

Clearly the police don't know about these remains, because, if they did, they wouldn't still be there. And also: how the hell did a bonehunter get into the Lallys' attic? I mean obviously there's where to hide anything in my parents' house, whereas you'd happily lose the Dead Sea Scrolls at Lal and Bridget's, but have to know both houses top to bottom to know that, and—

Jane Jones. She cleaned both these houses, for, what, half a year? She'd have known the layout like the back of her hand and that this house is spotless with no hiding places but that next door was a different story. I should call Mehreen Bindra, and I should do it right now.

But at the same time, I'm reluctant to involve myself any more deeply. If I tip Lal and Bridget off when they come back, they can report it themselves, and I get to stay out of it. I've got Billie to think of.

Not to mention that it will give them a chance to get rid of the possession-with-intent-to-supply levels of Class B drugs swinging from the rafters.

As I coast down the hill, two police cars and a van climb it. I flinch as we pass, as though they can smell that poor girl's bones on me, and feel relief when they're out of sight.

As I clear the lights, my phone rings. Number withheld.

'Eleanor? It's Jill from Children's Services,' she says. 'I'm here at our appointed time, but there appears to be another family living in the property?'

'Fuuuu . . .' I intercept the sound that comes out of my mouth just before it becomes a swear word. Moving to Horsfall made me forget about our social worker appointment. For the last year we've been so clever, meeting her outside 'for Covid reasons', and that's what we should've done today: turned up at Dylan's flat and given the usual disclaimer that he was sleeping off a night shift.

'Ah, yeah, he's got friends staying, friends from Bulgaria. We've decamped to my place for a bit.' The ease with which I can lie shocks me.

'All three of you?'

'That's right.'

'Because I can't get through to Dylan.'

'Yeah, he's between phones. His upgrade isn't due month. It's a nightmare!' My fake laugh sounds wild a

'Well, I'd like to come by and see where Billie's livi

'*Staying.*' Why did I say that? Now I've outright lied again. I give her the address and tell her it's a narrowboat.

'A *boat*,' she says; there's a little victory in her voice. 'Well. I'll see you there tomorrow morning at nine.'

Tomorrow morning. Crap, crap, *crap*.

I call Richard, crossing my fingers that my phone – currently on two per cent battery – will last the conversation.

'What've you got?' he asks, but his voice softens when he hears how upset I am. 'Alright, sweetheart, it's OK, I'm listening.' I know he's only using his old 'boyfriend' voice because he wants something from me, but right now I will take fake compassion and treat it like the real thing. 'I'm sorry.' I wipe my nose on my sleeve. 'I know I said I didn't want you to find Dylan but I really need him now.'

'When you say "now" . . .'

'Tomorrow morning.'

He whistles. 'I'll chase my lead again but, Nell, I don't want to get your hopes up. You should probably prepare for him not to turn up and also, finding him is one thing but if he's using, it might do more harm than—'

My phone goes black.

It starts to rain so I cycle slowly home via York Way, the new developments slammed up against ungentrifiable pockets of social housing and flat roof pubs. At a mini roundabout a car cuts me up and I swerve on to the raised domes of paintwork which are fine when it's dry but treacherous to cyclists when it's wet. I lose control of my bike and when I have to make a split-second choice between ploughing into a hulking Nissan Qashqai or a wall I ⌐oose the wall, buckling my front wheel. The driver doesn't stop. ⌐nker!' I yell after him, the force of it turning my throat to ⌐aper.

⌐d there stupefied for a moment before wheeling my wonky ⌐ half-mile to the Cycle Shop in Camden. A rebellious ⌐et trolley has nothing on a buckled front wheel, and ⌐take me five minutes on the bike or twenty minutes on foot fills the best part of an hour. I have to buy a whole new wheel and they're short-staffed because of Covid so they can't mend it for me until next week. Fuck it. If I can fit out the interior of a boat, I can change a wheel on a bicycle.

Back at the boat I put my phone on to charge, check in with Billie – she's fine, Kenza's mum's ordering Domino's, yes she'll come home first thing for Eyebrows' visit – then turn it off so it charges faster.

I work on the pontoon, grease and sweat loosening my grip, but I welcome the all-consuming physicality of the job. Moira brings me a cup of tea and a slice of Madeira cake that I cover in black fingerprints, and the way she talks to me makes me realise that I must be acting normally. That the turbulence inside hasn't reached the surface.

When I'm satisfied I take the bike for a test ride along the towpath. If anything, it handles better than before. I take advantage of my temporary reprieve from childcare responsibilities to sink a pint at the King Charles, a pub I like because it's got a stained glass window of a blond Elvis Presley. I sit underneath him and open the *Intimacies* catalogue at a random page, desperate for something that might explain what I've just unearthed. Sometimes you see things more clearly after a drink.

This is not one of those times.

The closer I stare at the pictures, the harder it is to focus. The same words whirl on the page, overlapping each other, crashing into each other until nothing makes sense.

I order another pint.

It's early evening by the time I get back to the basin and any wobbling is down to me, not my wheel. Once onboard, I empty my rucksack on to the counter with one hand and unlock my fully charged phone with the other, planning to check in with Billie, then call Dom.

There's one message from Billie – a picture of her teasing a string of melted cheese from her pizza – and six from Dom.

Call me

Call me now
Come on Nell it's urgent
Pick up ffs
Are you OK?
OK I'm driving back to London now but I'll be on hands-free.
Go to Mum and Dads as soon as you get this.

What could have gone wrong in a luxury hotel in Dorset? My immediate thought is Cora and which of her organs might have given out first. It's a race between the heart and lungs. The thought of her being in an ambulance, or worse, has my hands trembling so much I have to ask Siri to call Dom.

'I'm just five minutes away,' he says over traffic and honking horns. 'Are you there yet?'

'No, I only just picked up. What's happened?'

'I can't believe I'm saying this, but this afternoon the police searched Lal's house and found – they found more bones in Lal's attic. They think it's the waitress from Dad's party – you know, the *Intimacies* opening? And they've arrested both the guys on suspicion of murder.'

54

Dom's warned me that there's a reporter outside the front of the house so I take the Heath route, headlamp slicing through the dusk, tilted slightly downwards so I know to rise in my saddle when tree roots shoot across my path.

I decide not to tell anyone yet that I was in the attic. They'll find out I was there eventually; there's no way I eliminated every trace of my weird, identifiable-with-the-naked-eye fingerprints, and I'll have shed DNA on the rough string of the light pull and the other things I touched. But I have a Social Services visit first thing tomorrow morning, and missing it because I'm in a police cell is not the impression I want to make. I also want to wait until I know as much as possible about the investigation. How did the police know to search the attic? *They* can't have been looking for the catalogue. Even if the police had seen speculation about the catalogue online, I doubt they'd have taken it seriously, and even if they *had*, they couldn't have known it was in the attic. Only I and Cora and Bridget know that. Billie saw Bridget spirit it away, but she wouldn't have known where it went.

Dom lets me in through the back gate. He's dressed for Southwold in a Joules rugby shirt, cargo shorts and sliders. Sand from his hair dusts his shoulders like dandruff.

'Tell me everything,' I say. 'Who was she?'

'Leslie says they haven't released the girl's name yet because they haven't informed the next of kin. He's at the station with the guys. The police had a warrant to search the place and broke the door down. One of the neighbours called Mum and Dad back from Dorset, and when they got out of the car the guys were arrested.'

'Do you know *why* they searched it?'

'I do, yeah.' He looks from side to side, as if he too thinks people will be waiting in the bushes. 'I'll fill you in inside.'

The garden is a mirror image of the night the first bone was found; this time it's the Lally house the police are marching through with their evidence bags and their blue gloves. Silhouetted at my parents' kitchen window are Cora, Bridget, Oisin and Marcelle.

'Where are Rose and the kids?'

'Harriet's taking them back to our place.' He rolls his neck and we both wince at the sound of cervical vertebrae clicking together.

I sit at the table, accepting the glass of red that Cora slides my way then finding I don't have the desire for it. Rose has joined the party via FaceTime, Cora's tablet propped against a candlestick. Cora and Bridget don't look as though they've been crying but Oisin's pink eyes and cheeks tell me the tears have been flowing for a long time. He's got a couple of days' black stubble on his jaw but he looks like he did when he was five and he skinned his knee. I sink to his side.

'It's my fault,' he sniffs.

'Don't be silly, Osh.' I look up at Dom, waiting for him to placate or contradict Oisin, but he doesn't.

'The police viewed the tape of the *Intimacies* launch,' he says. 'The original VHS. It turns out that there was something on the end that Oisin trimmed from the digitised version. We dragged the full-length version out of the computer's recycling bin and – well it's easier to just show you.'

He flips open his laptop. 'So this is where the one we all saw ends,' he says, scrubbing through till he gets to the camera pointing at the kitchenette door. 'And this is what Osh cut.'

A figure lurches into the kitchenette. It's fuzzy but it's unmistakably Lal. He's wrestling a bottle of champagne from the waitress, and then he's brandishing it like a weapon. He then shoves her out of shot and disappears after her.

Oisin takes a long in-breath, snot rattling in his sinuses. 'I didn't want the production people to see Grandpa like that.'

I realise with a jolt that Oisin never knew that side of Lal. Obviously he knows that Lal can't drink any more, but no one has told him that the dent in the wall wasn't a one-off. He only knows his twinkly Grandpa Lal, not the monster he could be when he was drunk.

He takes a shuddering in-breath. 'Am I going to go to prison?'

'No,' says Rose. 'Absolutely not. It'd only be a crime if you'd done it *knowing* you were concealing evidence.'

'If this is the waitress from the *Intimacies* party, why are they after the guys when two Bonehunters crashed it? I know they took Stuart away but Jane wasn't arrested. She could've killed this girl on his behalf, his bidding, whatever, and put the body here years ago. There's no *way* she didn't have a set of keys cut.'

Cora shakes her head. 'We thought that too, so we had a locksmith come after we sacked her. He did this house and next door, same time we had the security cameras put in. I tipped him with an eighth of weed; he was ever so tickled by that, d'you remember, Bridget?'

How can she be so blasé? I guess she's used to having Leslie Napoleon magic the police away, like a wizard in one of the legends she loves so much. Who needs a magic wand when you have money?

Bridget twists the bangle on her arm. 'I do, but – oh, Cora, he only did the front door. I wanted to keep those gorgeous original locks, you know, with the monkey-tail handle and those lovely brass keys.'

'Oh, Mum,' says Rose on the screen. 'After all the security scares we've had?'

'Well – *we* haven't had any. It's all been the Churchers.'

'It's the same thing,' says Dom. 'It's the same *family*.' He gets up and walks a few paces away from Bridget, like he doesn't trust himself to be near her.

'Good God, Dominic, if I'd anticipated anything like this . . .' Bridget shakes her head. This vague helplessness is unlike Bridget, but maybe her husband being arrested for murder has finally breached the threshold of her competence where all the other tests failed.

'Speaking of keys, when I came back in here to get my phone, the attic key was missing.' I say this pointedly at Bridget, my anger at her for treating Billie like a criminal surfacing again; Lal hadn't been arrested for murder *then*. She nods, but doesn't offer an explanation.

'Leslie says they must have something else on the guys,' says Marcelle. Our heads turn towards her in unison, like we're all parts of the same machine. 'Something they're waiting to disclose. Can I play devil's advocate for a moment?'

55

'I say this in the context of Lal being one of my oldest, dearest friends,' says Marcelle. 'But I also think I might have a bit more detachment than the rest of you. The police are working on the assumption that the waitress was killed very soon after the last sighting. Which occurred just minutes before this video was taken. And we all know what Lal was like when he was on a bender. He would go after anyone who got between him and his next drink. I've *been* there.'

Bridget and Cora nod sympathetically; I take a beat longer to catch up. Never having known Marcelle in any other context than Frank's agent, it's easy for me to forget that they met when she was dating Lal. It dismays me that it is easier to imagine Lal hitting her than sleeping with her.

'He could be frightening,' Marcelle continues. 'And after the night in question, the night the police think this girl was murdered, he never drank again. What if that was his rock bottom; what if that night he did something so appalling that he never – don't look at me like that, Oisin, I'm just trying to think like the police here.'

Her words hang in the air for a moment, and then there's a swell of protest.

'OK, so he raised his hand once in a while, but *murder*?' says Bridget. 'He's not capable.'

'He *what*?' says Oisin. 'Did Grandpa used to hit Grandma? Did he ever hit you, Mum?'

Rose's sigh is so strong I expect the screen to billow like a sail. 'It was a long time ago, Osh,' she says. 'He wasn't well.'

Oisin looks as if he's taken a blow himself.

'We'll talk to you about it later, Osh,' says Dom. He and Rose nod at each other, their spousal telepathy as strong over FaceTime as it is in the flesh. You can see in Oisin's nod that their word means something to him. He trusts his parents to treat him like the adult he is. How Dom and Rose learned to be such good parents when they had such dysfunctional examples, I'll never know.

'And if Lal is in the frame, that explains why Frank was arrested too,' says Marcelle. 'The guys have a long history of covering each other's backs. Leslie's concerned that the police have found the barman Lal assaulted in the eighties and they know about Frank paying him off to drop the charges – which would obviously set a precedent for joint enterprise or whatever you call it. Don't worry, though. Leslie has a counter-investigation going on. Their investigator is finding everyone from the party. Including all his sitters.'

Five pairs of eyes strain with effort of not looking at Cora.

'No,' I say. 'I can't see Frank risking his reputation by getting involved with murder. And if he had, somehow, been involved, then he'd have got rid of the body *properly*. He's an engineer, he knows physics and chemistry. He knows all about skeletons, anatomy, and so on.'

'Just thinking back to that night,' says Marcelle. 'Those two hours when the police think the girl was killed. Lal missed the whole afterparty, didn't he? Came crashing in after midnight.'

Bridget brings her hand down on the table. 'Jesus, Marcelle, there's playing devil's advocate and then there's appointing yourself judge and jury and chief executioner.'

Cora puts her hand over her friend's. 'Bridget, she's right.'

It's the same blow, but coming from Cora it lands soft. Bridget's face crumples, scoring a million lines on her freckled skin.

'He took the car keys out of my pocket and got behind the wheel. I was terrified he would—' Her voice breaks. 'I was terrified he would kill someone.' She gives a horrified laugh. 'I spent some time pounding the streets looking for him but I gave up after about half an hour. Incredibly, he got the car home in one piece, but he'd blacked out and couldn't say where he'd been.'

Oisin says, in a voice that's years old than he is, 'And it never came back to him? 'Cos it might now. Like, the shock of being in with the police might jog his memory?'

'It doesn't work like that, poppet,' says Bridget. 'When an alcoholic has a blackout, it's not like they forget what they were doing. It's as if the brain never laid down that information in the first place.'

'It's true, Osh,' says Cora. 'Lal could drink enough to kill an elephant, and something in him just shut down. The body was present, he was present, you could have a conversation with him, I even saw him paint . . . but he just . . . wasn't *there*. And you couldn't tell. Why do you think we never told him where the jewels were hidden until he was sober?'

'It's on record, you know,' says Marcelle. 'The cameras were running when they were talking about the bender he went on. If the police have PD's footage, they'll know he went AWOL.'

'If, hypothetically, they did do it . . .' I begin.

'Not you as well,' says Bridget.

'Hear me out. There are two motives you need to think about. First of all, you've got the murder of the waitress in the first place. Second, you've got the motive of exposing it now. Whatever else you think, Frank doesn't benefit. It damages his reputation. It damages the reissue, and the app.'

'A Bonehunter who hates Frank would benefit,' says Dom slowly, 'And they'd enjoy turning the whole thing into an impossible puzzle and watching him squirm.' His speech picks up pace as his thoughts escalate. 'Someone who feels betrayed by him might even think it was worth killing an innocent woman just so they had a body.'

'But why would they drag Lal into it?' asks Bridget.

'The original hunt took over whole families,' says Marcelle. 'It destroyed relationships. If it's a Bonehunter bent on revenge, they might see it as poetic justice. All part of the fun.'

56

Horsfall Basin, London N1
7 August 2021

I wake up still in yesterday's clothes. After an ill-advised cycle ride home – at my mother's table I drank enough red wine to turn my teeth purple – I stayed up late reading the *Intimacies* catalogue. But the words kept skidding on the page as though it was a piece of homework in the wrong language. Now, it sits splayed on the side table. With its broken spine and dog-eared corners it is not the immaculate collectors' item it was this time last week. I am reluctant, in the light of what I found last night, to share it with the Glemhams. My guard is back up, and this time it's got padlocks on it.

I will take it to the police today and I will tell them everything we talked about last night, and then I will ask them why they aren't throwing everything they've got at Barney Badger and LetterstoIngrid and Jane Jones and yes, maybe even the Glemhams, instead of locking up two old men.

But first, Billie.

Her bike's on the roof when I come out of the shower block. I find her eating Shreddies at the breakfast bar, a trail of spilled milk and malted wheat destruction in her wake. She's taken advantage of the hairdryer and straighteners at Kenza's.

'You look lovely,' I say.

'Thanks.' She smooths down her hair, self-conscious but delighted. 'Any news?'

'They're still in custody, but I'm confident they'll be out in a couple of hours.'

She plucks at the scrunchie on her wrist, her eyes downcast, and then says, 'Ah, that's good. But I meant – I don't suppose there's any sign of . . .'

She means Dylan. I'm so wrapped up in my own sprawling family that I've lost sight of her tiny one.

'I'm sorry, kid. I did try. Let me make one last call.'

I pull the bedroom door closed behind me. Richard's mobile rings out and when I call his office, the woman answers.

'Can I speak to Richard, please?'

'I'm afraid he's not in the office at the moment. Are you an existing client?'

'No, I'm a – it's a personal matter.'

Her voice narrows its eyes. 'Can I take a name?'

It's ten minutes to nine. If Richard hasn't found Dylan by now, it's too late.

'It's fine,' I say, and end the call.

Billie's rinsing her breakfast bowl and trying very hard not to look hopeful.

'We can say he's at work. And I reckon we'll make a brilliant impression. The boat's gleaming, *you're* gleaming; I printed out your last term's reports. It'll be fine. I *promise*.'

The p-word just slipped out. I could kick myself. She nods, and turns her attention to the *Intimacies* catalogue on the work surface. She holds it up and says, 'It's *rare*,' in a good impression of Bridget, then sets it back down again. I put croissants in the oven even though it seems like a huge extravagance for a few lumps of pastry, fill the kettle with water for coffee and straighten the spices in their rack so the labels are all facing forward.

At five to nine, the buzzer on the pontoon sounds, harsh and urgent.

'Here we go, then,' I say.

I climb through the front door and catch my breath. It's not Eyebrows with her finger on the buzzer but two men, each of them a notch on my bedpost. One in a suit, greying beard, thick dark hair. The other with a buzz cut, in box-fresh trainers and a navy tracksuit that's a bit prison-issue but is smarter than anything I've seen him wear in years.

'Dylan!' I say.

'Dad?' Billie scrambles out of the hatch and my heart cracks open a little. Her eyes have never lit up like that for me.

'You're welcome,' says Richard, and it's only when I push the button to open the gate that I see that he has Dylan in a half-nelson. He shoves him roughly on to the boardwalk.

'Alright, alright, alright!' protests Dylan.

'I've got somewhere to be.' Richard turns to Dylan. 'Don't fuck it up.'

'Thank you,' I say to Richard. '*Thank you.*'

The look he gives me makes me wonder what he expects in return.

The pontoon thunders as Billie bowls into Dylan for a hug. He takes the impact but it feels like a punch to my gut. 'You came!' she says into his chest.

'Of course I did. Ooh, I've missed you so much.'

I bite my lip. Dylan looks clean, in both senses of the word. He smells of deodorant and he's shaved this morning. It's almost worse than if he'd turned up stinking and wasted. If he's in a good place, why hasn't he been in touch with Billie?

'You look gorgeous,' he says. 'So grown-up!'

'Thanks.' She glows.

'Dylan, are you—' I begin, but he doesn't let me finish the question.

'Four months,' he says, taking his Narcotics Anonymous chip out of his pocket and tossing it like a coin. Heads you win, tails you lose. 'Gotta stay clean for the little one, haven't I?'

'She's nearly as tall as you,' I say, drawing a line in the air between the top of Billie's head and Dylan's jaw.

'Nah, a *really* little one. Got another one on the way, with Nadja.'

Billie stops in her tracks. 'Nadja?'

'We got together in . . . I wanna say Lockdown Two? All a bit fast, I moved in after a couple of weeks, but she's a good girl. Be nice, little brother or sister for you, eh, Bill? You can come up and see us in Dunstable.'

'Right,' says Billie, as I quietly seethe on her behalf.

'Nadja's got her own maisonette, so I can keep my place on the Nightingale on.'

'Good for you to keep that income stream,' I say. The sarcasm sails over his head. 'And then you've got all Billie's child benefit.'

That one lands and at last he has the grace to look ashamed. He pulls a grubby fiver from his pocket. 'Get yourself something nice,' he says.

I'm about to shout, *Is that all you have to show for the last year and a half?* but the gate buzzes and I muster a smile.

'Let me take the lead in this, OK? I say, and then, as I buzz Eyebrows in, 'Jill! Lovely to see you, thanks so much for coming all the way.'

Her eyebrows are closer to her hairline than ever. Behind her back, Dylan places his forefingers over his own eyebrows and mouths *What the fuck?* to Billie, who bites back a giggle.

'You're not easy to find.' Eyebrows makes a big fuss about the difficulty of getting in and out through the front hatch – 'That low doorframe wants padding' – but, once she's inside, she can't hide the fact that she's impressed. She takes in the carefully laid floor, the tiles, the windows, the fairy lights around the mirror and the woodburning stove.

'Please, take a seat,' Dylan says, and the game of happy families commences. I make coffee, Dylan brews tea and Billie arranges the croissants on a plate. I don't like the example I'm setting Billie right now but I credit her with understanding that this is for her. It's about playing the system so that we can stay together. She certainly answers all of Jill's questions with aplomb. No, she doesn't mind the commute to school; it gives her time to read. Yes, she has a space to work, and it's so lovely to take a revision break and feed the ducks out of the window! No, she doesn't feel she's missing out. If anything, narrowboat living has taught her to value the resources we consume.

While she talks, I decide I'll cycle to Kentish Town as soon as Eyebrows has gone and tell the police about my trip to the Lallys' attic.

'And she hasn't tried to abscond again?'

'No, not at all. She's been good as gold.'

'No safeguarding issues, then.' Eyebrows ticks a box.

Here comes the blush, painting my lie red and rubbing it all over my face. No safeguarding issues, nothing to see here *unless* you count the psychopathic treasure-hunter who thinks that Billie is part of a bloodline that leads back to a woman who *never even existed* and she might be walking around with a golden bone in her pelvis.

'And Dylan,' says Eyebrows, 'how's work going for you? Any calmer, now that the numbers are falling?'

I'd forgotten to brief him. 'You know how it is,' he says easily and for the first time I'm grateful that he's a born liar. 'It's never quiet, really, in my line of work.'

'And the shift patterns?'

'Obviously it takes its toll.' Eyebrows looks to her notebook and Dylan shoots a grimace at me.

'Hospital porters are the unsung heroes of this pandemic, you know,' I say.

He catches the ball smoothly. 'Well, *and* mothers. Nell's a wonderful stepmother to Billie.'

'You're married?' Eyebrows brightens.

This is clearly a bluff too far for even Dylan. 'Figure of speech,' he says.

She closes her book. 'Well, as you know, I've had doubts about both of your backgrounds and, your, er, personal challenges. But your relationship is clearly stable and that's the most important thing. These unorthodox living arrangements wouldn't be ideal on a permanent basis, but they're only temporary? You'll be back at your flat in the Nightingale Estate when?'

'We'll probably stay here till the end of the school holidays,' I say, which buys me a few weeks.

When Eyebrows uses the loo I switch on the water pump so its drone covers my hissed conversation with Dylan.

'You'd better sort this out,' I say.

He waves a hand. 'It'll be cool. We'll just get the Dmitrovs to disappear for a bit.'

'Will you just get them to decorate for a bit as well? Because the last time I went there to pick up my post it was done up like a Bulgarian cathedral and the living room had two bunk beds and a cot in it.'

The toilet flushes and our smiles return. I show Eyebrows out, guiding her carefully through the hatch, and when we're back on deck I offer her a sprig of herbs from the raised flowerbeds on the roof. Dylan takes her hand to help her on to the pontoon. 'I'll see you to the gate,' he says, even though it's five paces away.

There are two figures in suits, a man and a woman, making their way down the boardwalk in the other direction. Dylan works out who they are before I do.

'Ah, fuck.' As soon as he's said it, it's as obvious as if they were in uniform. Dylan all but holds out his hands for the cuffs, but I know who they're really coming for. My legs go as weak as water.

'Eleanor Churcher?' says the man. 'I'm arresting you on suspicion of perverting the course of justice.'

Three jaws drop in unison. I don't know what my face is doing. Everything I've got is going into my legs, not letting myself collapse.

'Don't worry about Bill,' says Dylan. 'I'll stay with her till they let you go.'

The rest of the caution fades to a dull buzz. I am sure the social worker's face is a sight to behold but my eyes are only on Billie, the respect and trust draining from her face as fast as the fear floods in. She turns away from me as the cuffs click cold around my wrists.

57

Last time I was here, I turned right for an interview room; this
time the arresting officer steers me left for the custody suite, a
long corridor full of rectangles: cell doors, grids of bars, health
and safety posters. Institutional paint, the sick pastel yellow inex-
plicably known as lemon and a dark olive green. There's a tang of
urine in the air and it's cold. I feel as though I've been plucked
from August and set down in January.

Leslie Napoleon is waiting for me in my cell, just as he did in
Hampstead police station all those years ago.

'Eleanor.' His voice is rich and warm, shaped by wood-panelled
rooms and buffed to a shine by old school ties.

'Are the guys here?' I imagine Frank aiming for a seatless metal
toilet and missing. This is no place for old men, no matter how
young they like to think they are.

'They're exercising.' Leslie takes an expensive-looking silver
pen from his pocket and uncaps it to reveal an old-fashioned
nib. He writes my name, the date and time in the corner of his
yellow legal pad. Royal blue ink shines for a second before sinking into the paper. For some reason I find the ritual incredibly
reassuring.

'So what do you reckon?'

'The police have something up their sleeves,' he says. 'I'm just
not sure what. But we need to talk about you. What do you need
to tell me?'

'Well, I obviously was there,' I say. 'I did touch the body and I
didn't report it. There's no point in denying that. But they arrested
me for assisting an offender, which – that's not right, Leslie.
They're making out that I deliberately re-hid it because I was

protecting my father, and that's bollocks. It's Bonehunters. They're wasting their time with me.'

Leslie leans forward, elbows on his knees. 'You've been consistent in your allegations against the treasure-hunters, which will work in your favour. But I think the simplest thing to make this go away is that I offer a guilty plea to obstructing an inquiry and ask for a caution. You obviously knew the remains ought to be reported but you weren't actively shielding an offender, since you believe the others to be innocent.'

Unease bubbles up inside me like foul water. 'But that means I'll have a live caution again and then—' I cut myself off mid-sentence. So far Leslie has turned a blind eye to Billie. He's probably got some kind of duty to report it. If I put it into words now, do I put him in a position where he is forced to?

'Are you worried about the child?' This level of tact, this ability to read a face, is what my parents pay him for.

I nod. 'If they don't know about her, they can't take her away.'

I see him weigh something on his internal scales of justice. 'A guilty plea will preclude you having to say on record anything that might compromise your arrangement. If her continued stability with you is your priority then better a caution than a conviction. Better by far.'

Something to do with a 'developing situation' means they leave me in my cell for hours. With every clanging door I listen out for my father's voice or for Lal's but the only people speaking seem to be the officers themselves, discussing someone's leaving collection as though the custody suite were a normal workplace and not a badly painted purgatory. Desperate to get back to Billie but unable – for obvious reasons – to state that, I spend a long time fighting the urge to bash on the door with my fists.

I pass the time and try to take my mind off what Billie might be feeling by thinking about my theoretical chapel window. I close my eyes and let the shapes arrange themselves on the blank space behind my eyelids. I imagine it lit from within on a winter evening as well as what it might feel like to stand inside when the sun's beating down outside. When I've completed the image, I play around with different colours and textures of glass. I take a break for microwaved lasagne with oily orange cheese hotter than the surface of the sun, and bottled water that tastes of warm chalk, then mentally draft the letter I would write if I were into chasing high-status work, which I'm not. Even if I did want the work – and I can't deny the joy of designing, even in these circumstances – I wouldn't want the profile that came with it.

The square frosted window set high in the wall turns from white to grey. Is Billie still with Dylan? Has she eaten? There's no food at home. Did he take her somewhere with proper food or are they in some grotty pub where he's filling her belly with crisps and off-brand cola? It's what he's filling her head with that I should be worrying about. What if he tells her there's a home for her with him and Nadja? Would he do that, when he's spent the best part of her life avoiding responsibility for her? He can't honestly think she's better off with him. But if he does . . . I can't compete with a baby sibling, a ready-made nuclear family. Am I even right to try? Whose needs am I really putting first, Billie's, or mine? My thought-spiral gathers velocity as the hours pass, my sanity rushing down the plughole and into the sewer.

It's early evening when I'm led to an interview room. Bindra and DC Passmore are waiting for me. Keen not to waste any more time, I go on the apology offensive.

'I was *literally* on my way to come and talk to you when I was arrested,' I say, before I even sit down.

Leslie holds up a finger. 'All in good time,' he says. 'Take a seat.'

Bindra goes through the processes: formal introductions, the beep of the machine, the usual cautions. As soon as I know we're being recorded, I talk without a prompt.

'I know it looks bad, but I had my reasons for keeping the discovery to—'

'Let's take this from the beginning. Tell me what you know about the human remains found in Gerald Lally's home.'

'I keep telling you—'

Beside me, Leslie lays a palm flat on the table in warning. I shut my mouth.

'I'm not interested in your theories,' says Bindra. 'I mean, tell me why you went there. Talk me through that day, step by step.'

So I tell her. I was looking for a catalogue because I thought it might have a clue in it, then I saw that some stuff had been displaced, and when I saw it was a skeleton I went through it, and I don't know why I acted like that, I was in shock, I was worried about all the drugs and yes, now it's obvious that that's the least of everyone's worries, but still. I tell them about Bridget putting the catalogue there in the first place but I find myself leaving out the detail about her hiding the key because of Billie.

'And this catalogue. *Did* it contain the clues, when you found it?'

'I don't know. I haven't read it yet. I was setting it aside for when I had a clear head. I was a bit distracted by the whole "finding a dead body" business.'

My sarcasm focuses Bindra's laser. 'So where is it now?'

I look to Leslie. His nod says: if it's the truth, tell it.

'It's at home. In the kitchen, on the boat.'

She checks something on her iPad. 'That is not among the items found on the boat.'

My heart sinks. Billie wouldn't have sold it, but what if she told Dylan what it was? He knows that anything connected to Frank commands a price.

58

It is half past eight by the time they release me, and it takes them twenty minutes to give me back my phone. I text Billie before any notifications have had a chance to load.

Back in 30

I look at the screen, expecting at least one message from her, but there's nothing. A dark flower of unease blooms in my belly. I pocket my phone and step over the police station threshold to stand under the darkening sky and into the cool air of a Kentish Town evening. I close my eyes and inhale a lungful of second-hand vape and fried chicken.

When I open them, Bridget is facing me, her whole body clenched so that ropes of sinew connecting her square jaw to her collarbone stand out.

'Shitting hell!' I press my hand to my thumping heart. 'What are you—'

'How long had you known that there was a dead body in my attic, Eleanor?' In contrast to my yelp, her voice is cool and even. 'It feels like the kind of thing you could've called us about? My God, Eleanor, we are your *family*.'

'I can – it's – look, can we walk and talk? It's just that I need to check Billie's OK and—'

'Sure,' she says. We walk past empty shop fronts – *so many* empty shop fronts. Bridget's back is ramrod-straight, her steps measured and deliberate. I tell her everything as we turn from the side-street on to the main road and head towards Camden where I can access the towpath. Kids jostle each other outside McDonald's, glowing phones in their hands.

I text while I'm walking. *I'm coming home. Is Dylan still with you?*

'I understand your not wanting to tell the police what you'd found before the social worker and everything. But us?'

'I had Billie stuff to deal with. But also, I wanted to give you a chance to get rid of your stash. The last thing I wanted was *that* in the headlines as well. I didn't think it was worth dragging you back from your tasting menu. Obviously I didn't think the police were going to search it straight after I had.'

'Why the hell were *you* even up there, though?'

I explain that I thought that decoding the catalogue might shed some light on the jewel theft. 'Because – and this seems incredible to be even saying it – until yesterday that's what we thought it was, isn't it? Just your regular everyday priceless world-famous jewel theft. And remember I was trying to see if there was anything Bonehunters could interpret. I didn't believe Frank would've really put some Easter egg in there, right?'

'Mm-hmm,' says Bridget thoughtfully.

'What?'

She stops to give a couple of quid to a guy with no legs and a dog on a string. 'I'm not as convinced as the rest of you,' she says.

'Really?'

'When your father was sleeping with someone else, he always found a way to drop their name in conversation. He'd say, *I saw Adeola in the street today*, or he'd mention some anecdote about Lucy's husband, or if a song came on the radio he'd say, *This was playing when whoever was sitting for me*. He couldn't resist it. I don't think he even knew he was doing it, although *we* all knew. But you know how arrogant he can be, how in love with his own genius. It doesn't seem as out of character as the rest of you think. So honestly, I wouldn't rule out him hiding Easter eggs in his new work, just to prove what a clever bastard he was. People have no idea about half the things Frank Churcher gets his kicks from.' I'm surprised by the bile in her voice. 'The way he uses people to hurt others. Lal wasn't perfect back in the day. Christ knows, none of us were. But at least he had the guts to use his own body as a weapon, not other people's.'

Talking in riddles: again, Bridget's not acting like herself. I start to wonder whether the crisis isn't making her act out of character: rather, it has exposed a side of her I never suspected existed.

'He uses other people's bodies as *weapons*?' I echo. 'What, you mean he painted those women *just* to hurt their husbands?'

She looks away. 'In a sense.'

I decline to probe further. Whatever she's circling is clearly more information about my father and I'm fucked if I'm going to *work* to excavate yet more bad news.

'Whatever it is, I don't want to know,' I tell her. 'I feel like I reached my limit for the day about ten hours ago.' I chop the air above my head to show her how far out of my depth I am.

She actually thinks it over and then she holds up her hands, like: *I give up, it's your funeral.*

We walk in silence for a while. I check my phone. Nothing from Billie. I look up and down the road for the yellow light of a black cab but there's nothing. Pubs are filling up with colleagues and couples; in one window, a man and a woman clasp hands over a bottle of red. For the first time in a long, long time, loneliness plucks a string deep inside me.

'What did you do with the catalogue, anyway?' Bridget's sharp voice bursts my bubble of self-pity. 'Do the police have it?'

'That's the thing. The police couldn't find it when they searched the boat. Worst-case scenario is that Dylan's already flogging it on eBay.'

She feels for the reading glasses that hang on a beaded cord around her neck, pulls up the eBay app on her phone and taps for half a minute. While she's doing that, I call Billie. The phone rings out.

'Well,' says Bridget. 'No search results for *Frank Churcher Intimacies 1997 catalogue*. If Dylan's selling it, it's not here.'

Since the conversation has brought us here organically, I might as well say it.

'You know, she wasn't after it.'

Bridget takes off her glasses. 'Who wasn't after what?'

'Billie. She was never going to steal the catalogue.'

'I never thought she was, pet.' Bridget's puzzlement seems genuine.

'Oh right. I thought – maybe I'm being paranoid, but I thought you kept the key in your pocket so she wouldn't take it and sell it.'

She looks wounded. 'Christ, do you really think that of me?'

I shrug. 'You haven't given her the warmest of welcomes.'

'I'm so sorry you think that. I'll set that right. I will. It's just been – what with Aoife and so on. I'm sorry.' Her brow furrows. 'For what it's worth, I put the key straight back on the hook.'

'But when I came back in to get my phone, when the Glemhams were out the front, it wasn't there.'

'Yes – the key *did* go missing that day. I thought nothing of it. I said to myself at the time, I said I'll go to Cora's and get her spare but then it slipped my mind, what with everything. And I hadn't needed to go up there since.'

'Did you tell the police that? That would lend weight to the idea that someone else planted the skeleton. That the guys had nothing to do with it.'

Bridget purses her lips, producing a starburst of fine lines around her mouth. 'I don't know that they *do* know that,' she says. 'It didn't seem like an important detail at the time. Sure if I'd have known there was some poor girl rotting in my loft I'd have mentioned it alright.'

She makes the sign of the cross.

'So go back now,' I say. 'Go back and tell them you've just remembered it. It'll point them away from the family and towards the Bonehunters. It could even be the detail that gets the guys out.' I pause. 'There's no need to mention Billie.'

'I will,' she says. 'I'll go right now.'

We've reached Camden Gardens, a scrub of green in the middle of angry traffic. I'm a couple of minutes from the towpath.

'Do you mind if I don't wait for you?' I ask. 'I really need to go and check that Billie's OK.'

'Sure, sure. Send my love,' she says.

He used other people's bodies as weapons. What did she mean by that? They've never been close, Frank and Bridget, but nor have they ever been outright hostile.

59

LAL UP

They take the life-changing call from Marcelle together, Lal on the hallway phone and Bridget on the extension in the bedroom. Afterwards, he charges up the stairs, picks up his beautiful, clever wife and whirls her around and around.

'We'll be able to pay off the house,' she says. 'And pay Frank back.'

He tries not to let that dent his mood. Lately he's wondered if she might not have a point about Frank getting a kick out of playing the benefactor. That she's right when she says he likes to lord it.

'This calls for a celebration,' he says. She looks wary. 'No, not that.'

Lal's a year dry. He gave himself a wee scare after that business with the barman. He uses the bedside phone to call next door. They hear it ringing on the other side of the party wall. When Cora answers, he says, 'Will you keep an eye on our Rose for an hour or so?'

FRANK DOWN

Frank sits across from an empty canvas, listening to the sound of Lal and Bridget's lovemaking drift through the open window. He can't remember the last time he and Cora were at it like that.

Before Dom, probably. The age gap has lately started to show itself. She is forty-two to his thirty-six. He's an engineer and an amateur anatomist; he should've predicted that she would sag before her time. He just can't get excited about her any more.

'Fuck me,' comes the sound of Bridget's voice from next door. '*Fuck* me.'

Frank isn't even hard. Anyway, it's not that he wants Bridget. It's a source of fascination, in a way, that his powers don't work on her. But she's very bony and Christ knows he's had enough of skeleton girls – and besides, he wouldn't do that to Lal. He wants to do better than Lal but he doesn't want to humiliate him, just to quietly remain one step ahead. He just wants to want someone that way again. Since Lal laid off the sauce he keeps saying that he feels things again and that's what Frank wants. He wants to *feel*.

60

I call Billie again. She still isn't picking up and she hasn't read my text.

I break into a sprint, along Kentish Town Road and down to the canal.

The fading light gives the towpath an eerie, Dickensian quality. The graffiti I admire during the day seems to writhe on the brickwork, suggesting the twisted faces of the vagabonds lurking under bridges as I run, flat-footed, towards Horsfall. The still water looks like a sheet of onyx.

Why didn't I swap numbers with Moira and Joyce? While I'm running I call Richard and ask him for Dylan's number. He doesn't answer: I leave a breathless voice note. Two minutes later he sends a text.

As far as I know Dylan doesn't have a phone. I went to get him in the car.

Fuck. They could be in Dunstable already. The thought of his new girlfriend welcoming Billie twists a knife in my guts. If he charms her back to him, I've got no right to see her.

You're welcome, texts Richard.

'Oh, piss off,' I say to my phone.

Panting, I come off the towpath at King's Cross. The lack of pedestrian access to the basin that once seemed like a godsend is now an obstacle between me and my girl. Left, right, left and I'm at the gate to Horsfall. I find my key easily enough but it's like I'm operating someone else's hands and it takes me three goes to get it in the lock.

Horsfall is quiet but for the flap-flap-flap of the pink satin skirt-flag waving from its mast. Both our neighbouring boats are in darkness – and so is *Seren*.

No Billie, no Dylan.

When I press the hatch, it swings open and my heart speeds to a whirr.

'Billie?'

The boat throws my voice back in my face.

I back my way in, putting my hands on the stairs for balance as usual. The snap underfoot registers at the same time that I bring my right palm down on something sharp. A scream flies from my mouth. My left hand finds the light switch and the bulbs blink on to reveal blood trickling from the chip of scarlet glass that's plunged its way into my hand.

The steps are littered with more.

I grit my teeth, pull out the glass, yell again, and only then take in the extent of the damage. Someone has emptied the pigeon-holes of every sheet of coloured glass and dashed it to the wall. They have destroyed all the Christmas ornaments Billie and I made together, shards and empty metal frames where hats and stockings should be. Because so much of the glass is red, it takes me a few seconds to realise that the pieces are dotted with blood. A trail of it disappears into the Persian rug then starts up again on the other side, a chain of rubies snaking all the way to Billie's bedroom.

'Oh, God no,' I breathe. Who has been here? What have they done to my girl? I pick my way across the hazardous floor, my phone in my good hand, hitting three nines on the keypad and my forefinger hovering over the call button. 'Billie?' I call again. I put my good hand on the doorknob. 'Billie, sweetheart, are you there?'

There's a daughter. The bloodline continues.

I should have quashed that rumour. Never mind that it doesn't make sense: that hardly matters to a Bonehunter with a point to prove. I should have stated online that she was not my daughter.

If the Social had taken her away, at least they couldn't find her here.

No, no. *Please* no.

Let Billie be in Dunstable now; let her stay with Dylan forever. Nadja can adopt her; I won't force her to see me. Let her have run away. Let her be huddling in a subway or begging outside a cash machine. Anything, as long as she has air in her lungs and blood in her veins.

61

Billie's bedroom is dark except for the lava lamp. In blue liquid, roiling yellow wax forms globules that swirl over bloodstains on the bedclothes. Her body is a crescent under the sheets and her hair is splayed over the pillow. I crouch beside her.

'Billie. It's OK, I'm here.' I put a hand to her shoulder, dreading cold flesh. Gently, so gently, I try to roll her over on to her back but she resists, going rigid pulling away from me, muscles locked in anger that confirms she's alive. Relief loosens my guts, turns my limbs to rubber. Only the carpet of broken glass on the floor stops me collapsing.

'Bill,' I said. 'Talk to me. Tell me what's happened. Come on, sit up, love. I need to see you're alright.'

She rolls over and I stifle a scream. Her face is pale, her lips cracked and her cheeks lacerated with tiny cuts.

'Who did this? Where's Dylan?

'You made a promise!' she shouts at me. 'You said it would all be fine and then the police came and took you away!'

She did this. I broke my word, so she shattered my glass.

'Oh, Billie. Oh, love, no. Look, I'm not in trouble, it's going to be OK.'

It's going to be OK. I'm doubling down, making it worse.

I stretch my left hand, the one that isn't dripping blood, out across the bed. She doesn't take it. Instead, she points at me.

'*You* don't get to be arrested. Do you understand that?' Her lips are still bleeding; her spittle is pink.

'Of course I do, I—'

'No, really. Do you understand, though? Do you get what happens to me if you're not there? You're all I've got and you're only *playing*.'

'Playing?'

'Getting off on being a rescuer for the poor little foster kid. You're so noble, saving me from my shitty life, you get to show all your family that you're not a snob like them, you're salt of the earth, you're better than them. And then you go and get yourself nicked, like it doesn't even matter. And you think you can relate to me?'

'Well – yeah, I think we do understand each other, to a point – I know we're different, but – and as for being arrested, it's not like I'm immune from—'

'Your family do your head in but has there ever been a point where they wouldn't take you in? You've basically got four parents, and they're all loaded. Do you realise how offensive that is, to people who don't come from money? To choose to be poor? You haven't got a fucking clue.'

Her words find the truth and sting, like lemon juice in a cut.

'Give me a second to just – I'm just processing this.'

I put my head in my hands to focus my thoughts. The first one shocks me, but there it is, at the front of the queue: I could really do with a glass of something strong for this. But this kid – and Billie is more of a child tonight than I have ever seen her – has had enough of adults reaching for something to dull the edges of caring for her. I look at her, love and shame filling me, reaching my outer edges.

'I'm sorry,' I say, cringing at how hollow the words are. You say you're sorry when you bump into someone on an escalator, not when you wish with everything from your head to your hands to your heart that you had done things differently, not when you would give everything you have just to put it right. 'I should not have made you a promise that everything would be alright. Because it might not be. The police are after Frank and Lal and ignoring what's staring them in the face. I did something stupid that, yeah, did put the way we live in jeopardy.' I draw a breath, about to tell her that I'm mortified that I've made her feel that I was using her to prove a point, when she lets out a wail, a wild animal noise, that reminds me of something I'd hear from Aoife. Big, snotty heaving tears turn into hiccups.

'I trashed your glass and I wasted your money and I *loved* making them with you and we were gonna go round the markets and all I've done is given you the – perfect – excuse – to – get – rid – of me.'

Her handbrake turn from angry to penitent disorientates me, but those last few words slice through the confusion. 'Get *rid* of you?'

'I've spent so long trying to be this perfect kid so you'd like me, all the cooking and the cycling and getting good grades and just living up to what you want me to be, and now you know what I'm really like.' She's crying so hard she can't string more than a couple of words together, snatching what she can with each ragged breath. 'You know – that I'm – salty and – violent and – mean – and who'd – want – someone – like – meeee?'

I sit next to her on the bed. '*I* want you. The angry and mean bits only make me love you more.'

It's the first time I've told anyone I love them since Richard. I hope Billie doesn't sense that I smashed the piggy bank to get these words out. She's known too much responsibility already.

She snuffles at me from under a wing of tangled hair. Carefully I pick a shard of glass out of it.

'Are you being sarcastic?'

'Absolutely not. I want you to be *real* with me. I don't want a mini-me. Actually that's the last thing I want.' My calves are burning; this is the longest I've held a squat since a yoga holiday in Ibiza a decade ago, but I can't relax: the floor glitters dangerously beneath me. 'Don't you think I know what it's like, to lash out at the adults?' I ask her. 'Man, at least you only broke a few Christmas tree ornaments. Come back to me when you've assaulted a police officer!'

She laughs through the tears and her right nostril blows a bubble that pops in her face. 'So gross,' she says.

'Disgusting,' I agree.

I slide my upturned palm across the bloodstained duvet cover, wordlessly asking for her hand in mine.

'I can't,' she says. 'They're all cut up.'

I rise on my haunches with a groan, fetch the anglepoise light from my desk and begin tweezering splinters from her hands and arms and dressing the cuts, keeping an eye out for anything deep. This girl wants to be a veterinary surgeon; these hands matter. After an hour, I don't find anything that warrants a trip to hospital. When I'm done, the boat has the distinctive fresh-blood, childhood-injury smell of iron filings and Savlon.

'Congratulations,' I say. 'In one afternoon, you got yourself a bunch of scars it took me twenty years to earn.'

I comb out her hair; glass falls like slanted rain. I bundle up her bedsheets and put a fresh set on, smoothing my hands carefully over the mattress so as not to slice my own palms. She tries to help with the clear-up operation but she can't hold a brush so I make her a cup of tea and she watches me do what I can with the dust-pan and brush. I put the hand-held vacuum on to charge so that I can finish the job properly in the morning when I can see what I'm doing. Then I pop some corn in a pan, pour it into the biggest bowl I own, and we watch *Heathers* on the sofa while the boat rocks softly. Occasionally Billie takes several inhalations in quick succession, the aftershock of tears.

It's midnight by the time we finish. Only when I'm wiping down the work surfaces does the question of the catalogue crawl from a corner of my mind back to the tip of my tongue.

'Billie, when I left, there was an art brochure on the worktop,' I say, hoping that no accusation has crept into my voice.

'It's in my bag.' She nods to where her cloth tote hangs on a hook. When I retrieve the catalogue, it smells of cheese-and-onion crisps. 'The police said we had to get off the boat while they searched it. I took the brochure to the pub in case we were there for so long my phone ran out. Wanted to see why it was so valuable. And try to, I dunno, appreciate it a bit more. I was right the first time. It *is* a load of wank.'

I set the catalogue back on the work surface. Whatever secrets it might hold have been safe for twenty-five years. Another couple of hours won't make any difference.

62

I sit next to Billie's bed until she falls asleep. Her skin already looks better. The clean-up revealed the nicks on her face as shallow, and she's young and full of collagen.

In the kitchen, I uncap a half-bottle of – fuck you, Cora – supermarket prosecco. I can't remember the last evening I didn't drink. I haven't put it away like this since I was travelling. When we are on the other side of all this I'm not going to touch alcohol for a good six months. I flick exhaustedly through the cheese-and-onion *Intimacies* catalogue. The exhibition was appropriately named. It's page after page of breasts, buttocks, inner thighs, pubic hair, underarms. Faces are only shown partially. Eyes, cast coyly down or meeting the viewer, pupils blasted with desire. Lips parted as if about to tell a secret. It's a stretch to think of it as a roster of work rather than one of women.

Frank was at least inclusive in his tastes. No skin tone or body shape is left uncaptured. There's arrogance in every brushstroke. *Look*, they seem to say. *I can do whatever I want, be a Renaissance master and a Modernist in the same painting.*

No. I'm thinking like an artist – or an art critic – when I need to think like a Bonehunter.

So. Are these clues supposed to be in the words or the pictures – or, as with *The Golden Bones*, in the relationship between the two? The text is dense and would not, of course, have been written by Frank, so I study the bodies. I look for patterns in the positions of the sitters' limbs, on the body parts he has painted realistically – he doesn't flinch from a stretch mark or a hairy big toe – and the ones he chose to reveal through more rough, Impressionistic strokes. If any pattern emerges, it's that some

265

models feature more than others. I make a tally of how often each woman appears in case there's a clue in there. A bible verse, maybe, some famous mathematical sequence, I don't know.

One sitter holds my attention for reasons I can't pinpoint. She is very thin and has sock-marks at mid-calf and – and here's the thing I think might be interesting – what looks like a sock mark on her upper arm, too. For a moment I consider that she might have been wearing some kind of evening gloves before she disrobed in the studio, but who'd wear evening gloves with the kind of thick sports socks that have left ridges on her skin? Is that contradiction a clue? The Glemhams would know. Maybe it's the number of ridges on her legs?

To my dismay, my eyesight isn't sharp enough to count them, even with the big light on as well as the anglepoise. Clearly we are heading for reading glasses territory. I take a photo with my iPad and zoom in on that, instead. Details leap out that I couldn't see before. Right at the top of the neck, a curl of dark reddish-brown hair. Freckles across the shoulders. And, hidden under a fold of bedsheet, a curve of gold wire that I recognise. It looks like the edge of that bracelet Bridget sometimes wears on her

—on her

—on her upper arm.

That's not a mark from a glove. It's the indentation from a bangle. Of *course* it's Bridget. I've seen that body a million times, sunbathing in the garden, swimming on holiday.

Bridget. Frank painted Bridget for *Intimacies*, which means they—

They—

They—

Fragmented images of arms, legs, arched backs – the whole would be too grotesque – animate themselves in my mind.

Frank and Bridget. Frank and *Bridget*.

His best friend's wife. His wife's best friend.

No *wonder* she locked up the evidence and threw away the key. Does Cora know?

Does Lal know?

Christ, do *Dom and Rose* know?

The picture is dated 1994. Christ. They were at it while I was away in Europe. How long did it last? Are they *still* at it? The few remaining picture-perfect memories from my childhood are painted over with rough, angry daubs. The knowledge turns all the leads I have about the Bonehunters into dead ends, but so many other paths collide here – the party, the waitress, the picture – that it cannot be insignificant.

People have no idea how Frank Churcher really gets his kicks.
He uses other bodies as weapons.

Was *her own* the body Bridget meant?

What if Lal recognised Bridget in this picture at the *Intimacies* opening, and that's what sent him plunging to the bottom of his glass? What if he took out his hurt and rage on that poor girl with her tray of bubbles and her gap-toothed smile?

What if it *wasn't* a Bonehunter?

Frank's words from the day of filming come back to me. 'We emptied the vault on to the kitchen table . . . Lal came over for breakfast, helped me look through it. There were things no one had seen for fifty years. Stuff from when you were little, stuff from the nineties. And obviously Lal's had so many "lost weekends" that some of them he was seeing as though for the first time.'

What if Bridget's wrong about his drunken experiences being irretrievable, and seeing the catalogue again the night before the film crew arrived brought it all flooding back? That it was all there, the party and the girl and the bag of bones, buried deep in some dirty dark chamber of the mind that could only be blown apart with dynamite? What if we're wrong about Lal only losing his temper when he's been drinking, and in the white-hot hurt of recall he didn't care what or who else he toppled as long as he took Frank Churcher down?

And what if Bridget has known this all along, and hid the catalogue to cover not her own sins but her husband's?

PART THREE

INTIMACIES

A new collection of paintings by Frank Churcher

The Veasey Gallery
Haverstock Hill, London NW3

20 JUNE 1997
6.30 for 7p.m.

RSVP to Marcelle Veasey

Strictly no admittance without this invitation

63

The gold bangle on her upper arm slides down and catches her on the elbow, striking bone. She has barely eaten for the past week, sick at the thought of this moment, and now it is here.

'Bridget?' calls someone behind her, but she doesn't turn around. They will see her face and they will *know*. The painting is of her back, but is so clearly her that it might as well be full-frontal and include her face. She approaches it slowly, as though she is playing Grandmother's Footsteps, as though her painted self might turn and look over her shoulder if she moves too quickly.

She hasn't seen Frank yet, but under the cigarettes and sweat and wine and paint she can smell him: Guerlain Vétiver, tobacco and pepper, so distinctive that she'd had to shower after sex. It transports her back to the secret afternoons, the paint-stained sheets, two bodies coming together with the power to break two families apart. She had the same dream seven nights in a row: a crack in the earth on their shared lawn that became a chasm, the two houses splitting from each other, their interiors exposed like doll's houses. Those dreams had helped her decision to end it. Well, them and the other thing.

Last time she saw the painting it was a sketch on canvas. Frank ~~d~~ threatened to finish it without her – he had the Polaroids, ~~r~~ all – but she thought that was something he had thrown out ~~e~~ heat of the moment, when guilt got the better of her and ~~t~~old him it was the last time. She hadn't thought it was ~~thing~~ he would actually do to her, to all of them.

How different that last time was from the first. She remembers it as if it were yesterday. On her way back from the dentist she'd run into Frank in the street. He was carrying a French stick and a wheel of soft cheese. 'Come and have lunch with me?' he'd said. He had red wine in a decanter, so having a glass seemed less of a big deal than if he'd opened a bottle. They drank it from little tumblers that had paint around the rim, as though they'd once held turpentine and brushes. The bread and the cheese remained untouched. Home was vomit and broken glass, and under Frank's hands she was a ripe peach splitting open, danger and solace merged in the act. It was wrong, it was fucked up, but he was gentle and safe.

She knows now, as she regards her portrait, that he is nobody's safe space.

Nobody knows. Nobody would suspect because it is so shocking, the wrongness of it all.

It was an intimacy that had something of the secret garden, or locked hotel room, about it. And this painting kicks down the doors. It will do what they never wanted: spill like watercolours into the others' lives, everything running and ruined. What the hell is *wrong* with him?

'Bridget!' says the voice again. This time she turns around, for one reckless second not caring that her face will give her away. The woman, whoever she is, says, 'Christ – sorry,' and turns away, presumably to make small talk with someone who isn't having a nervous breakdown in front of her own unsanctioned portrait.

64

Six mirrored pillars hold up the ceiling in Marcelle's new gallery. Each pillar has four sides and a shelf for glasses and ashtrays at elbow height. Dom, who absolutely does not want to look too closely at any of the paintings, uses one of these mirrors to watch the Bonehunters on the pavement outside instead. They are standing obediently – for now at least – behind a red velvet rope on the pavement.(Dom can't help but picture a knife slicing through it. Anything associated with Ingrid provokes horrible images). He recognises Stuart Cummins from Ingrid Morrison's trial. The guy's a creep but there's no law against him being there. He recognises Jane Jones, aka Mary, aka Anne, from when she worked in his house, folding his underpants and making his bed, and a shudder passes through him. One of them even has a placard. TELL US WHERE ELINORE IS BURIED. Fortunately Marcelle's girlfriend Harriet has a blacklist of names and mugshots. Harriet is five foot nothing of solid gristle and quietly terrifying.

Dom knew they were coming; he read about their plans on the new Elinore'sArmy.net forum. It's pretty basic html stuff but it's got potential. He thinks Frank should set up an official website for his new work so that when you put his name into Yahoo something other than *The Golden Bones* pops up. He's even offered to build the site himself as his project for his computer science level. But Frank and Marcelle think the internet is just a flash in an.

all the excitement Dom feels about the Web, he also feels bout the implications it has for someone like Nell, who lute privacy. For the past three years Nell has existed as a series of intermittent postcards saying things like, 'Living in a dry riverbed in Spain!' or 'You would love Berlin!', and each one only made him miss her more. He looks around the human kaleidoscope for her. He knows she's arranged to arrive via the back entrance. If she's seen that lot outside and made an early exit the same way, he can't say he blames her.

Frank walks past, talking to a man with a Salvador Dalí moustache. 'I home in on one detail that captures the essence of my sitter,' he's saying. 'It could be the small of a back, the cleft in a chin – and I build out from there, so it's as though a single drop on the canvas expands to . . .'

His words are drowned out by the huffs and puffs of Sid, the 'event planner' who helps out with Cora's more ambitious house parties and is currently scooting around the floor holding trays of miniature food. Dominic follows a plate of blinis but they're gone by the time he catches them up. He finds himself standing in front of a painting of a generous redhead being appraised by two women.

'Extraordinary how he conveys this sense of intimacy with this ruthless objectivity,' says the tall one.

'Mmm, mmm,' says her friend. 'And it's fascinating that by evoking something that's almost a carcass – there's a real *pungency* to it, don't you think? – he utterly conjures live flesh.'

'It's so indecorous – but isn't sex itself, when you think about it?' asks the tall one.

'Abso*lutely*. Look at the way she's clutching the sheets there. It puts the whole painting on high alert, doesn't it?'

Yah yah yah, blah blah blah. Who teaches them to talk like this? Dom can tell the painting is good – it's pretty clever the way it combines the precise stuff Frank used to do and the sort of more rough style he's come up with lately. Maybe there's terminology for it. He can't talk about art, that's his problem. It's all suc' subjective, shifting bollocks, people trying to score intellect points. He wishes that the Admiral were still alive. Say what like about the old bastard, at least you could have a real conv tion with him.

"What's your take on the – you know . . . the *rumour*.' The short woman has dropped the pitch of her voice but not the volume, the way some people do instead of whispering properly. 'Marketing genius, or do you think he really did sleep with all of them?'

'I don't know what to think,' says the tall one. 'Either way, you've got to admire his chutzpah.'

'One's almost offended that one wasn't asked oneself.'

The women burst into laughter and walk out of earshot, but Dominic doesn't need to hear the rest. He already knows and so, it appears, does everyone else. Just your average Friday evening, he thinks, stuck in a party full of women my father has fucked, then painted. Or maybe painted, then fucked. The order is probably integral to Frank's process but Dom doesn't care to know the details.

He looks around. They've let him and Rose invite a couple of schoolfriends but they're not there yet. No Rose, no Nell – and no Cora, either. Dominic's a bit worried about his mum. She has lost a *lot* of weight very quickly and been even more vague and floaty than usual.

'Dominic! There you are.' Frank claps him on the shoulder and for a moment Dom is replete with pleasure at the thought that his father has noticed his discomfort and taken a break from schmoozing to spend a few moments with him. But all he says is, 'Where's your sister? There are some people I want her to meet.'

When Dom says he doesn't know, Frank tuts and walks off. Dom looks at his feet because they seem like the safest place to put his eyes. Frank has never wanted anyone to meet *him*. Their dad likes Nell because she's a rebel. When he was younger, Dom thought that working harder and harder would make Frank approve of him, but actually, the harder he works and the better grades, the more Frank seems repulsed by him.

Dom has a son, he's never going to be like that.

65

Cora is going to be late for the party.

'That's come out lovely, that has,' says the hairdresser, pulling hard on the round brush and spinning straw into gold. Cora lifts her eyes from the page of *Marie Claire* magazine that she's been staring at for the last half-hour. The hair looks good. Too good: it upstages her face. Cora is fifty-five and she feels as though she has let her husband down by no longer looking the way she did when he first painted her. Her appearance feels less the product of time's march than a character flaw. At Frank's behest she went to Harley Street and got herself some slimming pills and she's dropped a stone in six weeks, but for the first time in her long history of dieting her skin had not come along for the ride, and when she'd looked in the mirror this morning she had seen her mother's jowls swinging in the glass.

So today, as well as the highlights and the blow-dry, she has had a facial with electric currents passed through a metal roller to tighten her jawline, and a manicure and a makeover. She has been dashing around London like Mrs Dalloway preparing for the party, only instead of getting a house ready she has been working on herself.

'Twenty minutes and we'll be done,' says the hairdresser.

Then another twenty in a cab across London and it's the rush hour now. Cora is going to be *very* late. Her entrance will be moment, and they will all pause their guessing games to g her reaction to the paintings.

'I hope you're going out tonight; you look a million d don't want you wasting this hair on the telly and your s when Cora nods, 'Let's get you a glass of bubbly, then the mood.'

It comes in a flute, crisp and dry. It goes straight to her head but that's to be expected as she hasn't eaten for three days.

'So where's the do?' asks the hairdresser.

'My husband's opening,' says Cora but the hairdresser has turned the dryer up to deafening volume. Under cover of white noise, Cora says the words she's been keeping in for weeks. 'I'm going to be in a room full of women my husband has slept with,' she says.

'Sounds *lovely*,' yells the hairdresser.

'The most exhausting part is pretending not to mind. It was one thing in the sixties when I was letting men treat me like shit and calling it free love, but to still be putting up with it now . . . I'm *ashamed* of myself.'

The hairdresser is nodding away. Cora is emboldened.

'Sometimes I wait outside his studio and I watch as they leave. There's a café opposite. I get a cappuccino and a window seat and I study my husband's mistresses. He hasn't got a type. Black, white, curvy, bony, middle-aged, young – well, thirty, which is young from where I'm standing. I've seen them all. Saw one leaning out of the window wrapped in a bedsheet once, and last week—'

The dryer cuts out and Cora bites her lip. Last week, she had been going to say, I was sitting in front of a croissant that I couldn't eat because my veins were coursing with amphetamine sulphate while a girl with bright gold hair and sink-estate vowels shouted up at the window, 'You can't turn me away, Frank! Let me in! Talk to me!'

Cora had recognised desperation when she saw it. She'd envied girl for being able to express what she had suppressed – anger great man, the great artist. She had wanted to tell the girl wasn't worth it, but why should she do her husband's rk for him?

rdresser pulls a tendril then releases it to assess it for 'Another one?' she asks, nodding at the empty glass. replies Cora.

66

Lal jangles the car keys in his pocket. He's driven the T-Bird here tonight, despite the short distance and the ball-ache of parking, to force himself to stay sober. He'd known he wasn't going to make it as soon as he entered the gallery. Hell, he'd known it was a mistake before he fastened his seatbelt. But he wants to try for Bridget, or rather he wants Bridget to *see* him trying before she sees him fail.

Sure he'll stop after tonight. Bridget's right. They're all right. Even Father Paul's stopped offering prayers to the boozers' patron, St Max, and started using the word *disease*. Lal can't drink in moderation; it's got to be all or nothing. Tomorrow evening he'll go to the AA meeting at the Friends' Meeting House and he'll stand up and he'll say *my name's Lal and I'm an alcoholic* and the day after that he'll pick up Bridget's new manuscript and he'll start drawing again but by Christ he can't be expected to get through tonight without a few jars. Not with the way things stand with Frank. That last row – Frank kicking up a stink about the studio – was the worst one ever. Four years ago it was and things still aren't back to normal. On the surface everything's grand, it's not like the craic has gone or anything, it's just that there's this dark fizzing current of . . . *hatred*'s a strong word for a man you love like a brother, so Lal will settle for *antagonism*.

Sid carries a single glistening Perrier on a silver tray to where the man of the hour is in earnest conversation with a woman whose black dress is cut so low at the back that Lal can see the top of her arse crack. 'Thank you, Sid.' Frank makes a show of pouring the sparkling water into his glass. His eyes don't leave his female companion but Lal has the feeling that Frank is drinking the Perrier *at* him, to prove a point. *Look how controlled I am*, the clear drink suggests, *how pure*. Lal bristles. How dare he, when he's been dipping his dick in women like a paintbrush in turpentine? The contempt Frank shows Cora. The contempt he shows marriage itself. Why bother to get married in a church if you don't intend to respect the sacrament? And the kids. What kind of example is he setting for the kids? Lal hasn't been a great husband in some ways, he holds his hands up to that, but he's been true to his Bridie. Never been anyone else for him, not since the day he set eyes on her.

Someone has left a full glass unattended on a mirrored shelf. Lal tips it down his open throat.

Beside him, Bridget silently holds out her hand for the car keys. When he drops them into her palm, she slides them into the pocket of her jacket, which hangs on the coat rack by the door.

'We'll have to walk home,' she says on her return. 'I've already had three.'

'That's not like you,' he says.

She turns on him, eyes flashing, the snakes of her hair briefly alive. 'Did you ever stop to think for one second, Lal, that maybe you're not the only one who needs to take the edge off sometimes?'

Lal is astounded. What the hell reason does *Bridget* have to be edgy?

67

Richard Reid parks down a side road off Haverstock Hill. The approach to the Veasey Gallery is thronged with press photographers and Bonehunters. He flexes the invitation in his pocket. The stiff white card is embossed with another man's name. David Levy is a society reporter for the *Evening Standard* who uses Richard's services every now and again. He wangled himself an invitation that he passed to Richard in lieu of payment for a job.

This is the closest to penetrating the inner circle he's ever got. Fifteen years he's been chasing this piece of cheap gold. He's sure the stress of it was one reason his father had a heart attack two weeks into his retirement.

A woman in a wooden necklace sees him coming and waves excitedly. 'You're Mr Velasco's agent!' she says. 'Remember me?'

'Of course I do.' Richard shakes her hand. Jane Jones. The only Bonehunter to breach the Churcher homestead. Not that she found what she was looking for. Not that she *knows* what she's looking for. She went dark for a few years, Jane, got distracted by David Icke and crop circles, but this exhibition has brought them all crawling out of the woodwork. 'It's good to see you again,' says Richard, shaking her hand. Bracelets made of seashells rattle on her wrists. 'How's progress been?'

Progress. As though any of them have got an inch closer to finding the jewel since the seventies. Richard doesn't believe there are still clues out there, but Velasco does, and that's what he's paying him to amass. The treasure-hunters' stories are always interesting, if only for a snapshot of how far from reality the human mind can drift. They are otherwise intelligent, functioning people. What *is* it about this book that sends them nuts?

'I'm on the verge of a breakthrough,' says Jane. Richard braces himself for her reply. Has she used a teaspoon to dig a tunnel under Hampstead Heath? She gazes sagely yet wistfully at the gallery interior. 'I just need to get in there. The whole exhibition is one big meta-clue,' she says. 'Those paintings are *dripping* with hidden meaning.'

The way Frank Churcher carries on with his sitters, Richard thinks they're more likely to be dripping with something else, but he knows better than to say that to Jane.

Richard makes small talk with a few minor players in the ElinoresArmy fraternity – they're so much easier to keep tabs on now they're all migrating online – before engaging Stuart Cummins in conversation.

'How's tricks?' asks Richard.

Cummins – dapper in a white suit – pushes his glasses up his shiny nose with his middle finger. 'Faint heart ne'er won fair maiden,' he replies.

Cummins has always been one to watch. Mr Velasco believes that Ingrid Morrison had the keenest mind of any Bonehunter ever. Richard doesn't share Velasco's faith. He always pictured her both strait-jacketed and bouncing off the walls of a padded cell, all the horror-film clichés coming to life. Still, before she was sent away, he would always gather any Ingrid-related intel he could find. It kept Velasco happy and, just as even a stopped clock gives the right time twice a day, Richard figured that her scattergun brain might one day alight on something relevant and useful.

It's a balancing act, talking to Stuart Cummins. You have to humour him enough to keep him on-side but keep enough of a straight face that he doesn't sense you're mocking him, and some of the shite he comes out with makes that a real challenge.

'What a shame Ingrid can't be here to see this.' Richard invokes the name that casts as powerful a spell over Cummins as Elinore.

The man's lips twitch. He's clearly itching to tell Richard something.

282

'Stuart, you dark horse,' says Richard. 'Have you had a break-through in the hunt?'

'Next best thing.' Cummins hyperventilates a laugh. 'We've been writing to each other again. Keeping abreast of developments.'

'*How?*'

'I've got someone on the inside,' says Cummins. 'A courier, if you will.'

He's bribing a member of staff. So simple. Why didn't Richard think of it himself?

'So what do you write about?'

'I follow up her research. I'm her eyes and ears on the outside. I've just come back from a very rewarding weekend in the Mitchell Library at Glasgow.'

If Richard remembers correctly, the Mitchell Library houses a Scottish folk song archive.

'Oh, yeah? Did you find anything valuable?'

Cummins's face falls. 'No, but I ruled it out as a further resource, and that's just as important.'

'Remind me,' says Richard. 'What's the plan when you locate the bone?'

'We've already located it.' Cummins dips his head at the gallery where Frank Churcher's poor daughter numbers among the guests.

Richard finds he has reached the limits of what he is prepared to indulge.

'You need to let that drop,' he says. 'What do you honestly expect to do with it? Give it to Ingrid? Are you going to turn up on my doorstep with it all covered in blood in your hands and say, please give this to Mr Velasco. It's the *gold* he wants. The artwork.'

Cummins clicks his tongue. 'That's because he's thinking i purely material terms.'

'With respect, Mr Velasco wants to complete his artwork that's only because he's a scholar of the book.'

'He *aspires* to be,' says Stuart loftily, and then falters. '
– finding Elinore means so much to all of us, but Ingric

that bone. Sometimes – and please, you can't ever tell her this – sometimes I think any bone would do. I could *tell* her it came from Eleanor. It's not as though she's ever getting out of that place, is it? The authorities have made sure of that. She'd be *so happy* if she knew Elinore was being put back together.'

Richard is lost for words. This twisted logic would blow a gasket in someone who didn't understand it. He's as deep in *The Golden Bones* as anyone and Christ knows *his* gaskets are feeling the strain.

'It must be costing you a few quid, all this,' he says. 'The travel, the, er . . . the postage.'

'I'm absolutely *haemorrhaging* money,' acknowledges Cummins.

'What could I pay you for that correspondence?'

Cummins clutches the briefcase he's carrying to his chest. Richard didn't know he had the letters with him but he does now. 'I couldn't part with them,' he says. 'They're crucial to the investigation. They're . . . they're everything.'

'No need for you to part with anything,' says Richard. 'I can make copies. I'll give you five hundred pounds if you let me photograph that correspondence now.' In fact, he has a thousand in his pocket, and he's willing to get more from the cashpoint over the road if Cummins gets mercenary. 'We all want the same thing, don't we?' he wheedles. 'I know we don't always agree on the method and yes, our motives differ, but at the end of the day we share a goal. To put Elinore back together. See the lady *rise*, Stuart.' He has long since stopped feeling like a twerp when he talks like this. It gets the hunters on-side: works like a charm. 'I tell you what else. Five hundred pounds would pay for a lot of letters to Ingrid.'

ey do the deal behind a wheelie bin, Stuart tucking fifty-pound
into his socks, Richard using his Minox subminiature
a (God, how he loves a bit of kit) to scan twenty or so pages
written notes. Ingrid's writing is neat but cramped. He'll
ow the photographs right up to make them legible. But

it's something to show Mr Velasco. Sometimes Richard wonders if, on one level, Mr Velasco just likes the thought of him scampering around, of debasing him like this.

'A pleasure doing business with you,' says Richard, but Cummins doesn't reply. He is peering into the gallery, his wet lips parted in something that looks uncomfortably like arousal. When Richard takes his leave, he feels like there's a sheen of the man's grease all over him.

Richard stands in the queue. David Levy, he tells himself. My name is David Levy. He powers up his Palm Pilot to jot down what the Bonehunters have told him. He made notes more for the false confidence and the illusion of progress created by having written something down. God, this job. Velasco gives him a generous retainer but it feels like a piece of homework that will never end. He's turning thirty-six in a couple of weeks. God forbid he's still on this case when he's forty.

A taxi chug-chugs to a halt and deposits a dishevelled Cora Churcher on to the wide pavement. Richard's instinct is to take cover but of course Cora doesn't know him. She has no reason to connect him with the company, N20 Associates, offering ever-increasing sums for Elinore's pelvic girdle.

He takes one last look at Stuart Cummins. The man's a wisp, a puff of smoke. The worst he's going to do is press his nose up against the glass. Even among *The Golden Bones* obsessives, the odds of two nutters being so far gone they're willing to carve up an innocent young woman must be *vanishingly* small.

68

Cora cannot go in.

She *cannot*.

The walls of her hollow stomach seem to touch each other. She tips the driver and tries to make a ladylike exit from the cab, the knees-together swing, but her dress gets caught and after an undignified tug of war with her hemline she finds herself on the pavement. Stuart Cummins is within touching distance and Cora dips her head. A second of eye contact with that man could be interpreted as a communication from Elinore.

She's so distracted by him that she doesn't notice Jane Jones pawing at her arm until Harriet steps out and says, 'Behind the rope, please.'

Jane complies, which is encouraging.

Cora gets to thinking. It might not be the worst thing in the world that they're there. Maybe a bit of harmless heckling of Eleanor might even divert attention from her.

'Cora Churcher! You look *ravishing*.'

Even the glass of champagne Bridget's offering isn't enough to summon Cora over the threshold. She can see herself on the back wall, two-dimensional, spotlit, exposed; muddy oil-slicks of paint lay bare the pouches of fat on her belly, the swagging on her upper arm. Last time she stood in public before her own portrait was at the launch of *The Golden Bones*. The bookshop had blown up the cover big as a poster.

'I can't,' says Cora.

'You can. *We* can. Come on, you big eejit.' She slips her arm through Cora's.

As she enters, Cora sees pity in their faces. Elinore has let herself go. The age difference between herself and Frank is really making itself felt. He's growing into his prime while she grows away from hers. Time was she could have had any man in a room like this. Now she feels mumsy next to Bridget, who has, of course, got it right. She's in a slinky dress with hair loose, her arms wound with slim gold jewellery that would look ridiculous on anyone else, as would the flat sandals with leather laces criss-crossed up to the knee, but Bridget looks like a Roman empress. There's something a little off about her, though: a bird-like, dart-ing gaze that doesn't seem to settle on Cora for more than a few seconds, and an excess of nervous energy: Bridget is literally steering her around the room.

Cora doesn't overthink it. She's happy to abdicate responsibil-ity for where she stands or who she talks to. People congratulate her on being part of such an important show. When their glasses run dry, Bridget goes to the kitchenette to fetch a bottle. Sid's having a fag on the fire escape, leaving his only waitress run off her feet, poor thing.

It takes Bridget an age to return. While she's twiddling the stem of her empty glass between her fingers, Cora meets the eye of a man she recognises but can't place.

'Remind me how we know each other?' she says.

His face darkens and she wonders why he's having such a strong reaction. Christ, she thinks, is he a Bonehunter? Has one of those sneaky bastards made it past us after all the work we did on the blacklist? She's about to find Marcelle or Harriet when the man clears his throat and says, 'We, er – I collected my wife from your house,' he says, nodding not at a woman but a portrait. Onyx skin, generous curves: it's got to be her, the one who turned up at the Vale a few years ago, begging Frank to take her back. Ad was it? Adeola?

'Ah,' says Cora. They had regarded each other across th step, the spurned wife and the cuckolded husband, a their mutual grief and shame so perfectly reflected that to look away. 'So nice to see you again,' says Cora, and stumbles blindly into the crowd, only to see Adeola in the perfect flesh. Fire-engine lipstick and close-cropped hair, she's laughing with another woman. This one's petite and wearing a lavender sari and Cora doesn't have to imagine what the drapes of fabric might be hiding because there's a full-front portrait of *her* on the far wall.

'I honestly think in two decades' time there'll be a Churcher room at the National Portrait Gallery,' says Adeola. 'There's already a real cachet to being one of his sitters.'

'Immortality at last,' says the little one.

'Not to mention *infamy*,' says Adeola, and the women laugh again.

It's validating for them, Cora supposes. Most of them are married and probably surprised by how much they miss the relentless objectification they complained about when they were young women. God knows Cora does. Christ, what wouldn't she give to move through the world in her twenty-one-year-old body again. Give her a week in that skin. Give her one night.

She rests her glass on a shelf and is confronted with all fifty-five years of her reflection. Her nose is shiny and her hair is starting to frizz. Chiffon was not the right choice of fabric for such a stuffy room and the sequins are too try-hard. She closes her eyes and thinks, I am part of the first generation of women who can really truly have financial independence and choose whom I marry and control if and when I have children and somehow I have ended up here, playing second fiddle to a man whose idea of good art is to flaunt his adultery. I am *one more* humiliation away from leaving him. I mean it this time. Champagne turns to acid in her empty ʃut. Glazed in sweat, surrounded by pity and painted flesh, Cora ʃurcher is losing her fucking mind.

69

Frank is livid. Is it too much to ask that his family make the right impression? There goes his embarrassment of a wife, flapping through the gallery like a bin bag on a breeze. Isn't it part of the marriage pact that you don't let it all go to shit? Some women can afford to be lazy but Cora can't, not at her age. She's not like Bridget, strings of lean muscle still taut on an impeccable frame.

As for Eleanor. It's wonderful that she came home of course, but she looks like she's just staggered out of some kind of New Age traveller convoy with the matted hair and the multitude of earrings, which is fine, no artist wants a conventional child, but she is actively defacing herself and it's not like she had Cora's looks to start with. She won't even *talk* to the admissions tutor from Goldsmith's.

Mind you, Dominic looks as though he's just strolled out of an accountancy convention, which is far worse.

Still, it's a good turnout. All the right journalists, old friends from the Slade. Two dozen *serious* buyers, hand-picked by Marcelle. Her ambition for *Intimacies* is fierce and strategic. It is vital not just that one's first collection sells, but that it is bought by the right collectors, people whose taste is both barometer and forecaster for the rest of the market. There's a problem with th exhibition catalogues – glossy brochures that Marcelle ordere great expense which still haven't turned up – but that r people are really being forced to *look* at the work.

And then of course there are the sitters. His models, b They have stepped from their frames and into their b and in many cases they are arm-in-arm with husb telling themselves that it's just a rumour, some cooked up for column inches. After trying for half his life to leave the gimmickry of *The Golden Bones* behind and create something that engineers a visceral reaction, here Frank is again, having created a puzzle to solve. He is out of fashion, he knows. He's heard that Saatchi's upcoming RA show has sharks in formaldehyde and Myra Hindley's face made out of children's handprints, and Tracy Emin's tent with the names of everyone she'd ever slept with, and next to the so-called Young British Artists he feels past it. But Marcelle reassures him that people will always love painting.

Frank cannot pass anonymously through this crowd, but the small talk he makes with the people Marcelle introduces him to is so repetitive – and adrenaline has him in such a state of receptiveness, almost superhuman – that he's quite able to catch the background chatter, even while he's talking himself.

'Is it almost *too* idiosyncratic?' says a woman in an asymmetric dress.

Her companion wrinkles her nose. 'You do wonder if it's tiptoeing into outsider art.'

Frank dies a little inside. So-called 'outsider artists' make a good living, some of them make a killing in fact, but they are not serious players. The museums and big galleries don't display them. They don't get written up in the broadsheets. They are not part of the narrative of contemporary art. Marcelle's talking about the Tate, and if tonight goes badly, that dream is over before it began. He fears accusations of backwards, or naïveté or, God forbid, whimsy, almost more than he fears obscurity.

'The years haven't been kind to Lal, have they?'

This is more like it, thinks Frank.

now. And to think that at college he was considered the real

ot so much.

sn't know why it matters so much to best Lal, but it

rs fiercely. He needs someone to dominate – you

Freud to work out that that's a reaction to having

a domineering father like the Admiral – but, crucially, that domination must be hard-won. Cora, for example, is no challenge. It has to be someone he respects, is awed by, almost. It has to be a fair fight.

And it's also why, after he and Lal had their bitterest row, Frank crossed the ultimate line.

Christ, he still can't believe his own daring.

He looks at her across the room, those curls tumbling down her back. He knows what that thick hair feels like in his fist. It gives him a hard-on just thinking about it. He's waiting for the shame to kick in, waiting for the guilt, but so far all he has is triumph.

He keeps it in his back pocket, like a lucky charm.

Lal wanders in the direction of the painting and for a moment Frank thinks *fuck, no*, because the power is in having the secret, but Bridget comes to lead him away. The look she gives Frank is enough to shrivel a man's balls.

She's noticed, then.

70

The tiny woman on the door of the Veasey Gallery holds Richard Reid's invitation up to the light. The card is not only numbered but also watermarked.

'Thank you, David. Enjoy the show.' She crosses a name off a list on her clipboard, unhooks the rope, and Richard is in.

He accepts a glass of champagne from a passing waitress and places himself between two mirrored pillars. Ever-decreasing Richards stretch into infinity and each of them looks like an absolute *arsehole*. The designer stubble and highlights in his hair are bad enough but the Kermit-green Armani suit – borrowed from one of his flashier cousins – is beyond the pale. The point is, he doesn't look like himself. (He doesn't look like David Levy, either, but he'll cross that bridge if he comes to it.)

So: which of these nuts should he try to crack? Maybe the younger generation will be amenable to his advances. That's got to be Eleanor Churcher with the fair hair and all the silver jewellery. Pretty girl, if not quite the knockout her mother was in her heyday. She's fighting what beauty she does have with the weird hair and the sack of a dress. Richard thinks of Cummins, just a few metres away, and his conscience pricks again.

At the back of the room, a door twitches open and – oh, *hello* – Jane Jones is in.

Richard darts behind a pillar. If she outs him as Velasco's minion he's out on his ear. He watches as Jane takes a disposable camera from her pocket and starts on a point-and-shoot spree. The flash draws attention. She elbows a couple out of the way of one of the smaller paintings.

'So sorry, if I could just . . .' she says as though she's tiptoeing past people in cinema seats. 'I just need to see the clues.'

As if by mutual agreement, the Lally girl, the Churcher boy and their friends form a human shield in front of Eleanor. The tiny woman from the front desk takes the situation in hand.

'I'll have that,' she says, taking the camera from Jane's hand and dropping it in an ice bucket. Marcelle takes the woman's other arm.

'My clues!' cries Jane. Richard actually feels sorry for her.

'There are no clues in here,' Marcelle tells Jane, as they guide her to the front door. 'And if you set foot in my gallery again, I'll have you arrested.'

Jane Jones takes her miserable place behind the plum velvet rope.

Chatter fills the room again. One thing you can say about this evening, thinks Richard, there's been plenty to gossip about, and it's not even nine o'clock. He does another sweep of the gallery and observes Rosaleen Lally, standing with her back to Cora Churcher's painting, her glass empty, her eyes wide and her mouth pulled tight in the undirected smile of someone surprised to find that she has nobody to talk to.

71

Dom watches Rose talk to some smooth operator in a baggy green suit. How can someone he's seen almost every day of his life still take his breath away? She looks like a woman tonight. The strappy vests and denim cut-offs she wears with him have been replaced by a designer dress and jewellery that's not made of cotton or leather. The guy she's talking to – what kind of knob wears a T-shirt with a suit? – looks at least thirty. Dom kicks the base of a mirrored pillar. How can he compete with that? The age gap between him and Rose is only three months but it put them in different school years, and it's always seemed to set her apart.

He's had girlfriends, of course. He was seeing girls while Nell was still locked up like Rapunzel. He pored over his parents' ancient copy of *The Joy of Sex* like it was the Oxford Entrance Exam, and he doesn't think it's big-headed of him to say he thinks he'd get a first class degree in shagging. Not that he's ever *made love*, as *The Joy of Sex* would have him call it. All he's been doing is shoring up as much experience as possible so that when he finally gets together with Rose, firstly, he'll be the best she's ever had, and secondly, she will be enough for him forever.

On a good day, he dares to hope that's what she's doing too; ractising until the real thing. Rose has had boyfriends who can e, boyfriends who were at university, and at least one was a ate with a job. She's even had an abortion (she didn't tell s; he overheard Bridget telling Cora about it). Dominic is d of being jealous of the guy who got her pregnant but he it. He and Rose tell each other everything. He knows pizza with anchovies for her and she knows not to

294

order it with pepperoni for him. They can make each other laugh without talking. When they made each other mix tapes to listen to on their school trips, they chose all the same songs. Sex is all that's missing.

'Hey, Dom-dom,' says a voice at his side. It's Nell's old school-friend Suzy. His friend, too, he supposes. There's a gang of kids their age who were part of the artistic circles their parents moved in in the eighties and who went – still go, in Dom's case – to the same school. 'Are we having fun yet?' she asks him.

'The night is young,' he says. 'Have you seen Nell?'

Suzy nods to the corner where Nell – and Rose, who appears to have shaken off Green Suit – are in conversation with a Britpop dickhead. The guy has a feathered haircut and a packet of ironic, working-class Lambert and Butlers tucked into his rolled-up shirtsleeve. He's leaning over Rose, one arm propped against the wall.

'Who's that?' Dom's voice comes out sharper than intended.

'That's Ben!' laughs Suzy. Is it? *Jesus.* Last time Dom saw Suzy's brother, he was wearing a fleece covered in dog hair. One year at university has transformed him. Was *he* the one who got Rose pregnant? 'Let me go and get her for you.' Suzy twirls away from Dom without specifying who she's gone to fetch and Dom tries not to be disappointed when Nell cuts through the crowd to him, a champagne flute in each hand.

'Is one of those for me?' Dom asks, although actually he's not sure he should drink much more tonight. Jealousy is mind-altering substance enough.

'Piss off,' says Nell. 'That waitress comes round about once an hour, you have to load up. No, I'm a twin-fisted drinker tonigh*' She clinks glasses with herself. 'Those guys outside are mak' me edgy as fuck. I should never have come home.'

'*No!*' He can see that Nell's taken aback by the force reply. He is, too. 'I mean, I'm glad you did. It's not the sa out you.' But it's too late. He has laid out his lonelin sister to see.

'I'm sorry, Dom. I hated leaving you. But you still had Rose.'

'Did I?' This time it's bitterness that leaks out without his permission. Nell looks to the far side of the room where Ben is making Rose laugh. When she throws her head back, her neck is long and impossibly white. Nell looks back at Dominic and sees straight into his heart.

'Whoa,' she says. He braces himself for the lecture, the one Cora's given him: don't get too close, you can't go back to being friends afterwards. But to his surprise Nell says, 'D'you know what, I like it.'

'*Really?*'

Years ago, before Nell left, he'd hinted to Suzy that he saw himself ending up with Rose. She'd wrinkled her nose. 'Kind of incestuous? Maybe just try to stop thinking about her that way.' The suggestion presumes that there are moments when Rose is not on Dominic's mind. That he makes a conscious decision to think about her, when she is in fact his default setting. Actually? He doesn't think about Rose, ever. He *feels* her, all day long. She is a feeling that is extraordinary, but so ever-present that he takes it for granted. To notice it would be like noticing blinking or swallowing.

But of course Nell gets it. 'I mean, at least you wouldn't have to explain . . .' She points her finger and draws a join-the-dots in the air between the various family members at the party. Her eyes shine. 'And then *I* wouldn't have to worry about some annoying girlfriend judging us. So selfishly, yeah. It makes perfect sense for me, which is what really matters. Do you want me to say anything?' She looks giddy, playful.

'Under no circumstances.'

He has to do this himself, or it doesn't count. Better keep it as easy than risk rejection. He has to wait, and trust that Rose there eventually.

72

At the meetings Bridget goes to for the families of alcoholics, they talk about the addict hitting a rock bottom. Lal keeps finding new layers of rock, and it looks as if he's just broken through to the lava beneath. Has he reached that tipping point where he doesn't know what he's doing? It could be now or an hour ago or seven o'clock tomorrow morning, and there's no way to tell from the outside whether it's even happened.

She gives him a soft drink in the hope that it'll dilute the booze. He spits it back in her face. 'What is this shit?'

'Elderflower pressé.' Luckily she's wearing black so it doesn't show, and she doesn't think anyone has seen.

'Tastes like piss. Have they no spirits?'

'You can slow down or you can go home.'

'And miss the speech? I don't think so. Hoo, no.'

Bridget is sure he hasn't seen the painting. She's been by his side all night, and the state Lal's in, he wouldn't be able to control his reaction.

The waitress offers to top up their glasses. Lal snatches the bottle.

'Easy, tiger!' says the waitress.

'Away to fuck!' Lal zigzags off, bottle in hand.

Bridget slips a fiver into the waitress's top pocket. Her expression of gratitude makes Bridget wish she'd given her a twenty. 'I'm sorry about that. Please try not to serve him any more – and if you could tell the other staff.'

'You're having a laugh, aren't you? What other staff? There's only me and Sid here.' There's something honest, something 'old London' about her accent that Bridget likes. 'Don't worry. I've handled worse.'

Erin Kelly

Frank and Lal glare at each other across the room.

Angry as Bridget is with Frank, as much as she wants to dash her glass to the floor and tell everyone everything, she realises that in showing the painting he has done her a favour. He has given her no choice but to extricate herself. From her husband, from the Churchers, from the whole sorry tangled co-dependent mess. After tonight, how can she pretend in front of Cora? For a man who doesn't believe in divorce, Lal has given her more than ample unreasonable behaviour. Lal will be her cover story, Frank the true reason. With clever accounting and a good lawyer she could probably afford a little two-up, two-down in Muswell Hill or East Finchley. One room for Rose, another for her. They don't need more than that.

Across the room, Dominic is slouching but still head and shoulders above the rest of them. Bridget's heart cracks for him. I'll miss you, son, she thinks, but not as much as you'll miss Rose. If you two got together she'd never want to leave you, and then we'll all be tied to Frank fucking Churcher forever.

73

'Enjoying yourself?' asks Marcelle.

'I'd like it better if there were some red dots on the wall,' says Frank.

He's trying not to do the sums in his head but it's irresistible. One small painting would cover Dom's school fees for the next two years. That triptych on the far wall would be enough to put Nell up in some digs for art school (he's invited the admissions tutor from Goldsmiths back to the house in the hope she sees sense before the night is over).

'I'm working on it,' says Marcelle.

Adeola walks past Frank and trails her long fingernails lightly across his bare forearm. Her husband shuffles behind her like a puppy that's been kicked in the face The guy clearly knows that Frank could have Adeola again with a click of his fingers. Strange how he doesn't want her any more. The magic evaporated as soon as the paint was dry. It was like that with all the women.

With one notable exception.

Out of one eye, Frank tracks Lal. He's really putting it away, but that's no bad thing, it means he's circling the kitchenette – so that he can intercept the waiting staff when they come out with a new bottle. And the kitchenette is diagonally across from *the* painting, about as far as two points within the gallery could be.

'He won't see it.' The voice behind him is as familiar as his wife's and brittle with the effort of control. 'I'll make sure of that In between babysitting your wife and keeping an eye on the kid What I *can't* work out is whether you want him to see it or no

He turns to face her. It's the closest they've been all night looks incredible. Even in flat shoes she's nearly as tall as he i bones run like copper pipes under spare flesh. She wears cheap gold wire jewellery like diamonds. 'I don't think you do want him to see it,' she ponders. 'I don't even know if you wanted me to see it. I think you're getting off on the *chance*. The *potential* for danger.'

He is surprised that Bridget has the measure of him quite so much.

'What I don't get is why you're trusting me not to say anything. The scandal would ruin you.'

They are locked in eye contact, two founts of incendiary knowledge around which ignorant bodies revolve. He leans close, lets his lips brush against her hair and says, 'You wouldn't do that to Lal and Rose.'

Bridget sways a little. Lal? Maybe, the way things have been. But Rose? Never.

She pulls away from Frank, disgusted.

They both know he is right.

They both know he has won.

74

Lal watches as Harriet and her sister – he didn't realise she was a twin – close the gallery door. As they weave towards him they merge into one woman, who separates into two and re-forms again twice on the way to the Ladies'. Lal is wondering if maybe he needs glasses – he's fifty next birthday, he's lucky to have got away without them for this long -- when a bang silences the gallery and he finds himself looking to its source with sudden-onset 20:20 vision.

The guy does not look like your average door-kicker-downer; he's pale and wispy, soaped to a shine and snappily dressed. But the threat he poses is real. It's Stuart Cummins, the scrote who hung around the courtroom and wrote letters to the mad bitch Ingrid. Lal has the focus of a laser. Where's Eleanor? He needs to put himself between Cummins and the girl. He sees her pressed against one of the mirrored pillars, out of Cummins's sightlines, terrified. Her friends – Rose, Suzy and Ben – are slowly forming a protective shield around her. Across the room, Cora's hands flutter to her throat, her gaze fixed on her daughter. Look *away,* you dozy bitch, thinks Lal. Your eyes are a fucking signpost.

'Eleanor?' says Cummins. Sweat glistens on his upper lip as he reaches into his pocket.

Lal springs into the action he's been itching for all evening. snatches the knife from the guy's hand, drops it to the floor kicks it across to the corner of the room. Women scream a swear. The blade cuts the stunned crowd in two before c a halt at the base of a pillar.

Lal gets Cummins in a headlock. 'You've mess wrong man, fella.' Just as he dials down the North he wants to get served, he turns it up to eleven when he wants to be feared.

'Please,' yelps Stuart Cummins, as Lal frogmarches him across the room. It's no effort. The more the guy struggles, the stronger Lal gets. He could snap his limbs off like twigs from a tree. 'I can't go back to Ingrid without a bone, she'll never forgive me.'

'I'll rip off your leg and you can give her that on a plate, how's about that?'

'The police are on their way,' says Sid.

'You sad wee fuck. Listen to me. *The Golden Bones* was fiction. A *game*. You need to get yourself a life.' He turns to the pavement, where the Bonehunters are a row of open mouths above the velvet rope. '*All* youse need to get a life. It's only a fucking picture book, for the love of God!'

Harriet comes out of the bathroom. All heads turn her way as the door swings behind her. It's like a stranger entering a bar in a Western. 'What?' she says, and the room has permission to speak again. Lal manhandles Cummins through a reedbed of whispers. *The Golden Bones, Ingrid Morrison, gold skeleton*, the guests are saying. *Nell, hip, Elinore, stalker, knife, treasure, Bonehunters*. All the words Frank wouldn't want to hear tonight, but Nell's safe and that's all that matters.

Outside, Lal throws the guy to the pavement and pins him there until the coppers arrive and arrest Stuart Cummins for carrying an offensive weapon.

'Attempted murder, more like,' says Lal, as they try to wrestle the guy into their squad car. Lal got him out here single-handedly but the police are doing it properly, that's their problem. All restraint this and by-the-book that. 'He needs manhandling,' he says, as they do that thing where they push him into the back the top of his head. A third officer bags up the knife and in an evidence bag which goes into the car boot, and his bear Cummins away. 'I love that girl like she was my 'Is after the car. 'Like she was my own,' he repeats to 's remained outside the gallery.

Lal dusts off his palms. He could do with a glass in his hand, to take the edge off the reception when he goes back in. He'll be hailed as a hero. All eyes are on him as he stands in the doorway, but before he can get a drink, before he's even fully inside, Frank has him by the upper arm. His grip is light, which seems to knock the wind out of Lal more than if he'd lamped him.

'Is Eleanor alright?' asks Lal.

'She's fine,' snarls Frank. 'What the fuck was that? Bringing up *The Golden Bones* here? Tonight?'

'*Me* bringing up the book? Jesus, I'm not the one who broke in with a knife talking shite about bones, Frank!'

'But you didn't have to *say* it. In front of these people? Jesus Christ, Lal. Don't you *ever* embarrass me like that again.'

He leaves Lal standing alone. His arms are jellied with adrenaline but the fists that dangle at from them are dense as iron.

Disembodied gossip floats from the other side of a pillar. 'I knew we'd have a bit of drama tonight but I wasn't expecting that,' says a man.

'Well, that's Frank and Lal for you, isn't it?' says a woman. 'Always cleaning up each other's messes.'

Not any more, thinks Lal. That was the last time.

75

At the centre of the scrum of teenagers, Dom holds on tight to Nell. He can feel his sister's fear coming through her skin like a fever. Her dreadlocked hair is rough as hessian tickling the underside of his neck, an itch that would normally be unbearable but is presently welcome because it means she's right where he can see her. Right where he can protect her.

When the police arrive, their little huddle collectively exhales and spreads out. Suzy speaks for all of them.

'I can't believe it's happened again.' She rubs her arms as though she's cold, even though the air in the gallery is warm and thick. 'My car's up the road. Let me go and get it; I'll drive her home.'

'It's OK,' Rose tells Nell. 'We've got you.'

Bridget is comforting Cora.

Frank is moving through the room telling people how relieved he is.

Neither of them have approached Nell directly.

Jesus *Christ*, thinks Dom. Who are the adults here?

76

The questions come at Frank like rapid machine-gun fire. 'Yes, a terrible shock. Oh, she's a resilient girl. Yes, he was on our radar but we didn't think he was dangerous, or we'd have . . . some kind of restraining order, yes.'

All the talk is about Eleanor and she's *fine*. Not a mark on her, and the kids have assembled like a troupe of teenage superheroes, creating a force field around her that Frank himself would not dare to broach. Obviously it was terrifying to realise how close Cummins came to her, but if the scuffle remains the focal point of the evening, then honest to God . . . the man might as well have papered the gallery walls with pages from *The Golden Bones*. He feels that Elinore has been in here, danced bloodied footprints across all the canvases, ruining them forever.

And as for everyone's favourite piss artist . . . Frank concedes that he might have *looked* inert when Cummins drew the knife but in fact he was thinking hard, working out how best to deal with the man *discreetly* when Lal went charging in, giving it the full Gerry Adams. Far from defusing the situation, Lal turned it into a bar-room brawl.

Marcelle has left the office door open and is ostentatiously yelling into her phone. 'We've got interest from the Sheikh. If Charles was interested you know I couldn't tell you, but . . . waiting list?' It would be impressive if she didn't have one finger holding down the hook. She's talking to thin air. 'You can, but he took on a handful of commissions as word got round about tonight, so you're looking at a good three years. But you're welcome to come and meet him, although again, the diary's filling up.'

She's trying to boost buyer interest but at the expense of Frank's confidence. What if no one buys a single painting?

He takes a moment in a corner to go over his speech. He's got it down to just a few key words on a single index card. It's a little near the knuckle but for Christ's sake, what's the point in him taking two decades to find his voice as an artist only to mince his words in the speech? It *has* to be uncompromising. And after that performance earlier, he's in no mood to spare Lal's feelings.

'Champagne?'

Frank glances up from his notes to see a tray of glasses at eye level. The hands holding it are calloused, the nails bitten and cuticles ragged. Frank pans down, takes in the body beneath – good tits, nice waist-to-hip ratio, thick ankles which is a shame – before shooing her away with a 'No, thank you.'

'You sure, Frank? You look like you could do with it.'

It's a rough-around-the-edges voice that his body, at least, recognises: sweat springs from nowhere to plaster his shirt to his back. He's as damp as if someone had thrown a bucket of water over him. 'And if you don't now, you will in a minute.'

The tray is lowered, and Frank Churcher looks into the wide blue eyes and gap-toothed smile of Verity Winship.

77

Lal is making progress towards the waitress when Marcelle tinkles a fork on a glass and a chorus of 'Speech!' goes up. Frank climbs on to a stool and the crowd condenses around him. Lal is borne forth on a wave of bodies, about as far from the next drink as he could be without leaving the gallery.

Hip flask, he thinks. He should've brought a hip flask.

'You're standing on my foot!' says the woman behind him.

'Sorry, darlin'.' He shuffles forward, loses his balance, and for a second it's only the crowd that's holding him upright.

Lal sees Frank as a blur, a kind of Impressionist version of himself. It must be the heat in the gallery affecting his eyesight. It's awful close in here.

'Thank you so much for coming,' begins Frank in his officer-class voice, and the gallery falls silent. 'It's especially heartening to see that oil on canvas can still draw a crowd. I had worried about the lack of animals floating in formaldehyde or outsize pictures of serial killers here tonight.' The crowd laugh. 'Although perhaps my work shares common ground with a certain piece of camping equipment.'

The wave of laughter turns to gasps and someone whispers *I cannot believe he said that*. It takes Lal a beat or two to join the dots and, when he does, Mother of *God*. Frank means Emin's *Everyone I've Ever Slept With* tent. What a kick in the tits for Cora. Bad enough that she has to endure one infidelity after another, but for Frank to play it for cheap laughs? Lal's hands ball themselves into fists. Sometimes you spend all your violence with the first punch, but sometimes it flows like beer at a free bar, and it looks like tonight it's the latter.

Frank waits for the whispers to die down before continuing. '*Intimacies* is, of course, a collection of portraits. I've known since I was a boy that there was a photographic element to my painting, that I could capture a likeness. What I've done here is to go beyond likeness and into *truth*. To express with a different kind of brushstroke the essence of the human condition and set it alongside a more conservative, surface way of painting . . .'

On he goes. All heads are tilted his way, listening with misty-eyed adoration, the way people get during the father-of-the-bride speech. Lal feels a belch rise and clamps his lips closed, but the belch has other ideas. As the acrid gas of Laurent-Perrier and stomach acid escapes, a little moat of floor space appears around him.

'And what a liberation it's been at the age of forty-nine finally to make art for art's sake,' says Frank. 'I mean, illustration – can it ever be more than juvenilia? Pictures to explain text? You might as well be working at an advertising agency. Fine art on the other hand is an idea, a concept, brought to life.'

He might as well have hung neon arrows above Lal's and Cora's heads. Lal is used to Frank denigrating his 'little Celtic doodles'. But to flaunt his promiscuity in front of Cora and now to shit on *her* work as well? She's holding her head high, is Cora, rolling her eyes, *silly old Frank*, which is almost worse than if she'd started crying. Lal remembers that old story about Lucian Freud keeping a pane of window glass in his studio and deliberately piling increasing weight on it, curious to find its shattering point. It occurs to Lal that Frank is doing the same to Cora. His blood rises to a rolling boil.

'Prick.' In Lal's accent, the word is a dropped bomb. There's a ripple of nervous laughter. Lal stares a couple of people out. If they want to start something he's more than ready for them.

Then Bridget's fingers are cold on his arm, as though she can draw out the fury imperative with her touch. If only. If only.

'Not now,' she says. 'No more scenes. Have it out with him in the morning.'

Morning, as a concept, doesn't really exist for Lal right now. He is standing on the edge of a black hole, his night approaching the tipping point where he continues to act without laying down memories as he goes. When he is in this state there is only the present – there can be no past, because the past *is* memory. He shrugs off Bridget's hand, and on legs of rubber goes looking for that uppity little bitch of a waitress. If she tries to get between him and his glass again, he'll show her who's boss.

78

Frank barely registers the applause that follows his speech (which he thinks, on balance, he got away with). Verity is hovering. Regret is a physical feeling: a drag on Frank's internal organs. He should've invited her up when she doorstepped him at the studio that time – well, not invited her up, he'd had Sarita in his bed – but he could have gone downstairs, bought the girl her coffee, heard her out.

'There was a list,' he hisses. 'You were on a blacklist.'

'That was for guests, not staff.' She nods to Sid sweating over a corkscrew in the corner. 'Not that it would've made much difference. He doesn't even know my last name.'

The clapping turns into chatting. Conversations shift the bodies throughout the gallery, men and women swapping places and changing partners as smoothly as in a ballroom scene from a Regency drama. The arts critic from the *Sunday Telegraph* is making a beeline for Frank. He doesn't have long.

'Are you in cahoots with . . .' He jerks his head towards the Bonehunters outside.

'Nah. They gave me the idea that I was owed something but we're not in touch. Last picture they've got of me I'm like three years old.'

By unspoken agreement, he and Verity have decided to adopt tone and body language at odds with their words. She's leaning close to him, hand on her clavicle, classic flirting pose, and he finds himself smiling broadly at her. Even while panic sluices his insides, he takes a second to reflect that this probably looks good. Frank Churcher, down-to-earth, not above talking to the little people.

'Verity, we've been over this. I can't be responsible for your father's misinterpretation.'

'It's not my fault either, though, is it?' Verity smiles and flicks her hair over her shoulder. 'I grew up in care because of your book. I'd lived in twenty different places by the time I was sixteen. *You owe me that bone.* I deserve a bit of stability. And it's not like I've got anyone else to turn to.' Just for a second her voice cracks the façade of flirtation, but she recovers herself quickly, starts purring at him like a Bond Girl again. 'Frank. *Only you* can give me what I need.'

Instinctively he looks for Cora and finds her close by but oblivious, laughing with Harriet. The *Sunday Telegraph* is making slow progress, thank Christ. Frank steers Verity away from the mêlée so that her back is against one of the pillars. The girl's got lovely colouring: the same apricot-jam hair as Botticelli's *Venus*, pink lips and the kind of skin tone that usually signifies rosy nipples. In different circumstances . . .

'Frank. There's a bond between us whether you like it or not. I don't think it's something either of us wants out in the open . . .'

No. Frank certainly does not. *The Golden Bones* has already intruded upon tonight once. He will do anything – *anything* – to stop the book coming up again. He has cash in his studio, a couple of grand that Cora doesn't know about. That'll shut the girl up for tonight, at least.

'We're having an afterparty back at my place.' He gives her the address. 'Don't come to the front door: there's a gate in the back garden that I can slip out of. I will try my best—'

'I'll wait for you,' she says. 'All night, if I have to. I'm staying on a friend's sofa; it's not as if anyone'll notice if I never go home.'

'Frank!' The *Sunday Telegraph* holds out his hand. 'What a bloody triumph. Listen, I'd love to know about . . .'

It's the kind of conversation Frank has been waiting to have for twenty-five years: an exchange of ideas, rigour and regard in equal measure. They ping-pong on the meaning of art, his process, whether, given the influence of art history, any painter can ever *truly* begin with a blank canvas. When that journalist has gone, there's another behind him asking if she can grab a quick word. Verity Winship and her tray of glasses are nowhere to be seen.

79

When he has seen Nell and a handful of their friends safely into Suzy's car, Dom excuse-mes his way through the press of bodies, the mirrored pillars making a house of fun that is anything but, fucking with his sense of direction, and it's by accident rather than design that he finds himself within striking distance of Frank. He's talking to the waitress and something in their intensely locked eyes and their body language waves a red flag. Dom retreats unseen to the far side of the pillar and picks out their words under the hubbub.

'Only you can give me what I want,' says the waitress throatily, and Dom goes cold, as she continues. 'We have a bond, whether you like it or not.' Her voice is husky – she's actually very sexy, in a rough-around-the-edges sort of way. And then – Dom cannot believe this – they make a rendezvous. At his own party, held in the house where his wife and children live, Frank is going to nip out on to the Heath for a shag with the bloody cocktail girl.

Dom has never lost his temper with Frank and maybe that's part of the problem. He should've started talking back to him a few years ago, calling him out when he made his little digs at everyone, but the son's acquiescence to the bullying father had become their dynamic. Dom visualises himself shouldering his way through the crowd where his father is deep in conversation with some chin-stroker in a corduroy suit, felling Frank with a single punch, and ruining this whole creepy, tawdry exhibition.

Instinctively he scans the crowd for his mother. Cora is mercifully out of earshot, shiny-faced and laughing far too loudly at something Harriet is saying. Nothing's *that* funny. Dom makes it his mission to stick to her like glue for the rest of the night.

'Are you coming?'

Dom turns to find Rose tugging at his sleeve. She sets off the usual flare inside him. How, *how* can such a powerful attraction not transmit itself to her? 'Suzy says there's room for you in the Mini – if you don't mind me sitting on your lap?'

The thought of having Rose sitting on his lap almost makes him lurch towards her. The thought of Rose sitting on *Ben*'s lap sends him into a panic. But Cora's his *mum*. And he can't break his promise of moments ago, even if it was made only to himself.

'You're alright,' he says thickly. 'I'll catch you up later.'

80

Bridget has kept Lal away from the painting all evening but naturally her eyes have been on Nell and the kids for the last few minutes, and he's given her the slip. She searches the party for her husband. He's not in the Gents', or the kitchenette, or in the corridor between the gallery and the fire escape. As a last resort she tries Marcelle's office. Red wine rings on the white desk smudge at the touch of her finger so someone's been here recently, but it's empty now.

It's cool and quiet; Bridget allows herself to take a breather. Her eyes roam around the room: paperwork and portfolios. No sign of *The Golden Bones*. Bridget takes a tissue from a box, wipes the spilt wine before it can stain and drops it into the wire wastepaper basket, where it settles on top of a crumpled letter, a pink lotus floating over a white one.

Bridget isn't snooping but she's a writer, she absorbs words whether she wants to or not, and she can't help but take in the letterhead and the first paragraph.

In an instant, she understands how to take the painting out of circulation forever.

She picks up the receiver and punches a long number into the phone. It will show up on Marcelle's bill, of course, but that won't be through the letterbox for a good month, and, if Bridget's plan works, this will merely be the first of countless calls to and from this number.

81

The line of well-wishers seems never-ending. Next up is a white guy about Frank's age in those oversized glasses with heavy black frames that all the media wankers are wearing at the moment.

'Dean,' he introduces himself. 'Lucy Fincham's husband.'

It takes him a few seconds to place Lucy. Natural blonde. Caesarean scar. Never came despite Frank's best efforts and didn't bother pretending to, which felt like bad form. She was a good conversationalist, though. He remembers now her telling him that her husband was a serious collector. Owns a Basquiat, a couple of early Frank Bowlings.

'Good to meet you,' says Frank, as Dean pumps his hand a little too aggressively.

'Likewise, likewise. Frank, I want to buy the portrait of my wife.'

I want to buy. Until that moment, he never knew how beautiful those four words could be. *I want to buy.* An infusion of love for Dean Fincham fills Frank's veins. Whatever else happens tonight, he will have sold a painting to the right kind of collector.

'Well, that's great,' says Frank.

'It would be, if some other bastard hadn't beaten me to it.' Dean points to Lucy's portrait and Frank sees that something wonderful has happened. There is a little red sticker next to it. And the one beside it. He turns a slow circle. There is a little red sticker next to every painting in his eyeline. The sticker is part of a sheet from W.H. Smith's, each dot costing a fraction of a penny but representing tens of thousands of pounds.

He looks around for his agent. She is there with a mile-wide smile and a sticker sheet, empty but for three dots in the bottom left corner. Frank does not dare to think what this means for his collection: instead his mind goes *dot-dot-dot*, Morse code for the letter S, and he begrudges the Admiral's inevitable trespass into the moment.

'It's a sellout,' Marcelle confirms. 'A pre-empt.'

Thoughts of the Admiral disappear. Frank forgets he ever had a father. His mind bulges with questions. Who and how and when and how much?

'What, even Lucy?' asks Dean, although he of all people should know what a sellout means.

'Congrats, Frank,' says Marcelle and then, out of the side of her mouth, 'We'll have a debrief in a bit. Got some disappointed collectors to manage.'

'But it's my *wife*.' Dean Fincham is indignant, as though her image is somehow a piece of intellectual property that only he may own. You'd think a collector at his level would understand that Frank has made Lucy *his*. That he possesses these women in a way their husbands never will.

'I'm sorry, Dean. The good news is that Frank's taking commissions.' Marcelle leads him by the elbow and drops her voice conspiratorially. 'Let me see if I can bump you to the front of the queue.'

Frank approaches his painting of Cora. The starting point for this picture was the mole on her hip: sable brushes, a finish smooth as satin that contrasts with the ruthless broad strokes he used to evoke the texture of her thighs. He touches the little red circle beside it with his forefinger and presses it as if it's a magic button. And in a way, it is.

Frank's joy is pure as white sugar. It sets his teeth on edge.

He has sold out. He has fucking well sold out.

82

The young people – apart from the Churcher boy – left through a back door before Richard had a chance to talk to them. About twenty of them piled into a Mini Cooper as if it were a clown car, its chassis scraping the asphalt as it climbed Haverstock Hill. He's edging towards the exit himself – time to call it a night – when a fork tinkles on glass and the room falls silent for the second time that evening. This time all eyes are on Marcelle Veasey.

'I'm thrilled to say that the entire exhibition has been pre-empted by a private collector.' Hushed gasps precede a smatter of applause. The buyers eye each other suspiciously. 'I know there are a lot of disappointed buyers here tonight, but Frank is taking commissions. In the meantime, please, have another drink and feast your eyes on these paintings, because there's no telling when they'll be shown in public again.'

Opposite Richard, Bridget Lally breaks into a jubilant smile. Richard's always found her a bit angular and square-jawed for his liking, but for a moment she looks beautiful; delight for Frank has turned her into a young girl. Richard wonders just how close they really are.

Jane Jones is no longer outside the front of the gallery. What feels like instinct but is of course experience sends Richard to the fire exit, the site of her last breach. He presses the bar carefully, braced for an alarm, and when it doesn't come he pushes it fully open. A security light blinks on to show him a back alley, dumpsters, lock-up garages, a motorbike and a couple of cars, empty tins of cooking oil from the restaurant next door.

The waitress from the party is smoking on the short metal staircase.

'D'you want one?' Her accent is what Richard's dad would've called real cor-blimey. She raises an open pack of Marlboro Lights. One cigarette has been turned upside-down.

'No, thanks, love.' Richard does have the occasional cigarette when he needs to earn a fellow smoker's confidence, but the other day he found himself craving one at his desk. He's sworn off them for a month – let the nicotine leave his system. He'd make an exception if he thought it could land him a really good contact, but this girl's nobody in the grand scheme of *The Golden Bones*.

'You enjoying yourself, are you?' she asks.

'Ah, yes,' he says. 'Just came out for a breather.'

Even in the dark this girl's blue eyes bore into him. She *knows* he's not one of them.

A clattering sound makes them both jump. There's a shifting of shadows in the alleyway, just beyond the range of the security light. Richard flashes back to Stuart Cummins's earlier lunge at Eleanor Churcher. Who's to say he was working alone? The police officer only has the front entrance covered.

'Is anyone there?' he asks. He doesn't want to make an enemy of a Bonehunter.

'Oh, it's you,' says Jane Jones, stepping out of the shadow.

Richard takes a moment to congratulate himself on his prescience.

'I don't suppose you could get me one of the exhibition catalogues?' she says. 'I saw them being delivered ten minutes ago; they can't have run out yet. It doesn't seem fair that only the chattering classes get a chance to see them, whereas the rest of us – those who've devoted our lives to the search – don't get a look-in.'

'What the hell' – Harriet's voice carries from behind him – 'are you doing back here? Go on, piss off.'

'You know where to find me,' says Jane, then scuttles away.

'Piss *right* off,' says Harriet, 'before I have you nicked as well. Go on.' Jane's footsteps fade to nothing.

Richard turns back to the gallery. 'I wouldn't stay out here on my own,' he says to the waitress. 'Some dodgy people outside.'

'Some dodgy people inside an' all,' she says, but she grinds out her cigarette on the metal step and follows him back into the party.

Richard does one more slow circuit of the room, ears half-heartedly pricked for *Golden Bones* intel, before leaving. On the way out, he slips an *Intimacies* catalogue under his voluminous suit jacket, for his own benefit, not for Jane Jones. Well, not *yet*. You never know when you might need a bit of Churcher merch to exchange with a Bonehunter for information.

His car is parked a couple of blocks away, as is his habit on a job. He turns the key in the driver's door of his two-year-old Vauxhall Astra. When the light over the rear-view mirror comes on, he catches his reflection and thinks *arsehole* again. First thing in the morning he'll go to the Turkish barber, get a hot towel shave and get this bouffant hair buzzed off. About the only good thing about his failure to make any meaningful conversation with the family is that none of them would recognise him if they saw him again.

83

When she learned that Velasco had fallen for it, Bridget was so relieved that she couldn't stop smiling. She'd caught sight of herself in the mirror, grinning manically, but physically hadn't been able to relax her cheeks.

That was a nice, what, ninety seconds of peace before she remembered the catalogues: high-resolution prints of each picture. They arrived late and have only just been unboxed, but enough have been distributed that the picture will be at large.

Now that people are leaving, they'll be taking them away. The unmasking is inevitable after all.

She has to act quickly. She picks up a catalogue that's been discarded on a ledge and approaches Marcelle.

'I feel like we should get these out of the way,' she says.

Marcelle nods her approval. 'Artificial scarcity. Only adds to the buzz.'

So, while Frank is giving an interview, she and Marcelle and Harriet work the room, gently asking people to surrender their catalogues. 'It's for Eleanor,' Bridget says. 'We can't be too careful, given what's just happened. Anything that fuels the fire . . .'

The guests hand them over in a flurry of *God, of course*s and *how's she doing*s and *we thought that had all died down*s.

'Thank you so much for understanding,' says Bridget as the incriminating volumes pile up in her arms. At the fire escape, she finds Sid scowling into the dark.

'Don't suppose you've seen my bloody waitress?' he asks.

'Sorry.' Bridget shakes her head. 'I need to get rid of these.'

She tips the catalogues into the industrial dumpster and, when she's done, her heart soars to see the Chinese restaurant next door throw in filthy packaging and food waste to cover her tracks. On her return, she sees Marcelle and Frank having a hushed, tense conversation in the office. Has Marcelle seen . . . ? Well, what if she has? Her loyalty is to her commission.

The gallery has pretty much emptied out as everyone heads back to the Vale for the afterparty. Should it even be happening, after the attack on Nell? Dominic, clearly thinking the same thing, is enlisting a handful of the guys' old friends from the Slade to take turns on the door at the Vale. *Bless* him. He seems to have been relatively sober tonight, so hopefully he'll get both Lal and Cora home without incident. The main thing is that her husband isn't behind the wheel.

She unhooks her jacket from the coat-stand but, when she puts her hand in her pocket, she finds that the car keys are gone.

A tremor rocks Bridget. When Lal's on a bender, his fists are weapon enough. Behind the wheel, in the mood he's in, the amount he's drunk, it's like letting a sniper loose. She wraps her jacket around her and heads into Hampstead village, looking in the narrow English streets for an old American car with an out-of-control Irishman at the wheel.

84

Lal tosses the car keys from hand to hand and drops them.
   Sold out
   Fallen under the car fuck's sake
   Christ Frank's going to be *unbearable*
   Oof. The old knees aren't what they were
   Unbearable and fucking *minted*
   Takes a couple of goes to get the key in the ignition
   'A certain piece of camping equipment' what a *cunt*
   The empty bottle of champagne rolls in the passenger
footwell
   Actually a *better* driver after taking a drink, more relaxed
   Bad enough the women in his house trying to control him but
as for that little bitch of a waitress, the fucking cheek of her
   Mirror signal manoeuvre
   Handles *beautifully*
   Wrestling
   Gossip wrestling with—
   Poor wee Nell, such a shame
   Red
   A knock on the window
   'Are you sure you're OK to drive there – oh, it's *you*.'
   Amber
   A body slides into the passenger seat
   Green
   St Christopher swings from the mirror, silver and blue

85

Smoke hangs in a pall in the centre of the gallery. It's just Frank, Marcelle, Harriet, and Sid chasing fag butts and little slivers of gold from champagne caps around the floor with a wide broom.

'We've made the social pages as well as the cultural one,' says Marcelle. 'The party's going to be in the *Standard*, in Londoner's Diary. I've taken the stance of "neither confirm nor deny" with the arts journalists but they're speculating about the big names; the Geffens, the Zabludowiczes, the Cohens, Niarchos . . .'

Even as she speaks, Frank is taking apart the sentence. If *any* of those collectors had bought a piece, she would be trumpeting it from the rooftops. His earlier joy begins to congeal.

'Marcelle,' he says, both wanting and not wanting to know the answer; both knowing it and not knowing it already. 'Who bought my show?'

'The most important thing is that he *is* a serious collector and you absolutely need to trust me when I say that I believe this is, long term, a good thing for your career. Fritz Velasco exceeded the asking price by twenty-five per cent.'

'I'm sorry,' says Frank. 'For a moment there I thought you said you'd sold the work that was supposed to redefine me as an artist and set me free from *The Golden Bones* to the guy who's *obsessed* with it.' Something inside him has broken loose and is spinning out of control. 'You only took delivery of the catalogues this evening. You can't have FedExed one to Manila already. You're not telling me he made a pre-empt on the basis of a *fax*?'

Marcelle blinks behind huge red glasses: waits for him to get there on his own.

'He bought it blind,' says Frank. He had been a fool to think he could extricate himself from the book. Velasco's purchase is not a reflection on the work. It's simply a gesture of, what – spite? Ownership? Frank poured his soul into those portraits and they were bought by a man who never even laid eyes on them. Why would he – oh, no. Of course. Of *course*.

First Cora staggering about the party like the Wife of Bath, then Verity fucking Winship and now Fritz bloody fucking sodding Velasco. Will he ever be free? He knows he's no angel but seriously, what's he done that's so bad that everyone is out to ruin his career?

'Marcelle.' Frank sees himself reflected in her lenses, the room behind him bent out of shape. 'I'm going to ask you a question and I want you to answer me honestly. Has Velasco bought into the notion that these paintings are somehow an extension of *The Golden Bones*? Clues, if you will?'

To her credit, she doesn't bullshit him, just comes straight out with it. 'It didn't come from me. And there's no need to get all morose. There's a real buzz in the room. People are already excited about what you're going to do next. You've got enough commissions to last you the next two years. Frank, you're rich again.'

'And I guess you more than broke even too.' He is horrified to hear a sob in his voice. 'I thought you had faith in my *painting*.'

'It's my job to sell your work.' Marcelle is unrepentant. 'Also: in the long run you don't want to get a reputation as someone who just paints pictures of women he's fucked.' Her words pierce as only the truth can. 'I've spun this so you'll become a serious portrait painter, OK? It's kind of in your favour that the pictures don't see the light of day. Get this collection out of the way, it becomes kind of legendary, but you move on. Trust me. Not having these paintings exhibited is a good thing.'

She looks him in the eye so directly that for a moment he thinks, shit, she *knows*. She knows what that painting means, its terrible power, and this is her way of telling him she's got it out of the way. He waits for her to challenge him on it. He knows, at least, that their working relationship will survive. Marcelle is a shark in shoulder pads.

Harriet's at their side, a crate stamped with the Laurent-Perrier logo in her arms. 'There's a couple of dozen bottles left over. Thought we'd take them back to the Vale.' She nods to a further three boxes on the table behind her. 'Make yourself useful, Frank.'

Marcelle says nothing about *the* painting. Is this her poker face or does she genuinely not know? There is no way for Frank to find out.

He loads the clanking boxes into the boot of Marcelle's car but declines the offer of a lift. 'You go and get the party started. I'll walk.'

'You're not *sulking,* are you, Frank?' asks Marcelle.

'I'd just like to clear my head. It's only ten o'clock. Most of Cora's parties don't even get started till eleven.'

He does walk, but once Marcelle has driven past him he doubles back on himself and walks the perimeter of the Heath to Gospel Oak. In his studio, he unlocks a filing cupboard and pulls out the top drawer where he keeps cash, a credit card, condoms and lube. Cross-legged on the day-bed, he counts out just under a thousand pounds in twenties. That should keep Verity quiet – and keep talk of *The Golden Bones* at bay – for the rest of the evening, at least. The more he thinks about it, the angrier he is with her. As if he didn't have enough people conspiring to trap him in his past tonight!

There's a stack of fresh canvases stacked against the wall, hundreds of pounds' worth of supplies. Frank takes his craft knife and slices into them. Fuck Marcelle, fuck Velasco, fuck Verity, fuck Lal, fuck 'em all. When the frenzy dies down they are mummies' bandages hanging from wooden squares. He thought he'd feel better afterwards, but if anything it's galvanised his anger. He throws the knife to the floor in disgust and pockets the roll of twenties. He takes the shortcut back across the Heath, his tread heavy as he passes late-night lovers in the bushes. At the Vale, the champagne will be flowing but the aftertaste will be bitter.

PART FOUR

86

I wake up with a thick head and red wine clots in the corner of my mouth. It comes back to me in flashes.

Police station.

Fixing my bike.

Getting the call from Dom.

Coming home to blood and broken glass.

Recognising Bridget in Frank's painting.

I feel a lurching sensation even though the boat is still.

I sit up in bed. Now, with sunlight blasting through the windows, I realise how much glass I missed in the clean-up operation. The catalogue is still on the worktop, surrounded by a million tiny jewels. The rug glitters like tinsel and there's a smear of blood on the tiles. I put on my slippers then attack every corner of the boat with the hand-held vacuum.

The noise wakes Billie up.

'Let me,' she says. 'It's the least I can do.'

'It's done now,' I say, putting the vacuum back on to charge. I throw the hatch open. It's a cold, crisp day. The water is looking-glass smooth. The reflected wharf creates a parallel world of underwater luxury flats. I imagine mermaids in designer clothes swimming from their windows.

'I'll pay you back. Out of my cattery money.'

Six months ago I'd have said don't worry, that that's her money, but Rose says teens respond to boundaries. 'We'll go halves on it,' I say. It seems to reassure her.

She starts to redress the ancillary damage: hooks the fairy lights back over the stove, turns the spice jars so all the labels are facing the right way. She finds the curling Post-it with HONESTY HIDES TRUTH'S BONES IN KING'S CHASE scrawled on it and asks, 'What's this?'

'Oh, just some clue the Glemhams showed me when they were here the other day.'

'The ElinoresArmy people? When were you talking to *them*?'

'You were at Kenza's. They tracked me down.'

'Fuck!' she says, and then. 'Sorry.'

'It's OK, I think that warrants a *fuck*. They freaked me out too at first, but d'you know what? I think they're on the level.' Not so on the level that I'm going to share the catalogue with them. I smooth out the Post-It, only for it to coil in on itself again. 'Anyway, that's what they wanted to show me. Some Bonehunter reckoned it was – let me get this straight – an acrostic, that turned out to be an anagram, on an old newsletter. It's probably bollocks.'

Her face assumes its 'thinking' expression, the one I see when she's studying.

A croak and a peep at the hatch tells me there are moorhens outside. 'Hello, you,' I say to the family who've swum up to the hull. Delicate black waterbirds with red crests, moorhens are half the size of the ducks and swans and often get shoved aside. I chuck a good handful of feed into the water and watch them peck, taking a moment to love the way I live. When all this is over, I'll never take any of it for granted again.

A text from Dom interrupts my moment of gratitude.

Can you get on Zoom in five? The usual link. Leslie's got an update.

It feels weird clicking the same link we used over lockdown to do virtual birthday toasts and quizzes to find out what's happening in a real-life murder case that somehow involves our fathers. Billie sits next to me and fiddles about with the filters until the cuts on her face are polished out.

'We look like *androids*,' I say, marvelling at my pearlescent cheeks, my uncreased brow.

The Skeleton Key

'Better than the reality,' she replies, gingerly touching a cut on her chin.

One by one, the squares appear. Leslie, clean-shaven and suited, in front of a case full of leatherbound books. Dom and Rose in Dom's man-shed-office that's nicer than most people's houses. Bridget and Cora in their separate kitchens. Marcelle at the London flat, a cat dozing on a window ledge behind her. I imagine pinning lengths of string between them, making a spider diagram the way they do in police investigations, only instead of linking their movements the lines would tell me who knows what. Who knows about Bridget and my dad? Who knows about the painting? When did everyone find out?

I'm certainly not going to mention the painting on Zoom. If I'm going to throw this grenade, it'll be into a room of live bodies.

'Looks like we're quorate,' says Leslie. 'Easier to update you all in real time. No charges have been brought but I'll be honest with you, the evidence is stacking up. The police found letters from the victim to Frank – not threatening as such, but asking for money, which could give him a motive for wanting her gone, and of course they have Lal on video apparently attacking her. They seem to be building a case for joint enterprise.'

'Jesus,' says Bridget. 'So if there are letters from the victim – they know who she was?'

'We have a name,' says Leslie. 'Not yet released to the press as still no next of kin traced. She was called Verity Winship. Daughter of – well, you can work it out.'

There are two or three seconds of what could be stunned silence or a bad connection. Then Dom and I say *Shit,* at the same time. That little kid with the unisex bowl cut in the photo. I never knew her name, tried to avoid reading the details of Winship's death.

'What was—' says Rose. 'What was she doing *working* at the party? It can't have been a coincidence.'

Leslie speaks even more carefully than usual. 'It seems she bribed Sid's usual waitress to call in sick, then offered herself as a replacement, to get access to Frank. Clearly she was determined that they meet. Er . . .' Leslie glances down at his desk. 'A specialist lip-reader transcribed their conversation and they were arranging a rendezvous later that evening. Since she was last seen at the gallery – she didn't collect her wages or return to the place she was living – the police are working on the assumption that she met her death that evening.'

'Who reported her missing?' I ask. 'Sid?'

'Well, no. He didn't want to get into trouble for employing staff off the books, although he says he did worry. Reckons he kept her wage packet for her for the best part of a year. She was eventually reported missing by her late foster mother – apparently they met every Christmas.'

Billie goes rigid beside me. 'She was fostered?' she asks Leslie.

'Yes. She'd had rather a peripatetic lifestyle after her father died. Bounced around from home to home, it seems.'

I reach for Billie's hand. We are hearing a different story from the rest of them. We're hearing that the dead girl was only a care-leaver, no one to love or look after her. I give her hand a squeeze that I hope conveys, *this will never be you, you have a family now*.

'Anyway, her DNA was on file; she'd left a hairbrush with the friend she'd been staying with. The DNA from the pelvic bone was too degraded for a match, but they retrieved some from her tooth pulp, once they had the skull, and the match was as close as it gets. And that, together with the letters and the footage, shone the spotlight on Frank.'

'So if they'd never found the rest of the skeleton they'd never have known it was her?' says Dom. I can tell by the furrow in his brow what he's thinking: if Marcelle hadn't insisted on including footage of that night, the police would never have seized the VHS and they'd never have seen Lal attacking Verity and the guys would never have been arrested.

Leslie clears his throat. 'Not necessarily. They would have made the connection between a missing girl linked, however loosely, to your father in the end. They would have pursued that. And there's other evidence, although they haven't disclosed that to me yet.'

I ask the question no one else has. 'Leslie, is there – are they just totally disregarding the idea that this is a stitch-up by Bonehunters?'

'I know that's what you want to believe, Nell. We all do. But there's simply no hard evidence to link anyone in the treasure-hunting community to the murder. But, look, Frank and Lal still haven't been charged, and that's significant. My parallel investigation is ongoing. All is not lost.'

He Xs out of the chat and the squares rearrange themselves. Billie appears to have zoned out; she's scrolling through her phone with one hand and doodling on a pad with the other.

'I mean . . . all sounds *quite* lost,' says Rose, her chin weighing on her cupped hand. The sound of Aoife wailing comes from some distant room. 'For fuck's . . . I'm coming, sweetie!' And she's gone in a blur of curls.

'This one sounds like a two-parent job,' says Dom, as the noise escalates. 'Let's catch up later.' His living room lurches as he shuts his laptop.

'Will I come over?' asks Bridget, but he's already gone. She leaves the meeting and for a moment it's just me and Marcelle, and Cora.

Cora clears her throat. 'Marcelle. On the *Intimacies* night. Does anyone else apart from Harriet *know* that there's a gap in Frank's evening?' she says.

The ensuing silence swells like a fattening drop of water. We all know what's not being said here. Cora is asking Marcelle to alibi Frank for the night of Verity Winship's murder.

Marcelle's eyes dart around behind her glasses. She reaches for her cat and strokes it while she thinks.

'If it contradicted something Frank has already said . . .' she says eventually, 'it could well do more harm than good. I think I'm of greater value as a character witness if I don't have a perjury charge hanging over me.'

It's a typical Marcelle answer: diplomatic but self-serving.

'Of course,' says Cora. 'I'm being ridiculous, I was grasping at straws, forgive me.'

'Forget about it,' says Marcelle. 'None of us is thinking straight.'

I can't shake the feeling that, if Marcelle had said yes to covering for Frank, she and Cora would be cooking up a story right now. Does that mean they think Frank is capable of this?

And if they'd gone ahead with it – what would that have meant for Lal?

When I close the laptop I feel a deep, physical exhaustion that can't just be explained away by a few bad nights' sleep. My limbs feel like wet sandbags. I let my head tip back and rest on the sofa for a few seconds. 'Whaaaat a shitshow.'

'Nell?'

There's a note in Billie's voice – tentative, scared, even – that snaps my head up and my eyes open. 'What's up?'

She glances down at the pad she's doodling on. Glimpsed from the corner of my eye they looked like meaningless swirls; now they coalesce into letters, barely legible sentences in looping handwriting. 'I had a play with that anagram thingy on the Post-it. Honesty hides truth's bones in King's Chase.'

'Oh, yeah?'

'Like you said, it could be bollocks. It's easy to find things like anagrams and acrostics even when they're unintentional.'

'But?'

'But to be honest means to be frank, right? And verity means truth? And your dad said Henry VIII used to hunt on the Heath, and chasing is hunting, right? It could be nothing, but it could mean . . .'

I finish the sentence for her. 'Frank hides Verity's bones on the Heath.'

87

The woman on reception – girl, really, she can't be much older than Oisin – is on the phone. 'Hello there, it's Rhiannon from N20 Associates, just chasing our invoice,' she says, in a singsong telephone voice very different from the one she used with me. 'If you could give me the sixteen-digit number on the card?'

I clear my throat. The look she gives me could turn milk.

'My name's—'

'Nell Churcher. I know.'

'So can I go in and see him?'

'Yeah.'

I've got a quip about Richard suing the charm school on the tip of my tongue but when I push the door I see him behind his desk, looking utterly despondent.

'What's happened?'

'He's let me go.'

'Who? Velasco?' The absurdity of the question puts a giggle in my voice.

'As of last night, I am no longer responsible for finding the last golden bone.'

'Crap.' I am momentarily shocked out of my self-pity. 'Does that mean he's got it?'

'That's the big question, isn't it?' he replies. 'He *says* he's got a better team on the case. That I've failed to carry out my duties. The terms of our contract say that if the jewel is discovered or he gets it some other way, he has to pay me a six-month retainer, but he can terminate the arrangement immediately if it's on the grounds of my incompetence.'

I sit on his desk and rest my feet on a spare chair. 'Do you buy it?'

'There *are* obviously bigger boys than me,' he says. 'Larger teams, better tech. But no one knows as much about this case as I do. No one else has got my contacts; no one else has three filing cabinets of paper turning yellow. Nah, I reckon he's got it. The jewel.'

'How?'

'I have no bloody idea.' He gathers himself. 'Anyway. It's not all about me. I'm so sorry about your dad, Nell. You must be in bits. What can I do?'

'If I tell you everything, I need you to promise you won't go public with it,' I say. 'I'm trusting you. God knows why, but I am.'

I tell him everything while he stays perfectly still, an ankle propped on the other knee. I tell him about my visit from the Glemhams, the fuss about the catalogue (aka the real reason I went into Lal's attic) and my concerns about Bridget.

'Your dad and Lal's wife?' he says.

'I *know*.' I shake my head and tell him about the King's Chase clue. 'I just want a way to make it all *fit*, Richard.'

His brown eyes shine; his voice is gentle. Somewhere in a cold corner of my heart, an old ember of our love emits a faint and dangerous glow.

'You want me to tell you Frank and Lal didn't do it. You want me to prove it's someone working with Stuart Cummins. Or any Bonehunter.' Even after all these years, he can still read me. 'It sounds to me like Lal had good reason to be angry with Frank, love. Everything you've told me makes it sound like this really was something close to home. I'm sorry. If I was a copper, I'd be working on the premise that it was joint enterprise back in the day, and then Lal lost his rag last week and did the switcheroo.'

'How does that fit with you being sacked by Velasco? Lal wouldn't have sold him the bone.'

'Wouldn't he?'

'It has to be a Bonehunter,' I say, close to tears, now. 'I *need* it to be them.'

'I'm sorry,' he says. 'It's really shit.'

An alert pings on his computer screen. 'That's telling me our old friend LetterstoIngrid's made a post. I suppose I can disable the alert now.' His hands hover over the keyboard, and then he lets them fall. 'Jesus. I don't know if I *can* leave this case alone. It's been my life.'

It feels as though either of us could dissolve into tears at any moment.

'How the hell . . . ?'

He turns his screen around so I can read it.

@LetterstoIngrid: Breaking! Velasco has sacked his private dick. Does this mean Elinore is finally at peace? We have a right to know!

'Who'd know that?' I ask him.

'No one,' he says. 'Let me check my computer for malware . . .'

He hits some keys and a security programme starts to run a scan.

'They're inferring that my being let go is definitive evidence that he's got the jewel.'

'Works for me,' I say. 'If they think the golden skeleton's all in one piece, that gets me off the hook.' I swivel the chair from side to side. 'I'm going to tell the Glemhams what's going on but ask them to keep it on the downlow till we know more.'

'Honestly, Nell, I don't know if I've got the energy.' He's deflating in front of me, a slow puncture that's painful to watch.

'I'll do it.' I bring up the text chain between me and Porter. His last message – *Nell, we're so sorry about your dad. We don't believe it was him* – was sent ten hours ago. It's still mid-morning here, so it must be the small hours there. I tap out a message.

*Hope you had a safe flight. Thought you should know that the
'scoop' on Velasco is that he sacked Richard Reid but he claims
to have hired another firm. That doesn't sound like the bone has
definitely been found to me, but until I can work out who's
behind these threats to me I'd like to keep those rumours going!
Sound OK? It would really help me out. N x*

In less than a minute, Porter's face is on my screen in the form
of an incoming video call. I hit the green button to accept.

'I'm so sorry,' I say, although he looks perky as ever. 'I presumed
you'd mute your phone at night. I didn't mean to wake you.'

'It's cool. I'm still on UK time. I was going to call you about
that exact post anyway.'

'You know how they found out?' Richard perks up.

'Sorry, no. Not the content. But the location. They slipped up.
They posted from a public connection. Soon as I get off the phone
to you, I'm gonna call the police and let them know.'

'You actually have a street address for LetterstoIngrid?'

'Well, like I said, it's a public IP, so it's just where they are now;
I doubt it's where they live. It's in London.'

'Oh, my God. Can you drop me a pin?'

Porter shakes his head. 'Nuh-uh. You'll go there and put yourself in danger.'

'More like, I'll know *not* to go there, and put myself in
danger.'

'I won't let her,' says Richard. I whip around to him.

'Excuse me, who made you my keeper? Seriously though,
Porter. Send me the location. I promise I'm done taking stupid
risks.'

'You're a hard woman to resist, Miss Churcher.'

I shrink Porter to a square in the corner of my screen and open
the Maps app when his message comes through. I laugh. 'Porter,
you're a genius but you're also a doofus.' He scrunches up his tiny
face. 'You've dropped a pin *here*. How did you even do that? Have
you got a bug in my phone?'

His frown deepens. 'I couldn't have – hang on, let me double-check.' His fingers fly over the keyboard so fast the accompanying sound is more like a prolonged whirr than a series of clicks. 'No, I'm right, Nell. That IP address is where LetterstoIngrid just posted at like nine a.m. London time, but because we moderate their posts it only went live fifteen minutes ago. I promise I'm not mistaken. It's a public wifi, it's registered to . . .' He reads aloud the street name and number of this building.

'Yeah,' I say, my mouth suddenly feeling as though it's lined with dried clay. 'That's where I am now.'

'Then . . .' Porter looks horrified. 'Then, goddamn, Nell, get the hell out!'

I slide off Richard's desk. I find that I am breathing hard, as though I have already started to run away.

'Richard?'

He seems to grow more defined, as though I've been viewing him through frosted glass and the pane has just shattered. I can see his pores, the veins that thread his eyes.

'I promise you this is nothing to do with—' he starts.

I stand up, place my hands on his chest and push him as hard as I can, but he's bigger than me and he barely staggers. 'I cannot believe I let you take me for a fool *again*.'

I push again, harder this time, but he's braced for it.

'Nell. Trust me. Sit down.'

I won't sit down but neither can I move. My feet might as well be a pair of anvils, riveting me to the floor.

'Should I call the emergency services?' says Porter.

'I'm on it,' says Lisa-Marie, suddenly appearing in the background. 'Nine nine nine, right?'

'For Christ's sake, no,' says Richard. 'Nell, set the phone down so they can see both of us.' He holds his hands up. 'Look, I'm not touching her, she's not in any danger.' He opens the main door and the windows. 'Nell, you get scared, you yell. There's a dozen other people working in this building. I'm not going to do anything.'

It is with a mixture of reluctance and relief that I drop into the chair. Behind Porter, Lisa-Marie holds up her phone, +44 999. God knows whether you can even call the emergency services from the States but if you can, she's ready to go.

'Porter,' says Richard. 'You say this was posted an hour ago?'

'That's right.'

Richard turns to me. 'I only got to the office five minutes before you did, Nell. I only came in to meet you. Look, my coffee's still hot.'

I follow his gaze to see a paper cup piping a thin curl of steam into the air.

'*She* could've got that for you just now,' I say, nodding towards the door.

A fog moves across Richard's eyes. It's as though he's listening to a voice only he can hear, explaining something only he understands. He looks to the coffee cup, to the door, to me, and then back at the open door.

'Rhiannon!' he roars at his receptionist. 'Get your arse in here *now*.'

88

The receptionist stands shaking in the doorway. She's very tall and athletic but her body language is that of a child.

'Dad, I can explain—' she says.

'*Dad?*' I echo.

Richard lets out a long sigh that seems as much an exercise in bodily control as outlet of dismay. 'This is my youngest, Rhiannon. She's in her first year of uni and she's doing maternity cover for my PA while she's on her summer break. And . . . it looks like she's got some *fucking explaining to do*!' He brings his fist down on the desk, making Porter flip on to his back. I set the phone back upright on its short edge, maximise the WhatsApp window. Porter is slack-jawed, Lisa-Marie strained.

'Hang on,' I say. '*You're* LetterstoIngrid? That was *you*, in the grey hoodie? *You* uploaded the video of me catching the bone?'

Rhiannon Reid squeezes a perfect teardrop from each eye. 'I was chasing a story.'

I sink deeper into the chair. It makes a little *poof* sound.

'How does sock-puppeting online count as chasing a story?' I ask.

Rhiannon fiddles with the end of her long plait. She's naturally dark, but the hair at the tips is pale blonde: I can see how, clipped up on top of her head, it could easily fall across her forehead like a floppy blonde fringe. I can see how it would be easier for Oisin to assume she must be a guy than to accept that he could be outrun by a girl.

'I needed a story for my second-year project and, y'know, *The Golden Bones* is newsworthy and we have this archive—' She gestures to the bank of cabinets.

'That's not tabloid fodder!' explodes Richard.

'I see myself as more of a broadsheet—'

'Don't be a smart-arse, Rhiannon. Those are my *case notes*. Which you know full well are off-limits to you.'

She pouts, and more years dissolve until it's all too easy to imagine a foot-stamping seven-year-old. 'You should've hidden the keys better, then, shouldn't you? Look, Dad, Frank Churcher's been profiled a gazillion times but there's never been a long read on Ingrid Morrison. Her love for Elinore. The lengths she went to. But no one's allowed to go and see her, so without an interview, how do you make a story relevant? You create traction. That's what you need to do these days. Otherwise I'll be looking at a future of twenty quid for a thousand words, or some shitty listicle that'll be out of date six minutes after it goes live.'

'This is a contravention of so many different things, I don't even know where to start.' Richard places a hand on his hairline, then examines his palm like he expects to have shed great tufts in the last couple of minutes. 'Do you have *any* idea how much danger you put Nell in?'

Rhiannon rolls her eyes. 'God forbid anything should happen to precious Nell.'

Richard darkens. 'Well, thanks to you, it nearly did. I take it *you* told Stuart that the Cecil Sharp verses were real?'

Rhiannon shifts uncomfortably. 'It wasn't supposed to escalate like that. I was working on the assumption that the bone was going to be the prize. How was I supposed to know someone would nick it?'

'You tell me,' I say. 'You seem to know a lot of stuff you shouldn't.'

'But when the bone *did* go missing,' says Richard, 'why didn't you just quietly delete your account? Why did you keep working Stuart Cummins into a frenzy?'

'I told you,' she says. '*Traction*. I overheard what he said to Nell in the street, before, about it being *an utter travesty*.' She quotes

Stuart's words in an uncanny impersonation of his voice. 'I wanted to get Ingrid's name out there again.'

My instinct is to slap her round the face but I overcome it. 'You were playing with fire,' I tell her. '*The Golden Bones*, it gets under people's skin, it drives them mad. You don't know what that book does to people.'

Rhiannon scoffs. 'I don't know what that book does to people? It ruined my childhood!'

Richard snorts. 'I'm sorry, what? What part of the private school or the horse-riding or the skiing was so onerous?'

I have felt as though I was in a parallel universe a lot lately but now I'm in a play where my ex-boyfriend and his daughter appear to be speaking lines that could've been scripted by Frank and me.

'Because you were never there!' says Rhiannon. 'And even when you were, you were always obsessing about the hunt, dropping everything to chase some lead or other. You've *wasted your life* chasing a stupid lump of metal. And as for you.' She turns furiously to me. 'He's been mooning over you for, like, twenty years. How do you think my mum feels, knowing she was second choice? That you were the one who got away?'

Richard's glowing cheeks mirror my own. I'm relieved when Porter, who I'd almost forgotten was a presence in the room, breaks the tension.

'Rhiannon, it's very bad form, what you did,' he says. 'A lot of genuine hunters have been led astray by these fake clues. But you were obviously pretty convincing. How did you convince Stuart Cummins that you were in contact with Ingrid?'

She sighs. 'Dad's got copies of old letters between Ingrid and Stuart. I lifted information from that, stuff only he would know. And she had a weird turn of phrase. Like, she said "birdy eye" when she meant "beady eye", so I used that, too.'

Birdy eye. Another piece of the jigsaw falls into place, neat as a bone in its socket.

Porter takes a beat to digest this. 'So once you earned his trust, how did you persuade him that the Cecil Sharp Verses were authentic after all? You'd have to discredit the Northumbria Papers to do that.'

'*Duh*,' she says. 'Dad's *archives*?'

Tumbleweed blows where some kind of parental rebuke should be. I turn to Richard, a challenge in my eyes, but apparently yes, he really is going to let Rhiannon talk to Porter like that. His mind is on the content of her words, not their tone, and his eyes are on his tall filing cabinet. Oh, no. He *didn't*.

'Richard,' I say heavily. 'Anything you'd like to share with the rest of the class?'

89

Whetstone, London N20
November 1998

Richard sits in his office, spinning the glass Hello Kitty suncatcher that Nell made for a niece who doesn't exist. He really should throw it in the bin, but he can't bear to when he thinks of her scarred little hands measuring it, cutting it, grinding it, her mouth pursed in concentration as she soldered and polished. Some kid or collector would love this cartoon cat; it should go to an appreciative home, but Richard can't give it to a charity shop either. It's a one-off, made just for him, and if it somehow found its way back to Nell he would have a lot of explaining to do.

A pane of the glass in Hello Kitty's bow has a hairline fracture in it. If he pressed it the whole thing would crack. Nell is like this, riven with so many fissures that one careless touch could splinter her into a million tiny pieces. Richard hates knowing that that touch will inevitably come from him.

He slides the suncatcher back into his desk drawer and thinks, as he does most days, of telling Mr Velasco that he's passing on the case. He's known for years that it's a fool's errand but he can't let it go. It's mainly the money but it's not only the money. It's the sentimental pull of his father's case and his own professional pride. What he can do for Nell is minimise the risks from outside sources, and it is to that end he has decided to get in touch with Stuart Cummins.

The restraining order that prevents Cummins from going within two hundred metres of Nell expires in a little over two years, but Richard wants to put an end to the threat now. The orderly who used to act as a go-between for Cummins and Morrison obviously got the sack, and Stuart will go back to prison if he contacts Ingrid again but when two people are as determined as they are, you can't be complacent. Richard needs to throw him off the scent – well, not off the scent, on to a different one.

He calls Cummins on the number he supplied at the *Intimacies* launch. The foreign voice that answers – Richard has to enunciate the name *Stuart Cummins* five or six times before he is understood – speaks of a shared house, a payphone in a corridor. A settled life turned transient thanks to *The Golden Bones*.

'It's Richard Reid, Mr Velasco's UK agent,' he says when Cummins finally answers.

'Is there news?' Cummins's excitement seems to transmit itself down the line, the receiver to emit a charge that makes Richard hold it an inch farther away from his ear.

'Yes and no,' says Richard. 'Could I tempt you out for a coffee?'

They meet in an espresso bar in Moorgate, the Italian kind with marble standing counters. Richard orders two macchiatos and waits, a scroll of paper under his right arm. When Cummins arrives he's glistening with exertion. He's wearing pressed chinos and a golfing jumper; it's the most casual Richard's ever seen him look. He homes straight in on the scroll, wiping steam from his glasses to get a better look.

'What's that?' he asks.

'A bit of background first,' says Richard. 'The bone remains undiscovered, but in the course of my investigation I came across something that's relevant to yours. Well, ours: it's a shared cause, after all.'

'Go on.' Stuart sips his macchiato and pulls a face.

'As you know, my work for Mr Velasco means that I have a budget that regular Bonehunters can only dream of.'

'Tell me about it,' says Stuart bitterly.

'I've had eyeballs on documentation from a private collection in Northumbria that suggests that the Cecil Sharp Verses of "To Gather The Bones" were fakes.'

'*Fakes?*' Stuart's knees buckle and for a moment Frank thinks he's going to have to catch the guy, but he steadies himself on a counter top. 'But Ingrid . . .'

'Well, *quite.*' Richard shakes his head to imply that he doesn't like this any more than Stuart does. 'You know what it was like in the 1900s. All those song collectors trying to outdo each other. It looks as if my source's great-great grandfather decided to have a little fun. Take them down a peg or two. I've got copies. Made with my trusty Minox.' He finds himself miming the taking of a photograph.

Cummins's nose twitches as he sniffs bullshit. 'I trust you have the originals to show me?'

'I'm glad you asked,' says Richard, as though he hadn't led Stuart to the question. 'I've had them verified by a chap from Cecil Sharp House but I wanted a second opinion from a Bonehunter. Someone with skin in the game.' He crosses his fingers and hopes that flattery will get him everywhere. The coffee machine hisses and spits as Stuart studies the letters detailing the fraudster's intent to 'smuggle in' a new verse of 'To Gather the Bones'.

'How credulous these Londoners have proved themselves, with their hunger for ballads of milkmaids and dragons,' Stuart reads aloud. 'It seems to me that anyone with a spare afternoon and ink in his pen could dash off a song and claim to have heard it in some coaching inn. I think it should be rather a wheeze to pull the wool over their sentimental eyes.' Richard drums his fingers on the marble countertop as Stuart moves on to the 'drafts' of the Cecil Sharp Verses, with inkblots and crossings out. The author of these pages was not, of course, an Edwardian gentleman looking for a good wheeze. The words are Richard's. The documents were knocked up by a contact who did time for producing counterfeit twenty-pound notes back in the seventies. Richard's notes to the forger are safely in his filing cabinet, along with Stuart's letters to Ingrid with their strange code language of birdy eyes and bones. Richard has also provided an out-of-work actor who does a good Northumbrian accent with a burner phone and a script to read from, in case Stuart calls his bluff. Richard hasn't shown anything to anyone at Cecil Sharp House, but he will cross that bridge when he comes to it.

Office workers choose, buy and eat entire sandwiches in the time it takes Stuart to scrutinise the pages. Eventually, his face registers dismay and Richard's spirits lift. It's working.

'Well, this changes everything.' Stuart looks close to tears. 'If those other verses are a fake, it means that Ingrid's theory about the Churcher girl is baseless. And I . . .' Richard sees the emotions pass across Stuart's face. Disappointment, guilt, anger at having been hoodwinked. 'She'll be absolutely devastated,' says Stuart.

Richard, whose thoughts are all of Nell, takes a few seconds to understand that he means Ingrid. 'Does she have to know?'

'I can't lie to Ingrid!'

'Technically, you can't *talk* to Ingrid,' says Richard. 'And I strongly advise you not to. You're no good to Elinore back in prison. But given that she's not allowed to consume any media about the treasure hunt, maybe it's better to let her live in hope than tell her it's another dead end? You can carry on looking, of course.'

'I'll have to give this some serious thought,' says Stuart. Even his immaculately starched collar seems to have drooped.

'Take these.' Richard hands Stuart a cache of facsimile pages. 'I want to keep the originals under lock and key.' When Stuart is reluctant to make the swap, Richard leans forward. 'It's not that I don't trust you. It's just that I've got *industrial-level* security in my HQ.' The more he layers on the drama, the more Stuart laps it up.

'So I guess this means . . .' Richard's pulse pounds at his temple, fit to break the skin. He hopes his stress doesn't show in his voice. 'You might want to make some kind of public statement renouncing the idea that Eleanor Churcher is, ah, uh, a . . .' A sudden image of Nell with a knife sticking out of her beautiful round hip enters his mind, robbing him of language. 'A target, if you will. It might help you mend your bridges with the Bonehunter community. Get online – that's where the interesting discussions are happening now. Declare your commitment to a bloodless solve. But what you *can't* do is reveal your sources.'

'I don't know about *that*.' Stuart shoves his glasses back up his nose, his signature move. Richard is suddenly overcome by the desire to snap the frames over his thigh. Just go and get them fixed, he thinks. There's a Specsavers down the road. It'd take an optician half a minute to tighten those bloody frames.

'Think about it,' Richard improvises. 'You are currently the pre-eminent Bonehunter in the world. You go spreading the word that Cecil Sharp House is full of forgeries and they might not give you access to those archives again. We can't risk anything that jeopardises putting Elinore back together, can we?'

'That's got to be my priority,' agrees Stuart. 'Good God. This is a *lot* to get my head around.'

Richard leaves Stuart poring over his new reading material, oblivious to the factory line of suits and skirts, coffee and pastries passing behind him. On the Northern Line back to Whetstone, he waits for the buzz to kick in. He has just saved his lover's life. Yet all he feels is the low-level nausea that has accompanied him since the first night he went to bed with Nell. It doesn't change the act, or the scale, of his betrayal.

90

Whetstone, London N20
9 August 2021

Richard's brown eyes are ringed with red. 'I know that can't have been easy to hear, Nell, but believe me, it wasn't easy to say either.'

'My heart bleeds,' I say but my voice cracks on the last word.

Rhiannon has developed a fascination with a paperclip on Richard's desk, unbending the wire to its full length. She uses the tip to push back her cuticles.

'When did you even get access to all this?' he says wearily. 'That's a secure cabinet. I keep it locked whenever I'm out of the office.'

'I took your keys from home,' she says in a small voice. 'We came at night.'

'*We?*'

She blushes a shade of red that even I'm impressed by. 'I mean me.'

'Rhiannon, I've been watching you lie for nearly twenty years,' says Richard wearily. 'Spit it out. And for fuck's sake put that down while you've still got some skin on your hands.'

She drops the paperclip, now tipped with blood, on his desk. 'There's this guy called Barney.'

I swallow while my brain waits for me to register the significance.

'Barney – Barney *Badger*?' I ask. 'From the film crew?'

'He asked me out when I was doing his invoices.' She seems shy and proud at the same time: a young woman with what could be her first serious boyfriend. 'He's helping me with the feature. We thought we might turn it into a true crime podcast.' For a moment she looks furious. 'He was up here earlier, we were writing the LetterstoIngrid post on his phone, but when you said you were coming in I bundled him out of the office. He must've used the wifi in the caff downstairs. I knew he'd fuck up sooner or later.' God. Even his girlfriend thinks he's a liability.

'Is Barney still downstairs?' I ask.

Rhiannon hesitates, then nods.

'Bring him up,' says Richard.

The four of us sit around Richard's desk in a family formation, as though we are two parents (we *are* angry with you and we *are* disappointed) admonishing their children. Richard and I have both folded our arms. Barney and Rhiannon each fiddle with something on their lap: for him, the drawstring at the bottom of his hoodie; for her, one of those bubble-popping fidget toys that Niamh and Aoife collect. They both seem incredibly young, although Rhiannon's only a year or two younger than I was when I started seeing Richard, and Barney must be mid-twenties; Dominic was a father at that age.

'OK,' says Richard. 'Cards on the table. You both need to be completely honest about everything. Got that?'

'Right.'

This is the kind of conversation you plan in advance and make a list for, and here I am doing it all off the cuff. 'Was that you two on my boat?'

They look at each other and clearly see no point in lying. 'Yes.'

'And you found out I lived on a boat . . .'

'By going through Dad's notes.'

'Right. What were you going to do with that knife before my neighbour interrupted you?'

Rhiannon looks at Richard. 'It sounds really bad when she puts it like that.'

'Tell me in a way that paints you in a good light, then,' he challenges.

'We were just going to, like, untie your boat. And let you float out a little bit, and then film it.'

'Why?' I ask. 'And if you say "traction" one more time, I swear to God . . .'

'I was just trying to get LetterstoIngrid to the top of the forum,' she says.

'And did you not think, at any point, what it would do to someone with my history, to have someone break into my home carrying a knife? Did you not think how fucked-up that was? How cruel?'

Richard is listening with his head in his hands. His devastation is genuine, but I can't read the baseline. Does he feel responsible for any of this, or is he just disappointed at how his kid turned out?

Rhiannon's eyes dispense more pips of salt water. 'It didn't seem real then. You didn't seem real. It's different now you're in front of me. I feel bad now.'

'Better late than never,' I deadpan. 'Right, what else. Are you two "Yorick" as well?'

They both shake their heads. 'We'd say if we were. Honest.'

'Was that you, in the pub, the night before, when Dom and Frank were shooting their mouths off?'

She's still shaking her head in response to the last question I asked her, as if her body's gone into default denial mode. 'We went bowling.'

For a second they beam at each other, a nauseating second that at least has the benefit of stilling Rhiannon's head. It was starting to make me feel dizzy.

'Probably got selfies and that to prove it?' says Barney.

'I think I can live without seeing those.' I fix Rhiannon with a stare that I hope looks more convincing from the outside than it feels on the inside. 'So you didn't know the jewel was in the tree.'

'No idea.'

Richard looks weary. 'Rhiannon, love. If you did . . . if you had it, if you took it, even if you've already sold it – you would tell me, wouldn't you?'

'I promise, Dad,' she sniffles. 'I wouldn't – I wouldn't do that to you.'

I don't know the kid well enough to know whether she's telling the truth, but Richard – who, to his credit, doesn't seem like one of those parents whose default position is blind faith in his child – appears to buy it. 'Yeah, I know you would,' he says.

'Also, I know you were in line for a bonus if you found it. I'd want my share of that.'

'That's my girl,' he says bitterly.

I'm determined not to let this father-daughter reunion derail my investigation. 'On the day the bone was found. What *were* you doing in my parents' house? Were you taking pictures of the girl at the window?'

'No!' says Rhiannon. 'Barney let me in round the side. I was trying to nick one of the books, or at least get a photo of a QR code or a serial number or something to put online and get a bit of tra – attention. But then that girl turned around and I bottled it, but Barney told me to hang around 'cos there was some big scene happening that everyone was being secretive about and we were like, why not film it?'

'Right.' I'm glad to see Richard making notes because it's going too fast for me to absorb. 'So, Rhiannon. Did *you* unplug the CCTV?'

'First I heard of it is when Barney got the blame.'

'So it *was* you?' I ask Barney.

He shrugs. 'Well, I must have, mustn't I, but not on purpose? Like, I don't remember doing it? It was just a plug? I would tell you now; I'm in the shit anyway.'

I throw my hands up. 'I'm out. I give up. I have no idea where we take this from here.'

My phone clears its throat. All four of us jump: we'd forgotten that the Glemhams were there. 'Right, here's what you're going to do,' says Lisa-Marie. 'You're going to go online and say that you were never in touch with Ingrid Morrison and that you were just fishing for attention. You can paraphrase but that's the gist. I also want you to tell Stuart Cummins that you lied to him when you told him that the Northumbria Papers were forgeries.'

'But they *were* forgeries.' Rihannon screws up her face and Barney says, 'Huh?' They can't see where this is going yet, but I think I can.

'We need Stuart to believe that the Cecil Sharp verses are the fakes,' says Lisa-Marie. 'When he believed that, Nell was safe. Right?'

'I didn't hear a peep out of him for years,' I confirm.

'So,' Lisa-Marie continues, 'Rhiannon, you need to post a statement under your LetterstoIngrid handle saying it was a prank that got out of hand.'

'But I showed him like all Dad's notes to the forger and everything.'

'You'll tell Stuart that you were behind all that,' says Lisa-Marie firmly. '*Won't* you?' Her threat leaps the Atlantic. Rhiannon throws up her arms.

'Oh my *God*. I mean, yeah, if you insist.'

Lisa-Marie nods. 'We'll pin it to the top of the page so it's the first thing people see when they visit the forum.'

I'm struggling to believe my luck here. 'You'd do all that even though you know it's not true?'

'Sure,' says Porter. 'Because Ingrid's claims never had any foundation in truth to begin with. Short of actually producing the golden bone, this is the best way to draw a line under this horrible chapter.'

'Thank you,' I say. 'Thank you, so much.'

'Got it,' says Porter. 'OK, you guys. We're gonna call it a night. Or a morning. Or whatever it is.'

'Thank you,' I say to them. 'For everything.'

'Genuinely, it has been our pleasure,' says Lisa-Marie.

'And,' says Porter. 'And I really hope your dad—' He falters. Even he, Frank Churcher's greatest fan, can't bring himself to say *didn't do it*. Instead, he settles for '—has a good outcome.'

The tiny Americans in my screen wave goodbye, then disappear.

'So after we've, like, uploaded the corrections and stuff, then what?' asks Rhiannon.

All eyes turn to me, acknowledging me as the wronged party, the one who gets to decide.

'I'm just trying to think whether she's actually broken the law,' I say to Richard, ignoring her. 'Whether this counts as, I dunno, perverting the course of justice or something. Malicious communications. Impersonating an offender.' I'm making it up, but there must be something. 'She could've cost me my life and I'm supposed to just take it?'

Rhiannon turns on the tears again. It's surprising how much water can accumulate on the lower lashes before gravity takes over. So much so that she has to blink to release them. Even Barney's face starts to crumple. Love's young dream reach for each other's hands.

'She probably has broken some law,' says Richard, and now *his* eyes are shining. 'But she's my kid, Nell. What would you do if it was *your* girl?'

A week ago, I'd have said that *my girl* would never have done anything like that, but I remember picking my way over broken glass. To let Rhiannon off the hook would not satisfy my urge for justice, but it might stop yet another line of dominoes radiating from *The Golden Bones*.

'It's your call, Richard.'

I know he won't do anything. I also know, as I close the door behind me, that I'll never see him again.

91

On Whetstone High Road, everything looks the same but everything is different. The air seems lighter now that there isn't a Bonehunter with a knife lurking behind every tree. Even the light seems different, as though someone has both turned up the sun, so that there are fewer shadows, and softened it, so the glare doesn't blind me. All those threats. All that *fear.* Vaporised.

Or have they?

Too many things still don't make sense. LetterstoIngrid may be accounted for but Yorick isn't. And, of course, there's Bridget. I keep flashing back to the day in question. Could *she* have unplugged the CCTV? And if so, what would she have been hiding? Where was she, when the bone was switched? It was therapeutic to unburden myself to Richard, but I need to take it to Dom now. I've taken it as far as I can without bringing the picture and what it means into it.

I pop my earbuds in.

'Can I come over?' I keep my voice light; the call is alarm bell enough. Even before the pandemic, we never had the kind of relationship where we'd drop in on each other unannounced.

'I'm at Mum's. Trying to keep her spirits up, you know.'

Is it the worst idea in the world to talk to them both at the same time? For all I know, they already know and think they've been doing me a favour, protecting me. It might be a relief for them to have it out in the open. Or maybe neither of them has the slightest idea and I'm about to blow what's left of our families apart. It's a carpet of eggshells I need to tread, and the gaps in my knowledge make me feel as though I'm wearing heavy boots.

'Nell? You still there?'

'Yeah. Sorry. Cool. I'll be there in a bit.' I click my cycle helmet under my chin and hook my leg over the crossbar. 'Is Bridget with you?' Super-casual, super-breezy. My left foot finds the pedal.

'No,' says Dom, not a trace of suspicion in his voice. 'She's at my place with Rose and the kids.'

I push off into the choking traffic, hoping it stays that way.

In Cora's sitting room, ivy tickles the window and casts lacy shadows over the walls.

'We've been having a bit of a heart-to-heart,' says Dom, evidently to explain Cora's tear-stained appearance. A kinder daughter might balk at kicking a woman when she was already down but it suits me that Cora is crying. She'll be easier to talk to when she's already let her guard down than she would be if I'd found her in one of her hello-birds, hello-trees moods.

'Got a bit of good news to share,' I say, sinking on to the pink velvet sofa.

'Get-out-of-jail good?' asks Dom, hopefully. Cora can't manage much more than a watery smile.

'Not that good, sorry, but the next best thing.' I tell them everything that went down at Richard's just now. It's still fresh enough in my mind that I can repeat the conversation verbatim. They listen intently, too shocked even to interrupt.

'The devious, irresponsible little *shits*,' says Dom.

'My first reaction was thank God there's no one out to murder me, but OK,' I say.

'Yeah.' He blows out his cheeks. 'Obviously. Sorry. Just – relieved. You know.'

'And we also need to have a conversation about something else. God, this is awkward.'

Dom draws his brows together. 'Go on.'

'I feel like . . . there's a few things about the way Bridget's been that don't quite fit together.'

I read them both separately. If either of them knows about her and Frank, here's where recognition will show. If they both know about the affair, they won't be able to resist looking at each other. But the two faces are blank as pebbles and their eyes don't leave mine.

'And I just think we should take this opportunity, where it's just the three of us, to think about a couple of things.' I draw breath from the deepest part of my lungs. 'Do you think Bridget might have had something to do with it?'

Cora flutters pink eyes. '*Bridget?*'

Is she really bewildered, or is she hedging? Can I really be the one to break the news? The thought of it sets off an awful, swelling riptide inside me.

'Just – on the night Verity Winship was killed, Bridget says she was out looking for Lal, and that's why she was late to the party.' I am a coward, bypassing motive and means and going straight to opportunity. 'And then, on the day of the filming, she was in and out of the attic, where the skeleton was, and the key went missing right after. And – when everyone went out the front, where was she?'

'She was out the front too, with me,' says Cora.

'Could you swear to that? With all the chaos? And what if she unplugged the CCTV to get rid of footage of her going out to the tree?'

Cora and Dom still haven't so much as glanced at each other. Their scrutiny is starting to feel oppressive.

'But *what* are you accusing her of, and *why*?' asks Cora.

'I can't say it.'

The break in my voice awakens Cora to the scale of the unsaid; I can see that she grasps that this is about more than Bridget being a bit off this past week by her reaction, the hooks of her fingers scraping at her little brass tin. When it clatters open, a blue plastic lighter falls out. She turns to Dom. 'In Bridget's kitchen, in the tea caddy.'

She doesn't need to phrase it as an order for him to get to his feet. She shoots him a look of pure adoration. When she turns to me it's with a flash of steel.

'Whatever it is can wait until he gets back.'

She knows. Does she? And if she knows, does she know *I* know? Jesus Christ, this *family*.

I decide to try one more time before she smokes her way to Cloud Cuckoo Land or Dingly Dell or wherever it is she goes. 'You're a hundred per cent sure Bridget didn't leave your side the whole time?' I press.

'Stop interrogating me, Eleanor. You're as bad as Sergeant Bindra! I said yes, didn't I?' She looks at the door, anxious to receive her supply. I give up. Even if she thinks she's telling the truth, what's her word worth? She was already high as a kite by the time the Bonehunters began their procession down the Vale.

'It's a shame the only recording belongs to Crabwise,' I say. 'Would it be really bad to see if Osh can get hold . . .' I trail off; my own words have tugged at the bedclothes of a dormant memory. *I* have film of the day on my phone. The one Billie made but I didn't bother watching all the way through because she'd pointed the camera at my family in the front garden, not the Bonehunters in the street.

I open the file now. It's four minutes long. Time enough for . . . what?

The main sound is Billie's breathing over the top of things, the voices on the street muffled by the glass. The picture definition isn't great either. It's hard to differentiate the crew members, what with the unofficial uniform of grey hoodies. But the guys are both there, which does nothing to exonerate them from the original killing but confirms that they could not have physically put the bone in the tree.

'Look.' I show Cora. 'I need to send this to Leslie.'

'*Oh,*' she says, in a way that could mean anything.

The camera only jolts a little bit when Billie shouts, 'Come on, you're missing all the action.' That moment, I know now, was when Rhiannon Reid was standing opposite me in her grey hoodie and her mask. Bridget is in shot throughout.

'You were right,' I tell her. 'Bridget didn't leave the front garden.'

'Of course I was right.' Cora sniffs. 'Just because I'm seventy-nine, it doesn't mean I've lost *all* my faculties, you know.'

Arguably she's been demolishing her faculties since before I was born, but now does not feel like the time to resurrect that conversation.

Dom comes back, a slim joint in a ready-to-smoke position between his finger and thumb, and although he sparks it for Cora he doesn't take a drag. Instead, he sits next to me on the sofa, away from the fug that settles over our mother's shoulders like a favourite shawl.

'What you watching?' he asks.

'Just – something from the filming day,' I say. 'I was trying to work out whether Bridget could've got up the tree and back in, what, four minutes?'

'You're not serious,' says Dom.

'What? She's a *young* seventy-three. And four minutes is a long time. You don't think it is till you're watching it tick past. Anyway, it's moot. She's there pretty much the whole time.'

On screen, a matchstick Niamh pouts and makes a peace sign at the TV cameras.

'The little minx.' I show Dom with a smile. 'She swore blind she was waiting outside your room the whole time. I might've known that was uncharacteristically obedient of her. Good job I forgot I had this, Dom. If I'd shown that to the police, that'd be your alibi gone.'

He flinches, like two wires have touched inside him. The look on his face lasts for a quarter of a second. Less than that. An eighth, a sixteenth, a thirty-secondth? A fraction so small I don't know the name for it. But I do know the name for the feeling it signifies.

Horror.

The idea of his alibi being blown, something that should have made Dom chuckle, filled him with a primal terror I've never seen on another human face, not even Aoife's when I held the bone in my hands.

'Dom?' I pack a million questions into his name. *Say I'm wrong, say this is nothing to do with you.* My brother and my mother have gone from being seemingly unable to make eye contact to unable to look away from each other. Dom's eyes ask Cora's permission to talk. She begins to shake, the joint in her hand a shuddering point of fire. 'Cora?' I ask, and then, in desperation, 'Mum?'

'Just tell her,' says Cora. 'She's halfway to the truth. You two always could read each other like books.' Her trembling becomes a full-body spasm and the joint drops from her hand.

'Mum, shut *up,'* says Dom. He bounds across the room before it can catch on the rug and pinches it out between his thumb and forefinger. He stays there, kneeling before her and whispers, 'Don't.'

His broad shoulders drop and become round, as though the angles have been planed away. My mother puts her hand on the crown of his head and pulls him close. It seems to steady them both but I find that I am trembling as Cora murmurs, 'I'm so tired, Dominic,' into his hair. 'I can't keep this up any longer and neither can you. Come on, sweetheart. It's time.'

92

The Veasey Gallery, London NW3
20 June 1997

Frank is literally carrying on with another woman *under her nose*. If he looked up he would see that Cora is almost close enough to touch him, but he only has eyes for the bimbo serving drinks.

'I cannot cope with this,' she says to Harriet, but her voice is weak and the words get lost in the chatter.

Ever since that man burst into the gallery with a knife Cora's guts have been tying themselves into knots, trapping acid in the kinks. The burning and twisting did not subside when the police came, or even when Eleanor's friends spirited her to safety. If anything, it is getting worse.

The gallery is too full of bodies. There are too many paintings: squares and rectangles rigid around paintings of curved flesh. There are too many different perfumes, as dizzying as though multiple radios were playing at once. The white walls jumble all the voices to gibberish. All except one.

'Frank,' the waitress purrs. '*Only you* can give me what I need.'

Cora uses her loudest laugh to hide the fact that she's zoned out of the anecdote that Harriet's telling her and she uses the push and pull of the crowd to hide the fact that she's steering Harriet closer to the conversation, even though it's making her stomach plummet. Harriet's voice momentarily drowns out whatever Frank's growling into the girl's ear. No one else seems to be listening: after all, what of note would the star of the show have to say to some waitress? The way they're standing is sex hiding in plain sight. A couple who are clearly sleeping together using the double-bluff of obvious public flirting. Cora takes a step closer, challenging them to look up, to notice her, to pull apart in shame. But they only have eyes for each other.

'We're having an afterparty back at my place.' He gives her the address on the Vale of Health. 'Don't come to the front door: there's a gate in the back garden that I can slip out of.'

A high-pitched ringing fills Cora's head. The past few minutes have been worse than the past few hours, which have been worse than the past few days, which have been worse than the past few weeks, which have been worse than the past year which, despite some strong competition, has been the worst of her three wretched decades as Frank Churcher's wife. It is not enough that the walls are hung with her husband's lovers; he's even brought one of them in as *staff*, and even in the middle of his own opening he's arranging a knee-trembler up against some tree, on the Heath. Outside the house where they have raised their children. Near the spot where he *proposed* to her. The picture Cora has of the two of them going at it is a mental one but she closes her eyes anyway. When she opens them, the girl is pouring champagne for a man in a toupée and Frank is in animated conversation with a writer from the *Sunday Telegraph*.

Cora turns to find Dominic at her side. She examines his face to see if he, too, overheard his father and the waitress. He's never been able to hide his feelings from her.

'It's all a bit much,' he says.

'You're doing really well. I know it's not your scene. Not long to go now.'

He grabs her hand and squeezes. Dominic has always been more sensitive to her moods than Frank or Eleanor. He sticks by Cora's side – for comfort, probably – as she continues to work the room, making meaningless small talk, over-laughing at unfunny jokes until her cheeks hurt.

She's not going to cause a scene here. She will go home, and she will follow Frank out on to the Heath. She will catch them in the act and cite that grubby tart in the divorce petition.

Back at the Vale, a couple of Frank's art school friends are guarding the front door.

'Your boy asked us to keep an eye,' says one. 'Don't want a repeat of earlier, do we?'

They're not your typical bouncers, drinking good Rioja in their linen shirts, and Cora doubts they'd be a match for a determined gatecrasher, but she appreciates the gesture. And Dominic: what a thoughtful young man he's turning into. He must get that from her, because it certainly didn't come from his father.

The party is in full swing, despite Cora's late arrival and Frank's absence. It is as though their reputation itself has become the host, a separate entity filling glasses and making introductions.

The temperature has dropped. Cora is as uncomfortably cold now as she was uncomfortably warm in the gallery. Is it that, newly thin, she no longer makes her own insulation? Or is it just that middle age has broken her internal thermostat? One of Frank's scarves is hanging over the back of a garden chair and she throws it over her shoulders. It sends up a cloud of Vétiver. Cora wouldn't mind if she never smelled that scent again.

She cannot shake Dominic off. He follows her from room to room the way he used to when he was three. What was adorable supportiveness has become oppressive. It's a relief when Marcelle and Harriet stagger in under cases of champagne and she can order Dominic to help them unload more bottles from their car.

'Where's Bridget?' Cora asks Harriet. She needs a friend, a real friend, not all these art-world strangers.

'Lal's gone AWOL,' Harriet mimes the draining of a glass. 'She's trawling the streets for him before he does himself a mischief.'

'Oh, God, really?' says Cora. She can't get through this after-party without Bridget. A breeze blows in from the garden.

Harriet looks around. 'And where's the hero of the hour?'

'If you mean me, I'm here,' says Dom, the ropes of muscle on his forearms standing out as he hefts a crate under each arm. He eases them on to the breakfast bar. 'If you mean Dad, I haven't seen him.' He turns to talk to a saucer-eyed Suzy. Cora wills him to follow her up the stairs and give her half a minute to think.

But no, he's staying downstairs, even attempting to follow Cora into the bathroom.

'Dominic, I know we're close, but I draw the line at going to the toilet in front of you.'

What's *wrong* with him tonight?

93

Dom rubs his neck. He's pulled a muscle, heaving both those boxes of champagne out of the car at once to minimise the time Cora was left on her own.

He seeks her out again now. Cora tries to hide the flash of irritation – she doesn't know why he's clinging to her – but she's too drunk to have mastery over her own face. Something dark is bubbling under her flushed skin. Up close, her breath is rank: the ketosis reek of days without food, the stable-floor smell of wine on an empty stomach. He pours her a sparkling water and follows her around the party until she drinks it. While one eye is fixed on his mother, the other is roaming the room, looking for Frank. He's not here, and Dom can't work out if that's a good thing or a bad one. His dad could be out the back right now, having a little celebration shag, in which case maybe it'll be over already and he'll walk into the garden any moment and Cora will never be any the wiser.

A bright-eyed Suzy tries to pull him up the stairs. 'We're in Nell's room,' she says.

'In a minute,' he says, disengaging Suzy's hand from his arm It's enough to know his sister's alright, that she's got people with her.

He follows Cora to the downstairs cloakroom, so lost in his thoughts that he doesn't even notice he's followed her right inside until she snaps at him.

'Dominic, I know we're close but I draw the line at going to the toilet in front of you.'

'Sorry,' he says. 'Miles away.'

She closes the door behind her. Dom takes a step back and folds his arms, the better to guard the door. Along the tiled floor, Rose weaves towards him. Once again, the new womanliness of her takes his breath away. She looks like a stranger. Far from making him uneasy, he thinks it's kind of hot. He likes her like this. Less . . . sisterly. Still, when she throws both arms around his neck, he recoils, just a little.

'Domenico!' Her pupils are huge black circles of ink stretching her irises to slim green filaments. She opens her mouth to show him a little white pill on her tongue.

'Come on,' she says, and leans in, not for a kiss but to transfer the pill from her tongue to his. She rests the very tip of her tongue on his lower lip. Her breath is as sweet as Cora's was sour. Rose turns champagne into apples and sweets. Every cell in Dom's body feels the tug towards her, but he needs to stay straight for his mum, and also, is this even a kiss she's offering? Very quickly, he licks his forefinger and pats the pill on her tongue so it transfers to his fingertip.

'Maybe in a bit,' he says, putting it in his pocket.

Rose pouts. 'I hate men,' she says.

'Good-oh,' he says.

She boops him on the nose with a forefinger. 'Dom! Obviously *you* don't count.'

'I don't count as a man? This just gets better.'

'You know what I mean.'

He doesn't have a clue what she means. All he knows is that her bare arm is on his shoulder and it feels like it might burn through his shirt.

'Tonight, right, I got blanked by some dickhead I used to date' – *Knew it*, thinks Dom. 'And old men in corduroy suits touching my bum and some slimy wanker in a green suit trying to chat me up and half the women were crying and all the husbands were staring each other out and . . . You'd never be an arsehole if you were my boyfriend, would you?'

What?

Things you want this much do not land in your lap this easily. It's too convenient. It's almost as though – and then it hits him. 'Has Nell said something to you?'

Usually Rose's a quick thinker but intoxication has slowed her down. 'She might've done,' she admits. 'C'mon. Whaddaya say?'

Now it's on a plate, he can't kiss her. Not just because she's off her head but because up close to the opportunity it is now crystal-clear that if he keeps his hands off her he gets to keep her, and he'd rather spend the rest of his life loving her from a distance than ruin it all with sex and lose her forever.

Rose stands on her tiptoes. Her lips touch his so lightly that she is at once hardly even there and also she is part of him. Her tongue prises his lips apart. Resist, resist, he thinks, but it gets to the point where not to respond would be an insult and he lets her in. *Boom.* They are running on the same voltage. 'Barbie Girl' starts thumping from the speakers. Hardly the sweeping orchestral score he had envisaged for this moment but even that can't spoil it.

It's only the rattle of the key in the bathroom door that stops him undressing her there and then. He opens his eyes to see, over Rose's shoulder, the expanding rectangle of light.

It is not Cora's silhouette but Bridget's, all pointy shoulders and loose curls. She could not look more horrified if she had caught them naked. Rose senses the change before she turns around.

'Oops,' Rose giggles into his ear, but Bridget is farther from laughter than he's ever seen her. In his fantasies of his future with Rose he always expected a *little* initial resistance, but not the devastation that drags at Bridget's face now.

'Rosaleen Lally.' Her voice is hard as stone. 'I would like to speak with you at home.'

She looks as though she's going to cry. This isn't anger, thinks Dom. It's – hurt? Disappointment? He feels as if it's some profound emotion only the real grown-ups have access to. 'You do realise we have to get married now?' is the last thing Rose says to Dominic as Bridget pulls her daughter off him and marches her up the stairs like a five-year-old who's been caught throwing stones. He stands there trying to process what's just happened while the guy in the song urges Barbie to go party.

All that matters now is that Cora is on the loose. Dominic casts desperately around the party – living room, hallway, kitchen – until he sees a movement at the end of the garden.

Her black dress has melted into the night; she is nothing more than a swish of pale hair and the sequins on the hem of her dress, winking like a hundred tiny eyes, as she disappears through the back gate and on to the Heath.

94

Cora closes the toilet door behind her and immediately opens it again. Dom is standing sentinel but he has his back to her: Rose is poking her tongue out – a little white pill, one of those Es they're all into. What Cora wouldn't give to be seventeen and high.

But she is not seventeen, and, while she may be on the outside of a good two bottles of Laurent-Perrier and double her prescribed dose of amphetamines, nor does she feel high. She is low, misery an extra newton of gravity that makes her want to lie down on the floor. It is an effort to move quickly enough to give Dom the slip, but she makes it, winding her way through the guests and darting through the dark parts of the garden. That blasted song about a Barbie Girl is mocking her from the speakers. There's a half-full bottle of champagne on the stone table and she pours a glass's worth down her throat, then grips it by the neck and unbolts the gate to the Heath.

On the other side of the fence it is twice as dark. All the better to listen. She strains to hear a giggle or a groan. The slightest shift of her weight makes the forest floor crackle, twigs snapping like little gunshots beneath her feet. Cora clears her throat: it turns into a deep, thirty-a-day cough that Frank says makes her sound like the old man from *Steptoe and Son*.

'There you are,' says the girl's disembodied voice. Cora finally puts her finger on the word she was looking for: *common*. 'I could smell you coming a mile off. What is that, Old Spice?' A nervous laugh undermines her joke. 'Anyway, come here. Show yourself. We can do this quickly. I doubt you want it to get back to the wife.'

'The wife already knows,' says Cora.

The girl screams. 'Oh, my God!' she says. 'I'm so sorry. You scared the shit out of me.'

Cora takes a few crunchy steps forward, following the girl's voice. They are underneath the big oak tree. The girl is a fuzzy shape in the dark, the only point of orientation the glossy droplets of her eyes.

'How long?' asks Cora. 'How long have you been sleeping with my husband?'

The girl laughs. Throaty. Sexy. Cora's eyes, adapting to the dark, sees the pale fuzz of the girl's hair.

'It's not what it looks like.'

That is what people say when it is *exactly* what it looks like.

'Please don't patronise me,' says Cora.

'I've said to him, the last thing I want is to get tangled up in your marriage. I wanted to keep you out of this. I tell you what, I'll come back another time, now I know where to find him. You're all pissed as farts anyway.' She lights a cigarette and for a moment she is a Hallowe'en mask, long dark shadows making caves of her eye sockets. The flame shrinks; the waitress takes a deep drag that brings a tiny dying sun to life before turning away. 'Sleeping with Frank Churcher,' she chuckles as her cigarette descends to hip level. 'Give me a *bit* of credit.'

Denial, Cora was half-expecting. But *mockery*? Something inside her comes unhinged. The loss of temper is such a strongly physical sensation that even in the moment she is surprised not to hear an accompanying sound, like the pop of a tearing ligament, or the snap of a breaking bone. She swings the bottle in her hand so quickly that nothing is spilled as it arcs through the air and makes contact with the girl's head.

Even in the dark, Cora can tell that she's hit her bang in the back of the head, as perfectly as a tennis ball landing in the dead centre of the racquet. The girl hits the ground with a heavy thud.

Cora drops the bottle on its neck. The remaining champagne escapes. When it hits the bracken it makes a snap-crackle-pop noise from the Rice Krispies advert. She is suddenly utterly lucid.

She stumbles through unseen branches, arms stretched in front of her, although it's her feet that find the girl first. She crouches in the dark, fumbles the length of the girl's arm and feels for a pulse. There is none. She puts her cold hand in front of the girl's mouth, hoping for the faintest trace of breath. Nothing. She opens her mouth to wail but it's like a scream in a dream, her whole body tight with the effort of making the noise but no sound coming out.

All the furious energy of a moment ago is spent, and Cora lies down next to the girl. She is shivering again, but can't bring herself to draw Frank's scarf more tightly around her. Something that might even be calm is seeping in. *Well,* she thinks. There you go. Frank's won. His saggy old wife's going to prison to save him the trouble of divorce. He'll get to keep the lovely house, and with me out of the way he can fuck who he wants in the master bedroom.

Ten yards away, the garden gate bangs. Here he comes, she thinks. She's too spent even to guide him towards her. Let him find them lying together on the ground, his wife and his lover (because despite her protests, who else could she be?). Let him trip over the pair of them. Let him break his fucking neck.

But Frank – a practical man, for an artist – has bought a torch, and a fuzzy yellow beam grows stronger with his every tread. Cora shields her eyes against the glare.

'I—' she starts to say, but she doesn't have the energy to finish. The Heath is spinning around, black leaves and branches and dirt and sky whirling around that dazzling light.

'Oh, *Mum*.' Dominic drops into a crouch beside her. 'Mum, what the hell have you done?'

95

Dom squats before what used to be the waitress and trains the beam of his torch on her face. He has never seen a dead body before, yet he knows that the girl on the ground is dead. It's in the eyes. Whatever it is that makes a person human has departed.

'Mum, get up.' Dom offers Cora his hand but she curls into a prawn shape so she's almost spooning the dead girl. She's gone: retreated the way she always does when things get difficult. She's like a child playing hide and seek for the first time, who thinks she can't be seen by others if she closes her eyes.

The awful night smells of dry earth and stale wine and Guerlain Vétiver.

Cora's own eyes are full of what makes a human. Fear and hurt and love and panic suspended in water and jelly and protein.

'I'm so sorry,' she is murmuring to the girl on the ground. 'Oh, you poor thing, I didn't mean it, I'm so sorry. It's not your fault.'

'Mum,' says Dominic, more firmly this time. 'Tell me what's happened.'

'He was fucking her,' she says as she takes his hand. 'I saw her, you know. Outside his studio. Calling his name, like they all do. And tonight, she was waiting for him out here – under the tree where he asked me to marry him – and she *laughed* at me.'

The geyser of anger that blasts Dom's veins is not directed at the girl.

Frank is responsible for this. He is as responsible as if he had struck the blow himself. He has belittled and exploited and humiliated Cora for as long as Dom can remember.

'What am I going to do, Dominic?' Cora's sitting up now, leaves and dirt in her blonde hair.

The real question couldn't be any clearer. What are *you* going to do about this? She is handing responsibility for what she has done over to him. Dominic finds that he is happy to take it.

'Give me a minute to think.' He sinks back on his heels and boxes off the little boy who wants to cry, letting the logical, adult part of his brain take over. The waitress is dead. She is dead, and calling the police and having Cora sent to prison for murder won't bring her back to life. If Frank is the cause then Cora's marriage is punishment enough. Cora's remorse is a life sentence. He overheard the waitress say, just a couple of hours ago, that no one was expecting her home. There won't be a search party for her any time soon. Enough damage has been done by *The Golden Bones* and the man behind it. This is Dominic's chance to put things right.

But.

If he covers this up, if he saves his mother tonight, he'll never be able to mention it to anyone else. His life with Rose, if she still means what her kiss promised in the sober light of the morning, will be founded upon a – not a lie, but a withheld truth. Not because he doesn't trust her but because it wouldn't be fair to ask her to carry this burden. Close as the two families are, this is Churcher shit, and it's Dominic's to shovel.

Cora is groping in the undergrowth for something: Dom watches her hand close around the neck of a green bottle.

'Is that . . .' he asks, but his torch picks out the answer. Grease, and the faintest smear of something darker at the point of impact. Dom takes it and uses the edge of his shirt to wipe the stains off and polish away Cora's fingerprints.

'There's a way out of this,' he says, although he doesn't yet know what that might be. 'This wasn't your fault, OK? Listen to me. Dad drove you to this. I'm going to make it go away for you.' He continues buffing the bottle as though preparing it for some kind of display.

'You're not thinking straight,' she says.

I'm not thinking straight? thinks Dominic. I'm not the one who just ended someone's life. And he *is* thinking straight. His aim is as pure as an arrow that shoots along the tight trajectory of keeping Cora out of trouble. He manages not to snap at his mother.

'Can you handle going back to the party?' he asks her. 'Can you manage to act like nothing's happened?'

She nods too quickly. Her judgement is shot.

'Scratch that,' says Dom. 'I'm going to put her in the studio for the night. Come with me. Keep out of the light and just . . . wait outside the door, alright?'

The girl is heavier than she looks and Dom's thighs beg for mercy as he staggers over the Heath. It was a mistake to put Cora in charge of the torch. No matter how many times he says, 'Point it at the ground, Mum,' the light swings wildly. It feels as though the whole Heath is swaying, but somehow they reach the back gate without him tripping and breaking his neck.

'Kill the light and open the gate,' he pants. They make it into the garden undetected. Whatever Dom did to his neck lugging those bottles out of Marcelle's car is getting worse by the second. 'Open the studio,' he says.

With shaking fingers – *for fuck's sake, hurry up, Mum!* – Cora punches in the combination.

'No!' says Dominic as she feels for the light switch, her fingers millimetres away from illuminating the tableau for every guest at the party. Dom's heart cannot take this. 'Bloody *hell*, Mum. Just – open the kiln and take the shelves out.'

'Oh, Dominic,' says Cora. 'I can't bear the thought of her—'

'Just for tonight, OK?' he says. He frisks the waitress for ID and finds only a twenty-pack of Marlboro Lights, but he can tell from the pack's heft and the way the cardboard bulges that there's other stuff jammed in there too. He slides it into his back pocket and then folds the waitress into a sitting position. She sits at the bottom of the kiln like a child on the carpet at storytime. Dominic thinks he might throw up. This is the point of no return. He knows from reading Frank's ancient pathology books that her blood will soon start to pool in her buttocks and thighs, and, even after the rigor wears off, no position they arrange her in will disguise the fact that they moved the body. He whispers his own apology.

'I am so sorry,' he says. 'You don't deserve this. Remember who really killed you. I'm sorry you ever met him.'

'What did you say?' whimpers Cora.

'Nothing,' says Dominic. 'Let's get you to bed.'

Dom bears Cora's weight as he leads her through the party. 'One too many,' he says to the guests that part to let them through. No one bats an eyelid. This is a Churcher party, after all.

In his parents' bedroom, he brushes his mother's hair. A drift of leaf fragments and dry earth settles on her dress. He takes a flannel to her face and, while his A-level chemistry doesn't extend to knowing how the hell women get mascara off their eyelashes, he is at least able to wipe the worst of the black smears from the crêped skin under her eyes.

He draws the line at undressing her.

'Change out of those clothes.' He shuts himself in the en-suite to give her privacy. On the sink is a little brown pill bottle. *Mrs Cora Churcher. 20mg Amphetamine Sulphate. Take as directed by clinician.* She's off her tits on speed. That explains the weight loss. You can get amphetamine psychosis; it happened to one of the boys in Nell's year. He started hearing voices. If that's what's happened to Cora, then how can she possibly be responsible for what she's done this evening? Surely it would count as diminished responsibility in a court.

Not that Dominic's going to let it come to that.

'Are you decent?' he calls through the bathroom door.

'Yeah.'

She's on her bed in her dressing gown, knees pulled up under her chin. She takes the toothbrush he gives her, paste squeezed on to the bristles, and sucks it like a dummy.

Dom rattles the bottle of pills at her. 'How long have you been taking these?'

Cora shrugs. 'Six weeks. It was your father's idea. Get me trim for the opening.'

It's the first time Dominic's ever understood Lal's impetus to punch walls. Another reason Frank is to blame for this awful mess.

'We *all* used to take them in the sixties.'

'I'm going to flush them down the loo,' says Dominic. 'You're going to need your head straight over the next few days and these won't help you.'

The chiffon of Cora's dress bundles up to almost nothing in his hands.

'Right,' he says. 'Pretty much everyone saw you come up. I'm just going to tell them you're sleeping it off.'

He folds a triangle in the corner of the bedcovers and pats the sheet underneath, the way she used to do for him when he was little. Obediently Cora lies down and puts her head on the pillow. As an afterthought, he takes the bin from the en-suite and puts it by the side of her bed.

'You're a good man, Dominic,' she says. 'Nothing like your father.'

He's braced for a long wait, for more weeping and wailing, but sleep claims his mother within seconds. Dominic wants nothing more than to lie down next to her, put his head on his father's pillow and then wake up and realise that this has all been a horrible, horrible dream, the like of which he didn't know his subconscious was capable. But he must go back into the party, make meaningless noises that people will read as small talk, represent his mother.

A soft knock on the door shoots a bolt of fear through him.

'Dom?'

Rose pushes the door open. Big black eyes like a lemur's that soften when she sees what he's doing. 'That makes sense. I was starting to think you were hiding from me.'

'God, no – Rose, I – she's in a state.'

She stands over him. Champagne sloshes from a coffee mug. Cora's always used running out of glasses as the metric of a good party. Rose's jaw is working slightly, an effect of the E. 'Now at least you can have a pill?' she says hopefully.

'Ah, I think the moment's gone,' he says. 'By the time I come up, you'll all be coming down.'

'Come here.' She takes both his hands and pulls him up to sitting. The air between them vibrates. Dominic is not sure his body can take much more of this. He is exhausted and turned-on and scared and angry and euphoric and it's a more dangerous cocktail than anything Cora or Rose have taken tonight. When she raises her face to his, the effort of not kissing her is greater than the effort of carrying the waitress's body over the Heath. But he cannot let his contaminated hands touch Rose's skin.

'Not like this,' he says. 'Not with me sober and you off your face.'

He can sense her frustration, but she forces a smile.

'Ah, Dominic,' she says. 'You're a good man.'

96

Somehow, Dom manages to go back into the party. On the floor, little wire cages that once held captive champagne corks collapse under his tread. Experience has taught him to read the shape of his parents' parties, to mentally plot the night on a graph, and he gauges, by the amount of bottles still undrunk and the songs currently playing – the playlist has entered its Motown phase – that the festivity is approaching its peak. He makes small talk with a succession of people whose words and names and faces he forgets the instant they are out of his sight. He shares a joint with Nell, inhales a lungful of paranoia and instantly regrets it. When the terrace turns into a dancefloor, he watches Rose wave her arms in the air and knows she's moving for him. It's almost as though he's conducting a psychological experiment on himself. There's a dead woman in the studio at the end of the garden, his mother is upstairs, a death on her conscience and possibly about to choke on her own vomit, and yet he has kissed Rose, and that is what floats to the top.

It's a good twenty minutes before he remembers that the murder weapon is still out on the Heath. He makes his excuses, again, and edges his way along the shadowy borders of the garden into the scrub, no torch this time, just feeling for the bottle on his hands and knees.

'You've deigned to turn up, then?'

Frank's voice comes as a surprise to Dominic. Not the fact of it – he was expected here, after all – but its tone. It is brusque, impatient. Hardly the voice of a man meeting his lover (and if it *is* – if that's the way Frank talks before sex, snappy and entitled – he's an even bigger prick than Dominic thought).

Dominic freezes on all fours, hardly daring to breathe.

'I've got a grand in cash,' says Frank. 'All I could scrabble together for now.'

He's got what now? Why would he be paying the waitress? Was she a hooker? But no. Something tells Dominic that's not his father's style. Why was he giving her money? Is it possible they weren't sleeping together? He recasts the conversation he overheard. Something only you can give . . . a bond between us whether you like it or not . . . what else could that mean?

Jesus, thinks Dominic. Abortion money. He's got the girl pregnant. He's got her fucking *pregnant*. Did Cora know that? Dom's no Catholic, but the thought of Cora taking one life carried within another makes him want to vomit.

Frank takes a step towards him, led, perhaps, by the thumping of his heart, which is louder than the bassline that drifts from the terrace. No, no, no, *no*, thinks Dom. This is not a confrontation I can bear to have. He tries to breathe quietly. Why has he never noticed the myriad noises of a human body at rest?

Time passes – it could be ten minutes, it could be thirty seconds – before Frank says, 'Fuck this for a game of soldiers,' and heads back towards the house. He passes Dom with centimetres to spare, but doesn't notice him. There's a noise somewhere between a ring and a thud and another 'Fuck,' as Frank's foot finds the empty bottle. He picks it up and carries it back to the house. He is briefly illuminated as the back gate opens. He is in silhouette, but the backlit bottle is a green bulb glowing in his hand.

Frank's fingerprints are on the murder weapon now, thinks Dom.

That's when he knows what must be done.

97

Late next morning, while Frank is at the gallery and the agency cleaners are magically erasing the party carnage, Dom – who managed a few hours' sleep on the studio floor – sits cross-legged in front of the kiln, the contents of the dead girl's cigarette packet spread before him on the floor. A tatty Marlboro Lights box isn't much of a handbag. Its contents aren't much to show for a life. Five cigarettes, one turned upside-down. £6.27 in silver and bronze. A notebook the size of a credit card which she used as an address book.

Beside the names are dates; some are crossed out. Dom guesses that these are the people whose sofas she has been sleeping on, and the ones who have been crossed out are the places she outstayed her welcome. That would be heartbreaking enough, but then tucked into the back page he finds her debit card, and the name that recasts last night into a new and even more terrible light.

Verity Winship. The dead girl on the other side of the kiln door was Pete Winship's daughter.

Her last name would have rung a bell anyway, of course, but Dom knows, because Cora is terrible at filing letters, that she'd written to Frank a couple of times, begging for money. No threats, no nastiness, just the desperation of a girl who'd lost her only parent early and hit one obstacle after another ever since. His gorge rises. Not that Verity deserved to die even if she had been Frank's mistress, but this is doubly cruel. *The Golden Bones* claimed her father and now, in a way, it has claimed her too. Tears prick his eyes. He presses the heels of his hands into the sockets of his eyes as if he can push them back in.

Erin Kelly

He can't blame his mum for getting the wrong end of the stick. That overheard conversation, which now makes a completely different kind of sense, well – what other conclusion was she supposed to draw? Her husband is a serial adulterer and she was in a room full of his lovers, out of her mind on drugs that he had forced her to take. Cora cannot go down for this.

And neither will he.

He has known since last night, when Frank picked up the murder weapon, that he must put his father in the frame for this girl's death. The shock of the girl's identity doesn't change this. Frank drove Cora to it so absolutely that he might as well have raised the bottle himself. The thing is, Dominic can't call the police *yet*. It's not just that he needs to wait until Cora's strong enough to corroborate whatever story he comes up with. Verity's body is a crime scene and she'll be covered in his and his mum's DNA. She'll have traces of the kiln all over her. What he needs is a way to deal with Verity so that her body remains but the evidence of who has touched her and where she's been disappears, and the only way he can think of to do that is to reduce her to her bones.

It's going to be hot and dry for the rest of the week. That give-away smell – they say that the stench of death is such that you recognise it even if you've never smelt it before – and a cloud of blowfly are only days away. Dom looks at the temperature dial on the kiln. A couple of days at five hundred degrees would get rid of the surface traces, leach the water from her skin, effectively mummify her: stop the stench in its tracks and make her portable. But it would also dry her bright hair into a witchy grey, and shrink-wrap her skin green around her skull. It's too close to something from a horror film. It's too close to that infamous picture of Elinore.

Dom makes it to the sink just in time to heave yellow foam on to the crackled white porcelain.

What he needs is to store Verity for long enough that the method is obscured and only the motive remains, find or rather plant some more evidence that puts Frank in the frame, and *then*

382

call the cops. How, though, will he pare her back to the bone? His whole life, adults at parties have honked facts and anecdotes about bones at him and Nell, as if they were fascinated by skeletons rather than sick to death of them. There must be something there that he can use. The word *skeletonisation* tickles something at the back of his mind. He tries a little word association. *Bones, macerate, fracture, marrow, pathology —*

Hang on—

A St Patrick's party a few springs ago. Dom would've been about thirteen. An old schoolfriend of Lal's had just got a job as a Home Office pathologist, of all things. Dom remembers now because at least when this guy went on about bones you knew you were getting expertise, rather than some random fact someone had picked up playing Trivial Pursuit. The guy had been telling him, Nell and Rose – yep, Rose was there too, it was the last year she'd agreed to wear her Irish dancing costume and perform – about a colleague of his who'd needed a closer look at a hairline fracture. 'And she just couldn't get the bone clean enough, but then she had a thought. Biological washing powder! She said, if the enzymes in that can get poo out of my kids' nappies, I reckon they can work their way through human flesh. So that's what she did! One of the best-equipped labs in the country and there we were in the mortuary dunking a femur in Persil Automatic!'

His wife had turned up then. 'Stop terrifying the children,' she'd chided him. 'It's St Paddy's, not Hallowe'en.'

'They *love* it,' the pathologist had said, but she'd led him off anyway, mouthing apologies over her shoulder. Dom never saw the guy again but he says a silent thank you to him now.

He wakes Cora with a cup of sugary tea and a slice of toast, heavy on the butter. For a second she stares at him blankly, then her hands start to flap and she begins to whimper.

'Nope,' he says. He has decided to be strict with her. 'Get this down you. You can't function if you can't eat, and I need you to be able to hold a conversation.'

'Where is she?' says Cora. 'What are you going to do?'

'Mum,' he says. 'You are not responsible for this. Dad is. Those pills he put you on – you're not yourself when you're taking them. He treats you like shit; no wonder you snapped.' He rubs his eyes but it only makes them feel grittier. 'I will take care of it. It will never come back on you. Do you trust me? I need you to promise you'll never tell anyone. Not even Bridget. And definitely not Dad. All I need you to do is not go near the kiln until I say so, alright?' Cora nods so vaguely that Dominic wonders if his words are going in at all. 'And for the next couple of weeks I want you to start eating properly, not drink, lay off the weed. Just get your head straight. Can you promise me that?'

He starts to run her a bath, pouring expensive oils and bubbles into the steaming water.

'Just the odd joint, to settle my nerves. Get me off to sleep.'

'Mum.' He turns off the taps and regards her through the steam. 'I'm not pissing about. This is serious. You have *got* to keep it together. You can talk to me about it whenever you need to, OK?'

She takes both his hands in hers. 'Thank you, Dominic,' she says. 'I'll do my best.'

He can tell she means it but he has no idea, as he closes the door on her, whether she is *capable* of keeping her word.

98

Dominic has a long shower, scrubbing himself until he's pink all over, then brushes his teeth, his tongue and the roof of his mouth. He still doesn't feel clean enough for Rose, but it's nearly noon and he can't leave it any longer. He tells himself it was the E talking, that she was loved up, she's going to be mortified this morning and thank God they didn't go to bed because it was only a little snog and they don't count; for all he knows she might not even remember it. What is *wrong* with him, that he can contemplate macerating a corpse in relative calm but now it comes to talking to a girl his palms are sweating?

Because it's Rose, that's why.

He crosses the terrace and fortifies himself with a breath so deep it feels like the first one he's taken since before the opening last night. As a courtesy, he raps on the back door before opening it.

'Hello?' he calls.

The Lallys' kitchen is in worse disarray than usual, which is weird because last night's party didn't spill next door as is often the case in the summer. There's a dent in the wood panelling of the wall and splinters on the floor. The kitchen's usual smell – rosemary and joss-sticks – has been replaced by the hospital tang of disinfectant and vomit.

'Everything alright in here?' he calls. There's no answer. He moves into the heart of the house. A plant pot has been overturned and soil has been trodden through the green carpet.

'Lal?' he calls. 'Bridget? Rose? Rose?'

She comes flying down the stairs in her dressing gown, wet hair tumbling out of a turban. When she hurls herself at him it's not in a sex way: she's been crying, she's clinging on for comfort. Dominic holds her as firmly as he can manage while angling his hips away from her to hide what's already started.

'Worst comedown *ever*,' she sniffles. 'I got in at three to find Dad had totally trashed the place. He threw up blood. I've been scrubbing red puke out of the stairs all morning. Mum's taken him to hospital.'

'Oh, *Rose,*' says Dominic.

'*And* she's being really weird with me. Like, she can't even *look* at me.'

He waits for her to finish the sentence: *because she saw us together*. But she doesn't. Maybe she has forgotten.

'She'll just be worried about your dad,' he says.

'Yeah.' Rose pulls away from him and tightens her dressing gown around herself. That's it, thinks Dominic. If she does remember last night, she regrets it. To his horror, tears start to burn under his eyes. He turns away from Rose and busies himself with the fallen pot-plant, tucking the roots back into what little soil is left in the container.

'Dom,' she says. 'I need to ask you something.'

'Go on.'

'Are we still getting married or what?'

They lie tangled in Rose's single bed, the view of the trees fractionally different from the one from Dominic's own window but it might as well be a whole new world. Pete Winship's daughter is decomposing in the studio and Lal is in hospital and Frank is a bastard and Cora is a murderer and Christ knows what's going on with Bridget but here, with Rose in his arms, Dominic is happier than he's ever been. If all these things can be true at once then perhaps compartmentalising for the rest of his life will be easier than he thought.

'In answer to your question,' he says, 'church or register office?'

'Church. You know my dad. St Mary's, in the high street.'

Dominic finds that he doesn't mind. The miracle of his presence in Rose's bed has rocked the foundations of his atheism. 'I wanna wear one of those big meringue dresses.' She sighs, and then asks, 'Lally-Churcher or Churcher-Lally?'

'Chally?' suggests Dominic.

'Lurcher.'

They both laugh. Outside, the agency cleaners are tackling the garden. Bottles shatter as they hit the recycling bin. Dominic wonders which one is the murder weapon. There must be fifty identical empty bottles in that garden. He slides his finger into one of Rose's curls, pulls it down as far as her breast then watches it spring back.

'Are we going to tell them?' she asks. 'If Mum's reaction was anything to go by it's going to be a bit . . . controversial. I sort of want to keep it between us before they all get their opinions all over it. But then, can you be arsed sneaking around, like your dad does?'

Dominic considers. 'In any given situation, I think we should ask each other what our parents would do, and then do the polar opposite.'

He feels her smile: the apple of her cheek firm against his chest. 'Deal,' she says.

They tell everyone that night. As predicted, the parents are a bit weird about it. Frank tells them they're far too young for anything serious, Bridget doesn't say much, Nell says that if they ask her to be a bridesmaid she'll never talk to them again. Cora says, 'Hair of the dog?' and cracks open a bottle of Laurent-Perrier that somehow survived the party. Dom takes this as a good sign. She is carrying on as normal, just as he wanted her to.

Lal, of course, is in hospital, undergoing supervised alcohol withdrawal, when the announcement is made. He won't find out until weeks later, when he's finally allowed visitors. When Bridget tells him, he is so happy that he cries.

Dom tells Cora repeatedly not to tell Bridget what she did,

but a couple of times he's worried that Bridget knows. She has been distant with Cora since the night of the party, in a way that can't only be attributed to the stress of Lal's recovery. The easiness of old, the flow between their two homes, has been invisibly dammed.

99

It's four days after the party before Dom finally has the place to himself. He has read the *Standard* from cover to cover every day and there hasn't been a single mention of Verity Winship. The anxiety that's been pounding under his happiness had begun to subside but as he makes his way down the garden it starts up again, punishing his chest.

From the scrub behind the studio, he retrieves one of the ancient metal dustbins, blackened from decades of bonfires. It won't be missed for a few months: it has been agreed that the traditional Bonfire Night party won't go ahead this year. Lal won't long be out of rehab and Bridget feels it won't be fair to put temptation in his way.

The smell is faint but unmistakable, even before he turns the wheel to open the kiln. Verity looks like a Chamber of Horrors waxwork. Dom is glad he closed her eyes in the dark. He feels like there should be some kind of ceremony. Not religious, obviously, but a reading or a song or something to honour her life before he gets on with what needs to be done. But there are no books except for craft instruction manuals and the radio is stuck on Capital FM; the thought of switching it on and getting Whigfield or a Carphone Warehouse advert is grotesque. For a moment he thinks about singing, or at least reciting, a few verses from 'To Gather the Bones', but he comes to his senses just in time. In the end he just says, 'I really wish it had all been different for you,' before he gets to work.

Right.

Her black dress is synthetic and it needs to go. 'I'm so sorry,' he says as he cuts it off her with Cora's sewing scissors. Removing her underwear is a further violation. He forces himself look at the grubby half-moons of her bra and the scrappy triangles of her knickers on the floor and not the flesh they housed. He treats her gently, as if she were sleeping, sliding his hands under her arms and lowering her, still locked in her foetal position, into the metal drum, which he then slides back into the kiln. He uses the garden hose to fill it to the brim with water and tips in six packets of Persil Bio that fizz and bubble and almost cover the smell.

He transcribes the names and addresses in her scrappy notebook into an old physics textbook that no one but he will think to open. Not outright: he's not stupid. He uses a basic cipher that a Bonehunter would see through at a glance. The notebook, her clothes, the cigarettes, he drops into various different bins across the Heath on an early morning walk.

100

Nobody is suspicious when Cora abruptly loses interest in pottery.

'That's just her way, isn't it?' she overhears Frank tell Marcelle, a week or so after the show. 'She flits from one medium to another one, gets bored as soon as she's mastered the skill.'

And if this time she doesn't take up another project immediately, no one thinks too hard about that, either. The success of *Intimacies* and Lal's progress in rehab means that no one is really thinking about the wives.

Dominic believes he knows differently. He presumes she can't face the studio and of course she doesn't want to set foot in the place, knowing what is happening inside the kiln, but that is only part of the reason. Cora stops making because her work might not sell for six figures and it might not be fashionable but it comes from the heart, so how could her secret not leak out in her art? It would be like painting with blood, weaving with entrails, making jewellery from a young woman's bones.

When she was a child, Cora was often praised for being a good girl. She was quiet and undemanding, in the corner with her crayons. The grown-ups never understood that she wasn't good – she wasn't *there*. She was up the Faraway Tree or carving arrows from branches in Sherwood Forest, or prowling a Cretan labyrinth with a mirrored shield. For as long as she can remember, it has been easier – necessary, even – for her to have at least one foot in another world.

But now she has passed into a new realm from which there is no going back. She lives in a place inhabited only by those who have taken another human life. It is a superterranean Hades that is superimposed on the world where the innocent live, a club so secret even its members do not know each other. When she is in any kind of crowd she will look at the assembled strangers and wonder who else walks this world with her. She is plagued by elaborate fantasies that one day a vengeful – or maybe just bored – god will decide to expose them all. Cora and the other murderers will look up to see a swirling stormcloud above their heads. Nobody can explain the phenomenon, and the murderers aren't letting on. Sometimes they allow a brief moment of recognition in the street and the expression is always the same. You? *Really?* I'd never have guessed.

Eventually the connection is made between the clouds that hang over convicted killers and the disproportionate number of cloud people who have a missing person in their lives. The cloud people are rounded up and imprisoned without trial. Cora's imagination incarcerates them in a motte-and-bailey castle. Their collective clouds merge to form one huge navy-blue cumulonimbus that hangs so low it soaks their clothes and hair.

And this is just Cora's daydream. The nightmares wake her up as though someone has placed electric paddles on her chest. When she sleeps, it is not a thunderbolt that marks the killers but their victims. The waitress begins to follow Cora wherever she goes. Cora has forgiven the girl for sleeping with Frank; she sees now that she too was a victim long before Cora got to her. The waitress is not a staggering zombie; she looks just as she did when she was serving drinks – unless Cora is unlucky enough to glimpse the back of her head, and there she will find a mosaic of broken skull and what looks like hot red tar embedded in the girl's bright gold hair.

Thank goodness for Dominic. She must have done something right to raise a young man like him. By standing within the circle of her guilt, he has shown her that the true fault lies without it. She clings to it, the knowledge that none of this would have happened if it weren't for Frank, when her imagination gets the better of her.

When the night terrors shake Cora awake, and she sits up in bed, her heart pounding fit to displace a rib, she looks at Frank beside her and she visualises the burden passing from her body into his. One day, she will find a way to make him pay for what he has turned her into.

IOI

Dom isn't sure when he first experiences respite from thinking about Verity. Even in the magic of those early weeks with Rose, she is there, a rotting corpse sharing the bed with them. But about a month in, he realises that the book he's reading is actually going in and the letters are no longer sliding off the page to be replaced by images of cracked skulls and glassy blue eyes. When the conkers and acorns start to carpet the Heath there comes a morning when he wakes up and it's a matter of minutes rather than seconds before he sees her face or imagines quite what stage of decomposition she will be at by now. By Christmas, he can go for hours at a time without thinking about what he has done. He dares to hope that, in the future, he might make it through a whole day.

Dom doesn't enact the final part of his plan until the following autumn. He has followed Rose to the University of Sussex, where they share a little cottage just outside Brighton, but there's a weekend when both sets of parents are away from the Vale. Under the pretence of going to a careers fair, he drives up to London. When he opens the kiln again he braces for the smell, his forearm a barrier under his nose, but while it's not fragrant it no longer smells like rotting flesh. It's boggy and stagnant, rather like the lake at the bottom of the Vale. He opens the lid of the drum to find it is full of a greeny-brown slurry, which he siphons off and tips on to the rose bed outside Cora's studio door. Here and there are traces of the flesh that held the bone together, but under the tap they come away like wet tissue paper. When Dom has finished, there is a beautifully clean skeleton, her only imperfection a spiderweb crack in the back of the skull. A horrible thought comes to him: this is what Rose looks like underneath. He feels a surge of protectiveness for her.

He spreads the bones on the stone table, out of sight of the security cameras. It's a warm day and they are touch-dry in an hour. He places them in a big blue IKEA bag, carries them gently up the stairs and unscrews Gertrude from her frame on the wall. He staggers into his bedroom and sets the frame on the floor before unhinging the glass front. If he had his parents' artistic flair he could sketch the arrangement for reference, but he has to rely on his memory. He unpins Gertrude from her red velvet backing, replacing the fake bones with real ones. It is painstaking work involving wires and pins. The teeth are a problem. Those gaps and fillings are distinctive. But Gertrude's head had been arranged at an angle, tilted down so she appeared to be gazing at her left shoulder, and by the time Dominic has finished he reckons you'd have to know what you were looking for to see it.

Actual Gertrude, the horror-film fibreglass girl, he burns in the garden, in the brazier where he macerated Verity's corpse. It makes a chemical stench that half-blinds him and fucks up his lungs so badly that when he gets back to the cottage in Sussex, he can barely manage the stairs.

The following spring, everyone remarks on what a good year it is for the roses outside the studio. Fat, double-headed blooms that last well into the autumn. Dom finds them deeply unsettling but he can't put his finger on why, apart from the obvious. In the end it comes to him in a nightmare. He wakes up, drenched in sweat and screaming. Beside him, Rose puts a hand on his shoulder, comforting him even in her sleep.

Dom's already forgotten the narrative of the dream but one image has seared itself into his memory. A single rose petal floating in murky water, the same peachy gold as the flowers that bloom outside Cora's studio. The last time he saw a colour like that was Verity's hair, waving like the fronds of a beautiful aquatic plant hand as he pressed her head down under the soap-scented water.

102

In summer 1999, Dom moves on to his next task: getting Verity Winship on the missing persons list. Her letters to Frank are one thing, but if no one has reported her missing, the police won't know whose bones these are. But once they know it's Verity Winship, well, it'll be an open and shut case.

All Dominic has to go on is the coded list of names and numbers in the back of an old textbook. While Rose is at a lecture, Dominic sits at their kitchen table and withholds the house phone number before calling. It doesn't start well: a couple of numbers have been disconnected, one person's never heard of Verity and another says she still owes them fifty quid and she can fuck off if she thinks she's crashing at their place again. But Dominic skims the bulls-eye with his fifth call, the name Hayley and a London number, and tells the woman who answers that he's looking to trace a Verity Winship.

'What's it regarding?' asks Hayley. There's a newborn crying in the background.

He's planned for this. 'I'm calling from Her Majesty's Revenue and Customs. She's due a tax rebate after an overpayment last year.'

'Verity actually earned enough to pay tax?' asks Hayley. 'Well, I never. But I can't help you. She was only crashing here the odd night. Let's just say that it wasn't completely out of character for her not to come home. I've still got a bag of her stuff – don't like to chuck it. You've obviously tried Marilyn? Sorry, I don't know her last name.'

'She's next on my list,' he says, and skips ahead to M. The voice that answers is old and wavery.

'I'm looking to trace a Verity Winship.' He gives her his HMRC spiel and gives Hayley's address as Verity's last known residence to convince this Marilyn that he knows all about her.

'I wish I could help you, love. But I've not seen her for a good couple of years now. It's been on my mind, to be honest. She never turned up on Boxing Day, not last year or the one before. She can be very flighty, can Verity, but she's always popped in on the 26th for a mince pie and a catch-up. Every year since she left.'

'Since she left . . .'

'I fostered her for a couple of months, just before she left care. You're not supposed to have favourites, but some kids you just – you know. She was the last one, as well. Bloody handful, she was. Made me realise I was getting too old for it all.'

He likes that. A foster mother. The police would take that seriously.

'That's concerning,' says Dominic. 'Have you reported her missing?'

'I thought about it,' admits Marilyn. 'But Verity didn't like the—'

She seems to remember she's talking to someone 'official'. Dom is pretty certain the word she swallowed was 'police'. The picture he's building of Verity is someone who lived on the margins.

He chooses his next words carefully. 'Because if you did, the police might be able to trace her and then I'd know where to send this cheque. I'd do it myself, only it's a breach of data protection. In fact, I shouldn't even be telling you this now. Do me a favour, don't tell them I suggested it. I don't want to lose my job!'

'Oh, *no*. I wouldn't want to get you into trouble,' says Marilyn.

'Well. Let's hope you find her, and we can send her her rebate.'

'I will do. Thank you, love.'

He rocks back on the kitchen chair. The conversation has left him hot; there are sweat rings under his arms. That is as far as he dares push it. Marilyn will tell the police Verity is missing. Marilyn will give them Hayley's number. Hayley has a bag of her things. Dom pictures a hairbrush, matted with strawberry blonde hairs, the roots little white bulbs packed with genetic code that spell out Verity's name as clearly as letters.

103

Vale of Health, London NW3
9 August 2021

For the past half-hour, the duration of Dom and Cora's confessions, I have been systematically plucking the feathers out of the raspberry-pink sofa cushions. There's a scene of avian carnage on my lap. The millpond calm I feel must be some kind of mental shutdown. Maybe I'm saving my explosion for when Dom tells me what he did with the jewel. Maybe it's the need to keep my mouth shut about Bridget and Frank until I know what *they* know. So far, they haven't mentioned her once.

Or is it that I am not, in fact, surprised?

Cora as a killer makes an awful kind of sense. With that as my starting point, it's not too much of a leap to accept Dom covering for her. He's always been a mummy's boy; he's always hated Frank. Why shouldn't my solid, clever brother be adept at dissolving bodies and pinning them to walls for his family to wander past every day?

'So for years, what we all thought was Gertrude was really Verity Winship? While we were all eating Sunday lunch down here, while we had your *wedding reception* in the garden, up there on the landing there were literal human remains?' My voice has risen to a screech. The purple shadows under Dom's eyes seem to spread and darken by the second.

'I am so, so sor—'

'*Save* it.' My sense of calm was short-lived. I would like to hit Dom. I could land a punch as hard as a man's and I would enjoy it. 'When I took her down off the wall that time Aoife had a melt-down, I was handling a real dead girl's bones? Jesus *Christ*, Dom! No wonder you wouldn't let your kids play with her. Oh, this is fucked. This is fucked *up*.' I start to sweep the feathers into a little pyramid on my lap, a delicate operation at odds with my body's all-over thrumming of adrenaline. 'I take it you put her in Lal's attic?'

'I could hardly let her be picked up by the bin men, could I?'

'No, that would *never* do. Can't have the bin men upset, can we?'

'Eleanor . . .' says Cora weakly, but Dom puts his hand up to show her he can handle me.

'That day,' he says. 'When you'd all gone and Dad was asleep in front of the telly, I took her out of the bin. Lal and Bridget were out so I just thought, I'll pop her in their attic while I work out what to do with her.'

Pop her in the attic, like she's a winter coat he won't be needing for a few months. I edge the pyramid's base with tiny white feathers as though getting the design right is the most important thing in the world.

'Verity was up there, what, ten years?' I ask Dom without look-ing at him.

'Give or take.'

'So why get her out again that day?'

'I wanted Dad to get the blame for her death. I used to fantasise about it. Seeing his face when he understood what he'd set in motion. Literally fantasise. I'd picture myself unlocking the attic door and—'

He's seized on the wrong part of the question.

'No, I get that you wanted to make him pay. I mean, why *that day*? You told me that working on the app had brought you and Frank together – you were getting on at last.' I put a little brown feather on the top of the pile. It quivers in a breeze I can't feel. 'And even if he was being a monster, you basically risked trashing your own app. I know it turned out to be good publicity but there's no way you could've known that. What was it? Did he make one of his snide remarks?'

God knows we've all had *that* experience.

Dom looks out of the window on to the Vale as though shoring up strength for what's coming next. 'It wasn't something he said. It was something I saw. You were *there*, Nell. I was on hold to Leelo and Billie put it right down in front of me.'

Leelo, Billie, Dom: I reorientate myself in Cora's kitchen: a pile of brownies, orange juice, coffee. He means the catalogue and honestly, thank *fuck*. If they already know about the painting of Bridget, I don't have to be the one to break it to them.

But someone's got to say it.

The three of us regard each other warily, knowing there's something huge to be said and all hoping someone else will be the one to say it, because it will change everything. After ten seconds of loaded silence, it becomes apparent that person is me.

'The catalogue.'

Putting it out there is like undoing a notch on a too-tight belt. Cora and Dom nod in unison. It's a reprieve for them too. His shoulders drop. She gives me a watery grimace. 'Your brother only showed me it last night. Once you see it . . .'

'If only it could be unseen,' said Dominic hopelessly. 'You don't know how much time over the past week I've spent wishing I'd never seen it. That I could un-know it.'

'Did you know about it at the time?' I ask Cora.

She shakes her head vigorously. 'Christ, no. Of course not, I'd *never* have let it carry on. Never.' This seems a strange choice of words: as if Cora ever had any control over what Frank did. 'Dominic told me the day after the bone was found. I've had a few days to come to terms with it. Lal hasn't a clue. Only Bridget knew.'

'Well, of course *Bridget* knew,' I say. 'She's the one in the painting.'

Dom makes a weird noise, like he's aiming for language but can't quite get there. Cora takes his hand and her whole face changes. In the act of mothering her son she has become thirty again, and my brother looks like a little boy.

'Eleanor, love.' Cora's voice is thick. 'The painting. It's not Bridget.'

PART FIVE

104

Rosaleen isn't sure how long she's been standing, still as a sculpture, in front of her portrait. She approaches the painting – it is of her back, but is so clearly her that it might as well be a passport photograph – in tiny steps, as though she is playing Grandmother's Footsteps, as though her painted self will turn and look over her shoulder if she moves too quickly. She cannot believe he has gone through with it. He threatened it, when she ended things with him – *I'm going to paint you and hang you on the wall* – but she had thought it was something he had thrown out in the heat of the moment, not something he would really do to her, to her dad.

The gold bangle on her upper arm drops to her elbow, striking bone.

'Bridget?' Someone behind her calls her mother's name. Rose doesn't turn around. Her face will give it all away. She has borrowed her mother's dress and jewellery in an effort to appear sophisticated. She dressed up like this for Frank, once, to show him she wasn't just some kid. It backfired then – he preferred her school uniform – and it's backfired in a different way now. She looks the part but doesn't feel like herself. She's playing at being a grown-up. Again. She should have just worn her Topshop slip dress and her Adidas Gazelles. Nell's wearing a kind of sack with a hole in it and her hair's a mess of dreadlocks. Nell has always been very good at being herself. Maybe you have to leave to do it.

Rose isn't quite sure who she is but she knows she is no longer the kind of girl who would go to bed with her father's best friend, her best friend's father. Not the age thing – age is just numbers – but the family-ness of it, that's where the wrongness was. The whole thing had been taking on a comfortable air of unreality in the two years since she told him it was the last time, but now here it is, immortalised in paint. And yet.

I have to leave, she thinks – no, she knows it. I have to get out of this fucked-up extended family.

'Bridget!' says the voice again. This time Rose does turn around and the woman says, 'Christ – sorry.' As she plunges back into the crowd, Rose catches her say to her friend, 'Peas in a pod, aren't they?'

New blades of panic start to rotate inside Rose. She'd been so horrified at the thought of anyone recognising *her*, she hadn't considered that they might mistake the portrait for her mother.

105

When her feet are sore from traipsing the streets looking for Lal, Bridget gives up. At the top of the Vale she says a little prayer to St Christopher: please let the T-Bird be there, its fender unbent and unbloodied, the driver in one piece. There are a dozen unfamiliar cars parked outside, but no Thunderbird. Come on, now, she urges St Christopher. Pull your finger out.

She thanks the men on the door then plunges into a party that's fizzing with dark energy. It's hard to separate the night into its constituent parts; the intrusion, the sellout, the showdown, the gossip. She watches Rosaleen lead a swaying procession of teenagers carrying bottles into Nell's bedroom, sees a little paper bag change hands. They've always been liberal about that sort of thing, believing that if the children are going to experiment, they may as well do it at home. Should they have been stricter, more traditional? Did this attitude carve a space for Frank to move in on? Tonight, Bridget only hopes they'll pace themselves. And God knows emotions are running high for these kids. They've just shielded their friend from a nutter with a knife. Is it that that's made Rose hold herself so rigidly, or is it that she too has seen the painting?

Bridget treads a path through the house, top floor to bottom, and then makes a circuit of the garden, alert for headlamps in the street, hoping to catch Rose alone, watching Cora for signs that she knows, and dreading Frank's arrival. She repeats the route over and over. Every time the party has changed; new bodies on the landing, different music coming from the speakers.

She finds Cora first; in fact they crash into each other, as Bridget opens the downstairs loo just as Cora comes bowling out of it. She is red and clammy, as though she's been exercising.

'How're you—' begins Bridget but Cora responds with a 'Not now,' and escapes into the garden. A hot flush, thinks Bridget. Poor Cora, dealing with menopause on top of all this.

Outside, 'I'm A Barbie Girl' starts playing and the whole house groans.

Bridget takes a moment to gather herself. She sits on the closed toilet seat and takes a few deep breaths that if anything make her heart race faster. She splashes cold water on her face the way people do on telly when they're stressed. Now she is stressed with a wet face and smudged mascara. She emerges from the loo to see Rosaleen and Dominic kissing by the coat rack. Her belly flips because, before her cognitive brain can leap to the part where this is the absolute worst thing to happen and the worst possible timing, her lizard brain is thinking how perfect they look together, how right, how this is clearly something a million times bigger and deeper than a teenage snog.

Dominic sees her first. He opens his eyes just a fraction, as if he too is looking for something, and upon seeing Bridget they snap wide and he freezes. It takes Rosaleen a few seconds to catch up.

'Oops.' Rosaleen giggles. She is no longer rigid: whatever's in her veins has made her loose and liquid. She giggles as though none of this will have consequences, and that flips Bridget into disciplinarian mode.

'Rosaleen Lally, I would like to speak with you at home.' She literally pulls Rosaleen away from Dominic. It's like disentangling two cables that have been snarled together in a drawer for years.

'You do realise we have to get married now?' Rosaleen calls over her shoulder. Bridget doesn't turn to see Dominic's face.

The terrace is a dancefloor that spans both houses. Bridget leads a loose-limbed Rosaleen into their kitchen and up to the girl's bedroom, where the bass thumps the soles of their feet, but they can hear each other talk.

'Right, so . . .' she begins, and is suddenly unsure how to continue. This is either a conversation that should be had in the cold light of tomorrow, or one that must be had now while her defences are down and her mind is open. She opts for the latter. 'Rosaleen, you can't start anything with Dominic.'

Rosaleen raises her chin, apparently for a nod, but leaves it tilted in defiance. 'Oh, sorry,' she says. 'I was under the impression this was *my* life.'

Bridget sighs. The problem with raising strong women is that they make formidable opponents. She decides to just come out with it.

'I saw Frank's painting of you.'

Rose takes a great, shuddering inbreath that might be shock or might be drugs.

'Were you really fourteen?' Bridget asks.

Rosaleen's pupils flare. The green of her irises all but disappears. 'What are you going to do?' she asks.

Jesus, this London kid, thinks Bridget. She makes you long for the convent. 'What do *you* think we should do?'

'Nothing.'

'Right. Well, I think we should leave.'

'Leave? And go where?' Rosaleen gestures around her room and then next door, as if these two houses, on this plot of land, are the only residences in London.

'Pet.' Bridget takes Rosaleen's hands. 'We can't live next to a man who abused you. Seeing him every day. Lying to Cora.'

Rosaleen tosses her hair over her shoulder. 'It wasn't abuse. I wasn't a virgin. I was up for it.'

Even in her horror, Bridget feels a glimmer of pride. There's no shame coming from Rosaleen, only defiance. But what a tightrope they're going to have to walk to keep it that way.

'I'm not a child, Mum.'

Oh, but she is. She doesn't understand what he's done to her. Never mind the act; one day she'll work out that it was never about her, that Frank was using her to feel power over Lal, and when it lands . . . Bridget will be there for the fallout. She always is. It's who she is; it's what she does. Despite all those books with her name on the cover, she's still a nurse to the core, and what else is nursing but coping for those who cannot cope themselves?

'Was the baby his?'

Rosaleen nods. 'Yeah.'

'And he left you to deal with it on your own?' For some reason this lack of gallantry, even in the context of desecration, sticks in her craw.

'Oh, no, he did help. He wrote me a cheque for it. But I could hardly use it in front of you, could I?'

Bridget's newly discovered slyness stirs. 'What did you do with it?'

Rosaleen opens her desk drawer and takes out a ragged copy of the *NME* with Kurt Cobain on the cover. Tucked inside is Frank's signature on a cheque made out to the private family planning clinic that performed the abortion.

Bridget puts it in her pocket.

'You can't show this to Dad,' says Rosaleen. 'God knows what he'd do.'

Failure washes over Bridget in a huge wave. Her girl has two father figures. One she's terrified of. The other molested her. 'How did I not *see*?'

It's an expression of guilt, not a real question, but Rosaleen answers anyway. 'You were on a deadline and Dad was on a bender. No one was really looking my way.'

Bridget thought she knew about guilt, but *this*. 'The two of us could get a wee cottage somewhere. Start again.'

'What about Dom?' says Rosaleen. 'What about Dad?'

Maybe this is one conversation that should wait until the morning.

The DJ's doing a Motown set. The terrace is full of middle-aged people frugging to 'Your Love Is Lifting Me Higher' by Jackie Wilson. Bridget's eye is drawn to spangles at the end of the garden, an encroaching starfield that reveals itself to be the sequins on Cora's dress when she and Dom step out of the shadows and under the strings of lights. Dom is holding his mother up: her face is a mess.

'Bit too much to drink,' he says, manoeuvring his mother through the crowd.

'Classic Cora,' Bridget overhears someone say. 'It wouldn't be a Churcher party without any casualties, would it?'

Bridget fills in the gaps: Dom's taken his mum to the back of the garden for a discreet puke, and now he's putting her to bed.

He's a good boy.

Bridget's instinct is to take over, but if Dom's caring for Cora then he can't be snogging Rosaleen, and even a half-hour cooling-off period might make them realise they're better off as friends.

Who's she kidding? She saw them. She knows what has been set in motion tonight.

Bridget wades through a thick treacle of small talk on her route from the terrace to Cora's bedroom. By the time she gets there, Dom has gone. Cora is bathed and dressed for bed and she is silently crying. The bodice of her nightgown is transparent with tears.

'Hey,' says Bridget. Cora lets her hold her in a way that Rosaleen never would.

'All those women,' is all she can get out.

All those women. If she'd seen the painting, she'd say, wouldn't she?

'You should throw him out,' suggests Bridget, realising as she speaks that that's the ideal solution: if they divorce, perhaps *Frank* could go and the rest of them could stay here.

'He'd never go.' Cora shakes her head. 'And I can't leave now.' She dissolves into messy crying, only the odd word intelligible: w*omen, studio, champagne, Frank, affair, studio*. She has lost control of what she's saying. Bridget pricks her ears for her daughter's name but nothing resembling it comes.

Cora doesn't know about Frank and Rosaleen.

But the knowledge she *does* have is burden enough. One night in the real world, facing up to the truth of her marriage, has nudged Cora further along the road to madness. The whole truth about Frank would fast-track her to the destination.

Bridget lets Cora cry herself to sleep. She is close to dozing off herself when she hears the T-Bird's brakes squeal outside. She watches through the curtains as Lal parks the car at a forty-five-degree angle to the pavement.

'You want me to straighten that up for you, Lal?' says one of the dads on the door.

'Sure.' Lal tosses him the car keys. 'I'm getting a thirst on me now.'

106

Twenty-four hours later Bridget is in the family room at a private rehab clinic where doctors explain that her husband has got himself to a point where stopping is as dangerous as carrying on, and that they are withdrawing him from alcohol under managed conditions.

Leaving him there is one of the hardest things she has ever done. In the car park she turns up Radio 2 full blast and lets middle-of-the-road rock music cover her screams.

She gets home in the early evening. Rosaleen has cleaned the house. Dominic isn't there, but Bridget can smell him on her daughter.

'Please don't make a big thing of it,' she pleads.

'Rosaleen, you've experienced a huge abuse of trust. It *is* a big thing.'

'Only if you make it. I've handled it for the last couple of years, haven't I? I haven't jumped off a building or anything.'

'Entering into a sexual relationship with anyone is a huge thing, let alone the son of a man who . . .' She tries to make her next words sound like wisdom. 'There's a day coming for you, my love.' She can see from Rosaleen's face that they have been received as a threat.

Rosaleen is scornful. 'The only thing that's changed is that you know. You're the only one who wants to blow this up. What's it gonna to do Cora? Nell? Dad? And we can carry this between us, can't we? Come on, Mum. We're stronger than the rest of them put together.'

That much, Bridget knows is true.

*　　*　　*

Bridget doesn't see Lal for another two days. When she is allowed to visit him she senses the shift as soon as she sets eyes on him. His skin is yellow and his lips are chalky, but something internal and fundamental has taken place.

'I'm gonna give it a go, Bridie,' he says. 'I've let the drink take me to some dark places, but this . . .'

She'll be staying married, then. She knows that she'll be safe from now on. The miracle she's prayed for has happened. But she must know what his rock bottom was.

'What happened at the opening?' she asks. 'What did you see that night?' She studies the face she knows as well as her own.

He shrugs. 'You tell me.'

'Oh, Lal.'

'Like I said. I mean it this time.' Seemingly for no reason, he breaks into a wide smile that threatens to crack his lips and says, 'Come here to me, you aul bastard.'

Bridget smells pepper and bergamot. Her whole body clenches. 'Hello, Frank,' she says without moving her jaw.

'Bridget,' he says. It's the first time she's seen him since the party. She can't look him in the eye so she stares at his forearms, exposed by the shirtsleeves he's rolled up to the elbow. They are veined and hairy, repulsively male and adult. I could murder him, she realises.

''Frank's going to be my recovery buddy,' says Lal. 'He's going sober in solidarity.'

Finally she raises her eyes to Frank's face. His expression is equal parts desperate and daring. *You wouldn't*, his face insists, and then in the next blink: *you can't. You're the only one who wants to drag this into the light, Bridget. We are too enmeshed. Cora and Lal are fragile: they need things to stay the way they are. And then there are the kids . . .*

Bridget bites her tongue while the guys toss love back and forth in the form of insults. Lal's responses come slower each time. Within half an hour, he is asleep. By unspoken mutual agreement, Frank and Bridget wait until he's snoring before they speak directly to each other.

'I never—' he begins.

She doesn't care what he never did. What he did is enough.

'Rosaleen kept the cheque,' she says.

She can tell by his face that he grasps the threat hidden in those four words. She has raised a guillotine that she will leave to sway over his head. It will have to do until such time as the others are strong enough to know the truth. When Rosaleen understands what happened to her, when Lal is a few years dry, when Cora is out the other side of the change, all Bridget will need to do is twitch the rope to bring the blade down on Frank Churcher's neck.

107

Vale of Health, London NW3
31 July 2021

Dominic surveys the swarm on the lawn. Oisin seems to be carrying the same length of cable from one side of the garden to the other. He hopes Crabwise are giving him something useful to do, not just pointless busywork.

He's got Leelo in one ear, talking so fast he can't keep up. Nell is bombarding him with questions about tracing emails. She's worried that the nutter online pretending to be in contact with Ingrid is to be taken seriously. He trusts that the other Bonehunters will shout them down.

Leelo puts him on hold. He shuffles the papers on his desk, fiddles with a pen – and is confronted with a picture of his naked mother on the cover of the *Intimacies* catalogue.

Christ.

The night of.

Over Sunday lunch, Dom once foolishly asked his father if there was any truth in Jane Jones's insistence that the *Intimacies* pictures contained veiled clues to the last gold bone. He'd been braced for anger but Frank had howled with laughter and said, 'As if I'd do anything to get that load of pricks back into my life! Christ, Dominic, for a clever boy you can be really fucking dense.'

Boy. He'd been thirty-seven at the time. He'd got drunk, gone home and fired off a posting on an account he hadn't used for years, one he had set up soon after replacing Gertrude with Verity. It must have been, what, 1999, when the forums started to take off. In a long-gone internet café off Oxford Street, he had enlisted with ElinoresArmy as @Yorick and begun to lay digital bread-crumbs that would 'prove' his father killed Verity Winship. That drunken, angry Sunday, Yorick let rip. *I know things about the treasure hunt that would make your eyes bleed*, he'd typed. *One day, when the time is right, I'll blow the lid off everything.*

God. He cringes to think of it now. The complete works of Yorick are all still there if you know where to look. He's posted on Reddit, too, and Quora. Dom's actually been meaning to delete the lot for a couple of years. Because they're in a good place now, him and his dad. Not perfect, but compared to how it used to be . . .

Dom flicks through the catalogue, for something to do with his hands really. The text is as incomprehensible to him now as it was then, but the pictures send him spinning back through the years to the night of, champagne and mirrors, paint and smoke. There's Adeola, navy blues and purples capturing the light on her dark, supple skin. The next page is a striking contrast: a thin woman, pale skin evoked with brushstrokes of green and grey which trigger something uncomfortable in Dominic. Is it that the colours mimic decomposing flesh? Keen to halt the stone that appears to be falling through his insides, he flips overleaf, to a close-up of a pair of small brown breasts that he remembers from the night, those nipples like eyes following you around the room.

Dominic's body understands who the pale woman is before his brain does.

His heart sends an electric shock to his hand and it turns back to the previous page without his permission; his eyes zoom in on the telling detail. At the base of the woman's spine, between the two dimples that top her buttocks, is a little white scar, a pucker-ing of flesh. He knows that scar. He has touched that scar, he has kissed it; he has looked at that scar with his heart in his mouth as his wife's body split open in childbirth. That's the scar Rose got when she fell off the rope swing when she was little.

He looks at the date. Frank painted this in 1994.

Rose was fourteen.

Dominic goes blind for a second.

He is sure that no one knows about it; the next second he is sure that they have all known about it, all along, and that they have been laughing at him: what a sucker.

She was *fourteen*.

He looks over at Billie and dry-heaves.

Just a year older than Aoife, for Christ's sake. The dry heave turns wet. He swallows a dose of his own stomach acid.

In his earbuds, Leelo starts talking about the back-end server and – later, he will wonder how he managed to do this – Dominic is able to take in what she says and reply in a normal voice. The only distraction is Nell and Billie, giggling like a pair of schoolgirls. That laughter should be music: this kid makes Nell happier than he's seen her for years, and he's so bloody proud of how his sister is raising her. But in the circumstances it's an unbearable sound. He mutes Leelo, just for a second, to yell at them.

'Will the two of you just pack it in? My head is about to explode here.'

Dom isn't a yeller, not with his family anyway, so Nell gets out of his way. Clearly she thinks he's worried about the app. Dominic stares at the wall as they leave because if he makes eye contact with his sister he knows he'll blurt out everything. Everything.

Without stopping his call to Leelo, Dom takes a photo of the offending picture, and the one next to it, and immediately puts it in the hidden album on his phone.

The next twenty minutes are spent hammering keys and trading information with Leelo. Dominic goes into a kind of fugue state where a part of him takes over that needs to save the app. It's like having two tabs on a computer open at the same time, both of them processing completely different applications simultaneously and at lightning speed. He views his brain as a diagram from GCSE biology. His prefrontal cortex is a machine of restraint, control and information delivery, scrolling through reams of code. His amygdala, home of emotion, is shorting out.

Questions drop into his brain like Tetris tiles.

Was it consensual? He cannot stand the thought that it wasn't and he cannot stand the thought that it was. But of course it can't have been. Frank would have been in his mid to late forties, a few years older than Dominic is now, and it is fucking grotesque. Rose was fourteen; she was a child. They had been sophisticated London children but she was still a child. Did he get her drunk – did he spike her?

He grasps at a straw. Perhaps Frank painted from imagination, which is a deeply unpleasant thought but one that cuts Rose free from abuse. Could Frank have seen Rose's scar? She was eight when she fell from the swing. Dominic thinks back to the summers in the garden running around under the sprinklers, but Rose was pale and prone to sunburn and Bridget always made her cover up in one-piece swimsuits that looked more like leotards. His dad had only seen Rose naked before the scar, as a child – here, the bile rises again: how can you fuck someone who danced in the sprinklers in your garden as a child? – and then he finds himself blaming Rose: how can you fuck someone who raised you like a father?

The world is blurring around him, his marriage warping.

There is the fact that it happened, and then there is the fact that she never told him. She never named the boyfriend who got her pregnant, just that he was some older guy

He looks at the date again.

Oh, Jesus *Christ*.

While Dominic is on hold, again, he closes his eyes and sees images, random body parts, of his wife, who he was in love with even then. The images are vile and they won't stop coming. His father bending Rose over the studio daybed, his father's head disappearing under the pleats of Rose's school skirt, while Dom was still dreaming about her in double maths and wanking over her in the shower.

A row of wine glasses stand on the work surface. Dom wants to smash one against the marble and plunge it into his father's heart. He turns his attention to the screen for a second and when he looks up Dara is there, his fat little arms folded around some picture book.

Dominic finds that he is able to open a third tab in his head, the window that makes him a father.

'Hey, little guy!' he says. 'Nice to see you with some clothes on.'

'Can I have a story?' asks Dara.

Dominic manages a gravity-defying smile. 'D'you know what, buddy, I would *love* that.' He taps his earbud. 'But I have to stay on the phone right now. Why don't you go next door and see if your grandmas are back with the girls?'

Dara wanders off. The window of fatherhood shuts down and a new one opens, playing the old revenge fantasy. It was never supposed to be enacted with a house full of strangers, of course, but it offers its own comfort.

Dominic closes his eyes and walks the route in real time. Up the familiar stairs to the Lallys' attic, cutting a swath through the crap, finding the pelvic bone and making the switch. It's more intense than just watching a movie; it's as though Dominic's wearing a VR headset and gloves: he can *feel* his fingers on the light switch, he can *smell* the weed in the attic, he can *taste* the dust on his tongue. Out the back door, up the tree, switch the bones, back down again before anyone has noticed. Another quick trip, the rest of Verity hidden in the studio when everyone breaks for lunch, or even in the lake. He lets the fantasy progress farther than he ever has before. He imagines the confusion and rage on Sir Frank Churcher's face as he is arrested for murder.

But the garden is full of film crew, and that great lunk Shane is standing guard, and the fantasy must remain just that.

108

'Have you seen Dara?'

Dom looks up from his page of code. His wife looks exactly as she did half an hour ago and she is also a completely different person. He can't answer with words. He jerks his head in the direction of next door.

'Is he wearing clothes?'

Dom takes a deep breath and chokes on it. Rose finally senses that something is wrong.

'Shit,' she says. 'Is it fucked?'

It takes him a couple of beats to understand. Like Nell, she thinks he's upset about the app. A weird laugh issues from his throat.

'Dom?'

His next words bolt from his mouth without warning. 'The older boyfriend you had when we were kids. Was it my father?'

Now Rose is struck dumb, but she goes very white and then a blotch appears high on each cheek, blank paper absorbing red ink from a dropper. It is all the truth Dom needs.

'How—' She can't get the rest of the words out.

He scans the desk for the catalogue but it has vanished under a sea of paper, so he pulls up the photo on his iPad. Zooms in on the little white scar at the base of her spine. He observes Rose's reaction to the image. She is rigid as a statue but her curls are shaking, almost vibrating. There's one question he has to ask, one piece of awful knowledge that will shape the rest of this conversation.

'Did he force you into it?'

Rose sits down. Someone drags a camera on wheels across the terrace, close enough to overhear. She drops her voice.

421

'OK, so what you need to know is that I've had my whole adult life to get my head around this,' she says. 'The way I think about it now is not how it was at the time. It obviously came up a lot in therapy and—'

Therapy. The weekly sessions she has to do as part of her own practice. Eleven years since she trained as a psychologist. Eleven years that some woman in Muswell Hill with a Poäng chair and spider plants has known his wife better than he has.

'Just answer me,' he says.

Rose interlaces her fingers and starts to play cat's cradle with her own hands. 'He did and he didn't. Physically, no, he didn't force me, in that sense I was willing. I wasn't a virgin. He didn't hurt me at the time. I was the one to end it. But equally . . . what I would have described as seduction back then, we would now call grooming.'

It seems grossly unfair that Rose has the advantage of years to come to terms with it. She is calm. She has become her therapeutic self. Whereas he is a raw mess and can barely get the words out. He hates his wife for how calm she is being.

'You remember what it was like when Dad was drinking. Mum was either working or looking after him, and I guess Frank just paid me a different kind of attention. I'm not making excuses. I'm just telling you how it happened. It was fucked up. Sex with someone who *can't* consent – there's a name for that, you know?'

She unlaces her fingers and looks Dom straight in the eye.

'What is he, a paedophile?'

Rose shrugs. She fucking *shrugs*. 'Legally, yes. But I don't think that's his kink. It wasn't about my age,' she says. 'Or not *just*. It was about getting one over on Lal. Literally, the dirty little secret was the point. I was just the vessel.'

The *vessel*. Rose's body, the flesh that houses her extraordinary heart and mind, reduced to a *vessel*. Dom clutches his chest as if he's been stabbed. He wouldn't be surprised to look down and see blood spilling on to his fingers. Rose tries to take his hands in hers and it's not that he withdraws from her to score a point, it's that he can't move. It's that the pressure of his hands on his chest are the only thing keeping his organs on the inside.

'I'm sorry if this all feels a bit blunt,' she says. 'I always said, if it ever came out I would be totally honest with you. Mum reckons—'

'*Bridget* knows?' This astonishes Dom almost more than the original revelation. If Bridget knows, why didn't she go to the police? How could she bear to live next door, be best friends with, spend Christmases and birthdays with, the man who had done that to her little girl?

Just because he doesn't know Rose any more, it doesn't mean that she doesn't know him.

'Yeah. She found out the same way you did,' she says. 'Just, twenty-four years earlier. She worked it out at Frank's opening. Saw the painting and recognised my scar. She was – Christ, she was devastated. She was all for us moving that night. Packing our bags at the party and just going anywhere to get away.'

'So why didn't she?'

'In the short term – because she was dealing with Dad. It was the night he threw up blood, remember? In the longer term, because of us. It was the night we got together. Don't you remember how horrified she was when she saw us kissing?'

'*That's* why she was so against us.' Dom is doing some painful mental arithmetic.

'Yup,' says Rose. 'She wanted to cut ties.'

'And you never wanted to go with her? I don't see how you could bear to stay living next to him unless you were still . . .' *In love with him*, he wants to say, although she hasn't said that she ever was. 'And you – that night – you kissed me because you were on the rebound from my dad?'

'Oh, love, no,' Rose says, and then, after a second's consideration, 'It was over a good two years before *Intimacies*. I sort of came to my senses, worked out he was using me, and ended it. I don't expect you to understand this, but Frank and I just didn't talk about it. We were in this weird bubble where we acted like it had never happened.'

The awful irony is that Dom does understand, because isn't that exactly what he's been doing for the last twenty-odd years with Cora? That part of it he gets. That part of it makes perfect sense. He acknowledges the parallel without being ready to confront his own hypocrisy.

'But he wasn't supposed to include that painting,' Rose is saying. 'Last I saw, it was just a sketch on a canvas. If there was a violation, it was that. Completing the picture. *Showing* it.'

A beam of sunlight catches the row of champagne glasses, spilling rainbows on the marble, as beautiful as any of Nell's designs. Funny how just minutes ago he thought he might need to turn one into a weapon. Dom now feels perfectly capable of crushing his father's windpipe with one hand. Of throwing him into the Vale of Health pond as easily as bowling a cricket ball. Of sprinting up the stairs and tipping Verity's bones at his father's feet and saying *look what kind of man he is*. Knowing what he did to Rose back in the day has somehow compounded Dom's conviction that Frank killed Verity.

She is openly crying now. 'Are you gonna leave me?'

Of course he's not going to leave her, that is unthinkable, but before he can voice it the make-up girl barges in.

'I will literally *die* if I don't get some coffee in my veins in the next thirty seconds.' She wedges a croissant between her teeth as she fills her cup.

Rose bites her lip. Dominic goes back to his laptop.

'We can't leave it like this,' says Rose, when the make-up girl has gone. 'Just – give me five more minutes. Come upstairs.'

He protests. 'I can't. There's—'

Again she shows how well she knows him. 'The wifi's fine up there.' She actually takes his laptop off him and marches up the stairs. Dom gathers his tablet and pockets his phone and follows his wife up the stairs.

His anger is directed at Frank. Of course it is. And yet, is Rose blameless? Not in the doing of it, she was a child, but in the with-holding of it?

He doesn't doubt his wife's regret. But before he can talk it through with her, he needs her to be in the same place he is. Shocked. On the back foot. Ears still ringing, skin still stinging from the blow.

On the landing windowsill is a silver-framed snapshot of all four kids on the beach in Southwold. He has never doubted their paternity before and doesn't really now – they all have more of Cora in them than Frank – but he can't resist. It's as if he's been handed a weapon that's the perfect shape and size.

'Are they mine?' he asks.

Of course Dominic has hurt Rose before, in carelessness or the heat of a moment. But this is the first time he has hurt her for the sake of it. He is ashamed of how good it feels. He snatches the laptop from her hands, steps into the bedroom and slams the door in her face. He can hear Rose crying, and trying to stifle it, when his phone beeps in his ear. He taps his left earbud once to answer.

'Leelo!' he says brightly. 'How are you doing with that patch?'

109

And then, Shane leaves his post and the only obstacle between Dom and revenge is gone. He keeps the conversation going with Leelo even while his mind is racing with hateful images. He takes a pair of vinyl gloves from the stash in the en-suite vanity unit. The small part of him that is still thinking observes that if only they'd had gloves to hand twenty-odd years ago he wouldn't have had to cover his fingertips with scraps of loo roll.

He knows what he needs and he knows where he's going. He tiptoes carefully past Nell and Billie, watching events unfold through the window. In the hallway, he catches sight of one of Frank's scarves hanging from the coat-stand and inspiration strikes: he picks it up with the very tips of his fingers. The garden is totally empty as he crosses the terrace from the Churcher house to the Lally house. In the kitchen he unhooks the key the kids can't reach and then he's in the attic. The difference between the fantasy of this moment and the reality of it is that the fantasy was comfort, a place he could retreat to, whereas the carrying out of it is power, a pure distilled charge that's almost sexual. Black bags rustle as his hands close around bones and when he tears the plastic the pelvis is the first one he touches. That bit of luck makes it feel like Verity's on his side. Like she's saying, *at last we've got the old bastard*. He wraps the pelvis in a fragment of the torn plastic shroud and tucks it under his arm. He shakes Frank's scarf out over the remaining bones and bags to give them a good dusting of DNA.

He is tapping his headset at intervals to answer questions from or give instructions to Leelo, then double-tapping to mute it again so she can't hear his heavy breathing.

He checks his watch. It has taken him under a minute.

Descending the stairs, his pulse is a drum. If anyone intercepts him, will they ask what's in the plastic? He doesn't have an answer.

It takes another thirty seconds to cross the empty garden and scale the tree. Another thirty to switch the golden bone for the real thing. Verity's pelvis just about fits in the cavity at the top of the tree. When it's covered with bark you'd never know anything was in there. The golden bone he puts in the key pocket of his jeans. All this fuss for something the size of his thumb. It seems to Dominic that he bounds from the top of the oak tree in one move but that can't be true. He gets to the back gate just as Shane is rounding the side of the house.

Just under four minutes have passed.

It is an inconvenience rather than a disaster to re-enter the property via the front door. He slips behind the Crabwise van and along the side return of his in-laws' house. He panthers his way down the passage and across the terrace. Shane is standing with his back to the houses: the crew are returning to their equipment. As Dom slips back into his parents' house, no one sees him. The tatter of black plastic he drops in the kitchen bin, then tears that liner so it will look like another fragment of the same. He replaces Frank's scarf on the coat stand. In his peripheral vision, the black box recorder for the CCTV flashes blue.

Crap. He hadn't factored in the cameras.

Luckily, Billie and Nell remain glued to the circus in the street. Even more luckily, Dom knows his way around the system and it's the work of a few seconds to erase the last hour or so's footage from the black box and then pull the plug. He's rather proud of himself when he has the brainwave of substituting the plug with Barney's charger. This is the kind of quick thinking and, yes, deceit, that Frank would be impressed with, if only it wasn't engineering his own downfall.

Back in his parents' bedroom, he resumes the call with Leelo and makes a show of pacing again. In fact he wouldn't be able to stop if he tried. He has an excess of kinetic energy that abruptly drains when Leelo confirms that the fault is patched and the app is good to go and he is free to enjoy the rest of his day filming.

He puts his hand in his pocket for the attic key, only to find it has gone.

'Shit,' he says. There's a hole in the back pocket of his jeans that he didn't know about. It could be anywhere from the Lallys' staircase to the foot of the oak tree. He peppers the air with four-letter bullets. The swearing gives him a sore throat but absolute mental clarity.

The missing key has acted as a brake on his actions. If he were fatalistic like Cora he'd say it was the universe telling him that today is not the day. There are too many people around, too many variables. The plate of shit he wants Frank to eat is a dish best served cold.

But it's easily remedied. The reveal is scheduled for four p.m., when the light on the Heath will be perfect. Dominic's job is to climb the tree and reveal the golden bone. He has the jewel in his jeans – he pushes at the seams of his side pocket to make sure it doesn't go the same way as the attic key. It will be the work of a moment to pull Verity's pelvis from the hollow and replace it with the gold. The leaves are thick enough to cover him and if he wears a baggy hoodie – there's one over the back of his chair – he can hide the bone there.

And then, in a week or two, when – hopefully – Sir Frank Churcher is back in the news, *then* Dom will deliver the blow. He'll plant the bone in the studio maybe. Leave the whole skeleton on the doorstep. Something theatrical.

Right.

Right.

Back to it.

He looks down to see that he has sweated drifts of salt into his shirt, and a raging thirst overwhelms him. Downstairs in his parents' kitchen, he fills a pint glass with water and downs two in succession. When he's wiping his chin with the back of his sleeve, Nell comes in.

'Is it sorted?' she asks, so naturally that for a moment he wonders if he has told her of his grand plan. He catches himself just in time. Again, everyone presumes his only concern is the app.

'I think I might be about to die of adrenaline poisoning,' he says, and then he realises that the house and garden are quieter than they have been since breakfast time. 'Where is everyone?'

Even before Nell answers, an invisible hand reaches into his guts and starts to pull.

'I've been texting and texting. They're out the back, doing the reveal.'

Dom is already running as Nell fills him in: Oisin's already halfway up the tree. When he protests, he can tell she thinks he's been cheated of the limelight. She can think what she likes as long as he intercepts his son. But Oisin is already a shadow in the leaves, and what seems like a single pound of Dominic's heart later he's screaming like a little girl. A second after that, Verity Winship's pelvic bone falls like a shot bird into Nell's hands and Aoife begins her banshee keen.

110

Cora knows, even before the bone is confirmed as genuine human remains, that it belongs to the waitress. It's the look on Dominic's face that gives it away. She uses Aoife's screeching as cover to say, 'Please tell me that you had nothing to do with this,' to her son, but they both know it's a rhetorical question.

'I can explain,' he says.

Cora finds herself sucking slow deep lungfuls of air. Even if she can't get the hit from a joint she can mimic the sensation of the first drag. 'You said you'd made it all go away,' she says, but even as she speaks she wonders if he did say that. His preferred phrase, in that one-night window they were open with each other, was, 'I've taken care of it,' which is not the same thing as making it go away at all.

He leads her to the stone table.

'I want Dad to go down for it,' he says. It is a surreal phrase to hear from her educated son's mouth. *Go down for it*, like a film about East End gangsters! 'I've got an idea. It won't come back on us. Look, I can't tell you everything. Not here, with all these people around and the police turning up any minute.'

The police. Christ. She can't last the rest of the afternoon without a smoke.

'The house . . .' she says.

'There's nothing in the house,' he says.

Good boy: he seats her right in front of her ashtray. She finds the remains of her earlier joint and sparks it. The crew are shocked; Dominic makes a show of disapproval, wafting his hands about.

The cold tingle reaches her fingertips and toes. She ought to pace herself but honestly, she doesn't really want to be conscious for what's about to happen.

By the time Cora has a chance to talk to Dominic properly, a great deal has happened. A florid police constable has been joined by a slick team of detectives and pathologists and between them they have taken over her beautiful home. They have dismissed her as a doddery old lady, which is fine by her. It's given her time to think.

Somehow over those unspoken years it is as though she and Dominic have come to an understanding that the girl's death was his crime, not hers. In letting her son take responsibility for the, the, the . . . *disposal*, she has also made him the custodian of her guilt. Of course the moral, the true responsibility lies with Frank, but his kind of culpability doesn't leave its fingerprints anywhere they can be picked up by dusting powder. It is a kind of joint enterprise, a triangle of conspiracy of which Frank is the unwitting tip. Unwitting, but not innocent. Cora thinks of the three Fates of ancient myth: one to spin the thread of human destiny, one to dispense it, and another to cut it. Which of them is responsible? One, none or all?

Cora and Dominic steal a moment on a bench under the fruit trees in Bridget's garden. Hard green apples are just starting to weigh the branches down.

'I'll tell you everything,' he says, just as she says,

'Whatever it takes to keep you out of trouble – I'll do it.'

They hold each other's gaze for a few beats, both knowing they're heading for a point of no return as momentous as the last one. Dominic starts talking. Cora suffers three blows, one after the other.

One. Verity Winship. Not one of Frank's floozies, but an innocent girl; that cabbie's daughter. Cora is sickened.

'But what's done is done,' says Dominic. He has had decades to come to terms with that. She thought that was the body blow but here it really comes.

Two. Rosaleen. Rose. Virtually Frank's daughter. Other women, yes, but *this*? Some self-preserving component of Cora's mind kicks in, pulling the blinds over scenes she can't help but imagine. When her heart breaks, she tells herself it's for Dominic.

Three. And Bridget knew. Bridget alone knew the depth of Frank's monstrosity and kept it from her. Bridget let Cora live with him. Bridget lived *beside* him. Cora stares at the old fence post, wound with sweet-peas. She remembers when it was the centrepiece of the marquee at the children's wedding. She remembers Bridget and Frank whirling each other around the dancefloor.

'They danced together at your wedding,' she says.

'I know.' He picks at a chip in the bench's paint. 'I can't get my head around it either.'

The bruise spreads to her heart.

'So look,' says Dominic, 'I can pretty much do this on my own. Those bags—' He gestures to the terrace, where an officer is lugging one of those bloody grey postbags that she used to deal with every day. 'Somewhere in there are letters from Verity, asking Frank for money and asking him to meet her. And I've done some work online, making accusations that go back years. You don't need to do anything except plead ignorance.'

He swipes at his eyes. A fleck of paint from the bench gets caught on his cheekbone. Cora brushes it away with her fingertips. Her boy. Her clever, loyal boy.

'Dominic,' she says, 'you have my absolute blessing.'

III

During the crucial first hour or so of the investigation, everything seems to go Dominic's way. It is a stroke of luck that for all their searching, the police don't make anyone in the family turn out their pockets. That little heart-shaped jewel is digging into his own hip the whole time. His daughters lie for him. They swear to the police that they stood outside his door the entire time he was on the phone to Leelo, that, while the Glemhams were causing a fuss outside, they were listening to Dominic pace and swear. Wherever they were, it wasn't with the adults. He suspects that Niamh enticed Aoife to abandon sentry duty and they're covering for each other, not him. Still he feels as though he's drawn them into his crime. That kid in the grey hoodie is another godsend: someone to place on the unguarded property at the moment of the switch. He feels bad yelling at Nell for not alerting them, but what can he do? And someone posting on ElinoresArmy that they were in the pub? That one actually makes him go cold, because he doesn't have full recall over what they discussed.

Cora says it's the universe's way of telling him he's doing the right thing. Normally he'd tell her off for spouting cod-spirituality bollocks, but for the first time he understands the comfort it can offer.

The real crisis comes when he understands what has really been happening online: LetterstoIngrid's revelation that the so-called Cecil Sharp verses were part of the original song after all has reignited Stuart Cummins's crusade against Nell. God knows where they're getting their information from. It almost doesn't matter. What matters is that Dom's beloved sister is in as much danger now as she was when they were kids. It's a horrific Catch-22. The online shit-stirring would have been harmless if the jewel had been left in the tree. Taking the jewel would have been harmless (to Nell, at least) without the online shit-stirring. He couldn't have known about the Papers being fakes: but that someone would try to revive interest in Ingrid is something he should have foreseen.

The problem of how to frame Frank has now become a fight to keep Nell safe. Setting up a new user is too risky at this stage so he reactivates @Yorick. His old posts fill him with something between nostalgia and horror.

> @Yorick: When Elinore's last bone is found, the truth will come out about Frank Churcher

> @Yorick: What he did to Elinore is the least of our worries

> @Yorick: He is a literal killer

They open the doors on other, half-forgotten acts: that time he helped Frank format a newsletter and edited it to hide *Honesty hides truth's bones in King's Chase*, deep inside.

The first thing he sees is people speculating about Nell having a daughter. He shuts that shit down sharpish. *Admins, can you step in? This is not in the spirit of the treasure hunt.* It's off-brand for Yorick, but fuck it. If they start getting ideas about Aoife . . . his knees buckle at the thought of it.

New Yorick must pour water on the fire that rages online and threatens to engulf Nell. But really he can can only mitigate. The real threat will only end when the jewel is restored. Put Elinore back together again and they'll all calm down. As everything unravels around him, Dom holds the golden bone in a sweating fist. It has never held such a terrible power. The police are refusing to classify its removal as theft, so this is the hottest not-stolen property in the art world. He needs to get it to Fritz Velasco as ⌐oon as he can, without anyone knowing it was him. He can't go via Richard Reid as he's always suspected the guy still carries a torch for Nell. Velasco might be open to a direct approach but there's still the question of a physical handover. And verification: they'd want someone at Sotheby's or wherever to look at it, and at some point someone's going to ask for ID or, worse, recognise him. So he keeps it in his pocket, puts out feelers for corruptible valuers.

When a press photographer doorsteps them at home – and of course it had to be Aoife who noticed him – Rose insists they hide out for the next few days at Marcelle and Harriet's place on the Suffolk coast. Dominic can't think of an excuse in time and anyway he doesn't want to be without his wife. The last few days have been full of crying and apologies from both of them. Heading for the coast means leaving Verity's body in the Lallys' attic, but he reasons that if the police were going to search the house next door, they'd have done so on the day. Dominic has been very careful to ensure there isn't a shred of evidence linking all this to his in-laws.

Well – apart from the obvious.

They haven't dredged the pond on the Vale of Health. When they get back, he'll put Verity in there. It's not what he wanted for her, but he can't think of anywhere else.

The phone call from Leslie Napoleon telling him the guys have been arrested comes when Dom's crabbing with Dara in Southwold Harbour. In shock, he drops the fishing line in the estuary and a crab drags the bait along the stony bed, a string of clear nylon trailing behind it. Dara starts to wail.

'Come on, mate,' says Dom, hoisting his son on to his shoulders.

It's not just *that* they searched Frank's house, it's *why*. If he had had the slightest idea that the old video from the *Intimacies* launch had shown Lal threatening Verity then he would have ripped the tape out before Oisin could get to it. But even Marcelle hadn't watched it to the end. There was no way any of them could have known.

Dominic takes Oisin with him to the Vale. He can't be angry with the kid. He was only trying to protect his grandpa Lal. Any of them would have done the same. But still. *Fuck*.

The third morning after the guys are arrested, Dominic wakes up to find that the jeans he carefully folded over the bedroom chair before going to sleep are missing. The scent of laundry detergent, with its gruesome associations, fills the house. He enters the utility room to find the machine churning and Rose sitting on the floor with her legs crossed, Elinore's little gold pelvis glinting in her palm.

'This had better be good,' she says. 'This had better be fucking *brilliant*.'

112

When Dom finally comes to the end of his account, his voice is hoarse. 'Say something, Nell.'

I let out an exhale that sends the feathers on my lap into a cloud that falls softly to the floor. In the charged silence, I swear I can hear each one land. The three of us watch them settle then study them as if someone's going to take them away, then ask us to draw the pattern they've made. Eventually – when the arrangement of feathers is imprinted on my mind, probably forever – I find my voice.

'*You* were Yorick?'

He nods.

'Shitting *hell*. This is the most fucked-up thing I've ever heard. Which is something, having grown up in this family.' I notice a loose thread on one of the cushion's buttons and start picking at it.

'I had been trying to mitigate the problem,' he says. 'Yorick's recent posts have been playing down the threat.'

'There wouldn't be anything to *mitigate* if you hadn't done it in the first place, you stupid prick! If the bone had been found in the tree as planned, LetterstoIngrid's posts would've been a blip. Stuart wouldn't have latched on to them. I wouldn't have spent the past week terrified for my life. And Billie's.'

'I am so, so sorry about that,' he says.

I can't remember life without Dom yet I feel like I'm looking at him for the first time. I have admired him so much, for so long. N

437

one had farther to fall in my estimation than him. I wait for the tidal wave of hurt but there's nothing there, although I find that I care desperately about destroying this cushion. When I speak my voice sounds mechanical, stripped of feeling.

'What did you do with the jewel? You didn't sell it to Velasco?' I find that I am thinking of Richard and how he deserves, at least, to know.

He shakes his head. 'I put it somewhere safe. It's better if you don't know.'

I let out a snort. 'I can't think where we've heard that before. Good old Yorick,' I yank aggressively at the button on the cushion. 'What a mensch.'

'I'm sorry I lied to you.'

Success! The last of the fat silky thread ripples through the buttonhole. I hold it up to the light. It's mother-of-pearl and rather beautiful. 'Well,' I say, 'knowing the truth hasn't exactly brought me joy, has it? For the love of God, Dom. How are the police *not* going to work it out? You'll be done for – what will they even charge you with?'

He rolls his eyes almost imperceptibly, a flash of arrogance that belies his humility. 'I know what I'm doing. If they were going to find me, they would have done by now.'

An idea comes to me. 'So – you reckon your identity as Yorick is watertight?'

His eyes narrow. He can tell he's not going to like this. 'Why?'

'Yorick could make a confession online. You've already laid the groundwork for him being one of those Bonehunters who hate Frank. You can write that you crashed the party, you set Frank up – and Lal with him, as he's involved now too. I mean, it's pretty close to the truth.'

'Lal was never supposed to be in the frame.'

'All the more reason for you to make it right. Then the police et a confession from someone they'll never trace, but the guys e off the hook. It won't undo the damage between us, but it solves that problem. If your VPN is as untraceable as you say, you've got nothing to lose.'

Dom and Cora look at each other, eyes frantic in some mother-son semaphore I've never been able to read. For a naïve second I hope they're thinking about logistics, but their expressions are stunned rather than calculating. They don't know what to do because they never thought I'd question their intentions.

'Come on,' I say. 'This is one hell of an olive branch I'm holding out here.'

Dom shakes his head. 'At the moment they just think Yorick is just another nutter,' he says. 'If they got an actual *confession* they might redouble their efforts.'

Although I'm sitting down I feel a whoosh of vertigo. 'But the guys are up on a *murder* charge.'

'They've been arrested,' says Dom. 'Not charged.'

'Yet!' I counter. I look for more soft furnishings to destroy and settle on liberating another button from its cushion. 'Look, let's bring the others over from your place. Between us we're bound to come up with something we can do to get the guys off the hook without necessarily landing you two in the shit.'

Dom shakes his head. 'The kids—'

I cut him off mid-excuse. 'The kids can watch a film. Give them iPads. Break the golden rule and Uber them a McDonald's. We need to talk.'

Dom shifts in his seat. 'Me and Rose didn't part on the best of terms this morning.' The whimper in his voice lays bare a howling understatement.

'Oh, *do* tell.' I put a finger to my cheek and round my eyes, the old childhood spite flowing freely now the dam has broken.

'She found the jewel in my jeans pocket—'

The mother-of-pearl button cracks between my fingers. 'Your jeans pocket! You said it was somewhere safe!'

'Well, no one thought to look for it there,' he said.

'Must be nice, being able to walk around not worrying someone was about to knife you for it.'

'Eleanor,' says Cora. 'Hear your brother out.'

I lean back in my chair and fold my arms. 'I'm all ears.'

Somewhere in Hampstead Garden Suburb, Rose is processing the same news I am, although she's had a few hours' head start. I wonder if her own years as a secret-keeper have given her better tools to deal with it than I've got.

'I basically told her everything I've just told you,' says Dom. 'She knows what we did.' The line he draws in the air between himself and our mother is repeated several times, as if to underscore their bond.

'And what's Rose's hot take on it all?'

'Eleanor, please don't be snotty,' says Cora.

'Fuck off, Cora.'

Dom holds a blink: one, two three. When he opens his eyes they are shining. 'Obviously she called me out on – you know, the hypocrisy, double standards, what have you. You know, keeping things from each other. Which I guess I deserved. Um, in the end I had to give her a bit of space. She's with Bridget now.'

I briefly long to be a fly on the wall in Rose's house. I've occasionally wondered whether she and Bridget, so competent and controlled, each have a messy version of themselves they show only to each other.

'So at least we're all on the same page,' says Cora.

My instinct is to respond with more sarcasm but actually, she's right. Each uncovered lie rips off a layer of skin but takes with it the hell of not knowing (me) and the stress of pretence (everyone else). Without warning, the fight goes out of me; either I've used up my day's adrenaline or that part of my brain is holding some back in reserve in case I need it later. 'Well – if everyone knows everything, all the more reason for us all to talk. Get everyone re.'

'Not Osh,' says Dom firmly.

agree that Oisin will be classified as a child in terms of -know, which makes me wonder how much of this I'll be able to tell Billie. Again I wobble on that tightrope between protection and condescension. I won't know until the five of us have thrashed it out.

Dom leaves the room to summon his wife and her mother to the Vale. I can't hear the words, just the pleading in his tone.

113

While we wait for Rose and Bridget and the kids, Cora lights the dinner candles – three tapers in churchy purple, wedged in a cast-iron trident – and plays music on the kitchen speaker. An acoustic guitar plays an almost unbearably plaintive riff to introduce a song she used to sing as a lullaby when I was little. It's about an exiled queen awaiting her fate in a castle. Cora closes her eyes and hums off key. She's not singing for my comfort now but her own. Looking at her, lost in the music of her youth, locking out the horror of the present, it's easy to imagine she might never come back.

I'm relieved when that song gives way to something heavier: electric guitar dragging us out of fairyland. I leave my mother noodling at the kitchen table and step into the garden. On the other side of the fence, joggers and ramblers and tourists talk and laugh as though everything is normal. I rub my eyes and stretch a bit, then call and make arrangements for Moira and Joyce to give Billie dinner onboard *Prevail*.

I sit on the terrace and see if the consequences of the showdown in Richard's office are manifesting online. I'm heartened to see that Rhiannon has posted as LetterstoIngrid for the last time, a long unpunctuated apology for having pretended to be speaking for everyone's favourite knife-wielding Bonehunter.

I apologise unreservedly for misleading lifelong Bonehunters by claiming that the Northumbria Papers were forgeries, it states. There's no way these are her words. I can just see Richard standing over her, dictating them. *The truth is that I have become hooked on The Golden Bones like so many before me, and this was my attempt to make my mark on the hunt. The contentious cil Sharp verses are the true forgeries. I regret the hurt and*

442

confusion I have caused in the Bonehunter community and I will no longer be posting on ElinoresArmy.

The idea of someone uncovering a true fake, only to shove the genie awkwardly back into the bottle, is as good a metaphor for the wreckage *The Golden Bones* leaves in its wake, the mental gymnastics it forces people to perform, as any I can think of.

Rhiannon has not identified herself, but the Bonehunters are clamouring for her unmasking. Perhaps she, too, will find herself on the sharp end of their scrutiny. It couldn't happen to a nicer young woman.

The main thing is that Stuart has bought it. He has posted as BelleDame, once again pledging his allegiance to a bloodless solve. That, along with the rumours that the bone is with Velasco, mean that I am safe. Something is going right for the first time since this shitstorm broke.

I look over my shoulder. Cora is swaying in her seat, a deranged smile on her face, long sleeves passing dangerously close to the candles' flames. Whatever's going to get us out of this mess, it's clear we won't be able to count on her. She has opted out, removed herself just as decisively as if she had walked out on to the Heath. It's up to me and Dom now. I put all my screenshots of Yorick's posts in one album, hoping that a pattern will emerge and inspiration will strike. No light bulb pings above my head.

I hear the front door open and the kids pile in. 'Ah, fuck it,' I say, setting down my phone. Dom made this mess. It's up to him to clean it up.

When the others arrive it's with pink eyes and clutching brown paper bags that exude the smells of McGrease and McPotatostarch. Rose nods a brief hello, then goes up to settle the kids in their bedroom with Disney Plus and fries, shakes and nuggets.

Once they're zoned out in front of *Coco*, we close ourselves in the kitchen. The back doors are open: the sky above the treeline turning from livid pink to uneasy violet. Bridget sits at the h of the table, arms wide and hands flat on the tabletop. Th something of the seaside medium about the pose and the candle-light that adds to the swimming, unreal quality of the situation. A bottle of Knappogue Castle Single Malt forms the centrepiece and a cut-crystal tumbler marks our place settings. There's three fingers of liquid in Cora's glass. If ever there was a moment she needed to face up to, it's this one. I make a show of declining the bottle when she tilts it my way.

'Obviously, as a family, we're over,' says Bridget. 'We can't go back to pretending everything's fine, even if we do get him out. He's going to have to know his dirty little secret – sorry, I mean him, not you, Rose – is out in the open. He can't come back and live here again.'

I find myself pushing my glass around the table as if it's a ouija board. It makes a satisfyingly abrasive noise against the table. 'That's the long term,' I say. 'We need to focus on what happens in the next few days. The next few hours. We need to get the guys out of the frame for this. I know I keep banging on about this, Dom, but there must be a way to make your little Yorick sock puppet claim responsibility.'

'Can you not?' Dom glares at the glass in my hand. I grind it noisily against the table in front of him. I'm even annoying myself. Why am I being so petty when I want him on-side? 'I can't immediately think of how I could do that, but if I did . . .'

'When,' I say. 'I'm not letting you off the hook.'

Cora has made short work of her drink. There's just one finger left in the glass, and its rim is printed with a series of greasy pink half-moons, one for each gulp she's taken.

'And if Dom *does* find a way to get the guys off the hook, what do we tell them?' asks Bridget. 'Do we go along with the idea that Yorick did it? They're not stupid.'

'How can we tell them even a *corner* of the truth without it *all* ʌoming out?' says Dom. His pulse twitches double-time in his ʌck. 'I suppose it's better if they both think the same thing?' he . 'If we could . . . minimise the upset, from here on in. The ʌ people know, the safer the secret.'

I resist the urge to make a snide comment along the lines of *that old chestnut*, or *where have I heard that one before*? The thing is, he's right. My family's collective lies are an octopus with flailing tentacles in everything. We should be chopping them off, not adding to them.

'Agreed,' says Rose.

'Grand, so,' says Bridget.

'And it stays here.' Dom waves his arm around the table. 'No Leslie, no Marcelle.'

Another round of nods. I pick up the empty glass and roll it silently between my palms. The fidget impulse is strong as my body, clearly not understanding why my legs have not received a command to carry me out of here, shoots nervous energy along my limbs.

'And it goes without saying that what Dad did to Rose – that never leaves this room,' says Dom.

I note his choice of words. Not 'what happened between Dad and Rose', or even just 'Dad and Rose'. He has cast Frank as the perpetrator, which is right, but it's giving him tunnel vision and blinding him to the fact that he and Cora did this. I marvel at the doublethink.

'Yup.' I mime zipping my lips. 'Lal obviously doesn't know about *that*, given that Frank's still alive.'

Bridget snorts into her whisky. 'Sure I didn't keep it from Lal for *Frank*'s protection but for his own,' she says.

'What do you mean?'

'Don't you remember how ill he was back then? Imagine it, pet.' She shakes her head and gives a rueful laugh. '*Imagine* if I'd told Holy Lal that his so-called best friend got his daughter pregnant on some kind of power trip and paid for the abortion? Sure he'd have drunk himself to death within a week. And his recovery, it was so fragile for so long. The truth would've killed him.'

'That it would have done, Bridie, my love,' says Lal from dark recess of the hall. 'That it would.'

114

Bridget claps a hand to her mouth. I go very cold and then very hot as Lal steps out of the shadow and into the kitchen. Even from my seat at the table I can smell the police station on him. His dark grey curls are as greasy as a Teddy boy's and his three-day beard is white.

'You're out.' I state the obvious. I look behind him for my father, wondering whether I should shout out, tell him to duck.

Lal doesn't respond to me. His eyes skid across our faces until they land on Bridget.

'Bridie, please tell me I didn't just hear what I think I heard.'

His words pull her to her feet.

'Lal, I can . . .' she begins, but she trails off before she gets to the verb. I can't think of one that would fit. I can *explain* this? I can *justify* this? I can *stop* this? None of those things is true.

Bridget, who has always known what to do, looks for guidance to Cora, who never has. The only thing for which Cora can be relied upon is to say the least appropriate thing, and she doesn't disappoint now.

'Is Frank out too?' she says.

Dom blenches. I study Lal. To the ignorant eye this is desperate concern for a beloved husband but, as of half a minute ago, Lal is no longer ignorant. His face is unreadable, a slab of raw granite. Of course he doesn't yet know what's at stake for Cora; that if Frank has climbed the ladder to freedom, she and Dominic are at the top of the longest snake on the board.

Lal doesn't move or speak, but the front door slams in answer Cora's question. Rose presses herself into the back of her chair. puts a hand over hers and I know that this marriage will hough it might well be the only one that survives the night.

'Frank?' quavers Cora.

It is not Frank who enters but Leslie. We all dredge the usual niceties from somewhere inside us, but, an expert reader of rooms, he can't miss the atmosphere. I presume that *he* presumes that the awkwardness radiates from Lal's wretchedness and Frank's absence.

'Shall I fill them in, Lal?'

'I have to—' A choked Lal leaves the kitchen, swiftly followed by Bridget.

'Poor chap. He's been through the mill.' Leslie slides into the chair recently vacated by Bridget. 'I can't stay long. I gave him a lift home because the last thing we want is another cop car outside the house. Now. Frank.' He looks at Cora. 'Are you happy for me to continue in front of Rose? I know how close you all are.'

Oh, no, he doesn't.

Dom gives a limp wave. 'S'fine.'

Leslie uncaps his silver fountain pen, even though there's no paper in front of him, and I wonder if this gesture is for his reassurance or ours. Clearly his is not easy news to deliver.

'The CPS have agreed that the police can charge Frank with Verity Winship's murder.'

'Based on *what*?' asks Dom, his knee bouncing. What Leslie will interpret as disbelief is, of course, nerves about whether his grand plan worked. I can barely look at him.

'Frank's DNA was found in the material used to conceal her,' says Leslie.

Dom's knee stills immediately. This was his doing. You can't plant fingerprints but -- 'Was it a hair?' I ask Leslie.

He consults his mental notes before replying. 'I believe so.'

'Well, that doesn't prove that he murdered her,' I say.

'It suggests that he moved her,' he says. 'And to move her he' have had to know where she was. The police also have letters fr Verity that could be construed as blackmail. And your father access to next door as easily as if it were his own property.'

Cora lets her head drop into her hands while Dom shakes his convincingly. I sit on my hands. I'm not going to sell them out just yet, but nor will I pretend to look shocked on their behalf. I can see the cogs grinding behind my brother's eyes. What would an innocent person ask? he's thinking. What should I say now?

Rose comes to the rescue. 'Why did they let my dad go and not Frank?'

'The evidence against Lal was always weaker, but the clincher was that we found him an alibi.'

Our collective surprise is the first unfeigned reaction since Leslie's arrival.

'Our investigator interviewed as many attendees of the opening as we could trace and we found one Ben Markham, who would've been your age at the time.'

Suzy's brother. I'd forgotten he was even there. He'd been in the first flush of (his idea of) cool, dressed like a member of Blur.

'We were at school with him,' confirms Dom, but tentatively. Wherever this is going, it's down a path he did not lay.

'So I understand,' says Leslie. 'He was apparently with Lal in that two-hour window between leaving the party and arriving back home. He – Ben – asked Lal if he could take the Thunderbird out for a spin and – long story short – they ended up on the M1. It was quite the road trip.' I remember now – he got out of Suzy's overloaded car to walk.

'And he's a reliable witness?' I know from Suzy that Ben's an anaesthetist now, married with two kids.

'His testimony was convincing,' says Leslie. 'He was able to describe the car's interior – the St Christopher hanging from the mirror, for example. And I can't see that he stands to gain anything in coming forward. The opposite, in fact. He admits he was both unqualified to drive the car and over the legal drink-ive limit.'

That's exactly the kind of thing Ben *would* have done,' Rose eslie. 'Who'd have thought he'd end up being Dad's saviour?'

eed,' says Leslie.

'If only *Frank* had a saviour.' I look pointedly at Dom. He has the grace to colour, just a little.

'Frank is being transferred from police custody to one of the London prisons now.'

'*Prison.*' I project the word, hoping it brings back the stories I told them about my time in Holloway: security vans with blacked-out windows, piles of clothes folded into squares, the way people cry for their mothers in the night . . . anything that makes the reality of what they have done land. But as if by prior agreement their heads are bowed, chins tucked tight into chests. I find myself tilting my own face to the ceiling, as though my body has decided to set me apart.

'We will do all we can to fight this, Nell,' says Leslie. 'As a caveat, before I go. There is already press interest. All and any media requests must be directed to Marcelle. She and Harriet will do what damage-limitation they can. The family must remain strictly no comment.'

He clicks the lid back on to his pen to bring the matter to a close.

115

We sit around the table – me, Cora, Rose, Dom -- the shrinking candles the only sign of time passing. On the other side of the sitting room door, Lal and Bridget are talking. Her voice is low, a river rolling over well-worn rocks. His is the low rumble of encroaching thunder.

Cora takes a ready-rolled joint from her tin and nearly sets fire to her hair as she bends to light it from a candle. She offers it around, an invitation for us to join her on that plane where everything's lovely and magical and the trolls stay under the bridge and someone else will slay the dragons. We all decline, but the sweet smoke finds its way in anyway, heightening my senses. I have the sense that these homes, our conjoined houses, are swaying and creaking around us as the foundations crumble underneath. That one wrong move and we'll be clawing our way out through rubble and dust.

I make coffee, as much to get away from the table as to sharpen my senses. I drink it looking out over the Heath. When the trees have stopped making faces at me, I go back to the others. It is with great care that I show Dominic what's on my phone.

'I've screenshotted Yorick's greatest hits,' I say. 'I personally can't think of a way to spin this to get Frank off the hook, but if we all put our heads together?'

'The irony being that this is Frank's territory,' says Cora.

'I think Dom's proved himself pretty capable,' I say, but my ᵊ͟er's eyes are sliding all over the place, looking anywhere but ͟screen glowing in my hand.

ͻrrow, alright?' he snaps. 'I'm too jangled tonight. I'll set for five and come to it with a clean mind. I mean it's . . .'

he shakes his arm until his watch emerges from his sleeve '. . . nine o'clock. There's nothing we can do now to change the fact that he's going to spend the night in prison.'

Here's one card only I can play. 'The first night's the worst one. I knew I was only in for three weeks. *And* I knew I deserved it. Let him be known for the monster he was, but not this.'

'How can we?' snaps Dom.

I kick myself. Of course we can't let the full story be known without dragging Rose's name into it. Or not her name of course, she would remain anonymous and the press – who would be all over the story – wouldn't be allowed to name her, but it would only take one identifying detail for the Bonehunters to make the connection.

'Sorry, Rose,' I tell her. 'It's gross what he did to you, it makes me feel sick, but how does this make it right? I made a promise to myself, when Richard betrayed me, that I would never do anything like that to another person. This is on that scale. This is worse.'

'Oh, Eleanor.' Cora waves her joint at me. 'If ever there was a time to get down from your moral high horse, it's now.'

Anger blasts through me with such force it's almost enjoyable. 'My high – my fucking *what?*'

'You know. Always thinking you're better than the rest of us with your floating gypsy caravan, your waifs and strays, all holier-than-thou.'

I'm cresting a wave of adrenaline: it's a rush, a buzz. 'Well, considering I haven't actually murdered a woman and hung her skeleton on a fucking *wall*, I think I'm entitled to a bit of self-righteousness at this point in time.'

'She was a child!'

Lal's raised voice punches through walls and doors, unhea~~ that way for decades but instantly familiar. Dom braces him~~ against the table and I know exactly what he's thinking. I~~ rediscovers his fists tonight he's ready to slide back his ch~~ make the intervention he never could as a boy.

'No,' says Rose, and I can read her, too: that if they come to blows, it won't really be Lal Dom is fighting, and he won't know when to stop. She keeps her hand over Dom's until his arms go limp. Her eyes flick to the ceiling, clearly waiting for the kids to clatter downstairs, for Aoife to react in a way that only Aoife can, but there's nothing but the burble of *Coco* through the floor.

'A *child*!' he echoes, and although I know it's nonsense I can't help feel that the repetition is aimed at me, a reminder that Frank Churcher is no innocent man.

After maybe another minute of Bridget's almost musical murmuring, Lal shouts again. 'How *can* we?' There's a crack in his voice that both unsettles and soothes me. It's anguish – not anger, although a stop on the road to it – swelling the bellows of Lal's voice tonight. When we hear the sitting room door-handle turn from across the hall, the four of us jump as though caught listening at the keyhole.

Bridget appears in the doorway. For the first time she seems little-old-lady small, as though the day's onslaught of truths are pressing on her, compacting her spine.

'Dominic. Cora. Could you come in and . . .' She gestures vaguely between them and Lal. 'I've taken this as far as I can on my own.'

'You've *told* him?' asks Cora.

That phrase could have so many interpretations tonight. I'm losing track of who knows what.

'I had to,' she says.

Obviously no one expected Lal to come home unannounced, and Bridget's dealing with all this on the hoof. Still, I'm staggered that she made a unilateral decision for full disclosure without debating the pros and cons of Lal knowing the true details of ▪rity's murder and fate. Quickly I run through them in my head. ▪ros: there has to be *some* explanation for this mess and the ▪ we give him might as well be the truth. He knows about Frank ▪se; for him, nothing can be worse than that. And if he knows ▪g, he can lend his own considerable brainpower to the jailbreak effort. And whatever happens, Frank is essentially excom-municated. Those of us remaining should be able to talk freely.

Cons: I wouldn't wish this knowledge on anyone. And there's a chance – however small – that he might take Cora and Dom's crimes to the police. Will his faith compel him? Isn't one of the Ten Commandments *thou shalt not bear false witness against thy neighbour*? Lal was arrested for this crime too, and has every right to be furious with Cora and Dominic. As do we all.

There's a prolonged wheezing beside me as Cora takes an inter-minable drag on her joint. I remember her whiteout when PC Chisholm was in the garden and take it from her hands before grinding it out in the ashtray. 'You don't get to swoon your way out of this one, Cora.'.

Unanchored by either glass or joint, her clawed hands thrash at the air.

'I can't,' she pleads with Bridget. 'I can't, I can't.'

She saucers bloodshot eyes at Dom but it looks as if the prince has had enough of Rapunzel at last. 'No, come on,' he says, rising laboriously from his chair. 'I haven't got the bandwidth for any more layers of deception.'

The door closes behind them. I wonder if they will calibrate their confession differently for Lal.

'And then there were two,' I say to Rose. She acknowledges me with a little dry husk of a laugh. 'Rose, I don't know what to say to you about Frank. I'm so sorry. Sorry he did what he did. Sorry things were so shit at home that no one noticed. Sorry *I* didn't see what was going on.'

I didn't mean it as a feed line; that only occurs to me as I finish. But Rose's expected response – *you had enough worries of your own to cope with* – doesn't come. She says nothing, just twists h~~ hands. Her fingers, always skinny, are loose in their rings.

'Can you lean on Dom?' I say. 'Get him to use this Yorick to get us out of this mess? I know it's hard and I'm not ~~ Frank deserves to get away with it, but *murder*? Can't w~~ some justice from all this?'

'I don't think we should talk without the others here.' She is all hollows: her cheeks are concave, her clavicle a tunnel to the point where her neck meets her spine.

My insides perfectly replicate the feeling of misjudging the final step on a staircase and falling, however briefly, through space.

'Rose,' I say. 'This is *me*.'

'I'm going to check on the kids.' She leaves me alone at my mother's kitchen table, staring at white walls that are nonetheless filthy with secrets and lies.

I pinch the dinner candles and dribble warm wax on the back of my hands and enjoy watching it set. When I've picked it off, I get up and stretch. I walk aimlessly through the rooms I am not shut out of. In the study is a shelf lined with copies of the all-new *The Golden Bones*, their gold spines glowing like a temple wall. I want to see if Rhiannon Reid's unmasking robbed the book of its power over me. I draw one from the shelf, hold it in my hands. It seems to throb but that's just my own pulse. I let it fall open at random, half expecting it to emit light. The energy it radiates is real, but it does not come from within: it is made of meaning others have given it.

I'm faced with the double-page spread of Elinore's wedding to her ancient husband, old Sir Guy, lined and grey. The mediaeval church is beautifully rendered, each brick and pane of glass as detailed as a photograph, the velvet of her dress so soft it's a shock to touch it and find only paper. There's Tam in the back pew, twinkle in his eye and trouble in his trousers. How did I never notice how like Lal Frank had made his hero, with his dark curls nd olive skin? I flip through the book until I get to that infamous ond-to-last page, where Elinore dances across the page, her s, muscles and organs visible through ragged clothes and g skin.

look how I feel, love,' I say, before closing it. A remnant of nk on my hand becomes sealing wax, my slashed finger- ole imprint on Elinore's cheek.

Across the hall, the sitting-room door handle clicks. I put the book back on the shelf, then angle my head around the study door to see the swish of Rose's skirt as she closes it behind her. Please don't judge her, Lal, I think. Please send your anger in the right direction. Rage at Cora, at Dom, at Frank, but don't put this on Rose.

I go back to the kitchen, think about sparking up Cora's joint, realise what a dreadful idea that would be. I wash up the glasses, hide the whiskey and wipe out the ashtray.

Billie texts me.

When u back

I look at the clock. It's past ten.

Home by 11 latest. M&J looking after you?

Yes they're nice

She sends me a picture of herself tucking into a huge plate of pasta in Moira and Joyce's kitchen. It's a live shot that she's set to bounce, and I watch her slurp and unslurp a string of spaghetti, the steam curling and uncurling.

God, I wish I were there. I wish they were my parents and Billie's grandparents.

Cora appears, hovers at my side, looks at the picture. 'You haven't said anything to *her*?'

I let this fresh zap of anger join the rest: I picture one of those plasma balls crackling in my chest. 'Does she look like someone who's just found out she knows a murderer?'

'Don't be flippant, Eleanor. We want to keep all this in the family.'

If she weren't so frail I honestly might hit her. Instead, I set my phone face down. Dom and Bridget join us at the table.

'He knows everything you do,' says Dom. 'Which is all of it. We thought we'd give him a moment with Rose.'

'Is he being all Catholic about it?' I ask Bridget.

'Not at all,' she says, then: 'Unless you mean the guilt. heart's in bits.'

'Did you mention the Yorick idea to him?' I ask Dom.

'Give him a chance, Nell,' he snaps. 'There's a lot to wrap his head around.'

Rose and Lal are still in the sitting room at ten-thirty, which is when I need to leave if I'm to keep my word to Billie. I'm in my hi-vis jacket with my helmet swinging from my hand by the time they emerge. She goes straight upstairs, followed by Dom. Lal leaves by the back door. I go to follow him.

'Give him a bit of space, pet,' says Bridget.

I will do no such thing. Alone, I can appeal to his sense of what's right.

He's closing the fridge door, a can of Pepsi Max in his hand.

'Lal,' I say gently.

'Hello, darlin'.' He looks a hundred years old, more decrepit Sir Guy than dashing young Tam.

Gently, I put forward my suggestion that Dom make a confession. 'I'm not asking you to *forgive* Frank,' I say. 'I'm just asking you not to let him go down for this.'

He cracks the ring-pull. 'Let me sleep on it,' he says, to the bubbles that leap over the rim.

116

Pentonville Prison, London N7
10 August 2021

The music of prison hasn't changed. The tambourine rattle of keys on a ring and the off-beat toll of steel-on-steel ring in my ears as one gate after another clangs behind me. The conflicting emotions of anger, pity, contempt, grief, and, yes, love – form a choir of drunks in my head. Pentonville is the same 'generation' of prisons as Holloway and I find myself remembering tiny details I thought were long forgotten: the metal water jugs and the plastic cups, the black mice, barely bigger than spiders, who only come out at night.

I spent the journey here rehearsing what I was going to say to my father and, as I walk the corridor between reception and the visiting room, I still don't know which of the dozen possible opening sentences I will go for.

Sir Frank Churcher sits behind a nailed-down table with a petrol-blue tabard over a prison-issue tracksuit. He looks his true age without his beard oil and his blow-dry and his carefully put-together outfits, but, as I slide into the nailed-down chair opposite him, I sense a change beyond the surface. It is as though his essence has been transformed in some fundamental way I can't put my finger on. Is this because the experience of being arrested has altered him, or because I know things about him now that have changed the way I will see him forever?

'Eleanor.' He goes to hug me.

'No touching!' yells a guard.

We both slide into our hard shiny seats.

'Thanks for coming.' He smells of toothpaste over coffee. That's the difference. It's not his appearance that's off, it's his scent. Stripped of his Vétiver, my father seems less of himself. He is poised for speech, leaning forward on the table. He has clearly been rehearsing some variation on the theme of I-didn't-do-it, and I know exactly how I must begin.

'Rose?' The force of my disgust pushes him backwards in his chair. 'How *could* you, Frank?'

It is so far from the conversation he was expecting – bones and trees and jewels and waitresses – that he seems to choke on his own shock. There are three or four seconds when his face goes redder and redder, then a sleep-apnoea rattle releases him from paralysis. When he's caught his breath, he says, '*Ah.*'

'Ah? Is that all you've got to say for yourself? She was *fourteen.*' The acoustics of this old room bounce the number off the walls.

The prisoner at the next table, evidently sensing valuable intel, leans slightly in our direction. I drop my voice accordingly.

'And don't give me any of that "times were different" bullshit. It was the nineties, not the Middle Ages. You *knew* it was wrong. It was literally illegal.'

I wish I had something to fidget with. In lieu of an old paper-clip to bend out of shape, I let my left thumb and forefinger palpate the scar tissue in my right hand.

'Of course I knew it was wrong.' His brow is creased, but a muscle at the right-hand side of his mouth twitches. He pulls at his jowls with his hands but it's too late. The opaque words Bridget spoke on Kentish Town Road come back to me, now crystal-clear in their meaning. *At least Lal had the guts to use his own body as a weapon, not other people's.*

'*That's* why you did it,' I say, 'the wrongness. You were using to score points against Lal. It was the ultimate one-ship.'

shakes his head, as though considering another man's e behaviour. 'I got caught up in a petty masculinity that was prevalent at the time.' He attempts to blow his fringe out of his eyes. His hair is so lank it hardly moves.

'You got caught up in your own arrogance, more like. You have no idea what you started.'

'Christ. Please don't tell me this is somehow connected with the Winship girl's *murder*?' I can see his brain working, eyes flicking from side to side, a high-stakes version of Billie's expression when she's trying to solve a problem or guess the answer to a clue. It lasts for maybe half a minute until he gives up and looks to me for the solution.

'Verity Winship wasn't killed because of you and Rose. But that's why she . . .' I grasp for a phrase that doesn't sound too ridiculously biblical. 'That's why her body resurfaced. God. I don't know where to start.'

'Who is responsible for my situation?'

I can't help my bitter laugh. 'That's the big question, isn't it?'

He looks at the wall clock. 'We only have forty-five minutes left, Nell; there's no time for philosophy.'

'So last night, while you and Lal were still in the police station, I was with Cora, and Bridget, and Dom, and . . .' I tell him his own story viewed through the prism of what I know: when we each found out about his abuse – that's the word I use – of Rose, and how we found out. I break down the beats of Verity's murder and the ensuing web Dominic has woven and drawn the whole family into.

The conversation is an excruciating exercise in control: too loud, and we're overheard. Too quiet, and Frank can't pick up what I'm saying. And there's the control I need to deliver the information precisely and without emotion. He listens without interruption, which lets me scrutinise him for signs of shame.

'So,' I say when I'm done. His eyes are liquid and I'm reli to see the remorse that makes my efforts to fight his corner it.

'Do you think they'll go public with this? It happ doesn't it? "Historical" allegations?'

He curls finger quotes the word 'historical', as if that dimin-ishes it, and I understand why the furniture is fixed.

'Is that all you're worried about? Getting Yewtreed? Although fuck knows you deserve it. I don't know. That's up to Rose, isn't it? I think you're a grubby old man. I think you're vain and cowardly. But I don't share Dom and Cora's view that you're responsible for killing Verity Winship and concealing her body, and I won't let you be convicted of that. I've given Dom a couple of days to find a way to blame the whole thing on this ridiculous alias he's created.'

'And if he doesn't?'

'I can't let you rot in here, can I?'

He smiles; I shut it down.

'Even in the best-case scenario, you're not going to be able to come home. I can't see Dominic ever speaking to you again. I think Cora's forgiven you for the last time, and I hope that Lal—'

The colour drains from Frank's face; it seems that the whole room turns grey. '*Lal* knows?'

'Yeah, I *said*—'

'No.' He shakes his head. 'You said it was just you, Dom, Cora and Bridget.'

I think back. It's true, I'd cut the story off at the part where Lal came in, leapt straight to Dom's plans.

Shit. Shit shit *shit*.

'Yes,' I admit. 'He overheard us talking about the abortion.'

I have never understood what people meant when they described the lights in people's eyes going out, but it happens before me now.

'Isn't that what you wanted?' I say. 'For Lal to know? Show him was boss?'

'long as *I* knew, that was enough,' he says. 'I was a different k then.'

not exactly the Dalai Lama now.'

es through his nose, aiming for laughter and missing.

'I presume it's all over the papers,' he says. 'I suppose it's too early to get a sense of how it's going to affect the perception of my work?'

Even after everything I've learned over the last twenty-four hours, it turns out I still can absorb more disappointment.

'I rest my case,' I say. 'Look, I've said what I came here for. I'll do my best to put this right. Don't expect Cora to take you back.'

'Will I see *you* again?'

He is a pathetic, rat-faced old man in faded blue overalls. But at least I know him. At least he hasn't broken character. The others are strangers to me now.

'It's going to take me a while,' is the best I can do, and I don't just mean him.

Back in the visitors' centre, I open my locker and catch the pound coin as it's ejected from the lock. When I get my phone back, the screen is cluttered with notifications: missed calls and messages that are still stacking up. For a second I dare to hope that Dom has come up with his get-out-of-jail-free idea, but there are no messages from him. What fresh hell? I think, as the home button struggles to recognise my one good fingerprint. Have reporters got my number? Is it the Glemhams, after the inside track?

Two texts from Billie and three unanswered calls from Eyebrows sweep those concerns away.

I cycle back to Horsfall so fast that I overtake motorbikes and cars.

117

This time, the police aren't there for me but for Billie. Or rather, they're there to provide a bit of brawn for Eyebrows, who clearly doesn't think either of us are the type to go quietly. She's not wrong. Billie is kicking and screaming, a copper at each elbow. Heads poke from the surrounding flats. One man in the old wharf smokes a cigarette; a woman in one of the new-builds is nursing a cup of tea.

'Enjoying the show, are ya?' Billie yells at the woman disappears behind a sheer curtain. 'Get the fuck off me!' she says to the police.

There's a dragging sensation deep in my belly, an umbilical tug for a child I didn't carry.

'Billie!' Her head snaps towards me.

'These pigs are trying to *abduct* me.'

'It's OK,' I say uselessly. 'I'm here. Just – hold still for a bit.' What I really want to say is, *will you shut the fuck up so I can think straight*. And that the last thing I need is to visit her in a young offenders' institution. Instead, I say. 'Come on, love. You're going to hurt yourself. Let me find out what's going on. Eyeb— Jill?'

To my huge relief, Billie stops thrashing.

'I'm sorry, Eleanor,' says Eyebrows, and she seems to mean it. 'I ⸻dn't ignore your involvement with a murder investigation. ⸻the police interviewed Dylan they paid a visit to his flat on ⸻htingale Estate. It's clear he's been subletting it and that

462

it's been over a year since he lived with Billie. Which means that she no longer has a legal carer.'

'*I* care for her,' I say. 'You've seen it. I love her. OK, we might not have done things according to the letter of the law—'

'That's the thing. When it comes to safeguarding, we *need* to adhere to the letter of the law. Procedures are there for a reason. We can't make exceptions. There's been one too many child neglect cases. You *must* understand.'

I could cheerfully headbutt her for using the word 'neglect' in the context of me and Billie, but one of us kicking off is more than enough. I pretend I'm Aoife and count in my head. By the time I get to seven, I'm able to ask, 'Where are you taking her?'

'She'll be placed in temporary foster care until—'

'If you put me in a home I won't stay,' says Billie. 'I'll run away.'

'Please,' I say. 'You're effectively throwing her out on the streets.'

'I belong here. Nell's my *mum*.' It's the first time she's ever referred to me like that. My nose starts to fizz with tears but I have to keep it together in front of her.

'Billie, you're fifteen,' says Eyebrows. 'It's not your decision to make. The state is your legal guardian and we have to go through due process before deciding what's best for you.' She turns to face me. 'Billie will be made safe tonight and we have a hearing arranged for tomorrow.'

A hearing? Are they going to prosecute me for putting her in danger? Am I going to end up on some kind of list? 'What does that mean?'

'In the light of my observations from previous visits I'm letting you make an emergency application to foster her. And I'll be recommending that Billie is placed with you. I want to be very clear that it's only a recommendation; it's the board's decision to make.'

Billie and I look at each other, daring to smile. Eyebrow notices, and goes into expectation-management mode. 'It's no foregone conclusion. The board will take into account issue stability, your lack of a fixed address and the fact that you co' in Mr Garrett's deception.'

'Go with them, Bill,' I say, and then, reading her expression as clearly as if she had spoken aloud, 'This *is* how I fight for you.'

I have never wanted to make a promise so much, but I can't. Relief or maybe disappointment makes her slump like a ragdoll between the two PCs and she doesn't resist as they guide her along the waterside to the waiting police car.

Once she's out of sight, my own legs go from under me. I sit on the prow of my boat and put my hands over my eyes, pushing the tears back in. The sounds of the canal swirl around me: geese quacking, water gently slapping, the chug-chug-chug of a tourist boat cruising past.

None of this would have happened if it hadn't been for the anniversary of *The Golden Bones*. I sit with my chin on my knees like a kid until a shadow blocks the light and drops the temperature. I look up to see Moira and Joyce a metre away on their own deck.

'We didn't realise she wasn't your biological daughter,' says Joyce.

I brace myself for their judgement, but instead she makes an offer.

'D'you need a bit of moral support at the hearing? We're happy to come, aren't we, Moi?'

Moira nods. 'I wonder if it'd help if we wrote you a character reference,' she says. 'We were both teachers before we retired. We've dealt with umpteen safeguarding issues between us. I don't know if it'll count for anything, but . . .'

I wipe my eyes with my sleeve. I doubt it would penetrate the airlocked compartments of Social Services procedure, but their kindness – their seeing a need and offering to meet it – is almost more than I can take.

'That would be lovely,' I say. 'Thank you.'

I turn back to *Seren*, but Joyce says, 'Absolutely not. You're ~~ing~~ lunch with us, and a glass of something to take the edge

~~re~~ making the stride to their hull I leave a voice note on the ~~W~~hatsApp group.

'It's me. Uh, the police have just taken Billie away from me. I know she's not your priority right now but she's mine, so, yeah.' I hold the phone away so they won't hear me sniff back tears. 'I might not be able to drop everything for the next couple of days. I'm trusting you lot to, you know. Sort out what we talked about.'

Through the open doorway of the boat next door, I hear the pop of an old-fashioned cork and the glug of wine into a glass. The sound triggers a Pavlovian warmth in my limbs, if not actual relaxation.

'There's a crisp and playful South African rosé with your name on it in here,' calls Joyce.

I leap the chasm and clamber through the hatch.

The inside of their boat reminds me a little of Bridget's kitchen. Not because it's full of crap – boaters can't afford to accumulate clutter – but the way it doesn't stand on ceremony. The wood is shabby and the rugs are threadbare but the plants are watered and the fruit bowl is full. It radiates welcome and capability and makes me feel the same way I did next door when I was little: mothered.

Over a tuna Niçoise salad, Moira and Joyce listen to the story of how I came to know Billie. I'm surprised how comforting I find it to talk about her. Maybe it's because talking keeps me circling the edge of the panic vortex rather than plunging straight into it. They peck at their glasses every few minutes. At Cora's place, we'd already be on the second bottle. Hell, drinking on my own I'd be at the bottom of my second glass by now.

'Anyone can see that child belongs with you,' says Moira.

'Thank you,' I say.

Just then, my phone plays Bridget's tune.

I don't pick up.

She calls back.

Twice.

'Excuse me, ladies,' I say on the third ring. Bridget's cryin hard and there's such a clamour in the background that I h ask her to repeat herself.

Erin Kelly

'Oh, Eleanor. Frank was found hanged in his cell an hour ago,' she says. 'They say it would have been instant. May he rest in—'

I cut the call without saying anything.

Of course it would have been instant. Sir Frank Churcher was a brilliant engineer and knew all about human anatomy. And suffering was something for other people to endure.

118

Vale of Health, London NW3
10 August 2021

There are press outside my family home, again. I take the back route through the Heath, again. I let myself in the back way and lean my bike against Frank's studio. I try not to think about what's on the other side of the wall: the sketches, the half-finished canvases, the brushes and tubes of paint destined for landfill.

The remains of my family wait for me at the kitchen table. They're all sitting on the same side, as though they're posing for a scrappy recreation of *The Last Supper*. In the centre, Cora is wreathed in scarves and smoke. The Lallys sit to her right. Lal has had a shower, washed his hair and shaved. Bridget has cried off her make-up; little blobs of black grease sit in the inner corners of her eyes. The Churcher-Lallys sit to Cora's left. Dom is dirty and unshaven, looking as if *he*'s just done a night in the cells. Rose's eyes glitter. Her colour is high and her breathing shallow.

I sit opposite them. Up close they feel less accidental Renaissance painting, more bench of magistrates. None of them is smiling.

'Oh, pet,' says Bridget. 'I'm so sorry.' But she doesn't reach out or stand up for a hug.

'Leslie told us you saw Dad this morning,' says Dom, as I take a seat opposite them.

'You're not pinning this on me,' I say.

'That's not what I meant,' says Dom.

'But we can't help wondering what you said to each other,' says Cora.

'She means, how much did you tell him?' says Dom.

What's the point in holding back? There is only one person here whose feelings I care about protecting and yesterday she wouldn't even talk to me.

'I told him everything.'

My eyes rest on Cora, daring her to tell me that my words sent Frank over the edge. My retort – that he wouldn't have been inside in the first place if she hadn't killed anyone – crouches on my tongue. But all I get in return are a few unfocused blinks. None of them speaks. The calm in the room is not the numbness of shock. It is pregnant with things unsaid. Or rather, things they have said to each other, but are holding back from me. My heart starts going in great, slow thumps.

Dom rakes his unwashed hair; it stands up in peaks. 'Do me a favour, Nell,' he says. 'Switch your phone off. Journalists have been calling us all evening; my nerves are shot from ringing phones.'

Given how many people now have my number, this doesn't seem like a bad idea.

'Sure.' I slide my phone on to flight mode and set it on the table.

'We've come up with a plan.' Each word is evenly weighted. I haven't heard him sound this decisive since the day of.

'Oh, you diamond!' A little bit of my faith in my brother is restored. He's found a way to clear Frank's name; justice matters after all, even if it must now be posthumous. 'I knew you'd think of something. *Thank* you.'

The look on Dom's face – cool, defensive – instantly makes a fool of me. A heavy machinery starts to churn inside me.

'The thing is . . .' He breaks off, runs his tongue over his teeth, takes a deep breath, tries again. 'It's just that . . .'

Lal takes over, his voice still scratched from his time in the cells. 'The thing is, Eleanor, the police already have their nice tidy ending.'

Whatever's in my guts continues to plough them.

'Verity Winship, God rest her soul, was threatening Frank. ey found his DNA on her. And he took his own life. Doesn't look like guilt?'

'Is this some kind of test?' I sound reedy and pathetic.

'He's a bad man, Nell,' says Bridget. 'We're all better off without him.'

A voice in my head: she's right. But this is still wrong. I take a short, sharp breath.

'He's the worst person I know. And Christ knows that bar's been raised in the last couple of days. But he *isn't guilty of this*.'

'If we're talking blame,' says Cora – her speech is indistinct and her pupils are dilated – 'who's the one person without whom none of this would have happened? He put me on pills that made me ill, Eleanor. He *flaunted* his infidelity. And what Dominic saw in the catalogue – it would've made any man lose his temper. You don't understand what it's been like for us. *You'd* have done what we did in our position.'

'You've never known who I am, have you?' Before she can protest, I turn on Dom. 'Did you not even *try* to genius a way out of it?'

'It just raised too many flags,' he says. 'Look, Nell, you're in shock. Give it a day or two and you'll see it's the only real option.'

'Well, maybe I'll get the police to look closely at Yorick anyway,' I threaten.

Contempt drops across his face. 'Yeah, but you're the girl who cried wolf, aren't you? Bombarding them with one paranoid theory after another.' I must have missed the point where he switched from defensive into offensive but he's fully committed to the tactic now.

'I wasn't paranoid! People *were* after me! No thanks to you!'

'I've *said* I'm sorry about that.' There's a sulk in his voice, as though he's been forced to apologise for some childhood transgression. 'What I'm saying is, they won't take you seriously. You can read Yorick as a conspirator or a witness to the crime on the night. Or you can read him – or her – as just one more lunatic shouting on the internet. Police work is a lot like Bonehunti There is significance if you want to find it. Those comme they're meaningless. They're buried deep. If they gave weig every theory online – you think they've got the budget to do all that, when they've got a story that ties everything up nicely?'

'But they haven't,' I realise. 'Frank couldn't have put Verity's bone in the tree. That video on my phone – the one that fucks your alibi, Dom – Frank's in that. It's the only point when the switch could've been made, and he doesn't leave the frame for long enough to do it.'

He looks at my phone, dead on the table.

'And don't get ideas about wiping it, 'cos it's on Billie's WhatsApp as well, and my cloud.'

Lal clears his throat again. 'He could've done it before the crew got here. Just after Dom did it. Sure he was a sprightly fucker, what with all the yoga.'

It's an effort to keep the scream out of my voice. 'You said you were all together the whole time.'

'After you left last night,' says Dom, 'Lal and I were re-evaluating everything, as you do when new information comes to light.' My brother does a good impression of someone looking me in the eye but he's a sliver off, as though he's staring at my temples or the bridge of my nose. 'As soon as the crew started to arrive it was chaos. There was a good half hour when the Crabwise van was right up against the front of the house, blocking the sight lines for the cameras. Lal was in the loo' – At Dom's words, Lal caresses his gut, a swollen reminder of his digestive issues. Who's he trying to convince, himself or me? – 'And I was on my laptop. The Crabwise vans were blocking the CCTV. He could easily have gone out the front and around the side. We didn't tell the police about the gap in his alibi at the time because it didn't cross our minds that Dad was behind it.'

'That's because he wasn't.' Self-control hasn't got me anywhere, so I give into the shrill. 'You seem to be forgetting the small fact that *you've already told me you did it!*'

My loss of temper seems to have a calming effect on Dom. 'We compared notes about the day, and used our knowledge of his work, and the clues he'd planted over the years, and we could only conclude that the whole thing was one, big elaborate stunt.'

He still can't meet my eye. I hold on to that. Shame. It's all I've got left to exploit.

'Don't do this.' I move my face so my eyes meet his. He trains his gaze over my shoulder. I turn in desperation to Lal. 'Don't *you* insult my intelligence as well as your own morality, Lal.'

He can't look at me either. 'Look, both of you, you're not going to convince anyone. His motivation isn't strong enough. Not for the murder – Verity wasn't even blackmailing him, she was just a kid looking for money. And then, this summer: he had no reason to self-sabotage. Drawing attention to a failure, a crime, is the opposite of everything Frank Churcher is.' I swallow the rock that's appeared in my throat. 'Was.'

'Not if it was a dying artist's last work,' says Cora.

'Jesus *Christ*,' I say.

'Verity's death had been on his conscience for years.' For the first time since this all started, Cora is not shaking or fiddling with her clothes or hair: she is still as a stone, only her lips moving. 'As his own mortality became an issue, he wanted to come clean – but a man with an ego like that couldn't resist doing it in a flamboyant way that made it all seem a bit less sordid. He was an artist to the last. He wanted to dictate the terms of his legacy.'

'Like when David Bowie followed God on Twitter a few days before he died,' says Dom.

'Frank wasn't David fucking Bowie!' I'm screeching now, in a register I didn't know was in my range. 'Also – and forgive me if I'm splitting hairs here – he wasn't dying.'

Cora shakes her head. 'He thought he had prostate cancer. He'd booked in for a test to—'

I'm not letting her get away with that. 'No, he didn't. It was routine screening. He told me that. He didn't—'

'He had erectile dysfunction *and* urine in his blood,' says 'He confided in me about it months ago, so he did.'

I shake my head. 'You'll need a whole lot of Hail Marys to get you off the hook for this one, Lal.' He winces but I'm not finished. 'They'll find out in the post-mortem that he didn't have cancer.'

'It's what he *believed* that mattered,' says Cora.

They're gaslighting me. The sweet smoke in the air and the breeze at my back and the dark vibrating energy in this room is all too much.

'He didn't leave any *evidence*. He would've left a suicide note if that was the case.' My voice is returning to normal. Is this the fight going out of me?

Cora doesn't answer, but slips into the study and returns with a copy of *The Golden Bones*. It is the one I was looking at last night. My fingerprint is a purple smear on Elinore's cheek.

'I was tidying up in the study this morning and I found this tucked into the book. It explains everything to the police.'

She opens the book at the picture of Elinore and Tam getting it on in the cornfield. There is a sheet of ivory paper that I did not see there last night. Would I swear it upon *Seren*'s hull? Billie's head? I don't think I could.

I unfold the page. It is covered with what could at first glance be mistaken for another alphabetic system – Arabic, maybe – but I know this text. It is Frank's mirror writing.

'What's this?' I ask.

'Just read it,' says Cora. Her breath is coming unnaturally fast.

There's a floor-to-ceiling Venetian mirror in the hall. I stand in front of it, turn the big light on and hold the page up to the glass. The others stand behind me, spread out as though socially distancing, all of them wrapping their arms around their own shoulders or waists. I let their figures go out of focus; even bounced back into legibility by glass, these words need all of my concentration.

n artist who merely observes is but a reporter and his work will
er have reach that extends beyond its frame. To be truly great, he
participate in the world. More than that: he must transgress.

The art must always come first. Obstacles to creation must be removed. A masculine impulse, perhaps.

It is for this reason that Verity Winship had to die. Her daily intrusions into my life – through the letterbox and in person – could not be borne. Her constant presence and demands threw a veil over my muse. I knew that my 1997 collection would be a rebirth and here was this grabby young woman, effectively with her hands around a baby's neck. Her presence at my opening was beyond tolerance: I had to kill her to free myself.

And to create my greatest work.

I held on to her, my second skeleton girl, knowing that when the time was right the work would suggest itself. What better time than 2021, my own health failing, my body of work complete, my profile high again. Verity became puzzle, installation, performance art. I threw the stone not knowing how far the ripples would spread: it was the great delight of my final days to see people engaged and talking and looking again, my denials a crucial part of the performance. Verity achieved so much more in death than she ever would have in life.

The pen is not mightier than the sword but perhaps the paintbrush is interchangeable with the blade, and the list of great men who understood this is long. The murder for which Caravaggio is infamous was merely one crime on a long charge sheet. Van Gogh's genius cannot be separated from his madness. And these days Schiele would probably be listed on the sex offenders' register.

If you are reading this, then I too have begun that final journey to bone. This is my last work; let these be my last words. I shall impose no further meaning on the viewer, for it is in observation and contemplation that art truly comes alive.

Frank Churcher
The Vale of Health, London NW3
August 2021

119

A stinging sensation travels up my spine and spreads to my scalp. The letter is so convincingly Frank-like – not just the looking-glass hand, but his turns of phrase, the arrogance – that his voice narrates it in my head, and by the time I get to the end there is a corner of my brain – some synapse on the fritz – that believes what I'm reading and is grateful for it. Frank is a killer and Cora is not. Dominic had no involvement in Verity's murder and the right man was punished for it.

It lasts for less time than it takes me to crumple the paper in my hand. When it lands on the floor, I stamp on it, even though I know there are infinitely more where this one came from. I turn to face the row of liars and killers, writers and artists. Including the artist who, as a young man, spent days writing to Bonehunters in his best friend's writing. Who could imitate Frank's hand so well that even they could not tell which was the real thing and which a forgery.

I turn to him. 'All that trouble to get you out of prison and now you're incriminating yourself. Come on, Lal. This is nuts.' He doesn't say anything, but his fingers start working their way along an imaginary rosary.

'Nell, it's been decided,' says Dom. His voice is under control but the furrow in his brow – so much deeper than it was this time last week – is a monitor that displays the turmoil inside, the groove going from peak-and-trough to flatline and back again.

'Not by me it hasn't.' I try get each of them to look me in the eye but they're like the actors in a woeful piece of immersive the-atre I saw a couple of years ago. It was staged in a warehouse; the audience were encouraged to wander on to the set, but no matter how close we got the actors had to pretend we weren't there.

'No wonder you wanted me to keep my phone off.' I pick it up, turn it back on and drop it into my pocket. 'I'm sorry. I can't hack this. I love you all, I know why you're angry, I am too, but we can't do this. I've got that film. It disproves your alibi; it shows the girls were there.'

Rose stands up slowly, her chair scraping on the floor.

'You will not put my girls through that.' Her voice is forged with steel.

'Oh, Rose.' She wouldn't listen to me before, but perhaps she will now. 'There won't *be* consequences. As far as the girls were concerned it was a little white lie. Come on! Niamh's eight and Aoife's . . . well, she's Aoife. They don't make kids go to court any more, it's all done on video.'

'That's not what I mean.' In a snap, she's at the back door and blocking my exit, her arms stretched to span of the frame, long muscles rippling. I could duck under either arm but it's her expression that glues me to the spot. 'We had all four children in our room last night, crying because Frank was in prison. Even Oisin dragged his mattress in and slept at the foot of our bed.'

'Christ, the kids. Where are they? Do they—'

'They're at home with Oisin. He saw the letter.'

The blade in my guts is dull, rusty: it's pulling me apart. 'You mean you showed it to him, you let him think . . .' I close my eyes for a second. My rage is a red so dark it's nearly black. 'And you're alright with all the adults in his life colluding in a massive lie, are you? Jesus, Rose. You're supposed to be a parenting expert.'

She stands her ground. 'As far as he's concerned, his grandpa Frank is guilty and that's how it's going to stay. They all have grief and shame enough, Nell. What do you think it would do to them to lose their father and their grandmother in the same way? She's almost eighty. Frank didn't last twenty-four hours. How d'you rate her chances?'

Cora endeavours to arrange her features in a way that suggests great infirmity.

475

'How many more people do you think the kids can stand to lose?' asks Rose.

'This is shitty, trying to guilt-trip me,' I say. Shitty but effective; my resolve is ice in the sun.

'The press will dig and dig,' says Rose. 'Not to mention every Bonehunter in the world. Firstly, that means more attention on you. And what if they find out about me? You saw Oisin when he saw Dad on that tape. If he learns what Frank did to me that'll fuck him up for life. Every relationship he has. Another God knows how many women fucked up by a relationship with a fucked-up man. Aren't there enough of those in the world already? Not to mention *our* girls.'

'How could that possibly get out?' I ask gently. 'The only way that could happen is if someone in this room told them, and that's never going to happen. And even if it *did* somehow get out, aren't victims anonymous in cases like this?'

The slow shake of her head; she pities my naïveté. 'The press might not be able to report but ages, locations – it'd only take one person to guess and it'd be all over the internet. You of all people should know how dangerous that is.' Rose drops her arms so she's no longer blocking the door, and holds out cupped hands to me like a beggar. 'I can't lose Dominic. I need what's left of our family to raise my children. I need you on-side, Nell. If you've ever loved my kids, you'll leave things the way they are.'

My throat is closing up.

'I really don't want to do this,' says Rose, dropping her hands to her side. 'But if you go to the police, we'll make a phone call to Social Services.'

It is as though Billie is a chess piece she's sliding across a board: *your move*. My legs turn to sponge. I put my hand on the worktop to steady myself and this visible weakness emboldens her. She makes her hand into a starfish, each digit a point to be ticked off.

'You hid evidence – the catalogue,' she says, striking her little er. 'You knew what Cora and Dominic had done for twenty- hours and you didn't do anything about it. You have kept evidence from the police – that video – for the whole investigation. It makes it seem as though you were in on it. Are you willing to have police officers investigate you again, when you have a caution and a record? It'll take them months. God only knows where in the system Billie will be by then. And kids her age, they're hard to place with families. It'll be a home full of other teens, much more troubled than she is. It could knock her studies off course. All that potential – gone.'

'You wouldn't.' My voice falters. Rose is the last one I had faith in: the last one of them to fall.

'I don't want to, Nell. I don't *want* to have to go to the police and tell them that you didn't tell Social Services when you had a break-in on the boat.'

'She'd have done a runner. You really think she'd have been safer on the streets?'

'And you didn't say anything even when the Glemhams showed you content that could have endangered her life. How's that going to sound at your appeal?'

Rose has twisted her corkscrew into my heart with a straight face but at the end of this speech the masks slips; she pulls a face as if she's sucking on something sour. It only lasts for a second but it tells me she is as sickened by what she's saying as I am. I pounce on that.

'Rose. Come on. This isn't you. Your life is about protecting vulnerable children. You would not do that to a girl like Billie.'

She raises her palms. 'If you had kids, you'd understand.'

Something cuts loose inside me. Rose doesn't know it, but she's set me free. The decision is made, as simple as casting off a rope.

'I *have* a kid,' I say, getting to my feet. 'And I don't want her infected by this absolute *disease* of a family.' I throw up my hands. 'You win. I won't tell the police what you've done.' Relief make them sink as one, as if someone's lowered the floor. 'But I can't p along.' I wrap my shirt tight around me. 'You won't see me ag

Dom gets up so quickly his chair clatters to the floor h him. 'Nell, please don't,' he says.

'*You.*' I look my brother up and down: he's the right size and shape, but is only the outline of the person I thought he was. 'You are the biggest disappointment of them all.'

He follows me down the garden path. I can feel loneliness encroaching on me already as I walk away.

'You don't mean it, Nell. We're the only ones who know what it was like—'

His words throw a lasso around me. I stop, my bike lock swinging in my hand. If I leave now, I will never be fully known or understood by anyone again. In leaving behind the family, I am taking with me secrets I can't burden anyone else with.

I pick up my pace.

Dom's Adam's apple is a reef knot tied tight in his neck. 'What am I going to tell the kids about where you've gone?'

'That's not my problem.'

Oh, but it is. I miss them already. Tears are liquid fire behind my eyes. I put my key in the back gate, not daring to look back. Dom pulls at my shirt pocket and this is what I am leaving behind. Anyone else would try to wrestle me into a hug, but my brother would never, even in this desperate embrace, put his arms around me from behind the way Ingrid did.

'I've got to go.' I sniff hard as I push my way through the gate. 'See ya.'

See ya, like I'm nipping out for a bottle of wine rather than bidding a permanent goodbye to forty-plus years of siblinghood, with its shared baths and its shared cigarettes, its in-jokes and rivalries, its sandcastles and bike rides and car journeys and now its trail of lies and bones and threats.

I let the gate swing closed behind me, as final as the vast door that swung shut as I left Holloway.

I have never heard a man cry the way my brother does now. The ne of his howls – the long, even pull of them – makes me re him on his hands and knees in the dirt.

naybe it's just that that's the way I remember him crying were little.

What's left of the sunset is a thin strip of gold on the horizon. The Heath is lit with old-fashioned lamps and I cycle slowly from one white moon to the next, in no hurry to return to my empty boat.

Less than a fortnight ago, I thought that the great derailment of my life – the before-and-after that everyone has – was when Ingrid took a blade to my skin. Right now, that moment, and all the others – Stuart, Jane, Richard – God, even what Frank did to Rose, and Dom and Cora did to Verity, even Billie being dragged away from me this morning – seem little more than a kink in the tracks. This is the moment my life slides off the lines entirely. This is the impact, this is the wreck.

120

Lea Valley, London
October 2021

I check my face in the mirror for the last time. I must have been crying in the night again because there's a little salt drift on my hairline. I rub it away with a forefinger. Other tearstains are permanent. There are little deltas of burst blood vessels under my nostrils and on my cheeks from weeks of hacking sobs and nose-blowing.

Billie emerges from her bedroom. 'Is this OK? It's the only black I've got.'

She stands before me in her school uniform, plain blazer and kilt, open-necked shirt, hair smooth.

'It's perfect,' I say. 'What about me?' I pull at my own black dress. I felt as if the occasion demanded the kind of grown-up tailoring I've spent my entire life avoiding. Apparently adding an extra zero to your budget gets you a cut made to cradle rather than restrain the curves of middle age. It falls on the knee, a length I'd always thought of as conservative, corporate even. I have to admit: I look incredible. Forty-five in the best possible way. Powerful, artistic, sexy. If I'm honest, vanity played as big a part as respect in my choice of clothes. I desperately hope that there won't be any media there today but, if there are, I'd like to present an image of myself to counteract the sweaty, dishevelled woman catching a bone as it falls from a tree.

'You look *crisp,*' says Billie.

I check my phone. The Uber is one minute away.

'How does anyone wear stuff like this every day?' I grumble as I haul myself through the hatch without flashing my gusset.

'Most people have normal front doors,' says Billie, jumping on to the towpath and holding out her hand.

'Tights can get in the bin, while we're at it' I say, as I stagger from boat to land, hitching up the waistband. 'And high heels.'

Low courts that feel like stilts to me sink into the grass that edges the towpath. *My* patch of the towpath, home sweet home. White mist rises from the glassy canal and columns of smoke rise from chimneys. That offer of a spot on the Lea turned out to be true. This is where Billie lives, officially, permanently, close to the school that will nurture and challenge her. She is not my foster daughter and I have not adopted her. Instead, we have an arrangement called 'kinship care', which perfectly describes our status as each other's chosen family.

The mooring fees are easily affordable. Frank left me six finished paintings in his will. The value of his work has not decreased with the 'knowledge' that he killed Verity Winship. He is 'media cancelled', if the dozens of opinion pieces and the tens of thousands of tweets are anything to go by, but that's not the same thing as market cancelled. There appears to be a drive among collectors to own a notorious man's work that is similar perhaps to the public's ghoulish appetite for Dom's app.

During the day I tell myself that I'm happier estranged from my family. That they were never good for me anyway and the bits that were good were founded in lies. The one thing I valued – being known, being seen, not having to explain the past – turned out to be a one-way thing. They all gained, in the end, from Frank's death, and not only financially. They are all free from him: his bullying, his manipulation, his lies and his pettiness. Losing me was a price they were willing to pay.

The driver flashes his lights at me. I try not to picture my ankles snapping like matchsticks as I pick my way across the cobble The car takes us past my workshop, a converted dairy factory the edge of Hackney Marshes. An electric scooter parked ou tells me my apprentice is working inside. The night of F death, I went back to Horsfall, dug out the chapel windov and worked through the night. I scrapped the design I'd been tinkering with and poured my grief and confusion on to the page. I added more red glass, bolder shapes and grittier textures, breaking them up with slabs of opaque black glass that would throw shadows whose meaning changed as the sun crossed the sky.

I only went and won it.

As well as the workshop, I have a staff of three, and I no longer think it's noble to work for its own sake. I want my talent recognised. Cora spent her life in Frank's shadow. I refuse to do the same. Glassy Nell, with her suncatchers and her baubles, served her purpose for a long time, but it's time to let her go, too. Perhaps my family are not the only ones to feel freer without Frank Churcher in their lives.

The A406 shunts us around the east edge of London. The Central Line chugs overhead. The City and Canary Wharf loom in and out of view between wharves and warehouses and disappear as the Blackwall Tunnel swallows us up then spits us out in south London, where the yellow spikes of the building I suppose I will always think of as the Millennium Dome form a broken crown around the bubble of the roof.

'Will the others be there?' asks Billie.

I made the arrangements for today, not just because nobody else would but because I wanted to control it: keep it quiet. Do everything I could to keep the cameras away. And while there is no guest list for this event, neither has anybody been banned.

'Honestly, Billie? I really don't know.'

121

Nunhead Cemetery is the only one of London's 'magnificent seven' still to be receiving bodies. Mausolea and tombs give way to single stones in this city of the dead. There are notable figures but not the kind I'd have heard of. The trees are bare but evergreen ivy sucks names and numbers from old stone and strangles angels. There is a chapel, but we are not headed there. My heels clack-clack on tarmac paths as we study a map – one last map – to find the grave.

Pete Winship might not have been able to leave his daughter the gold he dreamed of, but he did bequeath her a place in an old family plot. His gravestone is black onyx, his epitaph etched in gold and dulled by moss.

> *Peter John Winship, 1930–1975*
> *Father, London Cabbie, Treasure-Hunter*

Newly chiselled in brighter gold beneath are words I chose. They are deliberately generic. I didn't want to impose upon their relationship but, when I remembered the picture of her as a toddler on his knee, 'beloved' didn't feel like a stretch.

> *And his beloved daughter Verity Jane, 1974–1997*

On the horizon the dome of St Paul's is framed in a porthole between two yews. Nunhead is a nice place to end up. Hardly anyone is still buried here. Verity must be one of the youngest residents. I like that for her. It's special.

I had been worried about media intrusion but the only journalists there are the citizen kind: Porter and Lisa-Marie Glemham, black-clad, pale and looking older, as though years rather than months have passed. DS Bindra and her colleagues are there in the black suits that police officers must have to keep in their wardrobes for all the funerals they attend in the line of work.

I turn a slow three-sixty, looking down the avenues between the graves, half-expecting to see Richard. He sent me a text a month ago to let me know that he'd found a muddy brass key in Rhiannon's desk drawer, and she'd confessed to picking it up from the garden on the day of filming. The missing attic key. The last mystery solved. I considered telling Richard how significant it was in what happened next, but decided against it. I don't want Rhiannon getting any more ideas.

There is a short ceremony at the graveside. A vicar says the words we are so familiar with – *earth to earth, ashes to ashes, dust to dust* – with as much care as if this long-dead girl had been one of his own beloved congregation. I thank him for it.

Bindra glides up to me and places a gloved hand on my forearm. 'I'm so sorry for your loss, Ms Churcher.' She means Frank, of course. 'How're you doing?'

'Ah, you know. Getting there.'

Her smile is professional; she must keep it in the wardrobe with her black suit. 'It's nice to see you all here.' She nods an acknowledgment to Billie and glances at the Glemhams. 'There's something particularly heartbreaking when the only mourners are the investigating officers. It's good of you to pay your respects, especially in the circs.'

'Well, I felt like the Churchers owed her something. I suppose there's an element of selfishness in it. Trying to get closure.'

The goodbye in her handshake is unequivocal. As far as she's concerned, this is over.

Behind me, the Glemhams are telling Billie how grown-up she looks in her uniform. Mortified, she makes a show of checking the time on her phone. 'D'you want me to stick around?' she asks. 'Only, I can get back in time for last period if I get the train now.'

'Consider yourself released,' I say with a wink. 'Seriously, Billie, thank you for coming. I'll see you back at the boat.'

Porter, Lisa-Marie and I stand in a triangle beside the grave.

'I'm so sorry you lost your daddy,' says Lisa-Marie.

'I'm so sorry for who Frank turned out to be,' says Porter.

'*Porter*,' says Lisa-Marie, mortified.

For a moment I want to tell them the truth. Give them another crusade. These kind, strange siblings who kept the flame alive for all these years. Then I think: Oisin, Aoife, Niamh, Dara. Aoife, Aoife, *Aoife*.

'It's a lot to come to terms with,' I say. And if it is not the whole truth, it is *a* truth.

'I hope you don't mind us asking – is it the real deal?'

They are referring to the picture that made the papers a week or so after Frank died. It trended on Twitter for twenty-four hours. Fritz Velasco, white-haired and designer-suited, arm in arm with Mrs Velasco, raven-haired, designer-dressed, with a little gold skeleton nestled in the crepe of her cleavage.

It was not Tam's love that put Elinore back together again, not the dogged persistence of a Bonehunter, not even theft. It was murder and lies. I can no more tell them this than I could tell a five-year-old that Santa's not real.

'It's really her,' I tell them.

Lisa-Marie and Porter turn their perfect smiles on each other. It's the closest to the fairytale ending they'll get. 'And Frank really orchestrated the whole thing?'

'Believe me, no one was more shocked by it than we were.' To corroborate Dom's cover story sticks in my throat but that's the choice I made. 'Actually, do you know what?' Having spent most of his conversation fudging the truth, I decide to commit to a lie. 'I'd love you to get the full story out. Frank gave me that last jewel in his will. He thought it was only right that I decide what to do with it. What else could I do but send it to Mr Velasco?'

Their eyes are filmed with water. 'That feels right,' says Lisa-Marie.

'As right as any of this *can* feel,' agrees Porter.

'It wasn't an entirely selfless decision,' I say. 'As long as that bone was at large, there was always the chance someone new would stumble upon Ingrid Morrison's batshit theories.'

'Those kids,' Porter growls. 'They did so much damage to the treasure-hunting community.'

'Not to mention what they did to *you*, Nell,' says Lisa-Marie.

'Yeah, well. I'm just glad it's over. Now all Elinore's bones have been reunited, I'm safe.' I find that I have taken their hands in mine. 'Listen, with Frank gone, you're basically the world authority on *The Golden Bones*. I'm trusting you with the legacy.'

For a moment they are too overcome to speak. Eventually Lisa-Marie says, 'You got it,' and squeezes my hand tight. Suddenly the hand-holding becomes awkward. We break the loop and take it in turns to study each other's shoes, the sky, the headstones around us.

'Well,' says Lisa-Marie eventually. 'Our driver should be here any minute. We're going to Gatwick. Can we give you a ride anywhere?'

'No, I'm good. I want to take a moment.'

'Sure.' We hug goodbye and promise to keep in touch. To my surprise, I mean it. I watch them leave, their breath white clouds in the air above their heads as they continue their endless volley of conversation.

I wonder what their lives would have been like without *The Golden Bones*. Would they still have travelled? Would they still be as close? Would they have families of their own?

Of course Frank didn't leave me the jewel in his will. The night I said goodbye to my family, I got back to the boat and put my hand in my pocket for my key, only to close my fingers around a tiny golden bone, dropped into my shirt pocket by Dom even as he begged me to stay. It was his apology and his way of acknowledging that I meant it to be a permanent goodbye. He knew it would set me up for life. God, I agonised about selling it. More than one night I stood on the deck with it in my fist, ready to fling it into the canal. But my heart cast the vote in Billie's favour. Velasco's money will put her through veterinary college. She will graduate without debt. We might not be in 'nice little flat' territory but that's OK, she wants to live on a narrowboat. Finally it feels as though *The Golden Bones*'s money is rinsed of its stain. As though I can pass the filth of my privilege on to someone who can wash it clean.

I think Verity would have wanted me to give Billie a good life.

Dipping as low to the ground as my high heels allow, I scoop soil into my left hand and sprinkle it over the coffin's lid. I repeat this until there's a thin blanket of dirt over wood and brass.

'Sleep tight, Verity,' I say, as the earth tucks her in.

EPILOGUE

Kilburn, London NW6
December 1969

On the beanbag, Lal snores, his breath surely flammable. Firelight renders Cora's skin in jungle stripes of dirty gold. A lump of coal jumps from the fire and crackles on the hearth.

'Cora,' says Frank. 'You must know how lovely you are?'

She dips her head. That same lock of hair falls loose again. This time when Frank catches hold of it he holds it and gently, so gently that it might not be happening at all, pulls her head towards his. Her smile is glinting and the gap between their faces is closing and she is so soft, but it is he who yields.

The bedroom is freezing, but somehow a lone candle is enough for them.

Cora falls into a deep sleep and Frank tries to join her but he is wired, replaying what just happened until he's ready to go again. He left a good half-glass of wine undrunk; maybe that will knock him out. He dresses and drapes Cora's Afghan coat around his shoulders.

Lal is out cold on the beanbag, Frank's empty glass at his side. Frank studies the room. Now that he's been to bed with Cora, her work – her *world* – takes on a new enchantment. He reads the lyrics she's reproduced in notebooks and runs his fingers over stitches she has sown. Wasn't he on the verge of an idea, earlier? He's damned if he can remember what it was.

'You got the ride, then?' Lal's voice in his ear nearly makes Frank jump out of his skin.

'Bloody hell! Don't *do* that, Lal. At least clear your throat or something, show us you're back in the land of the living. And well you may ask' – Frank doesn't bother to suppress his grin – 'but a gentleman never tells.'

He's standing before Cora's map. The legends it describes would lend themselves perfectly to his brush. It won't be serious art, but it might mean a flat with heating next winter. 'I was on to something,' he says. 'An idea. For a book, for Marcelle. Make a few bob.' He gestures to the map. 'Is there something in this, do you think? An illustrated guide book?' He scratches his neck. 'She said she wanted something different. I keep thinking of a book you can't take your eyes off, but how would I do that?'

'*Desire*,' says Lal throatily. 'Desire makes you keep looking, even if you don't want to. I'm not just talking about women. You have to be looking for something. Something you can't see at first glance. Like, a secret code in the book? Hidden messages?'

Frank feels a tug in his gut, as Lal takes an HB pencil from the box on Cora's coffee table and poises it over a blank page.

'That ridiculous song that she had us listening to. You'd take, like – say you could make a skeleton, and then scatter the bones, and that's the key to the book. You know, like . . .' He can barely speak and yet he draws with photographic precision. 'So, you could have one, like . . . I dunno, your folklore's shite compared to the Irish kind, it's all fucking milkmaids and farmhands.'

Frank laughs, and brings his candle to Cora's map. 'Not necessarily. We've got mermaids in Cornwall, a werewolf in, where is this, Staffordshire, ghosts off the Suffolk coast . . .'

The two men work through the night as smoothly as they did in the day. Frank feeds Lal place names and legends and Lal comes up with the rest, his incredible mind devising clues and stories faster than they can write them down. After an hour, they have hiding places for six of the seven bones, and clues for most of them.

When Lal passes out with a pencil in one hand and a cigarette in the other, Frank knows better than to try to wake him. He finishes the cigarette and sharpens the pencil and, as the mo slides across the window, he tidies up Lal's work, which is by t cramped and expansive as his pencil struggled to keep pace with his mind. Frank makes himself a cup of Nescafé. He unearths a new sketch pad from under a pile of fabric scraps and transcribes the words and pictures. He finesses the sketches and builds on the foundation of Lal's original idea. He is both thrilled and dismayed to find that his engineering training creeps in, dormant maths and astronomy and crossword skills gleaned from doing the *Telegraph* cryptic with his father lending a framework to Lal's fantastical ideas. The originals, he throws on to the embers.

Lal sleeps like the dead that night. At eight in the morning, the whistle of Cora's kettle wakes him from – well, others would call it a stupor but there were dreams, weird dreams of songs and girls and treasure that stay clear for one second then evaporate like his breath in the freezing room. He has cramp in his thighs and a rusty spring digging into his ribs. His brain feels loose in his skull. Dark spirits, that's the problem. Stick to drinks you can see through and you're grand. No more brown drinks, ever.

With some effort, he raises himself on to his elbows and opens his eyes.

'It's alive!'

Frank is standing over Lal, his shirt open to the waist despite the chill, Cora's hand reaching between the buttons. Frank's arm is around Cora's shoulder, one hand on her breast. Good on the fella. It's about time. Although he looks . . . nervous, is it?

'Cup of tea?' asks Cora, disentangling herself from Frank, throwing one of her quilts over her shoulder and moving towards the kettle.

'You're a darlin',' says Lal. 'Two sugars.'

Cora brings a pot of tea and three mismatched mugs on a tray. When she's poured hers, she raises it aloft.

'A toast!' she cries, and then, on seeing Lal's incomprehension, 'Oh, Lal. You slept through the whole thing! Have a look at this.' waves a sheaf of pages in his face. 'Frank had the idea for a book e night and it's the most astonishing . . . look, it's based on my map, and my records. He's sketched out all these plots and puzzles, it's so clever, I just know it's going to make him rich and famous.'

Frank's voice is shaking as he sets out the premise: a picture book, the like of which the world has never seen. A treasure hunt that will send readers on a chase all over England. He's going to call it *The Golden Bones*, he says. He watches Lal's face intently.

'Looks grand, so it does,' says Lal, flattered that his approval clearly means so much to Frank. 'Jesus, you're a clever bastard.'

Cora is right. Like all classics – like a song you know will be number one the first time you hear it -- it is original but somehow familiar, as though the idea was floating fully formed, just waiting for the right man to pluck it from the ether and set it on paper.

To Gather the Bones

A wedding day, a wedding day, in blazing gold July
Fair Elinore in kirtle green was wed to old Sir Guy
She raised her eyes to heaven as he dragged her down the aisle
And handsome Tam in the gallery returned her secret smile.
A wedding night, a wedding night, a husband's touch so coarse
The fine and feathered bed was as a ditch of thorn and gorse
At dawn she rose from bloodied sheet and creased her pretty
      brow
To gaze across the cornfield where Tam dragged his rusty plough.

Flesh will spoil and blood will spill but true love never dies
Gather the lady's bones with love to see the lady rise

A summer's night, a summer's night, the corn stalks flattened
      down
Young Tam beside the old man's wife, her skirt spread all around
Sir Guy out walking saw the pair, his heart grew hot and sore
When Elinore returned that night, he smote her to the floor
Before the sun, before the sun, Sir Guy went riding out
His axe slung o'er his shoulder for to scatter her bones about
Her spine he strew on the forest floor, her skull dropped down a
      well
Her ribs he tossed in the river deep, her limbs across the fell

Flesh will spoil and blood will spill but true love never dies
Gather the lady's bones with love to see the lady rise

A witch was watching in the woods, she damned Sir Guy to hell
She raised her arms and raised her voice and sang a rising spell
Witch's words alone, alas, lack power to raise the slain
With love's help perhaps the girl might tread this earth again
For his life, scared for his life, young Tam set out to flee
Fely 'cross the parish bounds, he fell against a tree

The Skeleton Key

'How shall I live without my love, how shall I cease to weep?'
He made his bed in heather and he lay him down to sleep

Flesh will spoil and blood will spill but true love never dies
Gather the lady's bones with love to see the lady rise

A silver mist, a silver mist, it from the forest came
The cloud it cleared, the witch appeared and called Tam by his name
'I cast my spell but could not save the Lady Elinore
I did all one witch can do but love can do much more.'
Tam staggered back, he staggered back, and crossed his breast in
    prayer
'But what know I of magic, crone? How come you from thin air?'
'Gather the bones, gather the bones of a cruelly murdered wife
And prove your love for her is true, she will regain her life.'

Flesh will spoil and blood will spill but true love never dies
Gather the lady's bones with love to see the lady rise

A wandering, a wandering, young Tam searched all the land
The fields he dug, the wells he drained till all bones were at hand
Upon his heather bed the bones he laid out, ev'ry part
Till all were there but the iv'ry cage that held her rose-red heart
A year he slept, a year he slept beside his true love's bones
Till came a flood that burst the banks and threw up earth and
    stones
And washed ashore the dozen ribs of lady Elinore
Tam laid them in the heather, singing, lady dance once more

Flesh will spoil and blood will spill but true love never dies
Gather the lady's bones with love to see the lady rise

She rose aloft, she rose aloft and spread her arms so wid
No hair upon her ragged head, her flesh a rough grey l
She twirled in rags, she stank of rot, no youthful ma

When Elinore approached her love, he recoiled from her kiss
He raved aloud, he raved aloud and called the witch a liar
The mist came up, the witch stepped forth from deep within the
    briar
'Young Tam, young Tam, did I not say fair words were not
    enough?
To bring a true love back to life will take a true love's touch.'

Flesh will spoil and blood will spill but true love never dies
Gather the lady's bones with love to see the lady rise

He closed his eyes, he closed his eyes and put his lips to hers
White skin grew over dirty bone as kiss it sealed the curse
Warm blood made roses of her cheeks, gold hair it crowned her
    head
Tam's living, laughing lady love lay in her heather bed

Flesh will spoil and blood will spill but true love never dies
Gather the lady's bones with love to see the lady rise
Flesh will spoil and blood will spill but true love never dies
Gather the lady's bones with love to see the lady rise.

THANK YOU

To everyone at Hodder: Jo Dickinson, who once again understood what I was doing before I did. To Leni Lawrence, Alice Morley, Sorcha Rose, Kate Keehan, Swati Gamble, Catherine Worsely, and Drew Hunt. Thank you Andrew Davis and Will Speed for making this grisly book so pretty on the outside. Thank you Linda McQueen for another eagle-eyed copy edit.

To everyone at United Agents: my indomitable agent Sarah Ballard, to Eli Keren, Jennifer Thompson, Amy Mitchell, Georgina Le Grice, Alex Stephens and Lucy Joyce.

To my first readers: Helen Treacy, Michelle Patel and Lucy Dawson.

To the man, the legend, the book hoover Stu Cummins for his generous bid in my name-a-character auction in aid of Oasis Domestic Abuse Services.

To the late, great Chris Wiseman for the insights into TV production. How I wish you were still here.

To Jess Wilder at Portal Painters for her stories about representing narrative, idiosyncratic artists, in the 1970s and beyond.

To glass artist Emily Hatzar of Crafty Glass London for helping me give shape and colour to Nell's working day.

To Paul Bromley and David Willis for letting me spend time on their beautiful narrowboat on the Lee Navigation.

To lawyer Hetty Gleave at Fladgates for unravelling the intricacies of the 1996 Treasure Act.

To pathologists Dr Stuart Hamilton and Dr Julie Roberts for telling me more about how to macerate a corpse than I ever wanted to know.

To Crime Scene Officer and author Kate Bendelow for her field guide to the 'Wombles'.

To DS Rebecca Bird and DS-turned-crime-writer Neil Lancaster for advising on police procedure. To Clare Lancaster for explaining how child safeguarding works (or doesn't). To CSI Kate Bendelow for talking me through the crime scene.

To Nick Wall and Malcolm Barr-Hamilton in the Vaughan Williams Memorial Library at Cecil Sharp House. Thank you for letting me spend time amongst your incredible bookshelves.

To those who have set, written about or followed treasure hunts: Ben Brewis, author of The Hidden Sun, Daniel Barbarisi, author of Chasing The Thrill, and Dan Amrich of the Kit Williams fansite bunneyears.net

To Kirsty Hillman and Kate Graham at Missing People for explaining how people can fall through the cracks.

To Dave Kerrigan and Fergus McNeill for patiently explaining what happens 'inside' the internet.

To Maxine Mei-Fung Chung for telling me what restrictions might be in place for Ingrid in hospital.

All of the above gave generously of their time and expertise to make this book more authentic. As ever, I let fact inform but story take the lead. Which is my way of saying that any inaccuracies are mine, all mine.

To Ben Walker and Kirsty Merryn for setting *To Gather The Bones* to music. I wanted the song to feel like a lost Fairport Convention album track and that's exactly what you gave me. I am in awe of your talent.

To Kit and Eleyne Williams, for such a gracious response to my fan mail.

Finally, family.

Mike, Marnie and Sadie: you make the world outside my study door a place of love and laughter. None of you bat an eyelid when I start muttering about bones and burials. Time, and possibly therapy, will tell if this is a good thing or not.

To my parents, Lynne and Mick, and my siblings, Owen and

Shona. Like Nell's childhood home, mine overflowed with books on the shelves, pictures on the walls and music in the air. Unlike Nell's, it also had unconditional love and attention. These are the treasures I pass down to my own girls, along with my well-thumbed copy of Masquerade.

READ ON FOR AN EXCLUSIVE
Q&A WITH ERIN KELLY

What was the inspiration for *The Skeleton Key*?

Masquerade was a picture book by the eccentric, genius Gloucestershire artist Kit Williams. I was three when it was published, and flipping through its intricate, fantastical, surreal paintings is one of my earliest memories.

When I could read, I fell in love with the story. It was an old-fashioned fable of how Jack Hare lost a jewel he was supposed to deliver from the moon to the sun. The first reader who worked out where it was would win real treasure: a hand-made, solid-gold, jewel-studded hare, buried somewhere in the English countryside. The first reader to interpret the paintings, the text and the riddles that bordered each page, could find its location. The back cover showed a picture of the jewel, half-buried in soil. I loved that idea: that a book, already a portal to another world, could offer yet another layer of magic. I never came close to solving the puzzle, but the effect it had on me never left me. It was almost inevitable that one day it would find its way out again in the form of a novel.

You explore the nature of obsession in this novel. Were readers of *Masquerade* similarly obsessed?

Absolutely. There's a sense of mischief in all Kit Williams' work and I think an element of madness and obsession was built into *Masquerade*. It didn't come with instructions, just the book itself. The reader had to work out what the puzzle was before they could solve it, so there were almost infinite directions it could be taken in, and thousands of different weird and wonderful theories. Gardens all over England were dug up by trespasser: people spent their life savings chasing the hare. One man's obsession with the hunt was even cited in his wife's divorce petition. You had to surrender a huge part of your mind to *Masquerade*. Some readers never quite got theirs back.

The depth of feeling was reflected when the treasure was found. In 1982, two physics teachers solved the riddle but before they could dig it up, Kit Williams' ex-girlfriend's new boyfriend' business partner (do keep up) had made an educated guess a claimed the treasure as his own. The bad faith find soured the hunt. To this day there remains a hard core of 'Masqueraders' who believe the treasure is still out there, and these were the inspiration behind Colin, Ingrid and the fanatics you met in these pages.

How did you do your research?

This was my first post-lockdown book so it was a real treat to get – as treasure hunters say – boots on the ground. The novel before had been researched almost entirely on screens. I walked Hampstead Heath so often I wore my own groove around its perimeter. I visited galleries and spoke to artists, I browsed the archives of folk song lyrics at Cecil Sharp House. My favourite part of research was getting the feel for life on the water. Part of *The Skeleton Key* was written during a few days I spent living on a narrowboat on the Regent's Canal, getting a feel for the joys and challenges of narrowboat living. I felt very close to Nell. Not only did I understand the rhythm of her days, but I also had an insight into what kind of person would choose to live that way. Canal life is an interesting blend of romanticism and almost primitive practicality.

Did you work with/refer to any visual elements while writing?

I ordered a tattered paperback copy of *Masquerade* on eBay, cut it up and plastered my study walls with the pages so that whenever I looked up, I'd be inspired. I also had a poster called The Great British Folklore and Superstition Map, a huge, illustrated map of the British Isles illustrated with the kind of legends that inspired *The Skeleton Key*. Cora is working on something similar to this when we first meet her in 1969.

Do you have a favourite character?

I can't say I want to go out for a drink with any of them. That said, did enjoy the writing the three generations of Churcher men. ank's old-fashioned, military upbringing gave him a sense of tlement, but no artistic confidence, leading to the monstrous arrogance that has him exploiting the people around him for his art. He vows not to treat his son with the same disdain the Admiral shows him, but when Dom pursues a professional career rather than a life in the arts, he can't hide his disappointment. Dom is uxurious, reliable, traditional, present: everything Frank was not. In Oisin, we see how conscientious, perhaps over-attentive, parenting, has created a different kind of entitlement. Dom is in turn frustrated at Oisin's frivolous career. And so it continues.

The book is based on the idea of a treasure hunt. Do you like puzzles?

I actually don't. I've never done a Sudoku square and cryptic crosswords make my brain melt. During the first draft of *The Skeleton Key* I intended to include all seven of the original clues in *The Golden Bones* but it was such an overwhelming task I only came up with one. I had to scour pages of online forums and puzzle books to see how others had done it. It was the hardest part of the book!

What is your writing process? Can you write anywhere or do you have a set routine?

I fill up the tank as much as possible before starting a new book: I read and watch things relating to my idea, visit places, interview people until inspiration reaches a kind of critical mass and bubbles onto the page. I might have a loose idea – a setting, a character, a twist, a moment – but I don't plot ahead, and I don't write in a linear way. I'll start with scenes, sketches, a few lines of dialogue, and then I'll build from there. For example, the first scene I wrote in *The Skeleton Key* was the one where Eleanor's final bone is about to be revealed – but instead a human bone is uncovered. It doesn't happen until a third of the way through the finished book, but once it was on the page, I knew I could build up to it – introduce the family, create a sense of dread about what was going to happen to them -- and lead away from it, making the reader long to know what would happen next? I delete and rewrite and reorder constantly, right up until my deadline.

As for my daily routine, I write five days a week, loosely office hours. With earplugs in I can write anywhere, although I tend not to because my workstation at home is a sitting-standing desk with a monitor at exactly the right height for my eyeline, and a chair I've carefully calibrated. After an hour hunched over a café table, I'm uncomfortable.

What's your favourite thing about being a writer? And what is the hardest aspect?

There's so much my career has given me – a raft of weird, interesting, loyal friends, travel, the chance to meet readers, the excuse to go down mad research rabbit holes and let us not overlook the fancy lunches. But the work is still the thing. The inside of my brain is a manic procession of thoughts, pictures, songs, lists, regrets, memories, ideas, and weird impulses. The absorption I feel when ordering the events of a story or choosing the right word is the closest I come to stillness. When it's going really well, it feels like reading a good book more than writing one.

The hardest aspect is all those hours at the desk – even my fancy ergonomic one – and the resultant RSI, arse-ache, back pain and poor circulation. I've tried a treadmill desk but it made me feel seasick, and voice activated software but my brain doesn't work that way. Anyway, I'm not sure dictation is a good idea for a crime writer. Imagine if I'd been out for a walk in the park, narrating a scene about macerating a corpse into a headset at the top of my voice? I'd be banged up within a week.

What do you do when you're not writing?

Feel guilty about not writing.

Who are your favourite writers and what do you read for fun?

I love fiction where rollicking narrative and really fine writing collide. So that's anything by Sarah Waters, Zadie Smith, Emma Jane Unsworth, Megan Abbott, Denise Mina, Susie Steiner and

Tana French. Recently I've loved *The Housekeepers* by Alex Hay, *Young Women* by Jessica Moor and *The Half Life of Valery K* by Natasha Pulley.

I increasingly enjoy memoir as I can truly switch off. With fiction, even if it's outside my own genre, my writer brain pops its head through the floorboards like an annoying sitcom neighbour, making predictions or thinking how I would have done it differently. In the past couple of years I've really enjoyed memoirs by Roopa Farooki, Fern Brady, Gavanndra Hodge and Lemn Sissay.

What are you writing next?

I've just finished a sequel to my debut novel, *The Poison Tree*. That book was set in 2008 and published in 2009. The follow-up takes place in the present day so my characters have had a good fifteen years to think about the consequences of their actions, and Alice, the little girl from *The Poison Tree* is all grown up and determined to uncover her parents' darkest secrets. I've never written a sequel before and I loved the process; the comfort of working with old friends – with every situation I put Karen and Rex in, I knew exactly how they would react – and the novelties of new settings and characters.

ENJOY AN EXCLUSIVE
EXTRACT

FROM THE BRILLIANT NEW
NOVEL BY ERIN KELLY

AVAILABLE FROM APRIL 2024

KAREN

'The things we do for Alice,' says Rex, reversing the hired van around a corner. The tarmac under the wheels turns to cobbles. The crate on my lap, carefully packed with beads and chains, starts to clack and rattle. A peacock feather stuck in a vase nearly stabs me in the eye.

'The things we do for Alice,' I echo.

He has no idea.

It's December, dark at four o'clock. This bit of Islington, currently dressed for Christmas in white lights and cut Hollie, was made for horses, not motor vehicles. Flagstones and wrought iron, alleyways and pubs straight out of Hogarth, antique shops and galleries. Even the modern boutiques are done up to look like something from a hundred years ago. Wooden windows painted lemon yellow showcase miniature clothes that cost twice what I'd spend on adult ones. A barber shop fitted out like something from the industrial revolution. A kid on an e-scooter with no lights on punctured the snow-globe illusion, shooting out from the van's blind spot so that Rex has to brake hard. Something in the back of the van shatters. 'The little…' he begins.

I lean out of the window. 'Are you trying to get yourself *killed*?'

The kid raises his eyebrows at Rex, as if to ask why he's outsourced his road rage duties to his missus. He can't know that Rex does not have the luxury of losing his temper. It's safer, when I pick up his anger, to funnel it through my lungs. Our dynamic is so ingrained I don't even notice it anymore.

'At least this is the last drop.' Rex inches the van backwards, tongue sticking out in concentration.

He fits the van into the space we've been illegally using as a loading bay all day and throws on the hazard lights. In the wing mirror we see our daughter approaching, dressed against type in an old sweatshirt and leggings that make her look a lot younger than twenty-four. Behind her, the logo she designed herself gleams gold and black on the window. It's her take on Leonardo da Vinci's

Vitruvian Man sketch, only instead of a spreadeagled naked man it's a young woman in a flowing dress, arms flung out so it looks like she's dancing. Above that, the shop's name: she's called it Dead Girls' Dresses.

'I still hate the name,' murmurs Rex, and of course he has good reason to. Dead girls are not an abstract concept for him. It has been twenty-five years – Alice's lifetime – since Biba was last seen alive, missing presumed dead after she abandoned a car – my car, she'd stolen it while I was asleep – at a notorious suicide spot. She had taken her life, like her mother before her. It's been ten since we had her legally declared dead. You can do it after seven but it had to be Rex's choice and I had to wait until he was ready. Biba was my best friend, but she was his sister. A year or two after his release, divers looking for another body found a single silver earring on the seabed. We'd listed it as one of the few items that might identify her. Those earrings were made just for her by Nina, Nina the silversmith. Biba never took them off. The lone twin earring is now in my jewellery box at home sea-smoothed and dull, Nina's hallmark worn shallow. It is worthless to most people but meaningful to us. I keep it in its own compartment, in a little velvet pouch whose ribbons I tie in a way that lets me know when Rex has taken it out to hold, to remember, to wonder and maybe to regret.

Alice has the back doors open before the engine's off and the three of us fall into place, a human chain passing the stock – or *the girls*, as she calls her pieces – from the van to the shop. Lace froths in my face: ribbons trail on the floor. When the van is finally empty, we are all panting.

'I'd better…' says Rex, nodding backwards at the van, which has miraculously escaped a parking ticket, but Alice throws her arms around our necks.

'Thank you both. So, so much,' she says. 'I won't let you down.' A lump forms in my throat and Rex appears to have something in his eye.

While he takes the van back to the hire place, I enter the shop, which still has its fresh-paint smell. 'I've made a start on it,' says Alice.

She has more than made a start. This morning the space was a black-walled shell, the only features a fitted brass clothes rails at eye level and a mound of charity-shop furniture under dust sheets. Now it's a . . . a . . . I want to use a word like *realm*. It feels like somewhere I have visited in a storybook. A chandelier glitters overhead. A stuffed swan's head hangs above a cast iron fireplace. Two gilt mirrors face each other, projecting Alices into infinity. A Chinese silk fan hangs behind an old-fashioned cash register and kitsch figurines wink from a cabinet of curiosities.

'I'm going for a sort of Dickensian hovel meets Weimar Republic boudoir,' she says. 'What do you think? Have I evoked a demimonde?'

What I think is that Dead Girls' Dresses is like Biba's old bedroom in the house in Queenswood Lane, that it's like going back in time, that it's uncanny. What I think is that all it would take is one of those songs from the old days and I would be a young girl in a bikini dancing in a garden again, rather than a middle-aged woman in a FatFace midi dress and special inserts in my boots to stop my knees hurting. What I think is that there's a hand pulling a scarf tight around my throat, making it hard to breathe. But what I say is:

'Very good. Very Instagrammable.'

'Well, what's the point of having a bricks-and-mortar shop if you don't make it a destination?'

'There's just so much to look at, wherever you – *oh*.' My eye falls on a dressmaker's dummy, bound tight in a corset decorated with a painting of what looks like a shepherdess. Alice reads my mind and rolls her eyes.

'For the last time,' she says. 'It was an *investment*.'

When Alice was in her third year of university, and she'd started getting serious about selling vintage clothes, she spent her student loan on a Eurostar ticket and a hotel because she 'clinically needed' this 1990 Vivienne Westwood piece that was going at auction. She didn't tell anyone beforehand in case they tried to talk her out of it. Her flatmates called the police and she arrived home, beautifully-dressed but three grand poorer, to find her door kicked in and me crying on her bed.

I finger the gold brocade on the shoulder straps. Even I have to admit that it's exquisite.

'It's already doubled its value,' she says. 'It's virtually a pension.'

'You're not going to hire that out?' She rents clothes to women who just want something special for a night out and to stylists and film companies too. Every now and then she'll send me a link to a video featuring some barefoot wraith twirling and chanting in one of her dresses.

'No.' Alice hugs the mannequin. 'Vivienne's *mine*.'

I turn my attention to the gallery wall of her fashion heroes: Marilyn in her Happy Birthday Mr President sequins, Princess Diana in her off-the-shoulder revenge dress, Kate Bush in a red gown, Billy Porter at the Oscars, a full skirt twirling beneath his tuxedo. 'All the major icons,' she says, then her eyes dart towards a picture and then hopefully towards me.

'Oh, *love*.' My hand flutters to my heart. Anyone Alice's age would think it was Alice; a bit of retro dress-up, run through a filter to give it a sun-drenched vibe. Anyone my age and older would recognise it as one of the most famous advertisements of the 1970s, the Natura shampoo girl with her gleaming dark hair in her white dress in the meadow. It's a multi-sensory experience, that photograph: you can hear the plinky harp music from the TV advert and smell the herbal tang of the shampoo. I had no idea, when as a child I sat in the bath and screamed as the lather stung my eyes, that one day I would marry the Natura girl's son and raise her grandchild. But I would never meet her. Sheila Capel hanged herself on the landing of the Queenswood Lane house when Rex was sixteen and Biba was twelve.

'I found it in an old *Vogue* and I thought . . .' Alice tilts her chin defiantly. 'It's a good picture. It's perfect for my brand.'

Pity tempers my frustration at her naivety. 'You must know you can't have this on the wall.'

'I can say it's me?'

The likeness is certainly strong enough. Sheila's pale face, with its huge dark eyes and strong nose is Alice's face, it is Rex's, it is Biba's. It passes down the generations like an heirloom. It bulldozes other likenesses out of its way.

'But it's a famous picture. It connects you to Dad's old name. It only takes one person to join the dots and he'll have to start all over again.' I could remind her what it was like when word of his conviction got out in our home town, but Alice was responsible for the breach and after everything died down we agreed we wouldn't use it as leverage. Still. She needs to know how serious this is. 'You don't remember how bad it was when Dad was first released. Your whole childhood, really. We kept the worst of it from you. Journalists were all over the family for years.' Gently, I take Sheila Capel down from the wall.

Alice's hands form fists. 'I'm not going to throw it away.'

'I'm not asking you to. It's a beautiful picture. You *should* own it.'

I set it face up on the counter. Alice capitulates. 'Right,' she dusts her palms. 'Let's hang some of these girls.' She looks at Sheila's picture, realises what she's said, and is horrified. 'Jesus. I didn't mean.'

'Good thing Dad didn't hear that.' I tear the cellophane off a pack of pink velvet hangers. 'Let's go.'

The clothes are already grouped by colour and size. I should know. I was up all night double-checking the measurements of bust-darts and waistbands. When everything is in place the shop looks less like Biba's bedroom. *Her* clothes were more likely to be found on the floor than on their rails.

My belly growls. 'Have you not eaten?' asks Alice, apparently forgetting that I've been on the move since dawn. My Fitbit tells me I've climbed fifty flights of stairs today. 'I'm going to go to the coffee shop over the road, introduce myself to the neighbours, get some grub.'

She grabs a peach kimono from a railing, throws it on over the leggings and instantly looks like something from an F. Scott Fitzgerald novel. She swishes out of the door, all tassels and hair.

Half a minute later, the brass bell above the door clangs as Rex pushes it open, a carrier bag in his hand.

'Bloody hell.' he runs the fingers of his free hand through his hair. 'It looks like . . .'

'I *know*.'

He moves a paisley scarf out of the way of a candelabra on the mantle. '*She* never had any fucking sense of fire safety either.' He coughs one of those laughs that's not really a laugh and looks at the door. 'I almost expect her to . . .'

'I know what you mean. But this is Alice. This is all Alice.'

It's not, and we both know it. Biba's ghost, never far away, has put on her best dress and slid in through cracks in windows, gaps under doors, through tightly closed eyes. She moves like mist, like poison gas.